I0691794

ACKNOWLEDGMENTS

Grateful acknowledgment is made to the editors of publications in which excerpts from this novel have appeared:

Eureka Literary Journal, Whet Magazine, Thieves Jargon, Sweet Fancy Moses, Smokebox, Skive, Working for the Man, edifice WRECKED and *Avatar Review.*

Ishmael Reed's untitled poem is from his *New and Collected Poems, 1964-2006,* © 1998, 2000, 2006 by Ishmael Reed.

Salt Lick

Brian Ames

Pocol Press
Clifton, VA

POCOL PRESS

Published in the United States of America
by Pocol Press.
6023 Pocol Drive
Clifton, VA 20124
http://www.pocolpress.com

Publisher's Cataloguing-in-Publication

Ames, Brian, 1963-

    Salt Lick / Brian Ames. – 1st ed. – Clifton, VA : Pocol Press, 2007.

       p. ; cm.

       ISBN-13: 978-1-929763-29-0
       ISBN-10: 1-929763-29-8

       1. Northwest, Pacific—Fiction.
    2. Rural Conditions—Fiction. 3. Black humor. I. Title.

    PS3601.M47 S25 2007
    813.6--dc22   0705

Surely I am more brutish than any man and have not the understanding of a man. I neither learned wisdom nor have the knowledge of the holy. Who hath ascended up into heaven, or descended? Who hath gathered the wind in his fists? Who hath bound the waters in a garment? Who hath established all the ends of the earth? What is his name, and what is his son's name, if thou canst tell?

– Proverbs 30:2-4

Today I feel bearish
I've just climbed out of
A stream with a jerking
Trout in my paw

Anyone who messes with
Me today will be hugged
And dispatched

– Ishmael Reed

FOREWORD

The unfolding of a paper ballot. The scritch of a barkeep's pencil. The buzz of a beer sign.

Mike Eagle Eye's smoke swirled around them.

"The vote is tallied, folks," Wellman Kinchlow said. He turned to Hector Aguirre. "Mr. Mayor, sir." Kinchlow aimed his gap-toothed smile at the game warden. The people had spoken. The bartender turned to Juniper Jamison. "And you, sir, will carry on the leadership work of an independent Tall Tree County." Juniper folded his colossal hands on the table. He nodded. Kinchlow surveyed the group. "That's what you all decided." There was nervous rustling as attendees to the ad hoc town meeting shifted atop their barstools. To even have acknowledged, in these successions, that the old bastard was gone seemed unbelievable.

Jacqua Druce sipped bourbon-laced coffee. She turned to Mallford Jenkins. "And you, Reverend, need to make plans to get him in the ground." The preacher's eye spun in agreement.

"Let the record reflect," Nick Oxendine said, "that the citizens of Salt Lick, Washington, appointed Hector Aguirre as town mayor and Juniper Jamison as leader of the Tall Tree County referendum on May the 28th, at 6:42 p.m., in the Year of Our Lord..."

"6:42? – I got 6:38," Mike Eagle Eye said, with a cloud of spent smoke. He turned to Gib MacNaughton. "What time do you have?" Gib's wristwatch read slightly different, and so on, around Lowell's Tavern.

Time circling on itself.

Over in Salt Lick, no two clocks told exactly the same time.

It's amazing that this was so, for in Lothar's lifetime, this never would have been countenanced. Lothar Sturmhund made it his first priority of business to ensure the clock on the façade of Salt Lick's Town Hall matched the time on his wristwatch. And throughout the day, he would check to make sure clocks he encountered – whether at Lowell's Tavern, in the Pie Apple store, in the laundromat, on the wrists of those he ran across – were synchronized with his. *Lothar time.*

In nature, a salt lick is a natural deposit of exposed salt that animals lick. There were none of these anyone knew of in or about Salt Lick.

But humankind had synthesized bricks of salt or artificially medicated saline preparations, and sold them to be set out for cattle or sheep to lick. From this notion heralded Salt Lick's placename: orchard workers used to place the bricks in the surrounding forest to lure deer and elk. No one could remember who named Salt Lick Salt Lick, and certainly that sort of thing – the unfair entrapment of game animals – wasn't going on there any more. Nevertheless, Salt Lick remained Salt Lick, and its name meant home for 38 foothills people. And for 37 of them, it meant subservience to the mighty Germanic warrior, Lothar Sturmhund.

When he left them, they folded like the wings of a buck-shot wood grouse.

In the forests around Salt Lick lived approximately 13,000 elk, according to state Department of Fish and Wildlife documents. This particular herd was of the Rocky Mountain variety (*Cervus elaphus nelsoni*). It was introduced at Cleman Mountain – just a couple klicks north of town, up by Kinchlow's peacock ranch – beginning in 1913. The government calibrated the health of this young, robust herd by measuring the ratio of male elk to females at the close of each hunting season. After rifles have gone silent and muzzleloaders have spent their powder, after bows have been unstrung and arrows re-quivered, there typically are twelve bulls – as male elk are called – for every hundred females, cows. Lothar Sturmhund would have liked those odds. He would have enjoyed in that distribution a metaphor for himself.

Another fact of interest: mature bulls who wish to copulate douse themselves with their own urine, then trumpet their musky readiness into the clear forest air. The stench of their urine is a perfume to cows.

This piss-drenched call of the bulls is known as bugling.

Salt Lick was a puzzle, like the sloughed bark of Ponderosa pine stumps, the edges of which resemble the cuttings of a jigsaw. The people and places of Salt Lick were a locus of old stories, as if the forest itself bred them. Stories rising from strange exhalations above ponds, from the prism of light refracted in frost thawing to dew on the blue new growth of Engelmann spruce. Stories that caromed from the staccato beakings of the northern flicker on hollow wood and lay in the resulting pulp-dust.

The deity formed from the dust of nothing the people and places of Salt Lick. And from this forging, from the magma that ran therein, the coursing and pumping through the arteries of an Almighty, rose Lothar.

In the Great Rift Valley of Yakima County, Lothar walked among us.

CHAPTER 1
in which Angus knows who the killer is...

There was a strong Germanic warrior named Lothar Sturmhund. One day when he was sixty-four, on the jobsite outside the trailer that served as his general contractor's office, he began to sweat profusely and had numbness in his extremities. This he ignored, as all are taught *not* to do. Later in the day his heart exploded. He fell across a coffee table in Gib MacNaughton's double-wide up Mud Lake Road, an abode which sat in a cleft below Manastash Ridge just after the turn onto Benton Road and above Mud Lake, and died. The last thing that swam in the sea of his Thüringian brain was *Uwe Uwe Oh!* He never knew what hit him.

There were a lot of people who were glad Lothar had been "called home," as Salt Lick's preacher put it, including the Reverend himself. Also in the community of secret Lothar-haters were his workers and former employees, neighbors, acquaintances. Even dogs, as anyone could have predicted.

They remembered him not as the general contractor, fire chief, police chief, and Salt Lick town mayor, but as overlord. They did not remember his 1988 Ford F250 pickup with four-wheel drive, shift on the fly, leather seats, power windows and a long bed filled with the implements of his general contracting. Nor that he cruised the roads outlying Salt Lick, building and repairing homes and summer cabins.

What they remembered was this: Lothar Sturmhund was the alpha male, the wily old royal bugling bull drenched in urine and musk.

Lothar's body lay in state. As mourners observed it – his fine features gone silent, his red beard and blond hair combed perfectly – each observer held a secret desire. Each felt an unbidden compulsion to do something nasty, to perform a desecration and mete out justice. For some, like his last few drinking cronies from Lowell's, just spitting on him would have been enough. For others, climbing up on the casket and defecating on his crossed hands, just over his heart, would have been more like it. Others thought cutting him up and leaving the parts to coyotes might be apropos. And still others could think of no indignity they could enact on the corpse punitive enough to redress their suffering.

Lothar's eight-hundred and seventy-five dollar beaverskin cowboy hat rested on the coffin. Juniper Jamison hoped Magda, Lothar's widow, would give it to him. Surely she wouldn't bury a nearly nine-hundred dollar hat.

Does God forgive a man like Lothar? His widow pondered this during Reverend Jenkins's eulogy. A God capable of such forgiveness would be the only kind of God that would have the right and power to rule the universe, she reasoned. A God with the kind of authority to forgive Lothar would rightfully be on its celestial throne.

A universe is only fair, Lothar's wife thought, if a wounded, wandering soldier like Lothar would be spared excoriation for the atrocities he had excreted. Ultimately we all want such a man as Lothar to be redeemable. Because then we *all* are redeemable.

The Reverend's wife led those gathered in a rendition of "Shall We Gather at the River" as Lothar Sturmhund's requiem.

This, Magda Sturmhund decided during the coda, would be the final proof that Heaven is, indeed, Heaven: If, when all of them – those Lothar loved and blacklisted and took hostage and shaped and abused – get there, Lothar himself waits.

To rule them.

Sensing strange tidings, a penful of peafowl up at Wellman Kinchlow's place stretched their necks and sniffed the cold breeze. On Cleman Mountain, something was not right.

There was a creeping, unnamed agitation roiling through the pen. Their scaly legs shuffled. They warbled wary *Aaaaaarrs* into the irresolute light of mid winter. In the dimness Kinchlow's retriever DelMar loitered nearby. Suddenly a cock sprung, neck as straight and hard as a battering ram, and nipped at the dog through the wire. The birds stamped their talons while DelMar yelped. They scored the dirt with deep, dragging tracks. The cocks opened up their trains in giant, brilliant fans. All of the colors of the spectrum shimmered from their feathers. Variegated light opened up the dim winter evening like a brilliant rip in reality's fabric. One cock, near out of his mind, charged a male rival. Soon all the cocks mimicked this aggression: anything that moved was a potential target – the peahens, Kinchlow's prize rooster, the rodents living behind the old ceramic bathtub that served as a water trough, all sorts of crawling dirtbugs.

2

A couple of cocks tore at the anchoring section of the fence. Together, they pulled with their beaks the jagged wire out of the hard dirt. It was like a prisonbreak.

Beyond the fence, out from under the protection of the plywood overhang, dark nimbostratus clouds hung close over Kinchlow's bare fields like a gray, inverted ocean. The land below them was white, interrupted here and there by fenceposts or wind rows of stripped poplar. Wind soughed through the naked trees, the hushed echoes of voices, the moldering remains of a long combination of autumn and winter. The two cocks broke loose of the yard. They slipped in the snow, punch-drunk, and took brief flight – not far, maybe twenty-five yards – in an iridescent arc of blue and green. They alit on a hundred-foot maple next to the Kinchlow house. There they turned west, bent their necks, bobbed, and scolded: *Aaaaaarr! Aaaaaarr!*

Their penmates poured out of the hole in the fence. The dog bayed as he raced away seeking solace where harrying birds might not follow.

The thing with Petey was that he was not technically a birthday present. He was, rather, a surrogate present, Angus MacNaughton having wanted a kitten. But a cat was simply not possible: in the presence of cats Angus's father, Gib, would develop a clotted nose and bulging cheeks that looked like eggplants. His eyes would squeeze shut and tear up. Gib MacNaughton's allergy to all things feline meant a cat was out of the question. And besides, kitty cats got chewed up at night – by coyotes or bigger, feral cats with gleaming teeth – in this part of the world.

"How about a dog, Dad?"

"Dogs tear things up," Gib said. Besides, he worried about the routine rootings-about one could expect from a dog – a snout burrowing around the loose dirt of his garden, claws dividing roots from loam, pulling up his plants, that sort of thing.

Angus tried other beasts on his father:

A ferret: "No."

Iguana: "No."

Llama: "No."

But a peacock? Now there was an acceptable alternative. Gib knew Lowell's barkeep, Wellman Kinchlow, raised them. Peacocks were clean, quiet, attractive.

Gib liked the looks of the Kinchlow farm. The grounds saddled the south half of Cleman's low summit. It had split-rail fences, a few

Holsteins pasturing, the folds of the Cascade foothills to the west and Lo Tower to the immediate northeast. Conifer forest ringed Kinchlow's farm, but his fields consisted mainly of bunchgrass and solitary deciduous trees, or a few trees in wind rows. This near-treelessness was an anomaly in these foothills, which were mostly coated by mature forests of hemlock, fir and pine.

Kinchlow's farmhouse was an immense log cabin, Abe Lincoln style, a bridge of windows with white trim and shutters facing south. Behind the house rose a massive maple, and further in the hillocky pastureland Gib saw the lines of tall, slim poplars – they must have been seventy, eighty feet high – planted in rows. When Kinchlow came out on the front stoop, he wore boots and overalls. It made Gib hopeful, seeing that a man could still live like this – out here in the open air, east of the constant rain, in a big ranch house – not merely a double-wide. He glanced down at Angus next to him on the bench seat. With an eager look of anticipation across his boy's face, Gib believed that being raised in a house trailer without a mother had, perhaps, not wounded his son as much as he sometimes feared.

"You ready?" Gib asked.

Angus looked up at him, then out the window at the farmer. The boy turned back to his father. A tiny Scot's smile spread on Angus's dry lips. A sparkle colony settled in his eyes, and Gib could yet discern – even after six months of little sun – the freckles on his son's nose. Faded, true, in the way that annuals die back, but still there, still ready to brighten when spring came. "Now?" the boy asked.

"Yes. That's Kinchlow."

"The guy with the peacocks."

Gib nodded.

"Cool," Angus said, lifting the pickup's latch and spilling out onto the gravel driveway. He gamboled like a freed colt to the farmer. "Where's the peacocks?"

"Round back." Kinchlow chuckled at the boy's excitement. He looked up to the approaching Gib, greeted him with a handclasp Gib almost missed for staring at the disaster of the farmer's teeth.

Wellman Kinchlow was owner and bartender of Lowell's Tavern, which sat across Mud Lake Road from Town Hall. So besides knowing how to raise and sell India Blue peacocks, he knew how to draw beer, mix drinks, and build a minor wealth from Lowell's. But not a nickel of it would he drop in a Yakima dentist's palm. Kinchlow sold mostly the mixed drinks and beer, not a hell of a lot of wine. A twelve-ounce tumbler of beer he called a "Peacock." He wouldn't draw a glass for someone who merely said, "Say, I'll have a beer." The person had to say, "I'll have a peacock, please." Inability to perceive and decipher this code kept many an out-of-towner from wetting his lips. And his grin never failed to amaze Gib – the barkeep's mouth was like a picket fence missing slats. It was an oral spectacle from which almost no reasonable person could tear his eyes. If that were not enough, it made the farmer whistle his speech from time to time, so that at unpredictable moments he sounded like the calls of his own birds.

"Birds are around back," Kinchlow repeated, gesturing that they should follow him. The pair fell in step, Angus's hand in his father's. They followed Kinchlow around the house, through a gate in the split-rail fence. They saw a barn – really just a large outbuilding – with the peacock pen abutting it.

The pen was of heavy-gage wire and 4x4 construction, wire affixed to the lumber with heavy-duty staples. The structure measured about thirty feet deep and forty-five feet long, maybe twelve feet high. A plywood roof slanted away from the barn and overhung the pen by a foot and a half. Peacocks overfilled it, peacocks sleeping, strutting, grooming, drilling their beaks into dirt, calling out softly *Aaaaaarr*. A few chickens were in with them. The smaller fowl appeared to be chiefly concerned with giving the peacocks proper respect – basically providing a wide, berth to stay out of the larger fowls' way.

"Awesome!" Angus said. The boy broke for the pen on a dead run. The penned birds scattered like gulls, their calls rising. A couple of them rose on flapping wings to collide with their ceiling and fall back to earth. They scrambled up, disoriented, then returned to the search for bugs, worms, or cornfeed at a safer distance. Kinchlow disappeared into the barn.

The peafowl grew placid again in a shorter time than Gib MacNaughton would have thought. Kinchlow reappeared, entered the pen. He selected a handsome bird from the closest group. The other fowl milled around his boots, questioning Kinchlow in their peafowl tongue. He brought out the chosen one for Angus to inspect.

"Is it a boy peacock or a girl peacock?" Angus asked. He touched the blue feathers of its neck while Kinchlow held it firmly. Its beak was jet black. Its eyes were like two little pieces of black flint. Kinchlow cradled the bird as would a running back a football, held it tight so the bird couldn't attempt a poke at the boy. Its train hung down behind Kinchlow's elbow, almost to the ground, in a graceful feathery arc.

"It's a boy, you can tell by the colors. Here's the deal: a female is mottled, black and gray and white, see?" Kinchlow pointed back at the pen, where several hens watched. "The boys are blue and green –

they're the ones with the pretty tails. They're the ones called peacocks. The ladies are called peahens. Together, we call them peafowl."

"Peafowl," Angus said, stroking the cock's neck with his fingertips. Angus looked up at his dad. Gib MacNaughton affirmed his son with a grin. The boy looked back at Kinchlow. "How come they got so many colors?"

"I don't know," Kinchlow said. "They come out of India, so I guess that's where they get them. They're just pheasants, if you want to know the truth, only out of India."

Angus didn't know where or what India was. Indians came from there, he supposed. Pony-tailed folks, such as Mike Eagle Eye.

"Petey," he said, looking at the bird.

"That's what you want to call him?" his father asked.

"Yeah, Petey."

Kinchlow loaded Petey in a small pen in the back of the pickup. Then he and Gib started to work out the money. Angus spent a few minutes next to Petey's carrier. Then he wandered over to the big pen for a last look. The birds scattered again, but quickly returned to investigate him. He noticed there was an old bathtub inside.

"What's the tub for?" he called over his shoulder.

"Water," Kinchlow hollered back. Returning his attention to the boy's father, he encouraged Gib to think about acquiring one of the hens as well.

"The deal is, cock's gonna get lonely," he said. For a moment Gib thought Kinchlow was making an off-color joke, as he would, sometimes, pulling Peacocks down at the tavern. Then he wondered whether Kinchlow was just trying to get more money off him. But he knew better. He'd known Kinchlow for a couple of years and never found him to be anything but square and decent. At face value Gib had to conclude the farmer was sincere. The peacock might pine away for a mate and be a sour match for his son.

Even so, in the end Gib decided he'd closely watch the male bird. He would see whether it seemed lonely. If so, he'd come back up Mud Lake Road sometime for a hen.

"I think just the one right now," Gib said.

"But you have my number."

"Yes, and I know where you work."

The barkeeper laughed with him. Gib called Angus to load up.

Then Angus, his father, and Petey were off to their place, Angus watching the bird through the rear window of the cab. Kinchlow's farm receded until the road's bends and the curve of Cleman Mountain's summit swallowed it.

6

At first, Petey was a disappointment. For Angus, a proper pet would display affection, friendliness – longing even – for its owner. But the peacock would not be lugged around the trailer or even gently fondled. An attempt to do either sent it kicking and shrieking off the back porch into the yard, train fanning wide with admonishment. Or it would fly up to one of the trees and look north, back up the mountain toward Kinchlow's.

What to do with a peacock? What were the rules of engagement?

"Come on, Petey," Angus would plead. The bird would blankly stare back at the boy and step backward or aside if Angus approached.

But in time the bird and Angus accustomized. They began, in small bits of progress at first, to understand what pleased or displeased each other. Over the course of these encouraging weeks, Gib discovered his son possessed a trace of patience in this regard. He hadn't known this of Angus – he had, in fact, always considered his boy somewhat restless. But soon the bird could be touched and rubbed by the boy and began to seek out this pleasing interaction.

Their companionship was cemented on a Saturday afternoon in March when Petey was attacked by Eli, the Jenkins' dog. Angus had left Petey out of his pen to exercise. The big Lab came stalking through the hemlock and spruce, suddenly bounding at the surprised bird in the unfenced back yard. Petey spread his train like the hood of a cobra and hissed, snapping his beak at the mutt, kicking out with its talons. Had Angus not heard the ruckus, the dog would soon have done Petey in. Those air-filled peafowl bones were no match for Eli's stout, snapping jaw.

Angus exploded from the double-wide with his Louisville Slugger. He hollered and took one swing, but the dog moved slightly at the last second. The bat glanced off one of Eli's ears. The dog backed off, posted up, and growled from somewhere low within him. Then Angus waded into the crouching dog. The boy screamed through sobs, "You stay away from Petey, you... you... you *fucker*!"_ He swung, bashing Eli in the snout.

This was enough for the dog, which had just wanted some fun anyway. The Jenkins's hound yelped loud and high, and sprung back into the woods running. He ran until he fell over exhausted and whimpering. Later, Eli slinked back to the Jenkins place, skull smarting, the casualty of Angus's well-aimed sweep of hickory.

Eli had gotten a bite or two in. Angus nursed Petey back to health, bandaging the wounds with a little bit of help from his dad, who had been away getting a few groceries at the Pie Apple. Angus was old enough now, Gib MacNaughton reasoned, to stay home during his father's errand-running. He could handle himself well – this proved it. Although Gib wondered, for an instant, about the spiritual consequences of bashing the snout of the preacher's dog.

After Eli's attack, Petey and Angus rarely separated except during the day when Angus had to catch the school bus down at the Pie Apple. During those long hours, Petey would watch the forest-line from where the dog had emerged. He would watch and never turn his back until he heard Angus's sneakers sloughing through the grass.

Gib MacNaughton went to work one day and his supervisor informed him that, along with dozens of other people, he would be losing his job. Like departments all throughout American businesses large and small, his was being forced to reduce its size. After a few weeks of heavy fretting and circling classifieds in the Yakima *Herald-Republic*, Gib secured an interview with a department at another company.

Every morning for seven years since Angus's mother had left them, Gib had climbed in his pickup truck and drove fifteen miles to Yakima, and then six miles further to Union Gap. Every day he tapped numbers and letters on a computer keyboard. Gib did not know what the data he entered was, what it was for, what it meant, or why it mattered. He only knew that every two weeks he received a paycheck. It was enough to pay the mortgage, buy Angus new schoolclothes every September, fill the gas tank, buy rolling papers, take his son out to supper at the Gleed Burger King every couple of weeks, and make sure Angus had a good breakfast of a couple of steaming Pop Tarts every morning. And maybe to rent a movie once a week at the Pie Apple.

The interview was with a firm in Zillah. If the interview were successful Gib would have to drive an additional twenty miles both ways, making his daily trek to work and back more than sixty miles. The added distance would play hell with his gas bill, maybe even make it impossible for the paychecks to last all two weeks. At best, he would have to stretch the money and erase every unnecessary expense. At worst, he would have to sell the double-wide and move closer to town. Maybe so close that there would be no place to pen and exercise a farm animal like Petey.

The interview was a success. He would be starting in two weeks. The sooner he said so long to Salt Lick, the sooner the gasoline bill and the rest of his finances would settle out. He could drive the sixty miles daily for now, but not for long. So gently he broke the news to Angus.

"I won't move, no matter where you have to work!" his son yelled. "I'll run away first!" Angus leapt off the back porch, sprung the latch on Petey's pen, gathered the fowl into his arms, and squeezed it. His tears splashed onto the bird's bright plumage. He sobbed and Petey cooed softly, sorrowfully.

A real-estate man brought a dozen prospects out to see the double-wide before anyone wanted a second look. The owner was doing all the right things – keeping the place picked up, the grounds properly policed, even setting bouquets of spring wildflowers on the dining room table, potpourri in dishes, lighting a small candle in the one tiny bathroom, and so forth – things to make the place look, feel and smell homey.

Meantime, getting to Zillah and back extracted from Gib's life an extra thirty to forty-five minutes in the morning, as well as an extra hour – on the best day – to return home. He couldn't find the money to have Angus watched by anyone in Salt Lick. So the boy remained alone in the mornings and afternoons.

Gib had made it clear that Petey was not allowed in the trailer. So when Angus let Petey in, it was an act of pure, willful disobedience. Even though spring's first day had come and gone, it was still cold outside, and constantly raining. Angus got to feeling that Petey must be more miserable each day. So he sneaked the peacock into the trailer twice a day: once in the morning, between the time his dad rolled out of the driveway and Angus had to depart for the bus, and once in the afternoons, after he got home from school, for a couple of hours before his dad was due. So far, Angus had successfully been able to return the bird to its coop, straighten things, and belabor homework or perform yard chores when his dad drove up.

One afternoon in May, the two were in Angus's bedroom at the far end of the double-wide when Angus heard the front-door open. It was too early for his father's return. He climbed onto his bed, looked out the window and saw the real estate man's car. When he turned around again, he discovered that Petey had left his room.

"Petey?" he whispered. "Petey?"

Angus arrived in the hallway at the instant Petey spread his feathers. He saw the backs of the real estate man and a woman through the film of Petey's open train. He saw that the man facing him was big

9

red-faced Lothar Sturmhund. He saw that the mayor saw Petey, and saw Angus. The mayor's mouth opened. His eyes looked like they were going to pop out. He looked surprised. Angus ducked back, trying to hide in the hall.

He heard a groan. The lady said, "Lothar, what's wrong?" The real estate man said, "Mr. Sturmhund?" He heard a loud cry that sounded like *Yoo-vay, Yoo-vay*, repeated, and then the mayor said, "Oh!" He heard a huge crash of glass breaking and something heavy dropping, and the double-wide's floor shook under him. Then Petey darted back past him in the hallway into Angus's bedroom.

Angus peered back into the living room. The lady was on her knees next to the mayor. Lothar Sturmhund had fallen through Gib McNaughton's coffee table. The lady was pushing on the mayor's chest and kissing him. The real estate man picked up the phone. As Angus emerged fully from the hallway, the agent started hollering into the mouthpiece, looking down at his own notes on a pad of paper to repeat the double-wide's address. Angus tiptoed away from the living room. He went back to his bedroom. Petey, hiding in the closet, trembled as if from cold or terror.

About twenty minutes passed. The lady did a lot of crying and the real estate man kept saying "I can't believe this, I can *not* believe this." Angus began wondering less about the weird scene in his living room and more about how getting Petey out of the double-wide without his dad knowing. While he puzzled over this, the sound of a siren grew louder. Angus peaked through the curtains as an aid-car pulled into the driveway. Two emergency men popped out.

Angus slid the window open. He lifted Petey, no small feat for a ninety-five pound boy, up and over the sill. Petey flew to the lowest branches of a tall, red cedar, perched there for a few seconds, then hopped down and disappeared on a heading for the back yard.

His pet safely out of the trailer, Angus ventured again out of his room and down the hall. He saw the emergency men working on the pop-eyed, gape-mouthed mayor. No one in the room acknowledged Angus – it could have been that they truly overlooked him in the hubbub, or that he was simply small and insignificant. In any case, Angus just stood there and watched them press on the man's round chest for some time. He watched while they put shocker things on his bare skin so he jumped up just a second after they shouted *Clear!* He watched as they shook their heads and told the lady *Sorry*. She fell onto the sofa bawling, and Angus knew the mayor, Lothar Sturmhund, was dead.

Angus didn't feel sad. There was one less buyer for the double-wide, which meant all the longer he could live there with Petey. And more to the point, this method – death by peacock-induced startling – might be useful again. For the next potential buyer.

One of the emergency men finally noticed Angus. He turned to the real-estate man. "Who's the kid?"

"Son of the owner." The agent looked down at Angus for the first time. "Didn't know you was even here."

"Yes, sir."

"When's your daddy get home?"

Angus looked at the clock on the paneled wall. "About six-thirty." That was an hour and a half off, yet. One of the emergency men stood up, stretched his back muscles, and walked over to peer out the back window.

"That a peacock?" he asked.

"Yes, sir."

"Pretty fella."

The agent's firm dropped the listing after three months, when it was time to renew the contract. It had been the worst listing the agent ever had in seventeen years of the real estate business. Just his luck, the only return prospect had dropped dead for no apparent reason during the second showing. The old guy's heart just blew up or something. Probably had something to do with the honey he'd been running around with that day – she clearly was not the man's wife. Half his age, no wedding ring.

Gib MacNaughton already had received a small raise at his new job. Although the commute wore on him, maybe it wasn't that far after all. Perhaps he could, in fact, tolerate the drive. It just took some getting used to.

Angus actually danced when Gib told him he was taking the double-wide off the market. The boy hopped up and down in a groovy little jitterbug as spirited and free of inhibition as only a small boy's glee-dance can be. He asked his dad to put on a Beatles record, asked whether he could bring Petey in just for a few minutes. So they could all celebrate. Angus's face shone like a polished gold medal. Gib and the agent had conducted a long, rational discussion whether anyone would ever buy the place. The two had concluded, after three months – as long as it was in the shape it was in, and with the legacy of Salt Lick's mayor dying smack dab in the middle of the living room – the double-wide

11

would be damned near impossible to sell. By then, it was really the conclusion Gib McNaughton had wanted to reach anyway.

"I wonder what made old Lothar croak right here," Angus's father said one night, for no reason in particular. "Why did he have to keel over right here in my living room?" He didn't expect an answer, certainly not from Angus. He'd just voiced the question into still air, staring at the spot where his coffee table had been.

Spring came to the valleys and hills of Yakima County in the way it always does on the eastern slopes of the Cascades: when it seems as if no more rain could possibly fall, it does, in sheets. Constantly, for weeks and weeks without even a glimpse of blue sky. Even when there was a respite from the rain itself, water still ran down tree branches and dripped – like cold, slow torture – from the evergreen needles everywhere. And everyone ran around saying, "I'll tell you what, I don't mind the rain, it makes everything so green, but this year's different – it's just going on and on. We could really use a break."

People who had depression disorders wondered whether they could hold out in the dark grayness, the soddenness, the eternity of cloud cover. Domesticated animals stood steaming in pastures as rain saturated their coats. Their wild counterparts – elk, deer, newly wakened black bear, steamed from their coats. Peacocks would stand out in the weather too – they don't mind it – and the saturation changes the apparent colors of their feathers.

Then the first buds popped out on maple and birch, and plum trees, cherry trees, apple trees exploded like popping corn in white and pink blossoms. The average temperature gradually climbed ten to fifteen degrees a month between February and May, and then came false summer – that teaser before kids get out of school and the return of rain during June. The freckles on Angus MacNaughton's nose would spread like a field of marigolds down his neck and onto his pale arms. Only then would summer come. It always began on the fifth of July.

Angus and his father finished the summer's first barbecue and lay in the grass of the backyard watching clouds. From time to time they would note the horizon-to-horizon passage of a commuter airplane, flying relatively low, toward the west. Gib MacNaughton drew on a marijuana cigarette, a recreational habit he had acquired to relax, rather than drinking too much alcohol.

"Maybe there'll be thunder and lightning tonight," Gib said, exhaling a pungent cloud.

"Maybe."

"You wanna bring Petey in if there is?"

"Uh-huh."

The pair reclined, hands clasped behind their heads. Angus watched the clouds coalesce and morph into a familiar shape. There, the high, hooked veils of cirrus: eye feathers. That dense, fleecy ball of cumulus there: a plumed breast. Whispy, drifting solo clouds joined as sword quills, wing feathers, legs, claws. For a moment, Angus saw Petey in the sky. Then the image dissipated.

"What do you see?" his father asked.

"I thought I saw a peacock. But then I realized it was nothing."

The pair glanced over at Petey, who was pecking for larva at the base of the barbecue kettle. He drove his sharp bill into the soil. When he excised it, a gray, impaled sowbug wiggled at its sharp tip.

The air over the grill waved, distorted with the near-spent heat of charcoal and ash.

CHAPTER 2
in which Reverend Jenkins wrestles with a eulogy...

Magda remembered, months back, maybe as long as a year and a half: she knew the evening would take an interesting turn when Jacqua Druce asked if she would like something in her coffee. Her friend, proprietor of the Pie Apple, didn't wait for an answer, but added a substantive splash. By "coffee," Jacqua meant two parts percolated and one part corn-distilled. Opening day of deer season was tomorrow. The menfolk of Salt Lick had all retreated into the hills. About now, they would be liquoring up next to campfires. Why not join them, at least in spirit?

"You know," Jacqua said, as they settled into chairs, "you could divorce the bastard."

Magda considered this, her eyes on the opposite rim of her coffee mug, face steamed with vapors of caffeine and booze. Jacqua was right, of course, as always. The Pie Apple's proprietress was, if anything, utterly practical. Magda's friend Jacqua was independent. There was her daughter, Tina, of course, to prove that she had once had a husband. Or at least coupled, though there is certainly all the evidence in the world that love is not required for this. Magda tried to imagine, in the silence that stretched, Jacqua as an impractical person. It wasn't a picture that leapt easily to mind.

There were some who said that Jacqua Druce had a mouth like a harrier: one of those types who could lick the skin off grapes. Magda had heard once – probably from one of the men down at the laundromat, or maybe from Helmut or Gunter – that an adult mountain lioness has a tongue so rough it is capable of licking the skin off a man. *Jacqua: you are like that. No wonder, of all Salt Lick's female_inhabitants, he does not mess with you. If only I were as strong.*

"I know," Magda said after the protracted quiet. Jacqua's cuckoo clock – one of those from the Old Country where birds pop out and lederhosen-clad lads pursue rosy-cheeked *Mädchens* in circles – ticked. "But you see, it doesn't really make any difference at this point, does it?

Lothar doesn't affect me one way or the other. He can do whatever he wants – he doesn't need me for anything and I don't need him. If he wants to go tear Hell off its hinges, let him."

"You've made your peace with that?"

"I have," Magda lied.

"Forgive me, dear, but bullshit." Jacqua drained her mug. She refilled it with three fingers of bourbon. "I think you got more hangups from that son of a bitch than my coat closet. You and I are going to drain this bottle dry and tell the truth."

Little Soldier hopped up into her lap. She offered him a sip of her coffee. The little chow poked his black tongue into the drink, smacked his little wrinkled lips, and hopped down breathing heavy. His tiny claws clicked on hardwood as he pattered away.

Whenever Reverend Mallford Jenkins had a job he knew he wasn't going to like, he'd seek solitude in the forest. There, in the deep, moist greens and browns, amid sword fern, lichen and the mossy boles of giant evergreens, he could usually close his eyes and hear, in the noise of the woods, God's voice. The throaty raven's honk might be an encouragement or an affirmation. The baying of a solitary coyote could indicate that a new direction should be taken. The long, low language of elk might point him to a relevant passage of scripture. The scolding of a squirrel might cause him to edit entire sections of a sermon.

And when the job was really tough, beyond him, he'd head for the timberline and above, for direct proximity to the Father.

So when the task of composing Lothar Sturmhund's eulogy fell about Reverend Jenkins' shoulders, he brewed a thermos of strong coffee, grabbed from his desk a spiral-bound notebook in which he made and kept sermon notes, climbed into the cab of his pickup truck, and drove to higher ground. The task of composing Lothar's eulogy might be unprecedented in degree of difficulty. Writing a sermon to commemorate the life of this man, of all men, might prove as perplexing for the Reverend as deriving solutions to complex calculus equations.

And for a conundrum as deep and wide as this, the Reverend knew that not any parcel of woods would do. He needed elevation. He needed to stand and sit and pace at the peak of a hill. He needed God's land to gather like the hem of a garment, and then fall away around him, with the sky and clouds within arm's reach. For the Spirit to move upon him, Reverend Jenkins needed to be as close to the Almighty as terrain would allow. And for that he needed Little Bald Mountain, maybe 20 miles, as the crow flies, to the west of Salt Lick. The answer, if it existed at all, would only be found at altitude.

What could you say? the Reverend brooded as he passed Town Hall. As he passed Lothar's office, gooseflesh lifted tiny peaks on his arms and neck. He shrugged it off, and turned right off Mud Lake Road onto Highway 410 headed west. *What could a person say?* As he followed the route of the tumbling Naches, as he passed hunting cabins and overturned jalopies with naked wheels and trunks and hoods sprung, as he wended the highway through canyons and bluffs, no answer came. The question churned between his ears like an engine that couldn't quite roar to life as he motored past roadside copses of alder and maple, and sipped his coffee.

He was to Eagle Rock and the Woodshed before he knew it. As he turned left onto Nile River Road, he sent a brief but earnest blessing the way of the crippled man with the cowboy hat – the Woodshed's operator. He crossed a bridge, the Naches rushing below him across rapids. He recalled an afternoon where, crossing this same bridge, a herd of elk had been wading the river – directly down its center – the animals on their way to lower ground or the feeding station. He had seen in them, their tawny hides and regal antlers, the denizens of Paradise. He had worked them into sermon notes for the following Sunday. But, he recalled as Nile River Road changed from asphalt to hard-packed gravel, he had opted during the sermon to leave this metaphor out. The comparison, the life message, seemed contrite and manufactured at that moment, as he looked out over the small congregation and made brief eye contact with Lothar.

The Reverend motored along the gravel, raising dust behind him like a farmer plowing furrows through arid soil. He passed ranch homes, great barbwire-enclosed pastures, Holsteins and Herefords and Jerseys licking salt, grazing, siphoning moisture from old mildew-green bathtubs of stagnant rainwater. Some of the cows would look up to note his passage, working their lips. He turned left on Forest Service Road 1600, climbed a small hillock, crossed a cattle grate, and entered the Nile game management unit.

As he drove further into the forest, the road surface became increasingly rough. His truck bounced, sloshing tepid coffee over his cup rim. At the tight, climbing curves, the constant compression-braking of heavy logging trucks had turned the gravel surface into hard washboard, so that the truck shook even more violently. For a while, he could think of nothing but negotiating through turns and keeping the tires in contact with the road.

"Oh Lord," he said, "if it be thy will, keep this bucket of bolts together."

On the straight stretches, when the road smoothed out, he could stop praying and glance out his dusty windows. Appreciation welled in him for the landscape that unfolded below and above. Some folks thought that the Almighty *was* nature – that this beauty and God Himself were one, unitary thing. The Reverend prayed for the souls of those misguided people. Although His creation was beautiful in an unrivaled sense, *it* was not the Father Himself. Such a notion was preposterous. Creation was just what its name implied – a *work*. *His* work, manifested for men, testifying to the omniscience and omnipresence of the Eternal One. Even so, the Nile valley opened, Mount Aix and Bismarck Peak and Timberwolf Mountain and Nelson Butte reigning beyond ribbons of clearcut on the far walls – and it seemed, for a moment, that God's face was in it. The sky was as light blue as a crystal.

At these times the environs of Salt Lick seemed to him like Eden. Paradise, this mosaic of land, the flora and fauna of central Washington. Grand fir lifted everywhere from the ground, little Hammond's flycatchers frolicking in the upper branches. Lodgepole pines stacked themselves together on mountainsides like happy sentinels. Juniper boughs moved in fragrant breezes, whispering the names of angels to ruffed grouse. The Reverend knew that nearby brown bears dipped fish from streams, from the clefts of water-smoothed boulders. Great gray wolves gazed wisely across the forestscape, and eagles soared above it. Antelope bitter brush, spiraea shrub, Oregon grape, longleaf phlox, mountain snowberry, arrowleaf balsomroot, cinquefoil, lupine, western yarrow, vetch, bunchgrass – these were the mattresses of white-tail fawns. God's sun shown down on all of this.

But what could a person say?

That Lothar Sturmhund was an *evil* man? That he was in no way connected with the notion of salvation? That of all the men who ever lived, for whom God had sent his Son as redeeming sacrifice, Lothar alone was excluded? That he, in his willfulness and bullishness and fulminance, was, alone of all men, *irredeemable?* When Christ Jesus cried out on the cross, the prime model of forgiveness even in His hour of great agony, "Father, forgive them, for they knoweth not what they do" – did the Savior mean everyone but Lothar Sturmhund? Could a person not say there were one or two positive qualities to Lothar Sturmhund? Possibly ... the firmness of his hand, his faith in the physical world, his leadership qualities. Would there be anyone who would object to the claim he was a good, patriotic American?

17

The Reverend passed Three Bears Camp and rolled his window down for a fresh blast of mountain air. It was cool and crisp, enervating, with the odor of evergreens and new growth in spring. It encouraged him to drive further toward his goal. He finished the last mouthful of cold coffee and screwed the cap one-handed back onto the thermos bottle. He passed a rockpile, Lindsey Camp, then navigated a tight turn to head up the north wall of Lindsey Canyon.

What could a person say?

Whirling in the Reverend's mind was his own role in the enormity that was Lothar Sturmhund. Had the Reverend not turned his eye from Lothar's legendary peccadilloes? Had he not happily given over power and authority – both temporal and spiritual – to Lothar's oversight of the citizens of tiny Salt Lick? Had he not, every morning, anticipated with no small amount of dread the moment when, that day, he would encounter Lothar Sturmhund and be queried about the time, and pull up his shirtsleeve and call on angels of succor that his wristwatch matched the time of Lothar's? Had he not been Lothar's sycophant also? The Reverend had modified sermons, *in situ*, from the pulpit, to accommodate Lothar's presence in Sunday morning services. It was as if a demonic and invisible squirrel barked orders of amendment from the shoulder of his black suit. In what way could a man – not just any *man*, but a Baptist *clergy*man – have been more complicit?

As he plodded up Forest Service Road 1600, now so rough and uneven that he had to drive slower than 10 mph to make progress, he wrestled with justification. Minuscule, resourceless Salt Lick had needed a firm hand on its tiller. Lothar's hand had been firm and relentless. The man, in every circumstance, knew what he wanted and what to do. Lothar's sons, Helmut and Gunter, had needed a strong father. And they had certainly had, if not enjoyed, that. Helmut Sturmhund would be the first to testify to his father's tough love, and limp away afterward. Magda, his wife, needed a provider. Lothar had fulfilled that responsibility, at least in the sense of economics. Indeed, in some ways, Lothar Sturmhund had been absolutely *dandy*.

But what would the young, innocent Flora Navarro, who had – as was fairly broad knowledge – been forced to lay under him as if she were his wife, have to say about him? What would Jacqua Druce say, or Mike Eagle Eye, or Hector Aguirre, or Nicholas Oxendine? How would thumbless Hoyt Stone assess Lothar's leadership and positive qualities? How would Jimmy Bayles testify? What tribute would Ivan Manley pay? Now Juniper Jamison ... there was a man who might speak of Lothar reverently. There was a moment flowing from this wellspring of questions and postulations when the Reverend was certain Lothar

Sturmhund, this instant, fried in the hottest corner of Hell. Where demons of flame jabbed him with red-hot sticks and the Accuser itself fed Lothar the bloody offal of his own offenses.

The Reverend's truck bounced over a high boulder. He heard the problematic crunch of metal on stone, his oilpan colliding with the rock. He said a short, earnest prayer. A cracked pan here, miles from anywhere, would constitute a real threat. Hiking out of here would take all day and most of the night – without water, without defense against coyote, black bear, cougar, rattlesnake. He pulled over at a wide spot in the shadow of the rockpile under the switchbacks that made the final approach to Little Bald's summit. He jumped from his cab to peer at the undercarriage, saw no cracks, no dripping oil, then uttered an acknowledgement of thanks Heavenward. He crossed behind the truck's bed to urinate in its exhaust cloud, and when his stream dwindled, zipped up. He heard, over his muffler, the approach of a commuter airplane.

The Reverend stretched his body, leaned back and tracked the craft. It flew east to west, the deep drone of its radial engines trailing the airplane by a few plane-lengths. All the way across and above the open bowl of the Nile valley, the Reverend tracked the craft. He recalled a flight of his own, from the Tri-Cities to Seattle, a few years back.

He had been preaching from his brother's pulpit in Pasco, a tiny white clapboard church amid apple orchards. From there, he was to attend a symposium of Baptist preachers in Seattle. After the Sunday sermon he had climbed into the tiny fuselage of the de Havilland Dash 8, took his assigned seat starboard, and peered through the portal as the turbopropellers coughed and caught and spun in a vertiginous, throaty whir. The airplane had jumped up off the Kennewick tarmac enthusiastically, banked and headed west. Reverend Jenkins had been put in mind of the ascension of Elijah the prophet in a whirlwind – a chariot of fire – in the book of II Kings. How dandy it must have been to rise to the Father that way, to have been "taken up," the only mortal man to never die. The Reverend, sitting peacefully as the airplane fought God's physics, had grinned his huge puppet grin. After twenty minutes or so, the pilot had come on the intercom and mentioned they would soon be over Yakima, and that passengers on the right-hand side of the aircraft might be able to have a good look at the city from their nine-thousand-foot vantage.

But Reverend Jenkins' own interest had not been on Yakima itself, but on seeing, from this exalted height, the structures and layout of Salt Lick. As soon as they were closer, he had seen the ribbon of Highway 410 fading into the foothills, and could certainly make out

Yakima and, twelve miles beyond it, Naches. He had observed the fork where Highway 12 departed 410. But slowly, as they approached Naches, they had begun to line up with 410, as if its route across the Cascades were a vector they must precisely follow. Naches' streets and outbuildings waved in the distortion of the window's lower edge, then were occluded by the sill itself. By the time he had estimated they were overflying Salt Lick, it would have been directly below the fuselage and invisible from his seat. At that moment, the tiny town passed, for a second or two, through the nadir of Reverend Mallford Jenkins. He had imagined his wife and son, going about their business below. And, of course, he had thought of Lothar, and for some reason it made him think of the fact that sometimes planes crash. And then he had thought what an odd thing it was to correlate the two, Lothar Sturmhund and the enormous kinetics of an airplane cratering into terrain.

He had offered a prayer for his town at that moment, imagining his Labrador retriever, Eli, alone among Salt Lick's life-forms, lifting his great black head and looking skyward, knowing his master sailed the lower reaches of the jetstream above. Knowing his master performed intercession in the great wide blue bowl of the sky.

The commuter plane disappeared over the cleft between Little Bald's summit and the rockpile. Its trailing sound changed tone and faded. The Reverend climbed back in his truck cab, engaged the gears, and assaulted the final approach to the summit. A series of tight switchbacks networking over a steep grade lifted him out of the valley. The sides of the road fell off precipitously – thousands of feet to the floor, now – first to his left then to his right. Little Bald Mountain and its open summit loomed in his windshield. Soon he crossed the treeline. High meadow grass, rather than giant evergreens, surrounded him. Here and there, like solitary vagrants, struggled shrunken, frost-blown trees gnarled inward and twisted from winter's wind and ice.

Again his physical surroundings, and the challenge of keeping the pickup righted and progressing, crowded from his mind the problem of Lothar's eulogy. Whether this was a good or bad thing was an internal debate, just now, for another time. He had enough to do to keep one of the tires from slipping over the almost-absent shoulder, teetering there, and the truck rolling in a fireball to the base of creation almost a mile below. Simply, the notion of reaching his destination, and faith that once he arrived the proper course would be revealed, propelled him onward and upward.

Finally, he crested the last rise and pulled into a turnaround at the bare mountain's apex. He killed the ignition and waited several minutes while the motor cooled. Its clicks and tocks metered the silence. He heard a breeze sough around the metal enclosure of his cab. Its gust moved the truck frame a little. His vehicle settled back on its shocks, and was silent.

What could a person say?

"Oh Lord," he said, "please give thy direction. Please allow me, your servant, a glimpse of thy holy answers. Amen."

He lifted his spiral notebook from the seat, opened his door to an onrush of cool air, and stepped from the cab. He crossed knee-high grass and passed dwarf-trees. He hiked downhill and then around the summit until his pickup was no longer visible. Then he found a huge boulder breaking through the clay, and took a seat. He arrayed the notebook on his lap, retrieved a pencil from his shirt pocket. Around him, breeze washed the maize grass in undulating waves. The only sound was its sweet hiss.

From 6,108 feet above sea level, a tableau of the eastern Cascades foothills unfolded before him. From his great height, the view reminded him of the folds of blankets and comforters laid over the ridge of the Cascade Divide, behind him, and trailing into the plains and potholes of eastern Washington.

He imagined that on the seventh day, if God had chosen this of all places in His world to rest, that he would have reclined here with his head on the future spot of Union Gap, arms flung wide, the right hand resting on Mt. Adams, the left over Wenatchee, sandals dipped in Tacoma's Commencement Bay. The Reverend imagined God napping there, moving in His holy sleep, dreaming holy dreams. He might have, on the seventh day, dreamed of His creation and all it enveloped, dreamed of new work to accomplish on the eighth day – new versions of physics or phyla with which to further enhance His handiwork. Could he have flailed in his Almighty dreams, dragged his left arm across the North Cascades, dug with his holy life-giving fingers the trench of Lake Chelan?

Reverend Jenkins noted the mustering of clouds behind him against the backbone of the state. He wondered whether the weather would change abruptly, as it often may in this high country. He decided that Lothar Sturmhund was fundamentally an evil man, and that this base fact must not, could not, be ignored. Then how to craft a eulogy around this? *What could a person say?* Maybe he should divert a portion of the eulogy to a Heavenward plea for Salt Lick, that a strong man would rise in Lothar's place to fill his substantial boots. But a kinder, gentler man. A godly man. Could this be Hector Aguirre, the new mayor?

The Reverend scribed a line down the center of his notebook page. At the top of the left-hand column, he wrote *Good*. At the top of the right-hand column, he wrote *Evil*. Then he began to make notes, finding that the *Evil* column filled up fast and he must turn the page and inscribe another dividing line. Low, fat cumulus gathered over him without his notice as his pencil scribbled and he wore it to blunt lead. He sharpened it on his boulder-seat, holding it at an acute angle and abrading the tip to a reasonable point. Then he began writing again, collecting an inventory of Lothar Sturmhund's character, a toting of his shortcomings and malevolences and hideousnesses. In devolving script, the Reverend charted a life of excess and rage, of unmitigated appetite, of small-time tyranny gone large and bizarre, of a macabre despot feared yet adored by his seduced subjects.

Reverend Mallford Jenkins resolved, at that moment, to expose Lothar Sturmhund and free the town from his clenched fist. There, above a silent Hell-bound corpse resting like an abomination in its half-open coffin, the Reverend would proclaim the truth, to God's glory.

What can a person say?

There was a cosmos-filling displacement of concussion and sound. A bolt of lightning frazzed the ground twenty yards from his perch, struck without warning and immensely so that its slam and the bright voltaic flash of its counter-stroke drilled through the core of Reverend Mallford Jenkins and made clear its divine message. Its violent clarity blew the preacher from the stone in a tumbling fetal bundle. Thunder clapped, reported and echoed so that he suffered a head-centered tinnitus for several hours, an aural tattoo of the Almighty's will. His body thrummed, lying in the tall grass, waiting for a second stroke. *Have I been hit?* He searched himself, his clothing, for telltale burn marks. He decided no, the lightning or its counterstrike had missed him, but he eyed the pall above him warily still. Because whether the crash had been the result of a percussive wallop of celestial timpani or the myrrh of an expensive linen napkin dragged across the beard of God, the directive was abundantly clear. And not something to be – in any way, shape or form – trifled with.

The Reverend crawled back to the boulder. His notebook lay flung against stalks of grass, its lined pages blowing. The Reverend retrieved it, scoured the earth for his pencil, still on his knees. Unable to find the writing instrument, he turned to rest his back against the outcrop, sat there on clay and grass with the boulder as his seatback. He tore the first five pages from the notebook, those encolumned, half-filled notes of slander and libel. He would start afresh, start with the Seven Virtues:

Humility.
Kindness.
Abstinence.
Chastity.
Patience.
Liberality.
Diligence.

Surely he could find the pattern of Lothar therein.

Well, then, dandy. He'd get started right away, as soon as he found the pencil.

CHAPTER 3
in which Ivan discovers a diaphanous passion...

Jacqua Druce was the first person in Salt Lick to get a satellite dish, and then all hell broke loose.

The white saucer canted toward the clouds from her back yard, out where chickens hopped around in grass and mud during the day and coyotes might come from the hills and mark its base at night. The dish allowed her to receive 99 channels, and in a town like Salt Lick – where residents were more used to three, on a good day, maybe four, snowy stations broadcast from Yakima, and where everyone had seen all of the Pie Apple's videocassettes two or three times each – word traveled fast as an unmitigated megahertz wave. The Lowell's crowd buzzed with the novelty of Jacqua's dish. Even Lothar thought it might be a good thing. Over half-finished drinks and resentful glances at the tavern's TV, the cronies waxed mournful over its poor signal. Nine Peacocks into the evening, one of them might get up and try out the karaoke machine, crooning like a stoned frog.

It wasn't long before folks were making excuses to come see Jacqua, bearing small gifts and plying her with absurd homilies such as *I've been thinking of you* or *How's business at the Pie Apple?* To witness Jacqua's hepped-up bandwidth became the desire of damned near everyone. Mike Eagle Eye was the first to ask for a key – not that Jacqua often locked up – so he could come around and watch the Sci-Fi Channel or American Movie Classics when she was tending the store and he was finished for the day with the town's work.

"Utilization," he explained. "You're putting up money for the subscription, right? Might as well get as much use as possible."

This argument appealed to Jacqua's sensibilities. She also had an inexplicable soft place in her heart for Mike Eagle Eye. So she had the extra key made.

"This rocks!" Mike said. Then, forsaking discretion, he took it upon himself to spread the word that Jacqua's underutilized 99-channel TV was now available for community viewing. Key grinders from

Union Gap to Cliffdell hogged out the cipher to the pins and tumblers of her front-door lock. Tina Druce, Jacqua's artistic teenager, would arrive home from school and find a small circus in her mother's living room – folks, empty beer cans, half-filled tortilla bags and scum-surfaced guacamole dip. Jacqua's ashtrays heaped with tamped-out cigarette butts.

Lioness-tongued Jacqua might previously have chastised the group. "Get this crap cleaned up and get the hell out!" she might have said. But lately some of the bile seemed to have drained from her, so that arriving home, she'd just shake her head, and go see how Tina's latest canvas was coming. Or she'd simply plop down on the couch. If all the seats were taken, she might unfold a lawn chair from its stowage place on the back porch. She would sit in the living room and stare at one of the 99 channels. Remarkably, she would offer no objection whatsoever if someone overused the remote, channel surfing. Many nights, if she didn't head over to Lowell's, she'd retire before everyone had left.

Ivan Manley, surfing during an increasingly rare moment when there wasn't a crowd, when he was alone, blipped onto a porn channel. Now *there's* some throbbing bandwidth! There, on the screen, a scant five or fewer feet from his face, raw acts of intercourse and ... beyond. Fascinating fare, these digital drillings, satellite-fed fellatio, close-up cunnilingus, tongues and flesh spinning. Unprecedented sounds from the TV's stereo speakers – the smack of glistening beefsteak. The pale skin bulging like that of freakish ground-bound mammals. It was unimaginable! And, *Oh my God, get a load of that lingerie!* The diaphanous tufts, pinks and pale blues, sheer, thin revealing fabrics that were sloughed quickly to the soundtrack of fusion. Silks shed like the skins of snakes. The TV channeled prurience into the unfulfilled parts of Ivan's brainstem, down those nerve bundles, snapping and fulminating the distance, to nest in its reptilian roots. Ivan Manley discovered the crocodile stem of himself although the poor man had no idea what to do with this treasure.

Before long, Ivan was battling for possession of the channel changer, wresting it from the fists of whoever preceded him to the couch. Once he snatched it from Mike Eagle Eye with such ferocity the town's fix-it man retaliated, shaking and spraying a full can of beer onto Ivan and Jacqua's sofa cushions.

"You're the one need's a shower," said Ivan.

Having won the remote, Ivan again clicked across media to locate skin and moans and copulation in inexplicable, complex positions. Mike Eagle Eye staggered from Jacqua's place, threatening to bring back

Lothar and see who, *then*, got the channel changer. Ivan collapsed into position on the couch, scooted aside a half-empty jar of pickled asparagus shoots on the coffee table with his boot. Brain-emptied, he stared out with close-set, black-rimmed eyes at the action.

For a while, Salt Lick folk put up with Ivan's monopoly. After all, life in Salt Lick could be quirky. Some people reacted to the town in odd ways. Perhaps this was at work in Ivan, with his white-knuckle grip on the remote.

After some time, for all but Ivan, the novelty of Jacqua's 99 channels wore away like the washboard surface of logging roads.

"Anything on?" someone would ask, humping through the front door.

"Not a damn thing."

Or, "Naw, same old stuff."

Mike Eagle Eye stopped coming around, turned his key back over to Jacqua. Then the rest petered away, slowly at first, finding other distractions, so that one week there averaged eight or nine people per night, then the next week, six to seven, and so on. Finally there remained Ivan, his hard-on, and Victoria Aguirre.

Truth was, Vicki, Hector Aguirre's daughter, was attracted to Ivan – especially his bitty eyes and strong, cocklike nose – in a powerful way. While the others faded from Jacqua's couch for other distractions, Vicki remained nymphomanically faithful. And this was not a trifling thing: Vicki Aguirre, in addition to possessing a beautiful soul, was as close to goddesslike on the exterior as any young *hija* anywhere near Salt Lick. Juniper Jamison once remarked, in Lothar's presence, that he would eat a mile of her shit just to have a look at where it dropped from. "Been there," Lothar had said. "Done that." Of course the Hirsute One had not eaten Vicki's feces, per se, but had enjoyed a very close, very intimate view of her backside and the surrounding blissful territory.

Jacqua arrived home one afternoon to find Vicki pressing her goddesslike frame into Ivan. Vicki's logger shirt was undone, bra unclasped, one breast in her hand pointed at Ivan like a nipple pistol. "I have one of those," she was saying, indicating some creamy scoop of flesh on the TV currently jiggling like a dollop of butterscotch pudding. "I can do that for you." She referred to the positionings, pistonings and moanings on screen.

Ivan craned his neck, peered around her. He shrugged her off, eyes imprisoned in pixels.

And, finally, Jacqua turned fits.

Ivan Manley sat with his bones at right angles in a hard chair, palms on the table. He examined his fingertips as if they might reveal how he got into this mess. Ivan hoped, somehow, he could gracefully extricate himself from this *delicate* situation. Across the table, an empty chair faced him. The walls around the chair and table were close, papered with community service and personal security posters. He glanced up from his hands, read the Yakima County Sheriff mission, goals and objectives. And there was McGruff the Crime Dog – WATCH OUT FOR CRIME. Ivan wondered for a moment whether McGruff meant to watch out for *him*, whether he – Ivan Manley – was included.

No, he decided. *Not me.* Yet the evidence of the moment seemed to the contrary: here he sat in what the policeman had called the "Inquiry Room." The officer had stated the name of this cell with a polite smirk, carefully unlocking the handcuffs, arranging Ivan in the chair.

"I'm gonna take these off and you gotta sit nice and quiet," the policeman had said. And Ivan had readily agreed: now was the time to start exhibiting what they called "good behavior." *Whatever happens, it's going to be all right* – he kept rolling this phrase around in his brain, as if repeating it again and again would negate his circumstances and roll back time a few hours. Better, weeks. Or a few months maybe.

He heard the doorknob jostle. The door hesitated on its jamb before opening inward. *That door isn't hung properly,* Ivan thought, as if observing this, for an instant, raised him above this predicament. He could point this out, demonstrate that he knew about these things. It might impress the officer that he was knowledgeable and able to contribute. He might then seem like a responsible, and not criminal, person.

"Mr. Manley, is it?" A new voice preceded its speaker through the door, not a voice as kind as the cop who had left him.

"Yes." A pause, and then it occurred to him to add, "Sir."

"There are no sirs here," the new officer said. He was smallish but wiry. His face was angular, with an aquiline nose and sculpted chin. The man strode the short space from the door to the chair opposite Ivan, and arranged himself on it. He met Ivan's gaze in a bored, detached manner, as if he were staring not at Ivan, but through him.

"You are Ivan Manley, thirty-nine years of age, living out in Salt Lick at 1204 Benton Road, a finish carpenter. Is all of that correct?" It seemed the totality of this query tumbled from the man's mouth in less than two seconds.

"Yes."

"Sad news of Lothar Sturmhund."

"Yes."

"He was a fine lawman. A fine deputy."

"Yes, sir... I mean, yes..."

"Detective. My name is Detective Pandoulis. That is a Greek surname." Detective Pandoulis spelled it rapidly for Ivan. "I am telling you this so that you know who you are dealing with. I will write it down for future reference." He did so on a pad of paper, tore the topmost sheet off with a tiny, flickish flourish of his wrist, and extended it to Ivan.

Ivan accepted the note. "Pandoulis," he repeated.

"Yes – you may address me as Detective, or Detective Pandoulis, whichever suits you."

"Thank you, sir. Detective. Pandoulis."

"Mr. Manley, you have been arrested and are being booked for theft of a commercial vehicle and property theft which, together, in this jurisdiction, are felony charges."

Ivan met the detective's stare with what he hoped was a comprehending and respectful manner. He nodded, as if affirming the detective's recitation of these facts might soon bode well for him.

"So you understand these charges are very ... oh, wait." The detective paused, drew an electronic device from his jacket, clicked a button on its side. "I would like to audio-record our proceedings here, if that's okay with you."

Ivan nodded.

"Of course, you have been told that you have a right to have an attorney present, and that one will be provided to you if you can't afford one."

Ivan nodded again, then realized the device couldn't record his head shaking. "Yes."

"You don't have to say anything without one."

"I'd like to." Ivan meant for it to sound earnest, and supremely cooperative. But he feared it had come out rather clenched, as if he had something to hide. So he repeated and elaborated. "Yes, I would like to speak with you – to make a statement. There's no need for a lawyer here, I'm pretty sure. I'd like to explain."

"Yes... good. So, where I left off before this..." – the detective gestured at the recorder – "...you understand the seriousness of the charges?"

"Yes, I do, Detective."

"You were stopped after driving away from the mall in a delivery truck full of clothing."

"Yes."

The detective looked as if he expected more than monosyllabic answers. There was a moment of stuffed silence. The detective sighed, and it made the sound of an automatic coffee pot that has just finished dripping a fresh carafe-full. Then he began a speech.

"Mr. Manley, the Yakima County Sheriff Department is going to try to reach out to you today." Ivan believed he might have heard this sort of script on a cop show at Jacqua's house, and was actually a little impressed – momentarily forgetting his situation – that he was hearing it executed so flawlessly in real life. "It's going to be up to you to be cooperative," the detective continued. "If you can make a statement that makes sense, maybe we can do something with the charges. I don't know, roll them down to malicious mischief or something non-felonious."

Ivan marveled wide-eyed.

"We can maybe work them down to misdemeanors or something, you just gotta give me something to go on."

It occurred to Ivan that the detective might suspect there was something bigger here than there really was. Did this Pandoulis think there was a huge operation, that Ivan was a minor operative? That he was the tip of an iceberg, some vast plan to pilfer women's undergarments and resell them on the black market? *In Salt Lick?*

"Oh..." Ivan shook his head. "Oh, you think... you think that... oh shit..."

"Mr. Manley?"

Ivan felt an urgent need to disabuse Detective Pandoulis of any wild notions of a broad panty-stealing conspiracy. It was really a great deal – a *huge* deal – more simple than that.

"Perhaps I should start at the beginning," Ivan said.

"Yes, that would be good."

And for the first time since entering the room, Detective Pandoulis looked at the subject of his interrogation. It wasn't that he had not glanced at Ivan once over or gazed *through* him, but only now did he *really* look. Only now did he really *observe* the unfortunate man on the chair in front of him. He decided that Ivan Manley had the face of an opossum – bitty eyes set half a facial-span too close to each other and a nose that projected as a flesh cone far from his ruddy gob. Manley had the look of a man who had once been surprised and never recovered, as if a giant golden horn had blown a startling glissando next to his ear and the next, most immediate position his face took had frozen there. A look of unmitigated stupefaction.

As the detective listened to the beginning of Ivan Manley's tale, he wondered whether he ought to pity the poor fool for his looks or slap some sense across his ugly face.

In Salt Lick's three-building business district, a laundromat squatted on Mud Lake Road north of the Pie Apple and Town Hall. Some rich person or persons in Yakima, presumably, owned it. No one ever witnessed it being serviced, nor did it seem anyone ever came to retrieve coins from the machines. But since foothills people do a lot of laundry, and most didn't possess their own washers and dryers, the place enjoyed a steady cycle of business. And there had to have been a great deal of maintenance, what with folks throwing coarse materials like saddle blankets and feedbags in their loads right alongside their delicates – underpants, socks, that sort of thing. Its maintenance, then, must have been accomplished in the small hours of night, with constellations spinning overhead and the clinkings of screwdriver turns rising like vapor to Vega. Either that or the laundromat's upkeep was one of the age's true enigmas – a perpetual-motion engine, a Foucault's Pendulum proving the rotation of earth, validating the same coreolis force that spun clouds over the foothills like limp dishrags, swirled water in the shafts of wells, made hunters walk in circles around horned owl nests and lynx dens when they'd lost their way in the surrounding woods.

Ivan Manley, sweating with the weight of two packed laundry baskets in his arms, nudged open the laundromat door. Phosphate-rich, muggy air washed around him as he nearly managed the doorway, but then lost purchase and spilled the contents of one of his baskets on the dusty mat just inside. He set the intact basket on a chair next to a rack of out-dated magazines, collected his soiled clothing into the tumbled basket. He breathed in and out the odor of bleach and buffering agents.

Ivan glanced around across a battalion of whirring apparatuses, all beige and yellow with chrome. Machines everywhere, hungry for quarters. Three other people waited for their machines to labor through cycles of soak, wash, rinse, spin. The bank of industrial-sized dryers along one wall was silent, except for two that spun their contents before the glazed expression of Mrs. Jenkins, the preacher's wife. She bit, without any sort of apparent consciousness, into half a chocolate bar, and continued watching the clothes.

He strode to the change machine, exchanged bills for coins, and plugged the detergent dispenser. A box skidded into a chrome tray at the bottom. He fed more quarters into the dispenser, purchasing enough soap for four loads, and migrated to four empty machines. Their lids yawned. Their coin feeders licked hungry lips.

He separated whites from coloreds atop two machines, then dropped half the coloreds each into their waiting drums. He plugged the machines with quarters, jacked them, heard the coins drop. He added the contents of two detergent boxes and closed the lids. Those cycles started. He repeated this with half his whites, then paused before emplacing the remainder in the fourth machine.

Because there, centrifugally wadded and clinging in a tight, white lump on the wall of its gray drum, remained an abandoned article of clothing.

At first, Ivan simply stared. Someone had clearly removed his or her load but somehow – perhaps it was that the lost article was thrown during the spin up against the drum's flange and escaped notice – had gone on to the dryers without it. He thought it might be an athletic sock, a pillowcase, a handkerchief or hand towel. For a long time he hovered above the open machine. It was only when the two machines with his coloreds clunked into their wash cycles and disturbed his trance that Ivan blinked. Then he reached down into the drum and retrieved the moist clump.

When he unkinked and spread the cloth across the top of one of the working machines, he had to perform a brief inventory of his personal experience. Up to this moment, Ivan had been devoid of any acquaintance with, or practical knowledge of, a pair of women's underwear. But this is exactly what lay before him, spread wrinkled but flat, and wet, across the cycling machine. Panties.

Ivan felt a tinge of embarrassment. He cast a furtive glance across the laundromat at its other clients. Had anyone seen him at that moment, they would have noticed the ruddiness of his face deepen. Splotches of rose-colored pigment framed his pointed nose and spread down his jaw onto his neck. But no one had seen him excise the panties from the washer. Or if anybody had, they were pretending to have not. Ivan probed the underwear with one finger, noted the material appeared to be cotton. The underwear had no design, were pure white, even at the waistband. How different they were from his briefs! And how... lovely. Yes, *lovely* – he actually whispered the word. He marveled that they were so small and delicate, that the holes for the legs rose so high from underneath to where the waistband would have collected them, snugly, against slim hips. There at the peak the material was, perhaps, only an eighth of an inch under the elastic, and sculpted so that the part which would have covered the bottom was much wider than the small V of material which would have covered the front. Ivan suddenly felt warm and not quite any longer sure about himself, or about what he was doing here, or about what he would do with *them*.

It took him a few minutes to decide. Suddenly he did, peeling the panties from the washertop. He dropped them back into the fourth drum, and followed this with the remainder of his whites. He closed the lid quickly, as if fearful they might take flight. And he fed quarters into the third and fourth machines, and could not take his eyes off the fourth. He imagined the foreign underthings mingling in warm, soapy water with his own. How the material would wind itself around and about that of his whites, would enervate them with the softness of the cotton, with what he imagined might have been left behind on them or in them, something bestowed by their former wearer. Who had she been? What had she looked like? What did people call her? And most of his thoughts were spent in this sort of conjecture: what mysteries had she covered with this garment?

He probably knew her! God – who was she? He thought he might never again look upon the womenfolk of Salt Lick in the same way.

Ivan floated in speculation and waited for all four machines to cycle. Then he fed their sodden contents into dryers and watched the clothing tumble through the hinged portals. As the clothes leapt, he caught a periodic glimpse of the panties, but as if they were shy they would disappear behind the fall of socks, T-shirts, trousers.

When the dryers had finished he removed the great, tangled wads of clothing and began folding. Three quarters through the piles he began to suffer a nagging fear that, somehow, they had vanished. Or that it had all been some sort of bizarre waking dream. That they had never been there at all. Ivan choked back disappointment by telling himself that, after all, this was a pair of women's underwear he was thinking about. Of what possible use were they to him? Even so, he found himself strangely upset as he neared completion of his folding, until this disturbed feeling evolved into something approaching a minor panic and then – *there!* – as he turned an inside-out sweatshirt right-side in, clinging with a minor static charge to the fleece.

The panties were warm and dry. They were as white as a small, gentle cloud. And they were *his* now, and no one else's. He folded them with tenderness, secreting them inside the crease of a hand towel. He emplaced the towel and its treasure in one of the baskets, finished folding the four or five articles that remained, and stepped out of the laundromat into a wet April afternoon.

When Ivan returned to his house up Sanford Canyon, he placed the panties in a bureau drawer under his own stack of briefs – *hid* them there, he supposed later – even though there was no one, no wife or girlfriend or female acquaintance of any sort who could discover them.

Ivan had no perverted plans to wear them or play with them in any odd, stimulating manner. They just intrigued him. He liked to remove them from the drawer, lay them on his bedspread and run his fingertips along the fabric. The cotton felt simultaneously cool and warm in a way he could not have explained. When he rubbed his fingers together with the material between them, he'd close his eyes and imagine what a woman must be like, here, especially when he handled the part that was doubled-plyed – the panel sewn in at the thinnest part of the base. He would put them away then, confused with an unfilled sort of feeling, an ache whose source he could not determine.

Still, as soon as he closed the bureau drawer, an image of the panties would fly cross his retinas like Cascades hawks or the airplanes that flew over town all day. The ideation of these underthings – so alien and compelling in all their occlusion – would not go away. The more Ivan wondered why, the more they colonized his mind so that some days he could barely keep from thinking of them, waiting, snugly under his briefs in the dark drawer.

It was shortly after this that Ivan found himself no longer able to quickly scan the clothing merchants' advertisements in Sunday's *Herald-Republic*. Instead, he would dwell on the photographs of women in underwear, and note that various department stores in Yakima were having some sort of lingerie sale or another. This kind of thing had never registered before in Ivan's mind. But he now found, upon waking Sunday mornings, that he eagerly anticipating the short trip down Benton Drive and Mud Lake Road past the looming windows of Town Hall to get a paper at the Pie Apple. Once he returned, Ivan spent a number of hours looking at the ads. He would do so without any cognition of the passage of time, without once glancing at his watch. Often it was well after noon when he finished scrutinizing the pictures and memorizing their details.

The advertisements fascinated him, of course. In them, models – women the likes of whom he could have only barely dreamed – sat in various stages of repose and languor. The small articles of fabric that covered them in those places became, for him, like a subpoena – utterly compelling. His desire to learn as much as possible about them, and to see as much of them as possible, became a special brand of personal zealotry. Too, he marveled at the words used in the advertising copy:

matching control brief, high-cut, scalloped trim, French cut, embroidered lace, demi, spandex. Sheer. *Nude.*

These words reached to him across a cosmos of inexperience, yet he began to understand them as he matched them, week after week, with their images on the slick ad inserts. He began to comprehend terms such as camisole, bikini-cut, strapless, jacquard, push-up, their meanings and functions, to distinguish one article of underclothing from another. Yet also, Ivan, by now, could appreciate they were all subsets of the large and wondrous set of feminine underthings, a set that drew him like a mirage draws an arid man toward what he imagines to be water. A water he has never tasted or swam in but whose sweetness and refreshing qualities he imagines to be unprecedented.

For some reason, all of this put him in mind of Jacqua's television and the feel of his fingerpads over buttons. And, perhaps, of Vicki Aguirre.

It didn't occur to Ivan to clip any of the advertisements, to keep them on hand pasted in a scrapbook for the sake of, say, reference. It was enough to await their weekly arrival and study them, and he found himself richly anticipating Sundays throughout his workweek. So much so that, in fact, the quality of his attention on his work tasks suffered, albeit mildly. He had to force himself to pay better attention before his boss might comment.

Whenever people in Salt Lick wanted to go anywhere, this essentially meant Yakima, fifteen miles distant. The Pie Apple, Salt Lick's tiny grocery, only stocked so much. Clothing? Yakima. Medical or dental services? Yakima. Automotive work, new tools, night life of any consequence, tropical fish, tattoo parlors, prostitutes, veterinarians – all Yakima. So Ivan found himself, one Friday afternoon two months after the laundromat discovery and a few weeks after Lothar Sturmhund dropped dead – after a drive he could not at all remember with any degree of clarity but must have made as an automaton – in Penney's Intimate Apparel section at a shopping mall in Yakima.

Row after row of undergarments on display called to him in soft, sighing music. It was like a dense, old-growth forest, but instead of trees, racks and racks of underwear – the most delightful leaves imaginable! Propelled through and among the racks, he fingered new sensations – here a tan-colored set of satin bikinis – his caress sensed molten chocolate and spun gossamer. He moved to a pair of sheer briefs with a trim of scalloped lace, tested the lining and cotton panel and see-through fabric. They felt so light, only a thin film of nearly nothing. His fingers came away with a sensation of having experienced warm, pleasing moisture, as if the briefs had been lightly anointed with exotic

34

perfumes. He moved to a display of bras, fingered their silky straps, examined the interior bowls of cups. Allowed himself further immersion in these sensations, gently rubbing the insides of his wrists, where his pulse was quickening and visible, against slight fabric. He was like a boy let loose in a pharmacy's sweets section.

"Sir, can I help you find something?"

The voice startled him, and he looked up in surprise at a saleswoman. Stunning, she smiled from full, red lips. Her eyes danced with customer service, though it was clear they sought, unsuccessfully, to steer clear of Ivan's prominent nose.

"I'm sorry?"

"Can I help you find something?"

Ivan understood she wanted him to buy something. The thought had not occurred, and he weighed it for an instant. Not a bad idea, really.

"I don't know," he said. "Right now, I'm just looking I guess."

"Just *looking?*" She gestured at the panties grasped in his palm. It made him wonder whether handling the garments was appropriate in a situation such as this. Whether a man was supposed to simply walk in, know what was required, and make his purchase. And whether she had seen him touching the undergarments.

"I wanted to see what they feel like." It seemed a perfectly reasonable pursuit, and her responding smile resurrected his waning confidence. Encouraged, he held them up for her to see. His fingertips were visible through the diaphanous material.

"Those are very nice," she said. "Your wife..." – she glanced at his left hand for a ring – "... uh, girlfriend? What does she like?"

Ivan paused for a thought. Nothing emerged. "I don't know." Yet he still sought a recommendation, for her suggestion that he purchase them, or some similar article, had lodged in his mind with barbed hooks. And the saleswoman was beautiful. She would have some idea how to proceed. She was obviously quite sophisticated and interested in the success of his endeavor. She could guide him through this.

"What do you think of these?" He indicated the pair in his hand. "Do you have any experience with them?"

"Pardon me?" Her smile remained, but a question now lay under it, a question that had nothing to do with Ivan's nose.

"Are these the kind you wear?"

She seemed confused by this. He had meant it as a genuine question, posed as any honest and frugal consumer. But her blush and half-step back betrayed he had crossed some border into a new country he did not comprehend.

Recovering, determined to remain helpful, she said, "Well, let's see, I have lots of kinds." She accepted them from his offered palm – he imagined a peaceful soughing sound as they slid away from his fingers. It was the sound the boughs of a pine tree make when moving across one another in a small, sweet mountain breeze. "Yes," she said. "I have worn these. They're really comfortable. Your girlfriend will feel sexy."

Ivan grinned. He wasn't sure what all of this meant, but the saleswoman said that last word with a new sort of smile on her face, one that had latent meaning, as if they two shared a fabulous secret. He liked the sense that she engaged him in some private, delicious plan. And he suddenly wanted very much to please her, this lovely saleswoman with her full lips and dancing eyes, this experienced, conspiratorial sophisticant.

"I'd like them, then," he said.

"Good, come over here and I'll ring them up." She motioned for him to follow and, like a faithful dog anticipating a walk, he did. And he emerged from Penney's with his second pair of panties.

Over the course of the next several weeks, Ivan purchased women's underwear at the rate of four or five pair per week. The mileage on his odometer ran up. His collection grew, and he moved them to their own separate bureau drawer, removing a bin of old work socks and placing the delicate items there like baby birds. At the height of summer, he bought a satin pair imprinted with tiger stripes at Nordstrom, imagining the sort of feral jungle woman who would pull them snugly into her wild place. He came home from Lamont's with a pair of thin, white cotton high-cuts. Red stripes were woven into their fabric, so that when he touched them his fingers came away with the smell and taste of peppermint. And he meditated fiercely on a sheer set whose tag had called it a thong. It was barely a strip of tanager-yellow silk, and he couldn't – no matter how long he thought about it or which way he held it up to the light – understand its application. Even so, he was drawn to finger it and imagine, with joy, its purposes.

What he had not counted on in all of this was the cost of the garments. The first, of course, had been free, and subsequent panties – purchased one pair at a time – were manageable. But when he began to have difficulty selecting only one garment and started buying them by the twos and threes, his carpenter's salary began to show strain and then, after a while, became wholly inadequate.

Parked in the Mall's lot outside Penney's, Ivan turned this problem over between his ears as August's dry heat made him light-headed. Through the glare of blasting sunlight, he saw a delivery truck pull up, execute a reverse turn and back carefully into the delivery dock. And from out of clear space came the notion that inside the truck, perhaps, were cartons and cartons of lingerie. That he had only to peek in and might find them there waiting.

Ivan was not a thief and was in no way acquainted with dishonesty. His subsequent act was nearly as involuntarily as succumbing to a stomach flu. He couldn't, later, explain why this idea grabbed hold of him and clenched. Yet he emerged from his own car. He closed the distance between his parking space and the truck's cab with a sprint. He lumbered behind the wheel. Ivan Manley engaged the gears and drove away.

Mall security was on him before he could manage the turn from the lot onto Peak Parkway. Yakima County Sheriff's deputies arrived shortly afterward.

"I see," said Detective Pandoulis after remaining silent for some time following Ivan's conclusion. "And that's it?"

"Yes," Ivan said. "That's it."

Pandoulis clicked the recorder to stop the tape. He leaned back and wiped his eyes. Ivan noted the man had been sweating under the arms, that dark circles had blossomed there as if the interrogation had made Pandoulis uncomfortable.

"I'll tell you what," the detective said. "I'll check with petty crimes and see what I can do. You've been very cooperative, and I want to thank you."

"You're welcome."

A knock came on the door. Ivan and Pandoulis watched as the jamb stuck again, then surrendered to the entering pressure of another officer. The new man beckoned to Detective Pandoulis, indicating he should leave Ivan for a private consultation outside in the hallway. "Excuse me for a moment, Mr. Manley," Pandoulis said. He rose and followed the other officer through the door. It shut softly but not fully – stuck on its jamb again – behind them.

Ivan waited for an indeterminate time, resting with visions of his bureau drawer and its dreamlike contents winding through his head like a happy river. Across the room he saw an abandoned newspaper on a shelf, wondered whether there was time for a look. And just as he began to rise and go to it, the door reopened with Pandoulis and the second officer entering.

"Good news for you," Pandoulis said.

"Yes?"

"Penney's will not pursue charges. Neither will Mall management. It seems there was an intervention on your behalf."

"An intervention?"

"Yes, a clerk at Penney's. A saleswoman. The head of the women's clothing department, oddly enough. Says she met you in Intimate Apparel. Apparently she was on break and saw you drive off in the truck. She asked for leniency."

"I'll be damned."

"Yes, you're free to leave."

"Yes, well then, uh... thank you."

"Not at all."

Ivan rose, free again, to depart. He wanted to say so much more. He felt that Detective Pandoulis had been, despite his rough look and tough-cop mannerisms early on in the interview, so kind and understanding. He paused to collect his thoughts, to figure forth an expression of gratitude.

"Mr. Manley?" Pandoulis said.

"Yes?"

"Mr. Manley, if you don't mind me saying so, there are people who can help you."

"Help me?"

"Yes, professionals. I'd recommend seeing one."

"Oh."

"And Mr. Manley, it's none of my business, really, but I think you need to get a girlfriend somewhere along the way."

"Really."

"Yeah, I'd say so."

Ivan thought this was a great idea. But he didn't know where to begin. "Thanks," was all he could manage.

Under a Horizon Air commuter airplane droning westward, Ivan Manley drove home to Salt Lick in sunshine, already extricating underthings from his bureau drawer, already future-tripping about the woman on whom he would bestow them as gifts. A *sexy* woman. First thing, he'd visit the lingerie lady at Penney's.

She'd know what to do.

CHAPTER 4
in which Stoneway Pouring conducts strange rites...

Lothar kicked dogs on numerous occasions, mostly for nothing, but just for simply being underfoot.

Odd, that such a he-mannish fellow would be such a mean prick to dogs. Particularly in light of his own surname, which translates "stormdog." Usually men like dogs, no? Dogs represent something emblematic for them, as opposed to domestic cats or other less masculine animals. There was ample evidence for this in Salt Lick, Washington, as there is in every town on God's green planet: imagine a group of men standing about in front of Town Hall with nothing terribly important to do. Imagine that a fine, tall male dog saunters toward the group, fresh from inspecting the garbage out back of Lowell's. The beast sniffs at the trouser-cuffs of each fellow, and moves on its princely way. If the dog has not been neutered, see if there is one man among Salt Lick's citizens – excepting Lothar, of course – whose eyes are not glued to that pendant scrotal sac, those canine balls shifting with confidence through the beast's stride.

A man is proud of his balls, but even prouder of his dog's.

But Lothar had surely received some dog's deep, infected bite as a small boy (if Lothar ever was small). Or he had borne witness – at some impressionable age – to gray-black lips pulled back in a doggish sneer over pearly, pointed canines. Perhaps there had been more than one of them, dogs, that is – a pack, as it were – of German shepherds.

Lothar, can you see the dogs now, herding Jews? Can you see the great gray beasts bite, the fearsome rolling of their eyes? See the whites disappear under heavy lids? See those mandibles snap at the leashes of the *Obersturmbannführer?*

Lothar: Here is a man who was not raised around puppies!

In Salt Lick, damned near everyone except the Sturmhunds had dogs. Everywhere Lothar would go or look: dogs. Dogs sniffing, barking, leg-lifting, dry-humping, shitting, grunting, testing the wind for the smell of game, panting, rolling their eyes up into their canine skulls, gazing sidelong into the dim woods at perceived movement. Watching him – yes, that's what those dogs were doing. Watching him, Lothar, the king. Looking for weakness. Because that's how dogs are – they sniff out weakness and exploit it. For they are usurpers, and spend their time plotting *coups d'etat*.

To take full inventory of the dogs of Salt Lick would require a notebook of many pages. There was Reverend Jenkins' great Labrador beast, the Biblically named Eli. And that golden retriever up at Kinchlow's, DelMar, the one always getting his ass pecked by the peafowl. Jimmy Bayles, the black fellow, had a mutt everyone just called Bastard. It lived in the trailer with him alongside Hoyt Stone's garage – probably slept, Lothar fumed, right up on Jimmy's nappy little cot. No one knew what breed of dog it was, but it was damned big, probably some sort of cross between a mastiff and a mule. Mike Eagle Eye owned a pair of stump-tailed, dock-eared Doberman Pinschers, Quoof and Pyewacket. And what about Jacqua's pukey little smashed-up, wrinkled thing, a chow he thought she'd once called it: Little Soldier? What kind of name was that for a dog? Several others had them of course. And if that weren't enough, there marauded bands of coyotes throughout the foothills all about them – rogue troupes of canine Pancho Villas with dusty fur where mange hadn't left them bald. Under cover of night, the feral dogs made raids on garbage cans, or meat hung by hunters, from the Cascades forests.

But how could Lothar admit to his people, those whom he ruled, to his doggish nightmares? Lothar had kicked each dog in town at least once, others twice, and a few several times. Each dog in town knew the shape, taste and feel of Lothar's kick. Even those Dobermans, who are not known for a kindly disposition toward a man's boot.

Hoyt Stone watched vine maple, aspen and birch rush past him through the windshield wipers as his truck started a climb up Mud Lake Road. He reached down to pull the rig into overdrive and listened to the rebuilt Road Ranger transmission shift out, grind for a second, grab and roar through the muddy floorboards. He lurched forward a little, finding leverage on the wheel, and eased back as the big motor's RPMs wound through his ears. Hoyt felt the truck shake then settle out through his gloves, through the steering column. He crossed over the center line on a curve at maybe 35 mph, pulled wide out of it and ran the rear tires out as inertia carried the whole left side over the shoulder, then centered out again. It was not a normal thing, fishtailing through the hills in a cement mixer weighing nearly ten tons, particularly across wet April roads.

But he was late again, damn it. And besides, it was hard to dump over a mixer with its low center of gravity. It was harder yet to get and keep a good pouring job, but he'd better damned well slow down, he thought, before he rounded the next corner and smashed through a wandering herd of elk or something. If Hoyt knew anything about this time of year, it was that forest animals intent on the rut were anything but cautious. Pranging his rig into a big musk-drenched bull was not his idea of a great morning.

He backed off the accelerator on a straight stretch that climbed out of Salt Lick, decided it was now warm enough in the cab with the thermostat finally jerry-rigged and working again to remove his gloves. Hoyt pulled his eyes away from the damp road long enough to contemplate the bright rash of scar tissue where his right-hand thumb once opposed his four fingers. He hooked those four fingers around the wheel, fished in the right pocket of his work shirt with his left hand, pulled out a lighter and a pack of smokes. Like one of those Vegas card-dealers shuffling the deck with a single hand, he managed to drive an 18,400-pound cement mixer, invert the cigarette pack to get one smoke out, replace the pack in his pocket – all while still holding the lighter in his left hand too – place the filtered tip of the cigarette between his chapped lips, and light it while running up past a yellow road sign that warned, in black: CURVES NEXT 8 MILES.

"When you gonna give up them fags?" Jimmy asked. They were the first words he'd spoken since they'd left Hoyt's place. "You promised Claire you'd quit."

"Damn right," Hoyt said. Both his hands were back on the wheel now, for the next curve. "And I will too, soon as I finish this pack." Hoyt glanced over at Jimmy briefly – noted, again, the young man's grin. Jimmy Bayles possessed a self-assured smirk that never left his face. It was an unwavering, broad, thick-lipped smile that made folks think he must know of a cache of buried gold bars somewhere or have prescience of the next winning Lotto numbers. His teeth shown at the center of that smile like pillared deposits of pure enamel.

"Right," Jimmy said, feigning enlightenment. "I see."

"Don't give me no shit, Jimmy. It's like this, see. I was smokin' while you were still pissin' your bibbies."

"You make my point."

Jimmy, eighteen years old, the only black man in a Salt Lick, was out of high school and out of his foster home in Yakima for five months now. The job with Hoyt – Stoneway Pouring comprising just the two of

41

them – was a good one by his reckoning. At least it meant he and Bastard could live in his own trailer out the side of Hoyt's garage. He'd lucked into the association – Hoyt Stone had just moved into the area as well, and had been looking for a top-notch assistant through the county placement agencies in town.

As for Hoyt – he was nearly as opposite Jimmy as a man could be, particularly from the standpoint of temperament. Hoyt Stone was arid-witted, wry in his rare humor, which he meted out drop by drop. Where Jimmy was entrepreneurial, Hoyt Stone was conservative in his approach, hard-working in a proletarian or Presbyterian manner. Jimmy wore his own brand of humor well. Hoyt was slightly less colorful than a loaf of white bread. Jimmy possessed patience far beyond his eighteen years. Hoyt, on the other hand, didn't suffer fools gladly. While Jimmy grinned incessantly, Hoyt Stone offered to the world a face perpetually netted in a grimace, creased and canyoned exactly as if he were permanently bearing down on a particularly dense stool. His face relaxed only when he inhaled on the paper throat of a cigarette.

Hoyt Stone and Jimmy Bayles covered the still-climbing road for five more minutes without further conversation. Hoyt blew smoke through the wing window. The rain slackened. Deciduous trees at the side of the road – ubiquitous, and showing new leaves and buds – thinned out now as evergreen woods took over. The route leveled off and straightened out, and Hoyt slipped the truck out of overdrive into a higher gear.

Further ahead the woods tapered off. The road divided small clearings devoted to pasture. If the plots had been maybe ten times their size, they might have properly been called pasturelands. Up here, the weather was breaking. Hoyt spied blue through an opening in the clouds. April in the foothills. The truck passed cows, horses and sheep grazing on the tiny plots, staring at some point directly in front of them while their herbivorous jaws worked grasses to spindly, digestible paste. In the air above them, great wheels of flock-birds turned. Hoyt asked Jimmy to consult the bid sheet and confirm the preacher's place was coming up soon.

"Yeah, should be," Jimmy said.

Hoyt was a tiny bit embarrassed. True, he'd not been living in Salt Lick much longer than Jimmy – eight months total – but getting acquainted with one's neighbors seemed sort of fundamental, especially in a town as small as this. But Hoyt Stone, if he'd lived in another time and place, would have been a hermit. Come to think of it, Hoyt would have realized what psychologists of a certain school called *self-actualization* as a frontiersman or trapper of the 19th century, coming

42

out of the wilderness only for provisions, brotheling, or having a fractured bone set. Hoyt had no need for human contact, or male bonding, or any of that kind of crap. What he needed was a wife, and Claire was fine for that, and one person to help him, and Jimmy ought to prove O.K. in the concrete-pouring department.

Jimmy pointed. "That's it. There."

Hoyt geared down again, the green house with white trim coming up on the right. Afront the property, behind a drainage ditch, ran a split-rail cedar fence. The house sat back from Mud Lake Road thirty yards. An empty dirt driveway ran to its one-car garage from a culvert next to the road. Hoyt hoped Jenkins' car was in the garage, because he was sure he had the appointment time right. Even though he was twenty-five minutes late, he hoped they had waited. Hoyt snuffed his smoke in the ashtray.

He slowed nearly to a stop, cranked the wheel over to the right, and pulled the rig slowly, like a great lumbering land mammal, into the driveway.

Jimmy and Hoyt pushed their doors open simultaneously, seats squeaking as they pivoted out of the cab onto the running boards, then down onto the dirt. They walked around the back of the truck to look at the condition of the driveway nearest the road, then together around the right side of the cement barrel. It was dense – just short of hardpan – all the way, soil compacted from repeated overpassings of the Jenkins automobile. In spite of recent rains, the surface was not muddy. It was too dense to absorb much water. This made for a damp surface only, and for this small blessing Hoyt Stone and Jimmy Bayles could thank the god who oversees concrete.

Without warning, around the front of the truck bounded a black Labrador retriever woofing and wagging its tail. It wanted to play, but Hoyt, backed away with Jimmy in between them.

"Get that damned dog away from me, Jimmy." There was the front of panic in his voice.

"Jeez, it's just a dog. Come here, fella."

Jimmy bent to take the dog's head in his hands, worked its ears over a bit as its tongue licked his fingers.

"Fine, you just keep him right there."

They heard the house's screen door open and bang shut, and a footfall on the porch.

"That's a heck of a dandy truck, sir," said a deep male voice.

Like eager infantrymen, the pair of pourers stepped smartly to the cab and around the front – Hoyt keeping Jimmy between him and the dog – encountering their customer for the first time.

Jenkins was a unique-looking fellow, with a lazy eye and tufts of hair that seemed to change direction a lot, even with no breeze. His mouth spanned the entire width of his face, his thin lips, smiling now, puppetlike. He wore a white shirt, black trousers with a crease, and rubber farm boots.

"Yes, thank you," said Hoyt, extending his thumbless hand.

"That's a 1972 International Boost-A-Load with a 237 horsepower Mack truck engine, eight-speed Road Ranger, with an Eaton differential," Jimmy said.

"And *that*," Hoyt said, pointing to his partner, "is Jimmy Bayles." Reverend Jenkins, oblivious that he had just been exposed to the cement pourer's rare humor, shook Jimmy's hand as well. "And I'm Hoyt Stone," Hoyt said. "And I'm sorry we're late."

"Not at all, Mr. Stone. Not at all. I'm just pleased you're here." Jenkins smiled from his clean-shaven face. His eyes looked, independently, at each of them. "I don't see you at my church." Jimmy thought the preacher had the voice of James Earl Jones.

"No," Hoyt said. He inhaled air that might propel an elaboration, but Jimmy cut in with a rescue.

"Sir, Hoyt is nervous about your dog." Jimmy pointed at the animal, which had run a few interested circles around the trio, then settled at Jenkins' feet. There, it consolidated its brown-eyed gaze upward at its master. Hoyt shot Jimmy a sardonic thanks-a-lot look.

"Eli?" Jenkins looked down at the Lab with one eye. "Don't worry about Eli. He's a good dog. In the true sense of the word. Why, if dogs had souls, Eli would be saved and sanctified indeed! Dandy! He wouldn't hurt anyone."

"It's no big deal," Hoyt said, further unnerved by the combination of the Reverend's continuing eye tricks and oblique religious overtones. "Dogs just make me nervous."

"How come?" asked Jimmy.

"Let's just say I had a bad experience with one a few years back."

"Well, we'll just put him in the house for now," said Jenkins. He turned and hollered up to the door. "Jericho!"

The door banged again and out popped a small version of the Reverend. The boy skipped down the steps by twos as Eli met him halfway, tail wagging and rump shaking.

"Jericho, take Eli inside," Jenkins said.

"Yes, Papa," the boy said, too enthusiastically, it seemed, to Hoyt. It was a suspicion he carried through life like his rig carried its spinning cement can: An agreement too easily or eagerly reached can't be good. One has to *work* for it!

Nevertheless, Hoyt's cynicism proved unfounded. The screen door banged again as Jericho and Eli disappeared lickity-split into the house. The men turned their attention to the task at hand, bidding out the concrete driveway. Hoyt discussed the process with Jenkins – they would measure and calculate the cubic dimensions of the driveway at seven inches thick, then take a look and see how much pre-grading they'd have to do. Jenkins would have to remove his car from the garage and park it out next to the road. They'd start laying in forms. After that, they'd probably have to get over to bid another job in Cowiche, so Hoyt said he reckoned they'd be back first thing tomorrow morning to pour.

"You won't be able to drive your car over it for a week or so," Hoyt said. "It's got to have time to set up."

"That will be all right," said Jenkins. "We can hike down to the church if the weather holds. A little walking for the Lord never hurt nobody." The three heard a telephone in the house. The screen door opened and the preacher's boy again emerged.

"Papa," he called from the stoop. "There's a phone call."

"Tell them I'll be right there." The Reverend turned to Hoyt and Jimmy. "Excuse me, sirs, if you will. Yes, thank you." Lazy-eyed Jenkins turned and left.

Jimmy turned to Hoyt, shrugged, and said, "Well, let's do 'er." He walked back to the cab to retrieve a measuring tape. As Jimmy began the process of measuring, Hoyt walked around back of the rig. There he unhooked metal clasps from the stow poles and started removing crusty two-by-six lumber for forms. His mind wandered through a tunnel twelve years deep to a construction site in Juneau.

It is bitter cold.

The crew is working hard and fast in the few hours of southern Alaska's autumn daylight. He's ripping a piece of plywood with a circular saw, the motor whine covering the beat of framing hammers. The cord to the unit is bunched up under his boots, limiting the run of the saw up the chalk-line. He reaches down with his left hand, still operating the saw with his right, pulls the cords out from under his boot. He loses balance for a second, switches hands on the saw's handle but still, for some reason he will never be able to explain, keeps the trigger depressed, and in stumbling, lifts the whirring saw up. He catches the root of his right thumb on the spinning blade. It slices through the web of his hand, the thumb's bone, the surrounding tissue. His thumb drops to the deck.

Still, he's holding up the saw. He examines the stub as blood fluxes from the wound, in time with his heartbeat, from a long distance.

The saw shuts down – he's finally pulled his finger off the trigger.

I need some help here.

Blood covers the plywood and extension cords and deck below him. The sleeve of his quilted shirt is sopping with it.

I need some help here!

"Hey, fellas. Can somebody give me some help here?" he shouts.

Pretty soon the whole crew has stopped whatever they were doing. They gather around.

"Dammit, Hoyt," someone says, he can't tell who, because the voice has come from far away and struggling uphill, as if calling from the foot of a canyon. He knows his body is in shock or soon will be, but he's perfectly calm. *No reason to get all excited. No reason to lose your cool.* Just move fast.

Someone pulls off his jacket and top shirt and winds the shirt around Hoyt's hand. Another crewmate has wrapped his hands like visegrips around the pressure point of Hoyt's right wrist, holding it up above the level of his heart.

My thumb.

My thumb.

"Somebody get my thumb, O.K.?" Hoyt voice sounds like that of a frightened boy, although Hoyt doesn't particularly *feel* scared. *No reason to get all excited. No reason to lose your cool.*

"Sure, Hoyt. Yeah. Here it is..."

Someone bends over and retrieves the thumb, stands up straight again, then holds open his hand with the nasty fragment enpalmed. Whoever this is seems to want to show it to Hoyt.

"Don't show me the fuckin' thing," Hoyt says, angry, embarrassed, feeling like passing out, turning his head. "Jesus."

"Just bring it with us," another voice says. They're going to take Hoyt right down the hillside to the clinic in town to see if the medic there can stitch it back on – or maybe they can find a bush pilot at a nearby tavern to fly him to Anchorage. That shouldn't prove too difficult.

The crew helps Hoyt down the stairs of the upper deck, out the future front porch and across snow and mud and scrap lumber and used nails – the general talus and scree of construction. He's feeling ... what would you call it? – *woozy.*

"Is somebody bringing it?" he asks.

"Yeah, I got it."

46

They're helping Hoyt into the passenger seat of a white Suburban – Hoyt remembers the moment as plainly as if it were all happening an hour ago: the white truck, its gray interior, seeing gouts of his breath as plumes in the cold air, and red rivulets coursing down his forearm. In the earnest focus on positioning Hoyt in the seat, the guy with his thumb, cradled in two handsful of snow, carelessly drops the severed appendage.

And a local hound, who's been hanging around the work site sniffs at the digit, finds the odor of Hoyt's meat pleasing. The brutish fiend snaps it up like a dog biscuit.

"Crap," says the heedless thumb porter. How the hell's he going to explain this to Hoyt?

"Hoyt."
Whuh?
"HOYT!"
"What? Stop yellin.'"
"I'm done taping this off," Jimmy said.
"Oh, O.K. Good. Help me with these forms then." A phantom itch returned where his missing thumb ought to be. The old, hard scar, and the knitted tissue just under it, ached. It was cold still, even mid-spring, with the mountain breeze and all its bone-penetrating dampness.

By noon, having first backed the rig out of the driveway, then paused as Jenkins removed his car from the garage and parked it on the street, they had basically finished hand-grading the ground. By 1:00, the forms were in place.

Jimmy walked up the sidewalk to the porch while Hoyt took a rest in the cab. He knocked on the door. Young Jericho answered. Although he had hailed his father from the group about the earlier telephone call, Jericho appraised Jimmy as if he had never seen a black person. Or at least not from so close.

"Papa!" he shouted over his shoulder. "The brown man is at the door."

"Jericho, mind your manners!" This admonishment came in the form of a female voice from inside a room down the hallway.

Jenkins came clomping down the hardwood hall in his farm boots, scruffed the blonde hair on his boy's head. He looked down at little Jericho and up at Jimmy at the same time, clucked at his son.

"Run back on in, Jericho," he said. The boy darted back down the hall. The preacher turned back to Jimmy. "Forgive my son. We've lived in the country a long time, and we don't watch the television. Or rent any movies."

"Probably a good thing," Jimmy said. "Look, we're about done here, and we've measured off and set up our forms."

"Great, great."

"Figure we'll be in around eight a.m., if the weather holds.

"Yes, great."

"We'll call if not."

"O.K., that will be fine."

"We'll see you tomorrow then."

"Dandy. Great."

Jimmy returned to the cab, Hoyt fired up the rebuilt Mack, and they started down the road for Salt Lick. They passed Town Hall. Jimmy wanted to stop at the Pie Apple for a can of soda. But Hoyt, noting the time on Town Hall's clock, said they had to press on or be late to the bid in Cowiche. Jimmy checked his watch to synchronize it with the clock in Town Hall's façade. They turned onto Highway 410 and headed east.

"Odd fellow," Hoyt said, once they were under way on the smooth highway.

"Yeah, maybe."

Next morning the sky was pushing clouds in a strong wind. Hoyt and Jimmy pulled up in the mixer, barrel rolling, behind Jenkins' cars. The blinds were drawn in the house, and the pair jumped out of their seats and headed up the driveway, stepping around the forms. They clambered up the sidewalk to the front porch.

Soon after they knocked, Jenkins opened the door. But his countenance had metamorphosed so completely in the span of a single night that it was almost as if they were being greeted by an entirely different Reverend Jenkins on this new morning. It was as if he had been replaced by an identical, but temperamentally opposite, twin reverend. The difference was no more clear than in the crestfallenness weighing down Jenkins's shoulders, the light that had fled, albeit temporarily, from his rogue eyes.

"We've had a tragedy," Jenkins said.

Hoyt and Jimmy heard soft weeping in the room down the hall.

"It's Eli," Jenkins said. "Eli has been run over."

"The dog?" asked Hoyt.

"Yes, Eli. The dog."

"I am sorry, Reverend Jenkins, sir. I am sorry," said Jimmy.

48

"It's a shame. Someone hit him with their vehicle, I suppose, right in front there," Jenkins pointed to the road. "Drove right off, apparently. Last night. And the worst of it is that there are only a few neighbors up this way, you know? It's likely that we know who took his life. It's likely they attend my church. They must not have known, or they would have stopped. Do you think that's possible? That they didn't know?"

"We could come back," Hoyt said, rather than postulating an answer.

"Oh, no. Please stay, it will be all right if you stay," said Jenkins. "We'd like to bury him while you are here, have a funeral for him, sweet thing. Entomb him in the concrete, yes, we would."

"Pardon?" Hoyt was sure what he thought he heard must have been a mistake. "It sounded like you said you wanted to entomb the dog in the concrete ... in the new driveway."

"Yes, well, we talked about it, and we thought there would be no better, more fitting resting place for Eli than right where we would be reminded of him every day as we went about our tasks.

"Under the driveway?" Jimmy asked, again with his unending smile. But in this case his grin was clearly forced, not the Lotto-winning or buried-treasure grin, but one affected as if with a broken-hearted clown's paint. A grin that was not sure it understood...

"Yes, sirs. Under the driveway, indeed."

"Well, now..." Hoyt said. "I'm not so sure we can do that, Reverend Jenkins. It's like this, see..."

The Reverend's face fell as if he were the captain of a vessel that would soon dash itself upon seaward rocks. Mr. Stone was saying something more...

"...you see, I'm not sure if it will meet code, sir."

"Code?" the Reverend repeated, this word from another language. *Code? Is this man speaking in tongues?*

"Yes, sir, the building code."

"Reverend Jenkins," Jimmy said, in an effort to help his boss out. "The building code says that concrete has to be a certain thickness – seven inches in this case. If we pour concrete around Eli he's going to, well... um, not to be gross, but... um, he's going to decompose, sir."

"Decompose?" *Decompose? What fresh Babel is this? Who has attempted another tower to Heaven?*

"Yeah, rot," Hoyt said. "Leaving a cavity which will collapse and you'll have a hole in the driveway, and that don't meet code."

"I see. Code. The Code. Yes, well this is very disappointing – Jericho – our child, you know, it was his idea and he is so sad this morning."

Then Jimmy's entrepreneurial bulb blinked on over his happy skull. An idea descended upon him like a dove from Heaven.

"Hoyt," he said. "You know, we could dig down a little, lay Eli in and cross over him with a couple rods of rebar. That'd do it, don't you think?"

Jenkins' asynchronous eyes brightened with a pre-glow like that of vacuum tubes commencing to power up.

"I suppose ... I don't know, but I suppose it would work," Hoyt said.

"We would be so grateful," the Reverend said. The statement rushed from his lips with the amplitude of something he had held in from the moment Hoyt and Jimmy had arrived. A degaussed radio finally and clearly transmitting.

"O.K. ... we'll try it."

"God will bless you, Mr. Stone."

"God bless us all," said Jimmy, his tongue, perhaps, too light for the moment. "Amen." Neither Hoyt nor Jenkins caught his humor, although the preacher readily and literally agreed: "Amen and amen," he echoed.

A moment of uncomfortable silence, in which someone could again be heard weeping, passed. Hoyt broke the quiet.

"Reverend Jenkins, we'd like to get started, I think."

"Yes, please do. Dandy. Amen and amen."

"We'll just be out front," said Jimmy.

Jenkins turned without another word and headed back into the hallway. He turned at the crying room and disappeared. Hoyt and Jimmy looked at each other, back down the hall after Jenkins, at each other again, and let themselves out.

"Where should we dig, do you think?" Jimmy asked, as the screen door settled behind them. "Right up next to the garage?"

"Fine."

Jimmy worked the spade for a few minutes until he hit serious hardpan and had to return to the rig and get a pick. The hole had to be about a foot deep below the level of the concrete, maybe three feet long and a foot and a half wide. Eli's final resting place – what a deal! He labored in this fashion for fifteen minutes, then Eli's hole was complete, and he signaled Hoyt. Hoyt knocked on the screen door again, informing Jenkins that they were ready.

Jenkins emerged in a black suit, carrying a Holy Bible under his right arm. Following him was Jericho, in a miniature version of his father's black clothing. Then emerged Mrs. Jenkins, a wispy creature in dark garments as well. She had a black pillbox hat bobby-pinned to her hair. A veil of dark mesh wavered in front of her face.

The Reverend walked around to the side of the garage, out of sight, as his family assembled next to the new grave. He returned with a bulging burlap sack. He set it down at the side of the grave and sought the open end.

"Will you join us?" he said to Hoyt and Jimmy.

The two joined the family, self-conscious in their quilted Carhartt overalls, workshirts and ball caps. Jimmy removed his hat, motioned to Hoyt to do the same. With love and gentle care, Jenkins brought forth Eli's broken body from the bag, laid the hound in the hole with all honors. It was as if he were placing a human infant therein. Jenkins reached down, grabbed a fistful of dirt from the berm next to the hole, and sifted it through his fingers onto Eli's black coat. He invited his wife and child to do the same, and they wept as the dirt sprinkled onto the dog like a coarse spice of sadness.

"We are here to grieve the death of Eli." His voice was toned like a massive iron bell. "Our faithful Eli, taken in an untimely manner from us, returns to the bosom of the Almighty.

He looked upward, and his face shown.

His two earthly charges – bride and first-born of his seed – did likewise, and Hoyt and Jimmy looked up too, but all they saw were scuddering clouds and a commuter flight moving on the eastern horizon toward them. Jenkins opened the Holy Bible of King James. Just then the wind picked up, blew his hair straight over and riffled through the pages of his Bible. He grasped the holy book again, found his page and his voice came through and over the breeze like it was a rockslide off of Mount Moriah:

"That which the palmerworm hath left hath the locust eaten; and that which the locust hath left hath the cankerworm eaten; and that which the cankerworm hath left hath the caterpillar eaten. The Good Lord giveth, and the Good Lord taketh away in His timing, and this hath mystery for us, His attendants. Ashes to ashes, dust to dust."

He paused to let these profundities sink in.

"Lord, unto thee we commit the spirit of our constant friend and loyal companion, Eli, which hath been named after your own servant." The preacher's voice came in a basso profundo that seemed to shake the earth beneath their feet. It merged with the droning of the aircraft's engines, now overhead but occluded by clouds.

A dog returns to its own vomit; a fool returns to his own foolishness, Hoyt thought, the only verse from the Bible he could remember concerning dogs.

"Would either of you two gentlemen like to say a word?"

Silence, except for sniffling and wind, then a throat clearing – Jenkins'.

"I say, Mr. *Stone* or Mr. *Bayles*..."

What?

"Would either of you like to say a word?"

Hoyt snapped out of a reverie in time to shake his head. Jimmy looked up at the darkening sky again, for inspiration, looked down again at the canine corpse and said, "Every dog has its day, and here's yours, Eli."

"Thank you." Jenkins turned to his family. Then he issued this short commandment: "Say goodbye to Eli."

His wife and son bade farewell, with more tears and the onset of running noses, and slowly disappeared back up the sidewalk, across the porch, and into the house. The screen door creaked open and banged twice. Then there was only Jenkins left, with Hoyt and Jimmy. The two had replaced their hats.

"Reverend Jenkins," Jimmy said. "We have to start now in order to get all the pouring done before it rains, sir."

"Yes," he said, from a very great distance. "You will have to start now. Please do. Dandy."

And Jenkins left too.

Hoyt and Jimmy had pulled the chute between the forms and released half the pour. The admixture of water, aggregate, and cement covered poor Eli. Suddenly Jimmy remembered the rebar, and shut down the flow. The pair laid two lengths of the reinforcing iron over the grave, then two lengths criss-crossed over that.

After they re-started the flow, the screen door articulated again on its hinges. Out popped Jericho, in farm-kid garb again.

"Be careful, Jericho," Jimmy said, moving between Jericho and the fresh pour before the boy unwittingly stepped in drying concrete. Jericho looked up at him. There were tears flowing down his little cheeks.

"Will he be all right in there?" The boy pointed to the setting cement over Eli's resting place.

"Jericho, he's ... not living. He can't feel it ... anything. Your daddy would say he's in Heaven."

"No ... I *know* all that. I mean will Eli's tomb be all right, will it last?"

52

Jimmy got down on his knees in front of Jericho, so his face was at the same level as the boy's.

"Yes, Jericho. It will last forever."

"Until the Lord comes?"

"Yes, even that long."

The boy smiled through his tears, sniffed twice, and watched as Jimmy returned to work. Hoyt was just shutting down the last of the mixture flowing from the chute. It was time to level it out and brush it for texture. They did this with a twelve-foot two-by-six, jiggling the setting mixture into a perfect plane, discounting the slope from garage to street, as they worked back on the vertical forms from the garage to the road. Tossing the two-by-six to the side, Hoyt gathered himself and stood, slowly from backache, removed his cap and wiped sweat from his graying head. He leaned on the mailbox and admired the work. A perfect pad of gray, thirty yards long, eleven feet, four inches wide, seven inches deep with the exception of one spot, where it was deeper.

The pair waited forty-five minutes. They snacked on pepperoni sticks and coffee in the cab of the mixer. Then they brushed out some texture with long-handled brooms and applied a coat of spray from Jenkins's hose-reel. They rolled out at sheet of plastic, staked the corners and points along the long sides, to keep unwanted moisture out and wanted moisture in.

"There it is," Jimmy said.

"Yep."

"It's nice."

"Yep."

"I mean the whole thing... it's nice."

"Yep. Now let's go get paid."

For the last time, Hoyt and Jimmy knocked on the Jenkins' screen door, were invited in for a last cup of coffee, and settled the account for $1,700.

"I'd like to ask you to accept another fifty for your extra effort today," Jenkins said.

"Oh, that's all right," said Jimmy. "We're glad to have been helpful during this difficult time."

Hoyt rolled his eyes. Jimmy hoped Jenkins hadn't seen it.

"Well, that's very kind of you, and I'm sure God will bless you."

"That's what I'm hoping." Jimmy smiled that Lotto smile.

"That's what we're all hoping, sirs!" Jenkins beamed as he rose to escort them to the door.

Hoyt Stone fired up the mixer. He did a three-point turn in Mud Lake Road. They headed back down to Salt Lick. Even though the rig fumed and roared through its gears down the road, there was silence in the cab.

"Strange," Jimmy said, breaking the stillness between them.

"Strangest damned thing I ever saw." Hoyt lit a smoke and exhaled out the wing window.

"Still," Jimmy said, "the man knows what he believes in."

"Yep."

Cigarette smoke blew from the cab, and the Road Ranger shifted from fifth to sixth gear.

"Yep, he does."

CHAPTER 5
in which Gunter receives an inheritance of machines...

Inasmuch as he was raised at all, Lothar was raised a carpenter's son. After he came to America, he became a carpenter himself. And when he had mastered all the finer points of the multiplier effect of wood and nail and hammer and the workings of other tools, when he appreciated all the facets of carpentry including the business end of things, he became a general contractor.

He settled on five acres of forest up Sanford Canyon in Salt Lick, at the core of the sodden state of Washington, in the middle 1970s. There, he took unto himself a wife: Magda, short for Magdaline. She was a Walla Walla girl – a Walla Walla Sweet, he called her at first, in honor of the onion. He met her while framing a new home in Selah. As a clerk at the lumber store, miles from home, she filled his nail order one afternoon and fell under his Lotharic spell. They married and Magda bore him two sons, two years apart.

Lothar liked to build and hunt and make others do what he wanted them to do. He was skilled in all of these pursuits, and he thought this made him a good man. He never doubted that he was *good*, never in all his life. He wondered about those around him from time to time, whether they were *on the right track*, as he often said of things that met his approval, things that represented *good*ness as he understood it.

Lothar demanded a great deal from those around him. His family, for sure, but also the workers who came to his job sites – glaziers, framers, drywallers, joist-jackers, plumbers, roofers, electricians, cement pourers, painters, insulation hangers, spacklers – as well as the servants of Salt Lick, the town clerk, the Pie Apple's proprietor, his cronies at Lowell's, the minister, the fix-it man, his fat protégé, Juniper Jamison. All of them. Lothar Sturmhund would have his damned way, because Salt Lick was a small town.

Lothar's will was the tip of a projectile. You either agreed with it or you didn't, but it came on nonetheless.

Gunter Sturmhund's inheritance was nothing more and nothing less than a ready-for-use machine shop.

His father left the house to his mother. Not that the house or its contents were any great treasure. Lotharless, Magda Sturmhund, now in the opening, confusing days of widowhood, found herself in sole possession of the four walls, plus the normal complement of household items. Among these were varied articles of furniture, the newest a quarter of a century old. There was a black and white television and a set of four TV trays. There was the queen-size bed on which Lothar returned to her after his myriad betrayals, and its two sets of bedclothes. A half-dozen bath towels. Pots, pans, dishes. All of Lothar's clothes and firearms. In summation, what was left behind Magda's drawn curtains was bric-a-brac and arcana of the sort that accumulates in more than two decades of marriage. And there was his fancy Ford truck. None of it was anything Madga felt she hadn't owned – except for the clothes and truck and guns, of course – more or less, already.

As for the matter of Lothar's clothes, these she offered to Reverend Jenkins for charitable deployment. And her husband's truck she decided to keep. She had no use she could think of for Lothar's guns and oily reloading equipment. These she bequeathed to Gunter's older brother, Helmut, who walked with a limp, and Candace, his wife. Nor could Magda imagine herself deriving use from the unattached garage, the machine shop.

Gunter had protested. "I just can't figure out what I'd do with it."

"You'll figure something out," said his mother. "Just spend some time there. Something will become clear."

So Gunter took possession of the shop. A few weeks after all the excitement of putting his father underground – it would have been mid-June probably, around Flag Day – he executed his first entry in years, so far as he could remember, into its strange mechanical environment. Gunter was twenty-one when his father took the sudden dirt nap and left his youngest son with a shopful of questions. After the burial, after the telephone call from his mother to stop by and get keys to the garage, he had made that first entry. Gunter had scanned the contents of his father's shop, the shop that was now – in spite of his protestations – to become his. And at first look, he had seen only machines, scraps of machines, scraps of machined metal, wood, plastic... plus an amalgamation of unmatched hardware large and small. His doubts persisted. They hung about him like vultures, glaring balefully down.

There were, of course, in addition to the doubts, all of those basic first impressions and the overimpression of a slightly dusty tidiness.

Some of the shop's articles of hardware seemed purposeless. Light from the overhead tubes fluoresced over their matte or steely surfaces. Gunter could only guess at their functions. But others seemed more obvious – on inspection, he could immediately understand what they did. Even so, the gift of the shop and its contents seemed unusable. To call his father's shop his own seemed superfluous in a life such as Gunter's, which was characterized at almost all moments by cerebral, sedentary pursuit.

Too, Gunter was mystified as to the shop's organization. True, its major tools were self-evident. He knew, for instance, when he saw one, the shape and function of a circular table-saw. And *there* was his father's, now his, at a constructed island at the shop's center. Its radial teeth glistened like the alloyed fangs of a wolf. He also appreciated the automaton-like countenance of the drill press. This boring tool stood as a watcher in the southwest corner of the shop, steel curls in its jigs and moorings like oily mechanical stubble. There was a booth in the southeast corner, festooned with electrical hookups, reels of soft, brassy wire and quivers full of flux like the shoots of bronze plants. This was clearly a welding cubicle. In a row along the north wall, in progression from east to west: a wood lathe; a mounted router, grinder and belt-sander; and another tall sentinelish object, a band saw. On the east wall: a door, then a long workbench. A vise rose through its pressboard surface. A full wall of shadowboard hung above it; hung thereon was every format and size of crescent wrench, monkey wrench, screwdriver, pliers, hammer (framing, claw, ball peen, and felted mallet), C-clamp, T-square, level, wire-stripper/cutter, caliper, drill motor, saw (coping, hand, hack, and jig). Also, a battalion of files. All of these tools were held in place by brackets or otherwise restrained before painted silhouettes of themselves. If one were taken from its place, its afterimage burned there in black. Gunter appreciated that if anything could be said of his father, the old bearded bigot was one son-of-a-bitching organized dude.

As if there weren't enough evidence for this, the west wall of the shop was a bank of drawers like a sheer canyon wall. Its face filled all the wall space from the drill press to the lathe, from floor to ceiling, with small drawers whose unlabeled faces were no larger than index cards. Gunter counted thirty-six drawers vertically and fifty-four horizontally, and the math wouldn't immediately come exactly, but he knew he was looking at well more than eighteen-hundred cubby-holes filled with God (and his father) only knew what. On Gunter's first visit to the shop after his father's death, he approached the wall of drawers with a feeling hybrid of awe and intimidation. He stood in front of it, this matrix of mystery, and thought in absurdities of a cruel game in which one of the drawers contained an incendiary device that would blow off his hands – *how was his luck running today? Would he pick, randomly, the bomb drawer?* He reached for a drawer's clasp and pulled it toward him. No explosion: rather, an ants' nest of cotter pins. In another drawer, lag bolts of all shapes and sizes. Sheet-metal screws here, molly bolts there, small gaskets and O-rings, carpenter's pencils, near-spent tubes of graphite, scraps of sandpaper, epoxies, hex nuts, washers, wire terminals, switches, gages, thumb brads, tiny tools with gleaming pincers. How could anyone know the meaning of all of these things?

There were no labels on the drawers. How his father had located needed objects within was an enigma. Had it been through the agency of an internal biological gift, an echolocation or photographic memory? Something slightly paranormal, perhaps, a sixth sense of knowing where lost objects are, an old man with the touch? Or was there a pattern to it, some algorithm of the various purposes of the spare hardware? For example, did *this* row comprise objects that fastened through bonding, *that* row objects that fastened through twisting compression? Were *these* drawers in this pattern, say, the pattern of a square or right angle, all filled with implements that measured the tolerances, lengths or other dimensions of objects? Perhaps it was a simple alpha arrangement. Gunter rejected all of these speculations – knowing his father, he settled on this explanation: the old man had simply demanded that the contents of each drawer imprint themselves on his mind. He would have bullied them into memory.

At first, Gunter's intimidation in the face of this riddle interfered with what might have occurred to him logically: to start with drawer No. 1, which happened to contain several spools of string and twine, and proceed to drawer No. 1,944, which enhoused the tumbler and other guts of a door lock, knob and bolt-engaging mechanism, as well as numerous randomly sized cork circles with adhesive on one side, used for protecting polished wood surfaces from the bases of commodities that would sit upon them. In between drawers No. 1 and No. 1,944, Gunter guessed lay all of the types of hardware that ever had been invented, in all of the world, in all of history. His father had collected and catalogued it – at least mentally – with a purpose that evaded Gunter.

A film of three types of dust – fibrous, resinous, metallic – lay upon everything. It all wanted a good whisk-brooming, and Gunter first set to the process of growing intimate with the shop in this way. He pinched a paper breathing mask in to the bridge of his nose and began whisking the dust into little piles. He collected the metal shavings under the press into a dust-pan. He emptied the sawdust reservoir under the table saw. He wiped down the mechanical devices with a rag that soon turned black with lubricant. He filled containers with the effluence of his father's handiwork.

He began to have the faintest appreciation for the machines and the parts only after the shop was swept and wiped, only after he had rendered this service of care. For several nights, not successive but two to four nights a week for the remainder of June, he simply drove the half mile up Mud Lake Road, took the fork onto Benton Drive to his mother's house after finishing work for the day. He would key the shop's padlock, enter through the door between the workbench and band saw, and take into himself the odors of the machines and components. He would switch on the fluorescent tubes and look around. Gunter began to form a notion that he might actually *use* one of the machines. He might exercise his own will on some object of metal, wood, or plastic.

During this same period, the Summer Solstice or thereabouts, Gunter discovered that he had started to look at objects in a new way. He would see the handle of an automobile's door, for example, and wonder which machines in his father's shop would collaborate to produce such a device. Not only the gleaming chrome projecting from the door's surface, but the complex mechanism inside, the parts hidden. He removed the cover plate from the underside of a coffee-maker in his mother's kitchen, examined the wires, capacitors, silicon boards. Through what conspiracy of implements was this miracle performed? He would pause passing Town Hall, gaze (with an odd, gut-clenched loathing he couldn't explain) through the truck's window at the clock on its façade. How could its internal machinery be fashioned so delicately as to predict, moment to moment, what the time would be?

He would have the urge to disassemble all sorts of mechanical and electronic devices, in the same way little boys and girls do as their childish awareness of tools and engineering evolves.

He would find himself poised at the entryway of his own home, half a mile across the ravine that fed Sanford Canyon from his mother's place, ready to depart for work but staring for moments at his own front door hinge. During the day, he would find himself daydreaming about the interaction of components – again, gears and cogs in the Town Hall clock, for example – and the elegant manner in which their intercourse produced something inherently useful. How they birthed value where had existed before vacuum.

One night Gunter entered the shop, walked directly to the band saw and – in a stunning display of uncharacteristic initiative and raw courage – levered the toggle switch to the on position. A jangling whir overfilled the shop's dense air as the steel band spun its circuit. And in the nest of the saw, Gunter was amazed to see that what before had been static – a jagged edge of sawteeth – now was intensely kinetic. The crenulated teeth had disappeared into a semi-solid horizon, a sort of change agent, which he knew he must now immediately satisfy. He glanced around the shop as the band saw whirred in its corner, located a neat arrangement of scrap wood he had noted during a previous visit, retrieved a piece of oak trim-moulding from the pile. He held it in place next to the terrible band, pushed it into, and through, a transformation. The band severed the piece, and Gunter held before him two components rather than one.

He began to appreciate, in the enormity of that moment, certain possibilities.

He toggled the machine off. The whir ceased instantly. The sawteeth, lightly dusted with wood fiber, reappeared.

This act marked the moment Gunter's mind began to change about the worth of the materials in the shop. Henceforth, he was more often in mind of the machines, tools and contents of the drawers during his daily tasks. He spent more evenings in the shop, examining things, turning on and off the machines, making exploratory cuts and drillings, joining together articles he found in the bank of drawers.

For an occupation, Gunter had chosen *planner*. He worked for a survey firm with offices in Yakima. At the end of the day, he would have produced a plan, tracked progress toward a plan, or estimated the resources necessary to accomplish things that were articulated in a plan. It was dry, unheady work, accomplished mostly by pencil and calculator, with nothing to point to at the end of the day or week or month and say *I did that*. In such a pursuit there was no exercise of the imagination possible but, rather, a rote vomiting forth of simple arithmetics. So Gunter began to view with disinterest this vocation and became further interested in his avocation, the exploration of the machines, the tools, the hardware – in a surprising way, they and their potentials appealed to him as tensile, corporeal, permanent. They seemed, at times, to be clad in flesh.

His planning work deteriorated, and his supervisor recommended an interview with one of the firm's human resources managers, a hapless bureaucrat assigned to employee-assistance issues.

"Do you have a problem with drugs, Gunter?" the bureaucrat asked.

"No," said Gunter.

The bureaucrat, seeking more, expounded: "Because your boss says you seem distracted. Your work... it's... not the same, he says. He doesn't understand..."

"It's not drugs," Gunter said. "I'm surprised you'd think that."

"Well, what are we supposed to think?"

Instead of answering, Gunter thought only of the contents of drawer No. 17, a chalk line wound about a wooden reel.

The bureaucrat grew frustrated; Gunter's file testified that he normally was an adequate worker. His boss had said the change came around the time of his father's death.

"Tell me about your father," the bureaucrat said.

The body that housed Gunter stood and the chair it had sat in tipped back. The body pointed at the human resources manager. "You don't know me or my father," it said. "He who knows me knows my father!" Gunter, the real Gunter – the entity that dwelt in the skull of the body of Gunter – meantime ruminated on how wire strippers were used to bare wiretips of plastic sleeving before soldering onto brass terminals. The shocked human resources bureaucrat finally found a word or two, but these were spoken into an empty vesicle. It was as if Gunter's mind pulsed on the surface of a distant sun-circling asteroid, as Gunter's body turned to depart.

"Gunter?" he heard from the other end of a corridor. "Gunter?"

One afternoon – Hector Aguirre had been named the mayor, his brother had gotten a new tattoo, Nick Oxendine had gone messy, and Mike Eagle Eye had wrecked the town pumper, so it must have been running on the end of summer – Gunter was boring a hole in a block of wood with the drill press when his right hand slipped and grazed the spinning bit. Gunter examined the bleeding wound for some time before taking any action.

While an anomaly, the incident seemed to Gunter destined. Perhaps, he wondered, machines must from time to time exact a toll from their operators. An even trade, all this service for an inconsequential wound. He thought of the time – six, seven hunting seasons ago? – when his father shot Helmut in the foot. After all, a pistol was a sort of machine, yes? He thought of another time hunting when he raised his rifle to sight on a passing commuter airplane. He had wondered, at that moment, about the possible interactions of one machine, the rifle, on another, the aircraft.

He bound his hand in an oily shop towel, poked the press's OFF button, left the block of wood partially clamped to the press's chassis, deserting the blood-dappled operation. As he washed the wound in his father's kitchen sink, it occurred to him that the random bite of one of the machines was an unprecedented intimacy. And that only through intimacy with his father's machines would he ever reconcile his own creative urge, his own longing – which he must now admit – to have known his father. He surmised that the shop's purpose might be to propel him toward a paternal, if posthumous, reconciliation. That only then, when that was properly handled, would he enjoy the satisfaction of making something with utility, indeed, with his own very life.

Over the course of fading summer, then as autumn set in, Gunter taught himself how to properly wield each tool in the shop. He would practice the purpose of that one individual tool on hardware he found in the drawers, then practice the connection of that tool's interaction with another – what the two tools might, either sequentially or concurrently, enact on these objects. Following this, he practiced combinations of work performed by various tools in random and patterned order, filling the interstices of this work with note-taking, the gathering of shavings or filings, the wiping down of machines.

Gunter made some interesting discoveries in the drawers, and in the process of connecting more things he found inside. He learned, for instance, that he preferred collections of components in the formulation of a useful object to an object of a single, solid state. He liked things built up of individual pieces rather than, say, castings. He found that the making of a purposeful amalgamation of objects was infinitely more satisfactory than the vaporous pursuit of *plan*-making. The human-resources manager recommended his termination from employment, so he was canned.

To celebrate, Gunter taught himself spot welding, arc welding, acetylene welding. He learned the intricacies of lathe-work, of grinding and routing. He learned how capricious a soldering gun can be, then taught the device respect for its betters. He learned the mysteries of electrical wiring, delving into the sacristy of cathodes, capacitors, current. He heaped upon his forehead ashes of sawdust and metal filings. The fumes of epoxy held his life together as he tinkered in his father's shop – no! *his* shop – making connections, penetrations, rippings, borings, torquings, screwings, fulminations of sparks. The onset of winter pressed in on the little shop, and he barely had the presence of mind to install a radiating heater, exhaling his own breath while laboring over the slippery intimacy of bolt, lock washer and nut. The heater glowed and dumped infrared energy into the space until

Gunter spied a required component in its filament and removed it with an Allen wrench. The heater was rendered useless then, more a host organism from which needed pieces could be cannibalized – a part farm.

Gunter began to see a distinct form taking shape in his mind, in the dreams he would have before waking and repairing to the shop for the day. The shape comprised components, to be sure, but it was anthropomorphic, bipedal. The shape was companionable.

He began, in his movements before and peerings into the bank of drawers, to search for pulleys and cables, ball bearings, fiberglass wrap, the proper sort of hardware that might serve as tendons, sinews, meat. He looked for, and found, a small treble speaker that might serve as an automated larynx. In the space above his head, he found rafters that housed PVC pipe – perfect for limbs and exoskeleton. He discovered old binocular lenses that might function as portals, rubber-tipped rods that could be digits, a steel funnel that must ultimately become part of the reproductive system and digestive tract, knobs and drawer handles which would serve as glands and nodes. He found viscera of mounting straps, threaded gaskets, solenoids, sockets, thermostats, collars, plug cores, terminal pins, sanding discs, valves, brackets. He assembled a brain of transistors trailing wire and twine ganglia through a length of spinal vacuum hose. He emplaced and shimmed a breastplate of brass studded with diode nipples. He installed a small electrical pump that would ensure the being possessed the capability to reject, to gag.

Gunter brought the assemblage into his mother's house, sat it on her sofa, brought it a steaming mug of coffee.

Gunter sat down.

Gunter waited to hear the voice of his father.

CHAPTER 6
in which Neat Nick suffers a breakdown of sorts...

Lothar was the originator of Tough Love.

Hunting country surrounded Salt Lick – millions of acres of national forest and logging land owned by huge timber companies and the federal government. Networks of gravel logging roads lay over the rolling hills and deep ravines. Massive conifers – yellow tamarack pine, enormous Douglas fir, ancient cedar – lifted from the forest floor. The odd cottonwood loosed its airborne puffs of seed like missionaries in accordance with the earth's cycles. Deciduous maple and birch, tangles of vine maple grew in copses along the Naches River. The roiling waterway ran parallel to Highway 410 for miles and miles, urgent in its flow to the Yakima River.

In autumn, hunters from across the state colonized the forest, fluorescent orange caps and vests for the rifle-bearers, camouflage for the archers. For weeks as frost clamped down on Salt Lick, residents heard from the west the echoed reports of large-bore rifles bouncing from ridge to cloud and back. Leaves turned brilliant yellow, and the first snows fell. Orion appeared high in the black bowl of pre-dawn sky, sword raised in pursuit of the Pleiades, and the tall cedars sent semaphore to Polaris. The full moon rose, gathering into its silver disk the waxing, thin light of day, and spin off haloes. Black bear would hibernate, and a dreadnought of snow and sleet and windstorm would push elk downhill to the lowlands closer in to the city.

Contracting slowed down in winter. The brilliant yellow western tanagers abandoned the forest canopies for better weather and left to the snows gray jays, mountain quail with their straight erect top-bobs, flycatchers, Oregon juncos, tiny pine siskins, hummingbirds. Seductive, honking ravens. And, of course, raptors – hawks.

With less to build or repair, Lothar Sturmhund could spend more time checking other people's time, imparting his will, flinging about the great hirsuteness of his Tetragrammaton, coiling under quilts with women, flying through the minds and business and stature of his townspeople like an often-returning comet or a collision with the earth of an asteroid.

And Lothar and his two sons would spend time hunting deer and elk in the Cascade Mountain foothills around Mt. Aix. The boys were a couple of years apart, both strapping Percheron-like bubs, both created physically in the blond Lotharic image of their father.

The older boy, Helmut, must have been sixteen or seventeen years old that autumn, because the younger boy, Gunter, was just sprouting his first whiskers – and this happened in Lothar's family, the signing of this genetic signature, at about fourteen or fifteen years for the men. The brothers had positioned themselves on opposing sides of a deep, green draw covered with a thick forest of larch pine, Douglas fir, and red cedar. It was getting on the end of the hunt for the day, that tick of the clock that marks quitting time drawing nigh. The oldest boy spied a four-point buck rubbing its antlers back and forth across the base of a cedar stump. The animal, at the base of the draw, turned to present a perfect withers-high target for Helmut. He lifted his rifle, drew a bead on the buck's heart, exhaled his breath and squeezed off a round. The rifle recoiled; the buck dropped to the forest floor, kicked once, then lay still. But a curious coincidence had taken place at that moment. For the younger brother also had seen the buck, from his cross-ravine vantage point, had hoisted his rifle, fired a round into the animal at the exact microsecond as his brother. When men complain about having no luck in life, they should think for a minute about that deer.

Both brothers let out a whoop of triumph and leapt, bounding out of control down the sides of the canyon. Both arrived at the dead deer simultaneously, with twilight falling, expecting congratulations from the other. Instead, what they each got, in turn, was a sort of shock.

Gunter claimed the deer. Helmut said, "Bullshit, I shot him."

"Fuck you, you know I did," said the younger brother.

It went on like this for a while, because neither brother had heard the other brother's shot, it being masked, as it were, by the report of his own rifle.

Helmut offered the idea that the disagreement might be settled by verifying the location of the entry wound. Both seemed to agree that the animal had been facing downhill, and each could certainly agree as to which side of the ravine – of the animal itself – he had been sitting. So the boys located the entry wound in the deer's chest, and then Gunter demanded the older's apology.

"Maybe it's the exit wound," Helmut said.

"You're so full of shit."

So they turned the animal over. They discovered that even in death it had retained its symmetry. In exactly the same place on the other side of its chassis, at exactly the same height above the forest floor, was the entry hole of a 30-06 bullet. And, exactly like the other side, there was no exit wound. Two bullets, their slaying energy spent, still apparently lie deep in the deer meat. And so the brothers each capitulated, if only temporarily. They began the long task of gutting the deer and packing it out of the ravine.

The brothers argued and scrapped for every inch of a thousand feet out of the hole. Helmut must have commanded Gunter not to jimmie-jack him around two dozen times. Halfway up, in retort, the younger Sturmhund son chastised the older for shooting an animal so deep in a canyon, forgetting for a moment that the deer's flesh enveloped two mushroomed lead slugs.

By the time Lothar heard the two brothers emerging from the woods with the animal slung between them on poles, the two were practically ready to drop it and use those poles to rain blows on one another. Lothar stood waiting for them at the side of his truck, shaking his head like a grizzly longsuffering of the foolishness of two bear cubs in springtime.

"You boys sound like a couple of communists," he said.

They got back to camp with the deer, strung up the animal to skin it, and immediately fell into a fistfight. Lothar let them go on a while. Then he grabbed the two boys by their necks and clopped their skulls together to get them to settle out. "Boys," he said, "you got your damned deer together, and that's a fine thing for brothers to do."

Although neither was yet of alcohol-drinking age, Lothar felt that a celebration was in order to commemorate the fine buck. All three began to drink peppermint schnapps. But the boys drank too much. They deteriorated once again into argument, and further into fisticuffs. Then Helmut broke the schnapps bottle and brandished it at his younger brother and told Lothar he would cut him. At his father, he shouted, "You shoulda rolled over off of mom and shot this fucker on the ceiling!"

That's when Lothar invented Tough Love. He would have no more of this disrespectful nonsense. It would end at this moment. He pulled a pistol out from the glove box of his truck and aimed its snub nose at the older boy's right foot. There was a sharp bang and a tongue of white fire – like the tip of an acetylene torch – from the tip of the pistol. About five seconds of silence followed, accompanied by the odor of gunpowder. The entire forest had been silenced by the blast, and there was time enough before anyone spoke or moved for a few small

66

birds to start chirping, and for squirrels to resume quarreling in their branches, and for a hawk or raven to dip overhead. Lothar had fired the round through the top of the boy's boot, through the foot, through the bootsole, into the forest floor. The odor of blood joined that of spent gunpowder.

All three of them looked down at this incredible circumstance and accepted it as the thing it was intended to be: a life lesson. The kind of life lesson that was perfectly within Lothar's character to administer. Helmut finally moaned a little. But even this small, involuntary cry came out clenched between his teeth and was truncated before it could build into any sort of mature protestation. Gunter helped his brother out of his boot. He washed and bound the wound. And the two made a solemn oath, there in the darkness of camp with Lothar sleeping already in the tent, never again to evoke one of their father's lessons through a disagreement. They became very fraternal indeed, and this pleased Lothar mightily.

"I'm proud of you boys," he had said on turning in. "Making up like you're doing. Mighty proud."

What began as a fondness for tidiness as a child had, for the grown man Nicholas Oxendine, blossomed into something of enormity. His mind obsessed with neatness. His brain had a neat arrangement. When he was not polishing and organizing, he was thinking about polishing and organizing. He shelved his books alphabetically by authors' last names. His silverware nested in a kitchen drawer, each sort of implement – small spoons, large spoons, forks, tableknives – gathered in their plastic trays. And what about Nick's closet? Shirts of a type hung together: T's, polos, dress-shirts, sweatshirts, flannel work shorts arranged on hangers by color. Then came trousers, corduroys first, jeans next, then chinos, and finally dress slacks. The shoes rested on pedestals on the floor, under the hanging garments. They were as orderly, and as evenly spaced, as tombstones.

Lothar had hired Nick Oxendine years ago, and Hector Aguirre knew a good organizer when he saw one. After they put Lothar in the ground, one of Hector's first acts was to affirm the continued employment of the city's two employees: Mike Eagle Eye, director of maintenance (so the paperwork read) and Nicholas Oxendine as town clerk (again, formally, on the papers). Nick couldn't have been more delighted.

People called Nick a "neat freak," or characterized him as "anally retentive," or both. "Neat Nick from Salt Lick" was an appellation conferred on him by the few "outside" folks – county assessors, grant money grunts, state bureaucrats – who came infrequently on municipal business to Town Hall. There, his desk area was spotless, with papers stacked and enfoldered without fail. When he was out of earshot, the puzzled visitors would mock his orderliness by suggesting this way to get a diamond: place a lump of coal between his butt cheeks, and wait.

Nick was not unaware that he had taken tidiness to a new, often extreme, level. But he preferred it that way – he was singularly plain in all other aspects. Neither handsome nor unhandsome, he was, nevertheless, well groomed. Not an introverted, quiet man, but also not a blathering, muscled extrovert, his manner was cooperatively affable. His projection was careful; he meant what he said, always, and his words, expressions and body language were precisely chosen, except for an idiosyncrasy he possessed, sometimes beginning sentences with, "Lookie here..." His vocabulary was not intricate, but the simple things he wished to say were always well and properly said. He met all the service milestones on his automobile, had the oil changed every three-thousand miles or every three months, whichever came first. He was a person who paid attention to tire rotation.

Every material object he owned had a proper place in his home, which was tucked neatly, like the cornerfolds of his bed sheets, under a bluff overlooking Highway 410. He changed the sheets on his bed every third day and preferred them pressed. The fibers in his carpeting had a preferred direction, attained with a deft hand at the vacuum sweeper.

Nick had no serious female entanglements, although rare opportunities had presented themselves. To the extent he cast an amorous net, he had to do so widely – throughout all of Yakima County – since Salt Lick constituted a somewhat finite playing field. Some women were drawn to his exactitude, believing it belied desirable character traits that he must possess. In his social life, they took the initiative more often than not. If they had spent some time with him and found him a prospective sexual companion as well, they, not he, were the aggressors. He liked it straight and clean. They – the women who had known him in this way – would have agreed that he was circumspect in this regard, always honorable, fastidious in his toilet habits afterward, respectful of their persons and personal things.

Each day Nick Oxendine followed an established routine. He rose with a single jangle of the alarm clock at 5:30. He would never stab at the snooze button – the notion of such a device didn't seem right to him. He would enter the shower at 5:31. (He washed his hair first, then head, chest, underarms, personal region, then arms, shoulders and hands, then legs and feet – always in that order, each shower an equation that, summed, equaled cleanliness.) He breakfasted on two eggs, toast, orange juice and black coffee at 6:05. He read the *Herald-Republic* front to back, eschewing only the daily comics, classifieds and Scene section. At 6:35, he dropped granular food into a tank of tropical fish, a specialty diet for his only real companions. Then he departed the front door at 6:40 after placing his dishes in the washer. He arrived behind his desk at a quarter of seven by the Town Hall clock itself, always fifteen minutes early.

There he would consult his work calendar and review goals for the coming day in that first, off-the-clock fifteen minutes. It was, this free time, a daily donation he happily made to the citizenry of Salt Lick. He believed a quarter of an hour invested in the town paid immeasurable dividends, cast him in a positive light from the perspective of his new superior. It satisfied him to do so in a way that management would appreciate but that union organizers and men sympathetic to the cause of labor – Lothar would have labeled them "communists" – would not.

His workday comprised report-composition and filing in the morning. The forty-five minutes prior to the break for lunch he spent reading, answering or composing mail. Then there was the lunch itself, which he toted in a brown paper sack (tuna-fish sandwich, banana, yogurt, spoon). Nick used the same paper sack for five consecutive days, folding it after each use and stowing it in his briefcase. (On Fridays, he discarded the wrinkled sack in the waste paper bin under his desk.) A brief meeting with Hector Aguirre and other town functionaries and businesspeople – most often Juniper Jamison, Mike Eagle Eye, Jacqua Druce and Wellman Kinchlow – followed lunch. After this, there was further filing, organization and data entry to be done. The day would end at four o'clock sharp. From 3:45 until then, Nick policed his area, previewed his calendar for the following day, and powered off Salt Lick's single municipal computer. He would pause on his egress from the desk area. Nick Oxendine would cast an eye of approval on its orderliness.

Nick would arrive at home between 4:05 and 4:20, depending on whether he stopped at the Pie Apple for provisions. Once or twice a week he'd step into Lowell's for a beverage or two, but this was not one of his favorite pastimes – he disliked that the often-unpredictable behavior of Lowell's customers after a few Peacocks made it impossible for him to exactly gage his arrival time home. They were always asking him to join them in a volley of darts or listen to one of them make a fool of himself with the karaoke machine.

When he got home, Nick would collect and read all the mail, even sweepstakes circulars, invitations to new heights of credit, missing children postcards. He would cook a supper, clean the dishes, start a load of laundry (Nicholas Oxendine was one of the very few residents of Salt Lick who owned his own clothes washer and dryer), then spend two hours cleaning, arranging or rearranging shelves or nooks or closets. A typical week might proceed as follows: One night he wiped dust from the top surfaces of picture frames and straightened them on the walls. Another he re-covered kitchen shelves with contact paper, replacing pots in order of size, making perfect geometric stacks with ceramic bowls, leaving glasses and mugs in pleasing patterns. He ran the vacuum sweeper the third evening and its tracks on the carpet put him in mind of Japanese rock and sand gardens, infusing him with serenity. On the fourth, he folded laundry and tended his closets, polishing shoes, running the iron along his work shirts and sheets and defining knife-edged creases in his trouser-legs. The iron itself hissed and steamed to accompany his labor, and he was pleased with the exercise. The fifth night he spent tending to the home's external matters – cutting grass in spring and summer, raking leaves or clearing downspouts in fall, checking insulation in the winter.

At the conclusion of each project, each night, he would select a task for the following evening. Then he spent one hour reading (he preferred nonfiction to fiction, but would occasionally indulge an exceptional crime novel). Finally, he watched the fuzzy evening news and retired. When he lay in bed at night his mind was populated by the fine points of order, the satisfaction of a life well and properly lived. Seldom, as he turned in, did he linger with fantasies of the smooth curve of skin, fundamental scents, the play of soft silk and taffeta fabric under fingertips, or the urgent, moist movement of companionship.

As far as he ever admitted, his dreams were never erotic but, rather, procedural and arithmetic. Unlike the dreams most people have, Nick's were well-connected, and celebrated the process of a neat life. Consecution came out in the vapor he snored, each exhalation an element of his own personal mathematics. His pores secreted erudition onto the flat, white sheets. His cellular activity was perfectionism in the darkness, and the red LED numbers of his alarm clock reached out into his well-ordered, algebraic bedroom and proclaimed the time.

That was then.

But what of the contrast since Lothar Sturmhund's heart blew up and he dropped like a stone through Gib MacNaughton's coffee table?

How is it that the Nicholas Oxendine everyone knew, Nicholas the predictable, the stolid, the accountable one, became the specimen folks encountered with a disappointed shake of their heads after Hector Aguirre's mayoral succession? Aside from a general ague at the absence of Lothar's guidance, how could it be that this transformed man was the same as Neat Nick. How had he fallen so far, from such a very great height?

What happened to Nicholas Oxendine was that he lost a sock in the wash. One mid-June evening, he finished folding a pile of laundry and there, in his hand, remained a single olive rayon sock with brown paisley shapes embroidered in the fabric. He held it up to the light, cocked his head, observed the mate-less article as if he didn't quite understand it. As if to ask: *A single sock of a pair is good for... for – what?*

Reasoning that static had fused the matching sock to another item of clothing, he extricated from the neat stacks of folded laundry those items which had tumbled as a group in the last load. This was an unfortunate detour from the night's plans, the unfruitful folding then unfolding then refolding of laundry. This sort of inefficiency was not exactly Nick's cup of tea; if he would that moment have consulted a mirror, he would have seen on his face a frown of disapproval. And even after all this inefficiency, the sock remained missing after he'd been through the load.

He must have overlooked the missing sock inside the dryer. He supposed this was possible. Surely the absent sock waited there for reunification with its mate, as it is a physical law that all halves must seek to be unified. But when he checked, the drum was an empty chamber.

Then it must still be in the washer. Nick thought, with no small amount of distaste, that this would prove further troublesome and disruptive: the missing sock, in that case, would still be soaked. He would have to delay the stowing of the folded and refolded clothes for the sake of one wet, wayward sock.

He opened the washer. But only emptiness and the odor of phosphates greeted his query.

"Damn it," he said, in the bright light of his laundry room. "This is *not* happening." He searched the dryer again, then the washer a second time, tried the hamper, ran upstairs to check his bathroom. The sock was nowhere. It seemed to have vanished from the world.

Nick lay down to sleep that night supremely troubled. He had the one sock. *"But what good is it?"* he asked of the evening. He had carried the single sock into his room with him, laid it carefully on the pillow. As he settled into the cool sheets, rested his head back on the pillow, he turned to look at the sock before putting out the light. He stared at it for a great while, then reached for the lampcord.

When his eyes grew accustomed to the faint light of the alarm, he saw the sock on the pillow next to him, a black lump – a sort of sarcoma. He remained awake for a long time, considering this. The lightest sounds kept him stirring. Just when his mind dropped into the cadence normally preceding sleep, some click on the roof shingles above, or a settling of the house's foundation, or an airplane passing overhead, would draw his mind back to the recalcitrant sock. And when he finally slept – sometime in the early morning – his restlessness tore the bedclothes from their tight corner-tucks.

Nick Oxendine dreamed erotically.

After that, people noticed incidents of slippage in Nick's ordered cosmos. For instance, in the week following the disappearance of the sock (which, as far as anyone knows, was never found), he arrived at work exactly on time for his contracted start not once, but *twice*. He forgot a spoon for his lunchtime yogurt and had to cross the street and borrow one from Lowell's. He left a folder on his desk with papers sliding out from under one of the covers. Small matters really, but Everests in the matter of Nick's hitherto total integrity in matters of neatness.

In the second week after the missing sock incident, he missed a dental appointment in Yakima without calling to cancel twenty-four hours in advance. He made a typographical error in a report he turned in to Hector. He forgot, one evening, to sweep his carpets. Then he pulled away from a self-service gasoline pump in Naches with the pump spigot still in the orifice of his automobile's gas-tank. The hose wrenched free, alarms sounding. The station attendant came running through the lot. The man waved his arms overhead as if the world were coming to a great unraveling.

All of this, while disconcerting for Nick Oxendine, was not yet so urgent to bring down on his shoulders any weird sense of doom. He remained, in general, in high spirits. He thought it a passing thing like a flu or virus. Perhaps it was some sort of memory and performance bacteriophage that had, through no fault of his own, assaulted him. One day he was fine, the next he was... well... out of sorts. It behaved exactly like an illness. And surely the ill cannot be blamed for their agues.

Yet his condition continued to deteriorate. There were days, of course, which seemed a return to his old, neat ways. Then it seemed as if the malaise was rooted in an unwanted, unbidden dreamland, an Erewhon of witchery and bedevilment. Here, now, in reality, it was simply a matter of mind over – well, over what he couldn't precisely

72

say. But on the good days, he fought a sinking notion that the general trend was not to the good, was in fact, a slowly waning curve that approached some small number, maybe a zero.

He went a day without shaving. He might as well have ventured onto Pinocchio's Pleasure Island. The day's growth of stubble could have been the sproutings of ass ears, a donkey's muzzle and tail. He could have commenced braying.

So the missing sock precipitated a spiral for Nicholas Oxendine. Sucked into a violent vortex of disorganization and miscategorization, his whole logarithmic approach to life was fundamentally altered. It was as if he had crossed the event horizon of a black hole. Only for him, it was fastidiousness – not light – that was held inside.

So he did a thing that seemed natural. In his alarm and desperation he reached out for companionship.

His new boss's daughter, Victoria Aguirre, was a person skilled in two mysteries: computers and coitus. Unbeknownst to Nick, she had been attracted to him for some time. Who knows why she never made her interest known before – perhaps she was the sort of woman for whom a liaison with one of her father's subordinates would have had special meaning or resolution. Or perhaps she simply noted a subtle modification in him – a modification brought on by the trauma of the AWOL sock – and interpreted it as an invitation. It was a change so utterly plain to him, but was simply a migration toward the "easy-going" from the perspective of his colleagues and acquaintances. He feared he was coming apart; they just thought he was loosening up. She may have thought he was coming on.

Vicki – as she came to be known to Nick informally – having been inexplicably spurned by Ivan Manley (that needle-nosed porn junkie), suddenly demanded his companionship. She insisted on driving for their outings, going "Dutch" for meals, throwing candy wrappers on the floor at the Yakima Cineplex during the movies. She had him over to her and her daddy's place out at the river after only the third date. Good thing Hector Aguirre was up the American River fishing. Back in the mayor's front room, she urged Nick Oxendine to experiment.

"Lover, this can be done in lots of ways," she laughed, her coiffe – arranged in the configuration of a famous Russian ice-skating princess – bobbing in time with her feral joy.

When Vicki had grown sexually attracted to him, which was very soon in their relationship, she discovered he was somewhat unimaginative or provincial, a "yokel," one might say, in his beliefs and habits regarding lovemaking. Notions such as "a man must be on top," or "the penis only goes there," would have to go, Vicki vowed. "Nick,

73

honey, from behind... there... *that's* right!" One must assume she had been an attentive and excellent student of Lothar's hairy, if malapropos, Thüringian Tetragrammaton.

But Vicki Aguirre was a messy woman. Nick grew extraordinarily fond of her, but he could yield only so much ground. He continued a fierce internal war against further deterioration. Against a metamorphosis from man to mule.

Nick's demise, from an orderliness standpoint, had been somewhat mitigated by Vicki's playful presence. However, he was only a mortal man, not a demigod. And as a mortal, he could not escape alien thoughts – ideas which seemed foreign to him at first, but which on closer reflection seemed to be more in accordance with the old, familiar Nicholas Oxendine. Letting her pay for bagels and vichyssoise at a café in Gleed was one thing, as was fucking her like they were two joyful Malamutes. He had stridden excellent strides in lightening up over these sorts of things. He could almost let her and her ebullient button-nipples parade around his house wearing only one of his T-shirts. It wasn't necessarily all bad to watch the twin cream dollops of her fine firm ass shake their way across his living room just below the hem. Nor was it objectionable to witness every bit of Christmas when she bent over with her back to him. No, like a showing mare, Victoria Aguirre clad only in a T-shirt had her moments. And he was making great progress in sharing his toothbrush and deodorant with her, clearing soft, black strands of her hair from his brushes, flicking her stark curly pubes off his ceramic toilet.

But should he have continued to allow her to leave dirty laundry on the floor, on his carefully managed and cultivated Japanese-garden carpets? Should he have fallen silent in the face of abominations such as milk-quaffing directly from the carton or toe-nail grooming as they, together, watched R-rated videocassettes from the Pie Apple late into the night? Can anyone say that he should have allowed all of these sorts of things, these trespasses against normalcy, these disgusting, twisted, broken, perverted, horrific acts, to continue?

"I just love your fish," Vicki said, dropping a scab of fried-chicken skin into the tank.

How could he have tolerated this? Who will stand and vilify him? To endure all of this would have been to finally abdicate the very last mote of arrangement he possessed. It would have been anathema to him, the drinking of hemlock. It would have been a denial of the Creator's purpose for him, for Nicholas Oxendine, for Neat Nick from Salt Lick, the anal one, the coal-to-diamond butt-crack alchemist.

He summoned, from deep within himself, a tiny fragment – perhaps a final fragment – of courage. With this fragment, he evicted her from his life. But by then, it was autumn and his fall was too advanced. His donkeyness marched inexorably toward a conclusion. He had crossed a river into a country from which there was no return. He was, finally, disorderly, depraved, a shambles. A beard trailed his chin like a filthy dishrag. He did nothing to stop it. Guilt steamed at him like a locomotive. Bewilderment, Despair, Terror, Humiliation: these were the names of his horsemen.

He ordered pizza delivered all the way from the Pie Palace in Selah, and let the boxes clutter his house. He left appliances plugged in. He let the dishes pile up. He refused to return Vicki's coy telephone messages. Captured by a snow-washed image on the screen of his television, he forgot one thing for another and let the vacuum sweeper stand in one place while operating; its beater bar burned a blemish into his carpet. It was the last time he swept.

Nick Oxendine ceased to change his sheets, to brush his teeth, to bathe. He dreamed horribly, of dirty animal-like sex and pure, enhorned prurience. Fish floated on the surface of his tank. About mid-August, when he ceased calling in sick, when they feared for his welfare and whereabouts, they came from Salt Lick Town Hall to check on him.

He answered the door on the third set of knocks, when they had begun to evolve from inquisitive, polite little tappings to zealous clouts.

"What?" He flung the door wide. Summer heat would have rushed in except for the odor of his residence rushing out. He stood in a stained T-shirt (a much different sort of picture, to be sure, than that presented by Victoria Aguirre) and briefs, hoary legs splayed like pale plinths of columns. They recoiled, the whole damned group. "What!" he repeated, firing twin lasers of madness from his pupils. His hair was an inverted cyclone, pocked brow and sunk cheeks lunar surfaced.

"My God, Nick..." Hector Aguirre said. "What has happened to you?"

And in response only silence from the creature, a blink of the sunken eyes. The sound of a car swishing past on 410. Nicholas Oxendine reached out with an unsteady limb that terminated in a now-gnarled fist. Unhinged the fingers, one by one.

The visitors peered as if he would reveal in his palm a brilliant gemstone, a diamond.

But there was only a single, mateless sock.

CHAPTER 7
in which the Breadman finds what may just be love...

Lothar was never much good at relationships. He preferred hostage-taking. There are several examples.

Lothar fancied himself a potentate of love. He imagined all women – certainly in central Washington, probably across the Pacific Northwest and, if he thought about it, probably throughout North America and Europe, the Civilized World – found him desirable. Perhaps this confidence derived, in no small part, from the fact that his blond hair remained thick and free of gray throughout his life. In terms of his own physical strength, he always remained much closer to eighteen years old than fifty. And his features were, admittedly, handsome. He wore dense, red facial hair when it suited him, shaved and showed his skin when not.

And it is true, he had many women. He took special pride in the notion that his name could be modified into *Lothario* because someone had once told him that was the name of a famous seducer of women. This interested him very much. He liked the notion that he could get whatever object he wanted, how he wanted it, when he wanted it, *now*.

If that object was an attractive, amoral woman who didn't happen to be his longsuffering wife, so be it.

Neither was Lothar concerned whether Magda found out about him fooling around. His wife was Hostage Number One. But he would return to her bed, always clean. Therein, he would convince her that she was the brightest star in his sky and reptile tears of false penitence would flow from his eyes. Underlying these lachrymal declarations, he always managed to convey – through the gentle speech that characterized his homecomings – a latent meaning: *What the fuck would you do about it, anyway?* He would spend himself into his bride, crying, *Uwe Uwe Oh!*

She was, it's true, dependent on him in every way. He had thus chosen her. And it wasn't that she was unintelligent, unquestioning, unambitious. She was simply a partner for whom a lifetime of all kinds of terrible intercourse with one unfaithful was good enough. Episode

76

after episode of heartbreak, followed by naïve, hopeful reunion, was the compost heap that comprised her, that enveloped her. She was "on the right track," Lothar would say.

Her love thus turned, in volume, to her two boys. In later life, both remained faithful to her like a pair of stupid dogs. Neither Helmut nor Gunter would suffer any unpunished indignity to come upon her, except those rained down by Lothar since, truth known, both of them were his hostages as well.

At the beginning of one summer, Lothar interviewed a prospective female employee, Flora Navarro. She showed up at the general contractor's trailer on time, sat down, and their chat began. All through the interview his eyes crawled on her. Her responses to his questions might as well have been vocalized in Esperanto; his ears heard nothing.

"Look there, on the desk there," he finally said. She followed his gaze. "That's where we'll find out if you're right for this job." She understood, and her olive cheeks reddened.

Flora complied; she needed the job, which was simple – just picking up scrap lumber and old nails from across the job site, really. She was responsible for the care of an ill, uninsured parent. So she offered this to Lothar: her virginity in exchange for the privilege of doing his bidding and suffering near-daily humiliations, at his hand, on the trailer's desktop.

Soon the newness of her no longer pleased him. He began to uncover certain deficiencies in her work. He developed an eye for her shortcomings, whether real or manufactured. So he fucked her once more, then fired her as they were cleaning themselves afterward. She was too in fear of him to protest, either there, at the moment of dismissal, or later with authorities that watch over such things. Who was a larger, broader authority than Lothar Sturmhund himself?

Lothar's wife protested his skirt-chasing only one time during their marriage of thirty-four years.

He blacked her eye and said, "You're on the wrong track," as she lay in a heap beneath him on the floor, and moved out for four months. During this time he slept in the general contractor's trailer and ate and showered at Lowell's.

He was telling her, in his own Lotharic way, what she had said hadn't suited him.

The Breadman didn't exactly have a sweetheart in every port. But at the bakery sections of well more than a dozen grocery stores, convenience stores, diners and traveler's stops he serviced on the route from Yakima to Cliffdell on State Highway 410, women anticipated his early morning arrival, his smile, the ingress of his loaves.

The women in a single store would hear the sound of his big diesel motor cut out, then his door closing.

"Ladies, the Breadman's here," the lead would announce. There would follow suppressed giggles and a general snapping to order. If counters needed swiping with a damp cloth, that was done hurriedly. If display items were out of order, they were set straight. Someone made sure, at that last moment, that any of yesterday's unsold bread was temporarily out of view. Then the pull-up door at the back of his van would roll with the sound of grinding chains. They'd listen as the Breadman tugged the aluminum ramp from beneath the rear bumper. Steel casters jangling down the washboard ramp would follow, and the glass door would swish open with pneumatic welcome. "Mornin'," the Breadman would say. "Howdy do."

The Breadman always wore a white short-sleeve shirt buttoned to the top and blue Dickies with creases ironed up the legs. His name, *Ed*, was embroidered on the shirt. Even on colder days he resisted a coat and hat, and his hair had begun the process of recession above his boyish face. No matter – the bakery women at the stores anticipated the Breadman's happy countenance each day like the unwrapping and eating of sweets. When his van pulled up outside, they smiled too, and waited like hopeful acolytes.

Typical of the Breadman's visits was this, on a mid-July morning, at the Gleed Super Six. The sun was barely up. There were no clouds, and the Breadman had followed the track of a plane westward from town – sunrise glinting off of its distant metal like starfire – as if his van were pulled along by a cable suspended from the aircraft. The air was sweet with that odor of summer morning before heat has grabbed all the nice smells and smothered them under a dense, weighty pillow. The Breadman rolled up in his van a few minutes early, pulled up the rear door, and headed into the Super Six with his first batch.

The Super Six's bakery women laughed and gathered around to take in the odor of fresh bread, handling the plastic-wrapped loaves with soft fingers. The colors of their polished nails stood out against the rich sienna of the crust, nestled in cellophane. The Breadman pulled trays of baked goods from his transport cases, French bread in paper sleeves, wrapped rye, pumpernickel, nine-grain, oatmeal, honeyed, cracked wheat, and white. He unloaded one case and returned to the van for another. When he returned, the women gathered around him in the same happy way children might surround an odd, old bewhiskered man blowing into a flute and standing on one leg. There was fresh joy and morning glory in their cheeks. They were, for these moments, like young girls again. The Breadman made it back to his van and returned with a few pastries and cookies, but mostly it was more bread, loaf upon loaf, baguettes, bagels and buns, until the kingdom that the Breadman labored for in the Super Six's bakery department was a kingdom of raised yeast, matured leaven and golden crust. In a way, he was a wandering vassal in service of the bakery women. To break into one of his loaves was their secret pleasure, indulged while the assistant manager busied himself across aisles and aisles of groceries, somewhere over in Produce.

When he was finished, the women banded together and followed the Breadman and his empty case like apostles. The group arrived at the sliding doors, and the Breadman offered thanks for their patronage and a friendly wink. It made him feel *good* to do so.

"You know," he said as he prepared to go, "sometimes I believe that if the whole world could only smell fresh-baked bread every morning, things would go on just a little bit better."

This homily, or rather, all of his homilies – those things he uttered that might have been stitched on a sampler but were, in fact, his own unique, daily creations – was one of their favorite things about the Breadman. For each day, at the conclusion of his provisionings, he could be absolutely relied upon to leaven them with a scrip of fortune-cookie wisdom such as this. Another day, he might say, "I was born a Breadman, a fella who gets to bring in the manna. Ain't no better thing to be born." In this way, the bakery women up and down the Highway 410 corridor were serviced by the Breadman. Each visit concluded with a saying or axiom, like these, that seemed – to the bakery women – eminently wise. And then he would turn and disappear from them for twenty-four hours and his absence would seem like a much longer thing than only a day.

The Breadman's unwitting hold over them was not a phenomenon of magnetism – his devotees among the bakery women along Highway 410 did not need or want the Breadman carnally. They were not mesmerized, as it were, by his innocent eruditions. It was, rather, a charismatic attraction. The Breadman always had something interesting to say, personally, to each of them. His daily words mattered. He was friendly and kind. And this mattered to them – a lot of their husbands or significant male acquaintances weren't. The Breadman was the opposite of most folks they knew – even themselves! – in what has come to be known paradoxically as the service industry. He made them know he looked forward to seeing them every morning, which was much more than their husbands, children, supervisors, neighbors and other acquaintances did. He may have appreciated things about them like their eyes, or the bloom of their cheeks, or the shapes of them – things other men noticed and sought – but if so, he was utterly discreet. He wore no jewelry of any sort. Sans wedding band, the women assumed him single. But not one was attracted to him in that way. Nuptially, that is.

The Breadman was, well... nice.

Jacqua Druce gave Flora Navarro a job while the young woman tried to take a few courses at the community college in Yakima. Flora liked the Pie Apple's owner – always had, really – and it was a pleasant way to pass a couple of early hours every day.

Things were starting to come back together for Flora, although from time to time she would fall back into depression. From there, it would seem that the light at a deep well's lips was so far off as to be unreachable. When she was enmired there, she was nearly inconsolable. Jacqua was a ready ear in all of this, a counselor of sorts, where her own mother was ineffectual.

"There's nothing to be ashamed of, you know," Jacqua said. "There are a lot of girls – women – who have suffered at his hand."

"I know that. It's just that everyone else knows, too."

Jacqua knew that this was true. There weren't many secrets in Salt Lick. And Lothar's transgressions, damn his soul, were certainly wide out there in the open.

"It doesn't matter what everyone knows or thinks they know." Jacqua re-gathered her hair into its pony tail and stretched a new rubber band around it. "They weren't there. And he's gone now. He can't hurt you – or anybody – any more."

Forgetting her gratitude for a moment, and that Jacqua Druce liked her – maybe *loved* her as much as she loved Tina, her own daughter – Flora bitterly told Jacqua that this sounded like something out of a greeting card. Jacqua stood silently for a moment. There were birdcalls and the waking sounds of the forest through the open screen door. The two women watched the world outside, through the Pie Apple's window. Dappled sunlight shown off Lowell's across the way. A hawk swept down Mud Lake Road, canted its wingtip slightly, and soared out of view.

"You're not the only one he's hurt," Jacqua said. "My god, think of Magda. His sons. Everybody in the whole damned town has suffered, one way or another, from him."

Flora knew in her brain this was true. But in her guts – where decisions about how to live and conduct oneself really are made, where confidence is manufactured – she wasn't convinced. She still felt freakish and unique. Bizarre. Filthy. All it took was one glance at Town Hall next door. Just one look and he would creep back into her, back onto her. She thought of his battering, his thrusts, his hairiness, his violations of her, his semen. She thought of his general contractor's trailer, the top of his desk. She heard the authority and command in his voice: *See there? That's where we'll find out if you're right for this job.* She remembered the first time, when it stung, and washing herself afterward. Flora remembered that no matter how hard she scrubbed and how blistering hot the shower pounded against her skin, that septic feeling would not go away. But she had needed the job. Her mother had needed her to have a job. She agonized over the thought his seed may have rooted in her.

She realized she would never trust a man, anywhere, anytime, again. A tear slid down her cheek.

"I'm sorry, Flora," Jacqua said. "But you need to know it. You can recover from him. Lots of people have, or are trying. We all are. Everybody here." She gestured with her arms to include the entire town, then invited Flora into their embrace.

The Breadman started every day when most others had only just fallen asleep. It was another way he was the opposite of most folks. His alarm clattered in a deep corner of his south Yakima apartment, and he rose to shower. Then he pulled on the clothes he had set out the afternoon before, wearing always the white shirt and blue pants two days, then cycling them with other sets. He had two slices of toast, walked through his front door into one a.m. darkness, climbed into his van, waited for the glow plug to tell him it was O.K. to kindle the motor, and drove out of the lot for the bakery. On the way to work he meditated on his many blessings, and offered a sort of prayer for these. In this way, the Breadman was intensely spiritual, winding through near empty streets – more likely to be populated at that hour by a lone wandering elk or deer than by his fellow humans.

The bakery was across town from where he dwelt, a huge kitchen of stainless steel attached to a warehouse that terminated in back-ups where the rears of vans pushed up to receive their cargoes of bread. The

Breadman's rig was no different – he entered the lot, backed up and slipped his van between two others waiting, as easily as a tableknife slips through a glob of creamery butter. Because of the diversity of breads and bakery products he would be obliged to deliver on a given day, and depending on the inventory requested by each store, it was important for him to follow a precise organization in the loading of his van. He clocked in, then received a yellow pick card from his lead, and proceeded to the appropriate lines: *FRENCH* on the far left of the warehouse. *SOURDOUGH* next to it. *CRACKED WHEAT*, then *RYE*, and so on, on bright cardboard placards, at the end of each line. The pick card had all the bakery products printed on it, and next to each of them on a blank line a written-in number, and a start time. This was so all the breadmen wouldn't stumble over each other in their race to fill the vans and get on the road to their first drops. The sooner they could start, the sooner the breadrun would finish. Then they'd be done for the day.

If the managers of the bakery believed in anything, it was in the sacredness of its orderly bread-loading process. A breadman who started to pick his breads one minute or even thirty seconds early was going to get written up. If he did it twice in a week, he was probably going to need to call his union steward, because the bakery was going to give him an unexpected day off. For this reason, nearly all the breadmen banded together in despising the lead bakery timekeeper, who ran around like a little female *Il Duce* with her eyes glued to the second hand of a wristwatch. She was a petite woman, who made up for her tiny size with large meanness and an abiding, biting scorn for others. Breadmen, to her, were just one step removed from single-celled organisms, although she didn't necessarily know what a single-celled organism was, or that there were such things. She just had a mental picture of them as very lowly and unevolved in comparison to her talents and contributions to the bakery. The timekeeper was one of those types who took themselves and their regulations, no matter how infinitesimally unimportant, much too seriously.

Still, the Breadman cheerfully complied with the loading regulations. The rules made perfect sense. He understood their utility – it would never do to have breadmen scrabbling all over one another, breaking new loaves of still-warm French, dumping baguettes onto the concrete, slipping in spilled frosting.

The timekeeper rewarded the Breadman's eager compliance, though, with a special kind of scorn, the sort reserved for those over whom one exercises a total brand of imagined power. He waited patiently at the roll-up door of his van on the freshly hosed deck, checking his watch, as anxious to begin his day as any other breadman, but outwardly patient. She pretended to happen by, saw him checking his watch, mocked his patience. "Got somewhere to go?" she asked. "I hope you can get control of your *enthusiasm.*"

Unbidden, a horn raised itself through his scalp, and for just an uncharacteristic second he began to think the word *bitch.* It must be understood that the Breadman was as likely to utter this foul word – even to *think* it, really – as he was likely to believe in an out-of-body experience or astral projection. It – this alien urge – fell away liked night mists dissipate when the sun rises. Instead, he blessed her with a silently aspirated prayer. *Love your enemies,* he thought. *Pray for them, and all will be well.* And this was the way it was for months, even years. The Breadman was a patient man, and fulfilled in every aspect by the noble vocation of transporting bakery products. At least this is what he told himself and, for a time, truly believed.

Jacqua hired Flora to work for a few of hours each morning as a thing called a *barrista* – an author and finisher of specialty coffee drinks. Flora was maybe twenty – if that – and wore half a dozen earrings in the lobe of one ear, a couple of clasps in the top of the other. Her eyes were the color of dark chocolate, and had the look of wounds and mistrust behind them – many years worth beyond twenty, it sometimes seemed. She wore dark cocoa fingernail polish and matching lipstick, and she wore her jet-black hair short, some of it up with plastic butterfly clips of various energetic colors. They were colors that belied her desperate mood. Because of the taut hairstyle, she needed no hairnet. It may be that this was the single characteristic of her that attracted the Breadman. He entered the Pie Apple one morning and his eyes fell upon the newly hired Flora across the videocassette racks. It was like those cartoons where movers are craning a grand piano out of a fourth- or fifth-story apartment, and the ropes break and it crashes to the concrete below in a cacophony of tight strings, black and white ivory and splintered hardwood. That's how hard his eyes – and the rest of him – fell on her.

The owner of the Pie Apple set down the tabloid, called him to meet her. "This here is Flora. She's new."

"Yes ma'am." The Breadman turned to the new woman. He sized her up. Was she a *ma'am* or a *miss*? An internal struggle that rivaled the greatest of this century's decisions of protocol waged above the white buttoned-up, _Ed_-embroidered, short-sleeved shirt. That face youngish for its years under the receding hairline screwed up with thought at this question: *Ma'am* or *miss*? Subconsciously, he chose what he hoped would be complimentary. "Pleased to meet you, miss."

Flora smiled, said one word, and her voice was a girlish melody: "Hi." The lipstick shape of her mouth was rich and genuine, and felt right on her for the first time in many months. She had no idea why.

"Have some of her coffee," Jacqua said. Flora's cheeks turned the color of roses; already this woman was overly complimentary of the magic she performed with ground coffee beans, steamed milk, and the bottles of flavoring. Now, here was a strapping, attractive – if *older* – fellow. And Jacqua was *foisting* Flora's coffee on him. Well, so be it. She got busy with the implements of espresso, while the Breadman made small protests about his timeliness in arriving at the next stops on his route.

"Don't be silly," Jacqua said. "It's only 6:20. You got plenty of time." The Breadman piped down then, made small talk with the Pie Apple's proprietor as the coffee machine whirred and grunted. Flora poured from various small silver vessels into a paper cup and stirred in some syrup from one of the bottles. She offered the cup.

"Be careful, it's hot," she said.

He noticed her fingers were lovely and delicate. The color of her nails was exquisite. The shade reminded him of soft deerhide. He accepted the cup, caressed its dry paper sides with his rough fingers. Then he sipped the top layer of foam and some of the steamy liquid below. In the same way the superheated coffee made contact with his mouth, so their eyes made contact – hers that rich Latin ochre, his blue and Northern. At that moment, Flora thought she might like to lay down with the Breadman sometime and listen to something by Jewel. He thought nearly the same thing, although the music would have been the Grateful Dead or the Eagles.

When the Breadman left the Pie Apple, he did so, cup in hand and the bittersweet aftertaste of caffeine, twenty minutes behind schedule, with his heart muscle flexing in overdrive. He loaded his empty cases up the ramp into the van, whistling melodies from *Workingman's Dead*. He did not notice he'd forgotten to leave the ladies with his usual – the verbal fortune cookie *du jour*. She had simply rendered him wordless.

"Breadman's got it hard," Jacqua said, out of Flora's earshot. She retrieved her copy of the *National Enquirer*, started to read an article about a carnival out in Rhode Island that had gotten decidedly out of hand. Something strange in the freak tent...

The Breadman spent nearly all of the next several days thinking of Flora. Her daily coffee drinks, though, set down into him with hooks. How she busied herself at the espresso bar, the way her reach extended the cup across the counter, the set of her eyes – these things sparked in the Breadman's mind and seemed inescapable. Here was a man who had, essentially, eschewed the intimate company of the opposite gender as a thing hopelessly removed, for good, from his experience. He remembered with no small amount of discomfort his high school and apprenticeship years – the awkwardness of seeking dates with his girl classmates or young women after graduation. How their cautious acceptances, unreturned phone calls, laborious outings, outright rejections had deposited a residue on his personality now too thick, perhaps, to chisel away. Question was, could Flora remove it, and – not an insignificant question in itself – would he *allow* her?

Lying on his mattress in his small apartment, miles from her, he decided that *yes,* he would. In fact, as he retired that afternoon, he had trouble falling to sleep. Midday sounds that ordinarily did not distract him – the whisk of cars passing on the highway, other residents of the apartment opening doors or closing drawers, the movement of water through pipes – intruded into the Breadman's head. And the thought of her and her fingertips, her earrings and earclasps, her dark pulpy lipstick, her raven hair, brown eyes. And yes, the shape of her. There was that as well.

He would ask for her company on a night out. He'd do it tomorrow morning. This so simply resolved as he lay between his sheets, the crease in his pants-legs freshly ironed and clothes set out for tomorrow, he wondered why sleep still escaped him. He rehearsed the precise wording of how to ask her many times. Two or three hours after he would normally have fallen asleep, he finally did.

The Breadman woke to the alarm exactly where he left off, in rehearsal. He practiced in the shower, as he brushed his teeth and applied deodorant, as he pulled skivvies on, donned the shirt, the Dickies. While pulling on sweatsocks, lacing up his sneakers. His drive to the bakery was a litany of Hail Marys, only they were Hail *Floras,* and the request was for divine intervention of a different sort. The pits of his eyes felt gritty, and he knew this was for lack of sleep. He felt tired – soon, though, a cup of Flora's specialty coffee would fix all of that.

When the Breadman arrived at the bakery, little Miss Mussolini the timekeeper strutted into his world like a loaded and cocked rooster. "We're running behind," she sneered. "Oven in the rye line caught fire last night. You can't load up till six."

The math came quick to the Breadman. It meant he'd be almost two hours late to the Pie Apple, where Flora would be waiting. But she'd be off shift and gone at eight.

"Uhh," the Breadman said. "My stores – I'll be late."

"They been called." The timekeeper crosschecked her clipboard. "You don't need to worry about it."

"But I gotta be at Salt Lick before eight."

"Tough luck."

The Breadman felt something foreign squirm at the core of him. *Say a prayer*, he thought, quickly, to cover what he suspected might soon rise. *Say a prayer.* "Look," he said. "I don't ever give you any trouble – a lot of the other fellas do, but never me."

She appraised him like a foot corn.

"Why don't you let me just kinda load up first, and I can get outta here?" he said. "Just this time?"

Her appraisal dropped into a smile, one that at first shoved a mote of encouragement into the encounter. But he quickly discerned it was really just her enjoyment of his predicament, his pleading – her own cruelty from her perspective of the tiniest, but firm, power.

"You're such a screw, Cubbens." She spat, still smiling. "You can wait like everybody else."

The Breadman recoiled as if one of Flora's steaming coffee drinks had been flung in his face. He cowered at the opening to his van while rooster woman strutted off. He felt his face reddening and perspiration popped out under his arms. He had to quiet the desire to take her apart, piece by piece, or at the very least, to respond in kind with harsh, insulting language. *Say a prayer.*

No! He would miss Flora, and today was it – *the* day. A prayer would not be good enough, and in its place rose a scheme that was so unlike him as to – in any other circumstance – be unthinkable. The Breadman would load his van. To hell with the timekeeper. *Just let her try and stop me*, he thought. And in rebellion, he went to clock in and retrieve his yellow pick card from his leadman.

But she, anticipating this move, had checked him by retrieving and holding the pick cards herself. As each breadman came in, she had tersely explained last night's fire, then, when it was time for them to start filling their vans, handed them each a modified pick card with the new times for each line scribbled in. Now, since she wouldn't give up his new pick card, he would have to try to fill his van from memory. He assumed he'd get it almost right and would be able to explain sweetly any discrepancies to his bakery women. He would redeem some water from the reservoir of goodwill he had deposited with each of them, the subjects of his doughy lumps of wisdom. "You have to understand," he'd explain politely. "There was a fire."

The Breadman crept to the *FRENCH* line with the first of his rolling cases, started loading the fresh loaves thereon. He filled several trays, moved over to *SOURDOUGH*, started transferring the loaves. Once filled, he returned the case to his van, and loaded it on.

"What in hell's going on here?" he heard as he locked in place the first case's wheelbrakes. She repeated, at higher volume, so perhaps all the other breadmen would hear and understand that an example was about to be made: "What in *hell* we got here?"

The Breadman rose from a crouch on one knee, started to stutter. "I... uhh..."

"Cubbens!" she shouted. "I can't believe my eyes."

He couldn't talk, could not explain the rebellion that welled in him like an eruption. He felt like his chest must burst. He began to see a prize slipping away, Flora's acceptance and company and perhaps caress and maybe laying down with the Dead, and *Say a prayer* wouldn't work because he thought just *NO!*

"Listen, you screw," he heard her acid voice growl from across an ocean of tyranny. "I warned you. I said 'don't load up till six.'" Her voice was rising. "I said it as plain as day, screw." An interested group of breadmen and linemen and bakers and even his leadman gathered at the Breadman's van.

"Better call the steward," someone said. "This one's gonna be trouble."

"Yep," somebody else said, but no one left to make the call. Everybody just stood and watched the timekeeper chewing on Ed Cubbens.

The Breadman suffered about two more minutes of this humiliation. Then, like the progression of an automobile accident – those moments where everything seems to go down in slow motion but the afterimages are burnt onto memory – the Breadman thought *No* one more time, sighed, squeezed his eyes together, coiled and struck.

The long and short of it is that he tried to choke her to death. In half a second he had her against the van's side panels, both hands at her throat, pressing all his weight up against her, grinding his pelvis into hers as he lifted. He compressed as if her pipes were the prize of Flora he felt slipping away, slowly tumbling, then out of reach, maybe forever and then, yes, he was certain, forever. But he kept squeezing and pushing against her form, the form of this small-time punk dictator on a small-time punk power trip. He imagined his fingers were twist-ties around the tops of plastic bread sacks, and that he must twist and twist to lock in – what? *Freshness? No! Venom! This bitch's venom! Snake bitch! Bitch! Fucking Bitch!* He squeezed even when a half dozen men tried to pry him from her, as they pulled at his arms and shoulders and neck and hair, and shouted in his ears, *"Let go, Ed, let go!"*

But he held and squeezed for good – if anything, he increased the rigor of this great act of justice. The eyeballs of the *Il Ducette* bulged like billiard balls, and in the last possible moment before he strangled her, before the final molecule of oxygen was her last bit of burned brain-fuel, the Breadman saw that they too, *Il Ducette*'s eyes, were brown like Flora's. He thought *Oh No* at the last moment before her swollen head would have blanked or burst from pressure, and he loosed her.

She dropped to the van's floor hacking, cursing him. A stringer of saliva dropped from her mouth. Her throat was violent red, especially where his two thumbs had ironed out her windpipe. Parts of her neck seemed as if an anvil had stove them in. The other breadmen clutched the Breadman to them, a group of them to hold and steady one of their brethren – like a spooked horse. While management rushed to phone the sheriff, other workers rushed to phone the union.

And Ed Cubbens, the Breadman, thought of missing Flora.

At the Pie Apple, behind the coffee counter, butterfly-clipped Flora fixed a coffee for Ivan Manley. She hoped to see the Breadman yet, although eight was fast approaching. She needed to get in her car and spurt down the highway in time to make the start of classes. She could maybe wait five more minutes, but it took a half-hour minimum to drive to Yakima. Where *was* he? Jacqua had told her the Breadman would be late – she'd described a report from the bakery of a fire. Not many loaves of bread got sold before eight anyway, so the only disappointment registered among the bakery women all along the Breadman's route was that of Flora's.

Still, she thought, he might yet come. *I hope*, she thought, just that simply. *Hope.* A bright bird the color of a marigold lit on the windowsill. It peered in, groomed its pinfeathers for half a minute, and flew away. Flora Navarro waited, as morning light rose up and bestowed again the gift of color to pines and cedars and birch trees and bunchgrass around the core of Salt Lick. She waited for the diesel signature of his van.

CHAPTER 8
in which the town celebrates its annual Jerky Fair...

On the day Lothar Sturmhund met Hoyt Stone, the new concrete guy, neither man came away overly impressed.

Lothar, for the fact that Hoyt's greeting lacked deference: eye contact too long sustained, the way the man rose slowly from the barstool. And then there was the thumbless handshake. Hoyt, for his part, observed this immediately of Lothar: he was a man of appetite and bullroarishness.

Lothar sat at the booth next to the door when Hoyt and Mike Eagle Eye stepped into the tavern. Not seeing Lothar there, the pair moved across the bar so Hoyt could be introduced to Kinchlow. The barkeeper greeted the new man without a handshake. His fingers were busy buffing bar glasses. While they sat, Lothar, behind them, wrestled the lid from a five-quart jar of pickled eggs. The seal was giving him some trouble, so he tapped the rim with a table knife, wrapped his mighty Teutonic palms around the metal, and twisted again. The lid gave way. He popped an egg, whole, into his mouth. Then he rose to inspect the new man.

"Lothar Sturmhund," he said, mouth full of egg. Hoyt slowly spun on his stool, took measure of Lothar, and offered his thumbless hand. "Hoyt Stone," he said. Lothar squinted at the stump with suspicion.

"What the hell happened to your thumb?" Tiny bits of yolk ejaculated like pepper from Lothar's stuffed mouth, speckling the breast pocket of Hoyt's overall bibs.

"Got ate by a dog," Hoyt said. "In Alaska."

Lothar grimaced. "Some son of a bitchin' dog, huh?"

"You might say that." Hoyt grasped Lothar's palm in his.

"Hoyt's a cement man," Mike Eagle Eye said. Then he lit a cigarette.

"Are you now?" said Lothar.

"Yes sir."

"Hoyt's moving to town, up Old Man Weesle's place," Mike explained.

"Is that right?"

Hoyt nodded. "Sold it to me," he said.

"The place with the busted up trailer out back?" Lothar said, well knowing Old Man Weesle's place and its sloppy environs. Weesle, dead in that derelict house two weeks before discovery. His own cats had started to nibble on him before Tina Druce, making a visit to check on the poor bastard, had found his purpling corpse. "I'd heard his grandkids sold it."

Hoyt nodded again.

"Lothar's a contractor, so you might get some work come your way," Mike told Hoyt. Lothar's smile was false and pasty. "He's also Salt Lick's mayor, fire chief, and law enforcement."

Hoyt, at this disclosure of Lothar's resumé, worried that he might be the victim of a strategic error. If this man Lothar was such a wheel, why hadn't Mike Eagle Eye introduced him first – gone straight to Lothar on crossing the tavern's threshold – instead of the barkeep? Hoyt doubted whether he would ever get pouring work from this blond-headed egg-stuffer.

"Where in Alaska?" Lothar asked. Hoyt fumbled in his bibs for a smoke, withdrew his pack and fished one out. He struck a match, applied it to the tip, and inhaled.

"Juneau," he said.

"Pussy Alaska!" Lothar roared. Hoyt took a step backward. Kinchlow and Mike Eagle Eye twittered like bob-jays. Their loud giggles were a display of brown-nosing for Lothar, Hoyt decided. The laughter was too urgent, too forced. Hoyt pretended he didn't get it, or hadn't heard correctly. It looked like he might ask, "What was that?" or say, "Come again," or make some other verbal cross-check. But, too soon for this, Lothar elaborated: "Pussy Alaska is south. Communistic. Not even really Alaska, more like Canada. Juneau," he said again, as if he were spitting. "People say they been in Alaska, I expect 'em to tell me they worked the pipeline out of Prudhoe Bay, or was a hunting guide up McKinley. Fished out of Anchorage or Kenai or Ninilchik or somewhere. But not *Ju*-neau. That ain't Alaska."

"Funny they put the capital there," Hoyt said.

"Proves my point, doesn't it?"

"How so?"

"Government people. Don't tell me you're one of those likes government people."

"Not overly so."

90

"Thank you."

Hoyt's capitulation, whether intended, seemed to salve the rising aggression. Kinchlow went back to buffing glasses, inverting each as he finished on a white towel spread on the counter. Mike Eagle Eye stubbed his smoke.

"Come on over here." Lothar motioned to the booth. "Have a pickled egg."

"I'll join you, but I'll pass on the eggs," Hoyt said. The two men sat; Mike Eagle Eye pulled up a chair at the end of the table.

"How about some of Kinchlow's kielbasa?" Lothar asked.

"No thanks, not just now. I've eaten."

"Mike?" Lothar offered.

"Maybe a nibble."

Lothar appeared suddenly pleased. He popped another egg between his lips and hollered at Kinchlow. "Wellman, fry us up some of your big wienie!" He guffawed and crushed the egg in his jaws simultaneously, spitting egg bits again. "Son of a bitch has the best wiener around." Suddenly serious, he peered at Hoyt over the egg jar. "I'm trying to get a read on you, Hoyt Stone," he said. Then he swallowed, finally.

Hoyt thought for a moment. Then he said, "I'm just what you see."

"Good," Lothar said. "I like a man who is what he seems. You can do some cement work for me – from time to time, of course. I got some other pourers in the area too. Got to spread the work around."

"That would be fine." Hoyt stubbed his cigarette.

There was a difficult silence, as if powers had been carried by brinkmanship to the edge of war but at the last moment declared a wary peace. The table formed a demilitarized zone between them. Lothar thought, *I'll be damned if you'll ever pour one teaspoon of concrete on one of my jobs.* Hoyt thought, *You can shove your jobs up your ass; there's plenty of work to be had hereabouts. I wouldn't pour concrete down your throat.* Their guardtowers were populated with itchy trigger fingers. They smiled pleasantly across a bloodless treaty.

Lothar fixed his attention on the egg-jar again. He hefted it in both palms, held it at eye level. The pickle juice inside looked briny, yellowish green, full of the round orbs of lime-colored eggs, hard-boiled, and potent with sulfur. Motes of spice leaves moved slowly through channels between the eggs. Lothar slid one palm around the front of the jar, pointed at a monstrous clove of garlic pinned by eggs against the glass. He looked at Hoyt, back at the tip of his finger, back at Hoyt, and asked solemnly, "Hoyt, what is that?"

Hoyt sat still as a window pane. Mike Eagle Eye craned his neck.

"I'll tell you what it is," Lothar said, lips broadening into a sly smirk. "It's a thumb, Hoyt Stone, it's your goddamned thumb! That dog never ate it, he spit it out into this here jar!" Lothar laughed deeply. Mike Eagle Eye broke into snickering spasms. Kinchlow brought himself and his picket-fence teeth from around the bar to see about the ruckus.

"Wellman!" Lothar hooted. "Wellman! You picklin' meat in with these eggs?" He held his belly and rolled over in the seat like a hapless child.

Hoyt Stone was silent, but a grin formed unbidden and spread across his face. Kinchlow clapped him on the back, between the shoulders.

"Welcome to Salt Lick!" the barkeeper shouted.

Candace Sturmhund bit into a strip of Hector Aguirre's elk jerky and busted off her tooth. It felt like a firecracker going off on her gumline.

"Jethuth," she mumbled, spilling out half-chewed jerky, saliva and blood into her upturned hand. And there, right on her palm's lifeline, a shard of enamel. "Owww!" She stood, tooth in one hand like an uprooted pearl, Styrofoam cup of black coffee in the other, in the parking lot of the church. She took a sip to wash away the coppery taste of her blood, and the hot liquid raised a throb that bounced around her palate, gathered, and collected in the new, pulpy orifice of her upper jaw.

Helmut, a few feet from her talking with Reverend Jenkins, heard her whine and hobbled across the gravel to attend. The Reverend was close on his heels, having heard the *Jethuth* part, the Lord's name taken lightly. *It can never mean a good thing*, he thought as he trailed Candace's husband.

"Honey, what's wrong?" Helmut lifted his arm to brace his spouse. "What happened?"

"I buthted my toof," Candace puled through the swelling. "I bit into thith pieth of jerky and it broke."

Helmut ordered her to open her mouth so he could verify her claim and inspect the damage. Reverend Jenkins crowded over his shoulder, and the sight of this, a man – a minister, no less, right up over the back of another man like a royal rutting bull – captured the curiosity of the others gathered at the church's annual Jerky Fair. Soon the mishap had drawn nearly everyone's interest. They gathered to crane their necks and peer into the maw of Candace Sturmhund's face, to point and comment on her bridgework, the straightness of her teeth and the disturbing opening, there, where her right-hand-side top incisor should have hung. Several winced and felt themselves horripilating, colons tightening. *There but for the grace of God go I.*

There was a general call for ice, and ten-year-old Angus MacNaughton abandoned his obsession, this day, for lighting fireworks to a zealous search for cubes. After scrambling across the lot and slipping in the wet grass, he found them at the soda tent, collected a dirty handful in a cellophane baggy, and returned to the scrum that persisted around Candace. Now her hand was clamped over her lips, tongue unable to resist plunging the new hole, ache welling in her cheek. Reverend Jenkins was trying to lay his hands on Candace's head, uttering mysteries, commanding that God should restore the tooth, calling down a righteous healing. His fingers splayed Candace's wet hair, and she seemed to want to duck out from underneath it, as if the great weight of restoration were too much, on top of the excised tooth, to bear.

Helmut was unsure of what to do next, but he had an idea it involved an interrogation. Where was Hector Aguirre? And why the hell was his jerky so tough that it could break somebody's damned tooth? Helmut stood on his tiptoes, felt an old pang in his hobbled right foot, looked around the lot. *There he is*, he thought, spying Salt Lick's new mayor near the smoldering bonfire. He took the ice from the returning Angus, popped a cube out of the bag and offered it to Candace.

"Here Honey, suck on this. I'll be right back."

Then he elbowed his way through the huddle of his fellow citizens, broke free from them and hailed Hector.

"Aguirre, what's with your jerky this year?"

Hector Aguirre, Washington State Department of Fish and Wildlife warden, recently appointed mayor of Salt Lick, shuffled his boots and tried, for a moment, to pretend he didn't hear. When Helmut stood before him, the mayor had difficulty maintaining eye contact, so mostly Helmut gave the third degree to a dark green Fish & Wildlife ballcap dripping rainwater from its bill. Water beaded on the wool top of the cap, and as Helmut demanded confession, Hector hung his head further and further, so that when Helmut finally shut up to provide the mayor with an accusatory silence in which to answer, the button at the top of his cap was like a single, guilty eye.

In the quiet, both men heard the approaching drone of a commuter plane wending the thick clouds overhead. And the dripping of rain from the trees.

Held on the Fourth of July, the Jerky Fair was Salt Lick's single annual civic event, unless the three or four residents who gathered to decorate the Town Hall with Christmas bulbs each year after Thanksgiving were counted. The fair was Reverend Jenkins' fund-raiser; he used the money to write two checks – one to an orphaned children's home in Yakima, the other to an ecumenical agency sponsoring missionaries in Indonesia. It was the church's single philanthropic – if such a term can be in any way associated with the smallness of Salt Lick – activity.

The townspeople would drive or hike down Benton Drive and Mud Lake Road, or cross Highway 410, passing Town Hall to gather at the church at precisely 10 a.m. on Fourth of July morning. There the Reverend and his church family would kindle a bonfire and erect a few striped awnings in the soggy weather. While rain dripped from the canvas, Salt Lick's residents might be joined by a half-dozen or a dozen acquaintances from the environs, folks from up the highway at Eagle Rock and Cliffdell, or down the highway toward Yakima. They would drink soda and coffee, sup deep ladles full of Jacqua Druce's beef stew, grow bloated on foothills-sized dollops of potato salad, nodule after nodule of sulfurous devilled eggs, huffing casserole dishes, apple pie, sweet potatoes smothered under a comforter of gelid marshmallow, Waldorf and aspic salads, blueberry puffs, and lemon meringue. And, of course, they would work their jaws numb masticating Hector Aguirre's elk and venison jerky. Everyone who attended would spend the better part of the day feeling as if they had swallowed a medicine ball or a gunnysack of stones. And, of course, there were those who could afford it, and returned home with still-bulging stomachs and the odor of fireworks smoke in their hair, and jerky – pounds of it, in vacuum-packed seal-a-meal cellophane.

The Jerky Fair was never a huge gala – proceedings provided for an average whopping seventy-five dollars for each of the charities – but it was, nevertheless, Salt Lick's single municipal celebration, and provided a preface for an evening, once darkness fell, of fireworks and drinking (secreted, for the most part, from the Reverend).

Washington State Department of Fish and Wildlife warden Hector Aguirre had, over the years, become the sole provisioner of the Jerky Fair. It was his special act of civic service to Salt Lick.

Hector had four chest freezers at his house on the banks of the Naches River, and a generator to provide power should a Cascades windstorm knock it out, as often happened. The freezers he would fill with game he confiscated and butchered over the course of each autumn's hunting seasons. When May rolled around and the first false summer blossomed its lies, and buds were coaxed from the tips of birch and maple limbs, Hector would have the new year's first thoughts about meat smoking. When June came, and the false summer had slipped away for another month of chilling rain, he began to clean his smokers – a vast construct of plywood and 2X4 arrayed out near his tool shed. He would use a pressure washer to clear the wood of its smoky deposits of tallow, which had frozen and thawed over winter, staining the timber and curing the wood. Down by the river, he would spray the stainless steel racks he'd had custom made and watch the film spread across the calm shallows like an oil slick and be carried away once it reached the main channel with the urgent current. He'd use steel wool and polishing unguents to bring the racks to a chromium shine, and set them on the river rocks to dry, if the weather cooperated.

These tasks of husbandry completed, Hector would turn his attention to the mixing of marinade. He had a 55-gallon oil drum he'd received from a poacher as propitiation one season, a drum the hunter used for burning hide, gut, hooves and bone in order to more efficiently steal concealed, illicit meat from the forest. Hector had stopped the poacher at Eagle Rock, the man's truck bed leaking blood in the intersection. The fellow had barely spoken English, proffering his explanations mostly in Spanish, but all of it amounted to the same thing – he had no hunting license, no tags, no proof of citizenship, just a rifle and poorly cut meat wrapped in a ripped-up tarp. And the oil drum, which the man gestured Hector might have a use for in exchange for a look-away.

Hector, after cleaning the smokers, would pour all kinds of ingestibles into the marinade. Worcestershire sauce and bug juice, gallons of both. Red, red wine. A dozen cans of Campbell's cream of mushroom soup. Maple syrup, sesame oil, brown sugar, corn syrup, Mickey's Big Mouth beer, cloves, paprika, beef and chicken bouillon, lemon peel, Shake-n-Bake fried chicken batter, cardamom, cumin, nutmeg. A fifth of Potter's whiskey. A 16-pounce jar of mayonnaise. Water drawn straight from the Naches. And just a dash of cinnamon. The swirling surface of the mix would rise in the 55-gallon barrel, spinning like a coreolis force, spice flotsam tracing psychedelic arcs and whorls on the surface. The odor wafting upward was strong; it urgently commanded the emplacement of meat.

Leaving off the marinade, Hector would retrieve wrapped parcels of meat from his freezers, one by one. He would set them to thawing on his counter. Then, as they became semi-malleable in the warmth of his kitchen, he would draw a long, sharp kitchen cleaver across them, slicing through the icy meat to create strips like rashers of bacon. Exquisitely thin, he would drop the strips, one by one by one, in the yawning barrel. There the juices of animal and tree and grape and man-made synthetics would commune and combine, and recombine, to form a sum greater than the parts. As he added new strips and thawed new parcels, the meat blotted taste and texture from its medium, so that when the freezers were empty and the barrel was full, and the concoction mewled upon itself for ninety-six hours in a gastronomic percolation, Hector had produced strips of meat as fine and thin as vellum, but latent with hillock-sized flavor.

Then he would bring the racks from the smoker into the kitchen and array thereon the meat strips with careful symmetry. As each rack was filled, Hector would tote it from the kitchen and slide the rack and its heady flesh into grooves cut in the smoker's supporting timbers. Slot by slot, the smoker filled with the odorous meat. Until, finally, it was engorged with elk meat and venison, and ready for smoke.

Underneath the smoker, Hector would assemble a fire, whose smoke vectored through a cambered sheet metal flue into two spigots connected to battery-powered fans that drew the woodsmoke into the chamber. When he had built the fire sufficiently underneath and clicked the toggles of the two fans, he stepped back and monitored the operation, folding his arms across his chest and experiencing the contentedness of a mountain man in direct contact with his deity. There was no better feeling of satisfaction, and he would tend the fire with a can of beer in one hand and a poker in the other, and stir coals and emplace new alder and cedar logs, and smoke would pour from the cracks in the plywood and overfill his riverside perch with savory, thick scent. The sound of the river rushing over stones, punctuated with the pops and cracks of pitchwood, would lull him onto the brink of paradise.

All of this had gone terribly wrong in the past winter, and the following spring.

First, there had been a particularly harsh winterkill. The late, lingering summer of the previous year had kept deer and elk in the extreme high country up Bumping Lake and the American River, so that the herds were still upland and out of the game management units Hector supervised until well after the autumn's hunting seasons had expired. When the hunters had gone home disappointed and the storms finally came, the elk and deer were caught unawares in the highest, most remote parts of their range. Snow covered their feed sources overnight, yet they were dozens of miles from feeding stations. They dropped of starvation as if from machine gun fire – far from the access of Hector Aguirre. The take for legitimate hunters had already been dramatically reduced from previous years and so, as it follows, had the take for illegitimate hunters – poachers – dwindled. There were simply too few animals in the surrounding woods, down low, and those that were taken seemed to have been done so legally. Hector confiscated only two deer – a spike buck and an immature doe – from a Yakama Indian man and his son. Their meat barely filled the corner of one of his six freezers.

To this meager store Hector was able to add a small juvenile elk he brought down himself with his Winchester Model 270 one afternoon hunting up Umptanum Ridge.

One Sunday in December, Reverend Jenkins had made a pointed reference to the Jerky Fair in a post-sermon conversation with Hector and Lothar Sturmhund, then town mayor and Hector's predecessor.

"This has been a tough winter," the preacher had said, his smile wide and wispy, untrained hair moving of its own volition. "Seems it wouldn't bode well for the jerky."

"Don't worry about that," Hector said. "It'll be fine. Like I say, it always is."

But the conversation had set a hook into him, like the hooks he often set in the lips and gills of steelhead in the Naches. He was concerned, a little, about the lack of meat. And his concern morphed and twisted on itself, evolving over the course of December, so that by Christmastime, he began to consider another potential source of meat.

From time to time in his game wardening, on at least a couple of occasions each season, Hector would run across a recently expired animal in the woods. Gut-shot usually, and having fled in panic, these animals would have eluded their human stalkers through a better, more fundamental, understanding of the terrain. Having perhaps staggered behind a massive cedar and finally given in to the calling of their wounds, lifeblood raining from them, they would take one last step, kneel to the forest duff, and collapse. Hector would usually find them eviscerated from marauding coyotes, all the softness eaten from them and presenting a husk of torn hide, bones, antlers and – if it was warm enough – odor. An arrow might remain, erect and pointing the way, tip buried in bone to the marrow.

Suppose Hector got to the dead animals soon enough, suppose he discovered them before the coyotes. If the temperature remained sufficiently frigid, the meat would still be good   – if a degree more gamy than fresh kill. It was certainly nothing his special marinade couldn't fix.

Although he was aware the game laws forbade this practice – in the same way it set prohibition on the taking of game killed in road accidents – he had certainly been one to bend the rules a little in the past. And so, as Christmas approached and the nights grew their longest and coldest, he dispatched himself into the woods around Nile Creek and searched. He crossed ridges and valleys choked with snow up to his neck. He crossed the deepest core of the forest and tangled himself in snow-clad boughs. He froze his ass off. His efforts produced, after a week of bitter reconnaissance, two white-tailed deer, one mule deer, and a partially eaten cow.

Hector brought them home and cut them up. And finally, one freezer was packed to its seal strip. But in spite of this small victory and his own resourcefulness, all Hector could think of was *Five to go, Five to go.*

So when Reverend Jenkins, in February, mentioned the Jerky Fair again – "How's that cache comin' for the jerky?" – Hector snapped monosyllabically at the minister – "Fine" – and immediately regretted it, wondering whether a new sector of Hell had kindled flames for him. Imagine, barking at the man of God that way. Thus began a series of sleepless nights as Hector's mind catalogued possible solutions. He could steal away to Yakima and buy pre-packaged jerky. But that was too expensive on his Fish & Wildlife salary. He could buy beef, and pretend it was elk meat or venison come July. No – people might know. There is a distinct difference in the texture and taste of the different meats. As February evolved to March and March to April, Hector became increasingly disturbed at the deficiency that mocked him from the five empty chest freezers.

So much so that in May, when Lothar Sturmhund fell over and died of a heart attack, and the townspeople of Salt Lick appointed Hector to the mayorship, he acquiesced without giving the matter even a passing thought. He had larger trouble on his mind. A bigger fish to fry. The matter of his brain was stuffed to overflowing with the problem of meatlessness. Or near meatlessness anyway. After all, the mayor of Salt Lick didn't have to do a hell of a lot, "mayor" being more an honorific title than anything. This, though, the absence of jerky meat, was an enormous, unprecedented predicament. As he sat behind Lothar's desk in Town Hall, he worried more about the missing meat than filling the old German's massive boots.

And then, as if Heaven had opened up and dropped manna, an elk dropped dead on Highway 410 in front of Hector Aguirre's place. Not that it actually dropped – it was more that the elk *landed* as the result of an extremely kinetic impact, colliding as it did with the front bumper of a Kenworth tractor and trailer flying eastward in the night like a cannonball toward Yakima. Hector heard, from his living room couch, the shriek of compression brakes and a sound like a pumpkin being dropped from eight stories onto asphalt. Then he heard the truck gear down, the trucker punch it, and roar his or her storming way toward sun-up. He grabbed a flashlight from its closet-hook and emerged into the night.

The elk was a jellied mess thrown up on the shoulder, as dead as a thing could be. Barely recognizable as a hoof-bearing mammal, it looked more like a pile of steaming dung. Blood drained from every hole in it, and the fluid collected on the shoulder and seeped into high grass. Hector searched for the head, the eyes or eye, found it – completely blank, a pitted glass marble of void. It was a minor epiphany – a half a freezer-full, at least. He looked up and down the road, trained the flashlight on a rod of flesh that might have used to be a leg, grabbed it and felt the flesh and tendons rotate under his grasp. He killed the light, and pulled the mass with all his weight and momentum toward his yard.

It barely budged, and the odor of it – fractured open as it was in all its vital and digestive areas – washed him. Hector went for his ax and chain saw.

Hector Aguirre filled his remaining four chest freezers with road kill: raven, beaver, rattlesnake, deer, another elk he pulled of the road west of Cliffdell, coyote, opossum, a lynx he found crow-pecked and maggoty up near Boulder Cave. He supplemented this tarmac fare with squirrel and cranes he brought down with a small-bore air rifle on the river. Impossible to completely fillet to his satisfaction, the smaller animals he marinated and smoked nearly whole, removing as much bone and gut and fur and feather as possible. If a tiny skull or femur or the kinks of a backbone remained, he thought of this potential as a minor issue, explainable as an unmixed quanta of seasoning or a misplaced chip of alder.

In time for the Jerky Fair, he smoked his meat, basking in the rivermusic and the rhythm of popping flame. Beer in hand, he thanked God for provision.

"Don't jimmie-jack me around, Aguirre. What's with your jerky this year?"

99

Hector folded into himself in Helmut Sturmhund's onslaught. He stared at a space of wet grass between Helmut's boots, watched rainwater drip from the bill of his cap. He smelled smoke – it seemed as if smoke had surrounded him, indwelt him, for months. The bonfire behind him struggled against the Independence Day drizzle, and he heard someone in the crowd around Candace Sturmhund proclaim, "A bone! It's a bone!"

"For crying out loud," Helmut said, poking the mayor in the chest. "You got bones in your jerky, Hector!"

"Maybe it's a wood chip," Hector mumbled.

"Let me see that," Helmut commanded over his shoulder. Candace broke from the ministering group, trailing them like a train of betrothal to Helmut's side. She displayed a half-chewed chunk of jerky sprouting a minuscule arc of spinal column – a chipmunk's, probably – in her open hand. "That ain't no alder chip, Hector," Helmut said, turning back to warden. "Now what is it?"

"It's just a tiny bone."

"What kinda bone?"

"Squirrel probably, maybe chipmunk. Maybe crow – hell, I don't know."

Eighteen bellies surrounding the three heaved. Hector looked up to a phalanx of white, pinched faces, as if someone had planted a dozen and a half satellite dishes here in the church's sideyard.

"Lord have mercy," Reverend Jenkins said.

"Squirrel," someone repeated, as if the noun sounded familiar but its meaning was not entirely precise.

Someone else: "And chipmunk, and crow, he said."

As if on cue, those in the surrounding crowd began to examine their meat, either the strips upon which they had been gnawing, or drawing forth from knapsacks or pockets the cellophane envelopes of sealed jerky, pressing on the contents inside to inspect for bone or bone shards. Or other foreign matter.

Tina Druce let out a shout, holding her bag aloft. "It's a head," she shouted, "it's a head!" She displayed the package limp-wristed and surely, with no doubt in anyone's mind, contained therein was the skull and beak of a small bird – an Oregon junco perhaps, or a large hummingbird.

"OK, *Mayor*," Helmut said with a thin-lipped sneer. "Spill it. What'd you smoke?"

Hector rushed into the open arms of confession:

"Some was elk," he said. "Other deer. But the winter was rough, so there wasn't enough. I got some raven, some beaver. Rattlesnake. Lynx. Some 'possum, some crow."

"Crow!" said Wellman Kinchlow, as he felt bile rise from the fullness of his guts.

"Holy shit, Wellman," Jacqua Druce said. "Maybe you better go count your peacocks."

"Roadkill, mostly," the mayor added, so as to have everything precisely disclosed, all out in the open.

Kinchlow gulped, sped for the treeline, made it three quarters of the way, doubled over, and voided his stomach on the grass. Seeing this, Flora Navarro threw up as well. The odor of vomit wafted among the crowd, and folks gagged on visions of small, furry animal meat and feathers, squashed two-dimensional forms they passed each day in quantity and paid no mind to, and imagined this tinctured, gnawed meat sliding down their own esophagi.

What followed was a chorus of stomach voiding, a Handel's *Messiah* of puking. An entire Western Canon of chow-blowing. Only Hector Aguirre, the wounded Candace Sturmhund, and freckle-faced Angus managed to clench their guts together and keep down their food.

The crowd retching around him, Hector, new mayor of Salt Lick, turned his full attention to Candace.

"I'm sorry about your tooth."

"It'th all right, Hector. I gotta go to the dentitht anyway. Might ath well do it thooner than later."

She tossed her unfinished, spinal-column-laden chipmunk jerky into the firepit and turned for the coffee tent to refresh her cup. Her cheek still throbbed, but the pain was dulling so that it was partly, at least, manageable. What she really needed to do was get away from the smell of all that puke.

Reverend Jenkins started looking around for Mike Eagle Eye. The side yard needed a good hosing down, if they were salvage anything of this year's Fourth of July Jerky Fair. He supposed his checks to the orphanage and the missionary agency would be somewhat smaller this year. He turned from his own pool of vomit and walked toward the church's side-door. He'd try Mike on the phone, see if he could get him down here with a hose.

"I'm sorry," Hector said to his back.

The Reverend turned, looked to Heaven for patience or inspiration, looked back at Salt Lick's mayor, and shook his head. The preacher's hair writhed like adders. His wide mouth had upon it a rictus of reproach.

"I'll pray for you, Hector," he said. "Yes, I will." He turned and left.

Angus sidled up to Hector Aguirre, put his young pigmented arm up around the man's waist. Pulled him into a sort of awkward but genuine side-embrace.

"Don't feel bad, Mr. Aguirre," said young Angus. His boyish smile beamed a promise of innocent companionship. There was a look behind his eyes that suggested he thought none of this – not a bit of it – was in any way a big deal at all. "I kinda liked the jerky this year."

The boy ran off to light more firecrackers.

CHAPTER 9
in which Helmut gives a tax man a lasting come-uppance...

Lothar's Tetragrammaton was LTHR, and he considered himself goddish.

His name was an ancient Fatherland rendering of Luther, or Lothair – *famous warrior*. He also liked to imagine links to Old Norse, claiming at times that his given name was rooted in Lutr and Llotolf and even Moðr, which meant *fury*. Lothar liked the notion that he was, indeed, strong, his countenance a thing to behold and flee from. He believed a mark of a real man was the dismay with which others would encounter his voice. He imagined himself from time to time in knight's armor, swinging clubs and crushing the skulls of bears.

Lothar went to church periodically but emerged unfazed – imagine surrendering, subjugating his own will to that of a greater force!

Lothar remembered, of course, the Jesus stories of his youth – full of crap like water walking, the manipulation of weather and wine, feeding thousands with loaves and fish. Turning the other cheek. Surely no carpenter's son had ever been such a weak suckling! For deities, Lothar preferred a sort of ancestor-respect for the warring chieftains of Old Germanic history – the Goths, Visigoths, Vandals, and so forth. By the full beards of all Thüringians! By the blarings of *Reichsklaxons!* If he must have gods outside of himself, outside of LTHR, they must be the great chain-mailed Teutons of the Ages.

When Lothar rose in the morning he would pause at his kitchen counter with a cup of black coffee and survey his country. The thought would actually enter his mind that in an alternate history, if he were to have been born and lived and died a thousand years earlier, he would have been the battling lord of a mid-European fiefdom. He would mount a fine charger on mornings such as this, and gallop across his land swinging a broadsword at foes. The notion appealed to him, and he would grin, take in a gulp of the hot coffee, and breathe out with satisfaction.

If one of the boys or his wife interrupted this meditation they would likely be abused, certainly verbally, possibly bodily. Once, disturbed so, Lothar pitched his coffee cup at Magda with all the speed of a Cy Young Award-winning pitcher. Just in time she ducked away. The cup glanced off the crown of her head, raising only a welt where he had intended a lesson in proper humility.

He also believed that many, if not all, the people who ever disagreed with him or held in reverence opinions opposed to his were communists. "Sounds like a communistic thought to me," was one of his most-repeated sayings. He would pronounce this summation at any time, even if it made no earthly sense. It was as if he suffered from Tourette's, but rather than cursing, he would pronounce someone Red. In this way he was like Senator Joseph McCarthy or Cecil B. deMille – always on the Right end of an issue, and always ready to issue a blacklist. He felt that he and the great actor John Wayne thus held two things in common. First, both were virile and viewed themselves as embattled gunslingers. Second, both were unmistakably *Americans*, and wondered – often for excellent reasons – about those around them.

Lothar once toyed with the notion of having his Tetragrammaton tattooed on his chest. He imagined it there, ink over his oxen heart, a semaphore of skin sending a message to those who beheld him shirtless in the summer. It was a pleasant thought, but faded.

Lothar's religion was that of Ptolemy: he found nothing at the center of the cosmos but Himself, LTHR. Lothar sat upon His royal seat and was attended by His subjects.

Helmut's first impression on coming to was that he must be in a nice jail. Most of them have filthy concrete floors, but this time his fingertips kneaded carpet – it felt soft and hospitable. Then he turned his groggy head aside to see the shadows of bars cast by wan sunlight. He closed his eyes, ran his tongue across a mouth full of liquor paste. Not again – Candace would kill him this time. Or just outright leave. He'd been in the can four times this year, in front of a judge in Yakima for three of those four. He knew he drank too much, but *damn* – he couldn't catch a break since his old man died. He dug his fingers further into the carpet. It felt warm and clean.

Then he heard the sound of a machine, an electro-motorish sort of racket, oscillating, closer, then further away. He reopened his eyes. Candace towered over him with the vacuum sweeper. What was she doing *here?*

He understood soon that he lay not at the center of a cell, but stomach down, spread-eagled on his living room floor. His jacket was bunched up around his shoulders like an old grocery sack. The bar shadows were cast by the back of Candace's rocking chair. She had pulled it over next to the window to sweep the carpet. He was relieved: He must have come home drunk as a storm and passed out cold.

"You gonna lay there all morning, have me sweep around you?" Candace asked.

"Naw, I'm gettin' up." Helmut pushed up. A stab of pain flared on his shoulder, in the skin above the blade.

"Ouch – what the hell's that?" He reached under his coat, felt sponginess at his skin, and pain underneath. The jolt shot around his shoulder, up into his neck. A bar fight, maybe? Had he been in some sort of *brouhaha?* The last thing he remembered was being over at The Dot. Hoisting beers and tequila shooters.

"Help me up," he said. "I think I got hurt." He stood. Dizziness washed through his head. The pounding in his temples slammed into his brain like a mallet rhythm, and his stomach felt queasy. And he had to piss.

Helmut shuffled down the hall to the bathroom. He relieved himself, shrugged out of the coat, tossed it out the door into the hallway. His face in the mirror was a hell of a thing: hair standing up, three days without a shave. He turned to his right and lowered his shoulder. There was a bandage under his T-shirt, starting over the shoulder and running part way down his back. He pulled the shirt from around his neck, snaking his arms through.

"Christ," he said. He peeled the bandage off, bloodcrust grabbing to reveal a mottled thing, blood and ink across gauze. A new tattoo. Like a car with a new bumper sticker, it sent this message to the entire universe: *CANDACE*. The letters were high gothic and enscrolled around a red heart.

"Hey, get a load a this!" he shouted to be heard over the vacuum. She didn't come; its noise drowned his call. He dropped the nasty gauze into the wastebasket, emerged from the bathroom. "Honey," he called, "look at this." She saw him coming bare-chested, his strong pectorals, that one ranging vein that rose down each biceps and coiled his forearms. He turned to show her.

Candace didn't know what to say, standing there gripping the sweeper handle. She toed the switch on the machine into silence. It was raw, blood oozing from the needlepricks. The edges of it were scabby. But she saw her name, the scroll, the heart. He thought she would be pleased with this, or at least not angry.

"Oh, Helmut," she said. "It's... it's... well, so nice."

"You think so?"

"Yeah, kinda."

"I got it for you."

"Obviously," she said. "Thus the name and all."

"You really like it?"

Instead of answering, she paused, then asked, "Where'd you get it?"

"Uh... well, I guess down at Skin Prints, in Yakima."

"How much did it cost?"

He looked sheepish. "Um... I don't really know sweetie." With no convincing story, Helmut was trapped not knowing the when, where or why of it. He didn't even remember leaving The Dot.

"I remember going into Skin Prints," he lied, "but paying – I don't know. I think the pain and all... probably with the MasterCard." He reached into his wallet – there, folded with a couple of bills, the receipt. Sure enough, it read Skin Prints, $85.00.

He handed the slip to her. Candace's eyes popped out like two pie plates.

"Eighty-five bucks! Helmut, you know we can't..."

"Honey, I'll work some overtime this week – it's no big deal."

Whatever, she thought. It was a nice tattoo, or would be when it healed. She had one of her own, a little brown mouse inside her upper thigh. Helmut drove her nuts whenever he put his mouth on it, worked upward to where that mouse would never venture. When he rubbed onto her with that soft beard, those bushy sideburns, when his tongue poked from between them and plunged – then there was no question of forgiveness. It just flowed from her. German ticklers, he called his whiskers. She found herself thinking about that rather than $85 gone AWOL.

"Go brush your teeth," she said. "I'll finish this later."

Later, on their bed, she drank the blood and ink from his shoulder as his sweat dropped onto her, the odor of cigarettes and The Dot in his hair.

Candace sorted through mail on her way back to the house from the route box. A couple of ad circulars, a missing kid postcard, and three bills. She shuffled through the envelopes to uncover one with a Washington State Liquor Control Board return address. It was addressed to Helmut.

She entered the house, strode across the living room to the dining table. She dropped the other envelopes and held the envelope addressed to Helmut. He hated it when she opened his mail. But she couldn't resist. She slid her thumb under the hasp and sliced the top open with her fingernail. It was a bill – *Body Art Tax*, it read, *$35.00. Due two weeks from receipt. Check or money order, please, send no cash through the U.S. Postal Service.* There was a return envelope with a cellophane address portal. No stamp, though.

"What the hell's a Body Art Tax?" she said. Maybe Helmut knew – she'd have to ask him when he got home. After he cooled down from learning that his wife had again pried into his mail. "We're husband and wife," she'd say. "Your business is my business." He'd snort and grouse, then come around, especially if she offered to bring out her mouse. Sometimes Candace thought her husband was relatively sophisticated, especially for a first-generation German boy in the middle of the foothills. But it was moments like this – particularly when his resolve melted with the promise of sex – where she realized he had all the elegance of a monster truck rally.

"I never heard of a Body Art Tax," he said, when he arrived home. "Sounds like bullshit to me."

"The date here is from a couple of weeks ago, when you got the new tattoo."

Helmut grabbed the bill. Sure enough, it was marked *For Services Rendered* and had the date. Two weeks had passed; the tattoo had fully healed.

"Well I ain't payin' it." Helmut had never heard of the tax. Someone must be playing games.

"It looks pretty official," said Candace.

"I don't give a crap. If this is someone's way of raising more money, I ain't gonna be any part of it." His lips pursed. His eyes focused on something beyond the walls of the room, as if he were brokering a decision with intense mental effort. "Toss it," he said.

Candace complied, carrying the envelopes and the bill to the kitchen garbage. She threw it in with the eggshells and a greasy pizza box and wondered whether in doing so she committed a crime.

Twenty-eight days later a second bill arrived. In polite governmentspeak, it read: "If you have made payment and our correspondence has crossed yours in the mail, please disregard this second notice. If, however, you have not sent payment, why not do so today?" Another return envelope was enclosed.

"Toss it," he said.

107

A month passed, and a third notice arrived. Its tone shattered all pretence at civility: "THIRD NOTICE," it threatened. "PAST DUE: Please make immediate payment before this bill is turned over to a collection agency."

Helmut drove to Yakima, took the bill to Skin Prints. Inside, the smell of sage incense nearly gagged him. The walls were covered with examples of skin art on white paper squares – tigers rampant, the Harley-Davidson logo, skulls, anchors, snakes, flags of Dixie, wide-mouthed sharks, women with perky balloon breasts and narrow hips. There were yins and yangs, dragons, Disney and Warner Bros. characters, all kinds of shit.

The *artiste* waited behind the counter. "You were in here before," he said.

"Yeah, you did a nice job too."

"Refresh my memory." The man had metal fobs and gewgaws stapled to his ears. His skin was a bestiary of ink. Even on his neck, where a black web had affixed itself, connecting the base of his ear with something under his shirt. His nipple, probably, Helmut speculated. He was a skin-headed guy, ugly fuck, but good with the needle.

"My shoulder," Helmut said. "A heart with 'Candace' on it."

"Oh yeah, you were a late-nighter. Drunk as a maggot. You happy with it?"

"Yeah."

"She like it?"

"Yes, she does."

"Heal up O.K.?"

Helmut nodded, fishing in the pocket of his jacket for the bill.

"So you come in for another one." The *artiste* gestured at the samples on the walls.

"No, not today. I gotta question for you though."

"Maybe I got an answer."

"You ever seen this?" Helmut pointed at the bill. The ink man scrutinized it.

"Oh yeah," he said. "The skin tax, sure. State politicos passed it last spring. More money for the coffers, I guess. They gotta get it some way, since the vehicle tax got lowered. Shit, man, you know your tattoo is helping fill potholes?"

"But thirty-five bones?" Helmut said. "For eighty-five bucks worth of ink? That's what percentage?"

"I look like a mathematician to you? But it don't matter, we can ask the tax man hisself." The ink man turned his head and hollered, "Hey Hank," back into the shop. "Hank's here during the day, 'cept for

Friday and Saturday nights, when he stays late, collects the tax right on the spot. He's an asshole." The *artiste* looked over his shoulder and lowered his voice. "Hard to get along with, being a government dickhead and all, and he don't stick around for the night customers during the week. Makes me give him the addresses, files his report – he wasn't here the night you came in. They're everywhere now, in all the art houses. Piercing, tats, scarring, branding – even got a tiny little tax for henna. It's shit, I know."

"Whaddaya want needle man?" Hank wallowed through the door to the ink room, folded his chubby arms over a huge stomach. He wore a short sleeve shirt buttoned up to his neck; skin wrapped down over the collar like a blanket. His eyes were black pinpoints. He looked like a comic-book character: Fat Ass.

"Customer here has some questions about your Skin Tax."

"Yeah? What kinda questions?"

Helmut stepped closer to the counter, pointed at the bill.

"This – who ever heard a this?"

The rotund tax man eyed Helmut with distaste. "Looks like *you* heard of it now, fella," he said. "But it looks like you're having some trouble understanding the concept of a bill. See there," Hank turned to the *artiste* as if seeking someone to testify to the truth of his claim. He pointed at the raw words on the notice. "Past due!" he read. "Third notice!" The fat man shook his cartoonish head longsufferingly, as if Helmut were one in a parade of idiots to whom he must perpetually explain and justify the notion of the Body Art Tax. If he would have been honest, the taxman would have admitted that about the second time he had to offer his apologies for the state of Washington, he'd already been sick and damned tired of it. So for this goat-faced, sideburn-framed puke, he'd offer just four words of advice. He turned to Helmut. "I'd pay it now," he stated.

"Like hell," said Helmut. The ink man winced.

"I'd do it," the *artiste* said. "It can go on your record."

Helmut looked at the two, ink man, tax man. "Jesus," he said. "A Body Art Tax? What a crock." He wanted nothing more at that moment than to whack the fat fuck's kneecaps with a ball bat. To watch him double over and cry to his mommy or his boss at the Body Art Tax Collector's Department. Nevertheless, instead, hands trembling a bit, he fished out his wallet. Tossed a twenty, a ten and a five at the tax man. He turned to leave, hobbled to the door.

"Lucky I don't charge you a late fee," the tax man called after him.

"I'd kick your ass," Helmut said, slamming the door behind him.

Helmut was doing some hard drinking. It was payday, and he had a wallet full of cash. He had called Candace a few minutes before to say he'd be home late. She had drilled him with objections, even invoked her little mouse. But he needed to hang out with his crew for while. "We had a rough day, honey," he said. "We need to bond."

He meant with Ivan, and the other fellows. Ivan had come down to The Dot after a not-so-successful interlude with the Penney's lingerie-counter woman, who had told him she thought, maybe, they needed to feel free to date other people. Ivan told Helmut he figured it had something to do with the way his eyes set on his face, or the prominence of his nose. He knew that she had found his face interesting at first. But she'd grown weary of it, he supposed, tired of this dick-looking probe on the front of him.

"My old buddy, Dicknose!" Helmut said. Ivan joined in the laughter, just to prove he didn't care about the Penney's woman. "Plenty a women out there want to put their hands all over your face, Ivy!"

"Yeah, I suppose," Ivan said. He signaled Nebby, the Spot's barkeep, for a beer.

The Dot was a hovel on Yakima's Fifth Street, a jukebox and beer sign honky-tonk like a million others. Since his daddy died, Helmut preferred the drive to Yakima for his R&R to the Lowell's crowd. Too many maudlin memories, too many toasts to the old, wonderful blond-headed bastard. And too much goddamned nervous wristwatch checking.

The bartender and Helmut had been cawing back and forth for an hour about the Body Art Tax.

"Gimme another shot, Nebby," Helmut said. "I'm just getting into this."

"You know, you're gonna drive yourself to drinkin' worryin' about shit you got no control over," Nebby said. He set a full shotglass on the counter. Helmut tossed it back and lit a smoke.

"Don't jimmie-jack me around, Nebby. The government can do whatever it wants to do, but it ain't gotta right to tax what I put on me."

"Well, they tax what you put in you." Nebby pointed at the empty shotglass, then at Helmut's cigarette. "They tax whatever the fuck they want."

"That's just it – they got enough a my money."

"Well you don't gotta buy the shit," Nebby said. "It's your choice, like playing Lotto. Noboby's got a gun to your head."

Helmut asked for another shot.

"You've had a few, big guy."

"Just supportin' my country," he said.

Before long he was boiled, his cheeks tight and stomach primed. He was eating everything in sight, bar chips, peanuts, pepperoni sticks. He wanted one of those pickled hard-boiled eggs. Nebby brought the jar and Helmut fished one out. It slid down his throat like a ball of paste, so good he got another. And more beer. His mates were buying pitchers and throwing darts. Helmut joined in, threw one and missed completely, buried its needle tip in a Miller Babes poster next to the board, right in the bikini model's smiley-ass teeth. He started goofing off with the darts, aiming for her tits. *Thunk* – one pierced her navel. His crewmates cheered.

"Oh!" Helmut shouted. "Piercing tax! Charge her, charge her! Send her a bill! She can't pay? We got ways a dealing with that too!"

Then he was in the bathroom pissing beer, and it was like water flowing through him. He was dizzy and lost. He felt those eggs bunch and push. A big sulfur belch ejected from him. The taste overfilled his mouth, banished for a minute the aftertaste of beer, tequila, cigarettes. "Goddamned tax man," he muttered, eyes red and heavy-lidded. "I'm gonna show that prick."

Helmut vomited in the urinal. When he was done, he thought, *Good. Room for more.* He staggered back to the bar. "Hit me, Nebby-Boy," he shouted.

"Helmut, mellow out," the bartender said. "I'm gonna have to cut you off pretty soon. Your wife'll drive down here and have my ass."

"Take it easy, Nebby. I'm gonna go get me some new ink tonight. Gotta be plenty blotto 'fore I sit through that."

"I'd say you're ready now."

Helmut and Ivan staggered together down Fifth Street. "Gonna get us some ink," Ivan howled, passersby crossing over to the other side of the avenue ahead of them. The pair, caroming off plate glass and bus-stop signs, was happier than pigs wallowing. They saw the Skin Prints sign. Before long they were at the door.

"After you." Helmut held open the door. He swept with his hand. Ivan bowed, skittered inside giggling. The needle man looked up from an underground newsletter he had been reading all evening.

"Hey fellas," he said. "Come in tonight for a tattoo, or just cruisin'?"

"Ink!" said Helmut. "That one." He pointed at a sample of an anchor, with a scroll on which anything could be written, indelibly, forever. "I want it to say, 'NO TAXES.'"

"And you, sir?" The *artiste* turned to Ivan.

"I gotta look for a minute," Ivan said. Helmut sensed hesitance. Ivan, as far as he knew, wore no tattoos. If he got one tonight, it would be his first.

"You chicken shit," he said, pointing at his best friend. "Don't you puss out on me tonight, Ivy. Get you a tattoo on that Pinocchio nose you got growin' there."

"Ah, fuck you Helmut – I gotta see what they got."

Helmut remained unconvinced. "Yeah, you take a good look, bub. There's plenty for you to pick from."

"Yeah, take your time," the needle man added.

Helmut was directed around the counter, through the door to the back. Fat Hank was sitting there reading a dog-eared copy of *Field & Stream*, wishing he had a big bass on his hook. He glanced up, saw Helmut. He couldn't quite place the guy.

"It's gonna be about sixty-five," the *artiste* said, "depending on how much time it takes." He was usually pretty close.

"Plus the Skin Tax," Hank said. He grinned wryly, remembering this puke now. Guy said he was gonna kick his ass! *Oh boy, it'll be a pleasure taking your money, you drunk piece of low-life scum.* God, how he hated these assholes.

Helmut stripped off his shirt, sat on a stool. The *artiste* assembled his implements, the needle gun, the small jars of ink, some pure alcohol, swabs and bandages.

"Where you want it?" he asked.

Helmut motioned to his right biceps and flexed the muscle. The vein rode its ridge. The CANDACE tattoo on his shoulderblade was in perfect bloom, and the *artiste* paused to admire his own work.

"That came in nice," he said.

"Mmm-huh," Helmut mumbled. The needle man dipped some gauze in the alcohol, its odor eddied under Helmut's nose. He breathed in – it smelled so clean. And it was cool, like ice, where the *artiste* dabbed and swabbed over the vein. He ran a disposable razor across the skin to prepare the surface. Then he swabbed on some transfer gel. He pressed an ink template there, over the biceps, let the design transfer onto Helmut's skin.

The needle gun clicked and hummed. The *artiste* dipped the tip into one of the ink pots. Helmut felt the first teeth as its motor rose. It spat blackness into his skin. He clamped his teeth, squinted. It still hurt, even through the booze. He watched as the *artiste* moved the gun in little wasp swirls. The pain ebbed and flowed, more acute at times, almost inconsequential at others. The needle man dipped the business

112

end of the gun again, completed the outline of the anchor and scroll. He changed tips, swabbed blood away with clean gauze. The wipe came away stained some unidentifiable, unheard-of color.

Then he filled the anchor with gray, the solid application of a wider inktip. It hurt worse because the hole being blasted in his skin was twice as wide. Helmut jerked.

"You better hold that fucker still," the needle man said. "I'd hate to draw a gray line halfway across your arm."

Helmut braced again, suffered through the gray until the *artiste* was finished. Then came time for the scroll.

"What you want it to say?"

"NO TAXES!" Helmut eyed Hank evenly. "All capital letters, with a exclamation point at the end."

"You got it." The needle man slipped the first tip back on the gun, dipped it in black again. He carved the message into Helmut's arm. The crossbar of the T bisected that big blue vein, and he was finished.

"You want color on the scroll?"

Helmut had had enough, so declined. "I want the skin to show through there," he said, as if this were some aesthetic preference. Truth was, he thought as he gripped the arm with a gauze bandage as thick as a maxi-pad, this motherfucker *hurt*, and he wanted no more of it. And the pain had affected his drunkenness too – rather than sober him, the adrenaline and beating of his heart had made it deeper and broader than when he had come in. It – he – rolled from it, wanted to sleep in it, wanted to strike out at the same time.

"I want that jackass to come get his tax money." Helmet pointed a wavering finger at Hank. "Come on, jackass."

"I think you know I'm gonna have no trouble collecting," said Hank.

"Well bring it, don't sing it," Helmut said. Both men rose. The needle man jumped from between them and fled to a corner. The two men squared off like pro wrestlers. Hank swatted the air with an exploratory poke. His flabby arms shook as he countered Helmut's first jab. They made a circle, danced through arcs. Helmut looked for an in, found it, lashed out and laced knuckles across Hank's cheek. It backed the big cartoon up.

Then Hank charged, ran right through the stool between them and upset the working table. The ink pots went flying, splattering the opposite wall and Helmut's chest and belly. Ivan Manley heard the crash and followed the sound of the ruckus through the door. His bitty eyes drew a bead around that long schnoz and saw some fat bastard bulling into Helmut's body like a locomotive.

"I'm here, partner!" Ivan yelled, forgetting he now had a sheet – a police record—and that Detective Pandoulis didn't want to *see* him again. He grabbed the needle gun by its pneumatic tube. The air pressure that spat ink was fed through this rubber conduit, but now it was the handle of a weapon, the brass gun whirling from it like a bolo in radii from Ivan's wrist. He pulled hard on the tube – a whip crack – and the gun smashed into the fat man's temple. Hank went over like a bag of salt, splintering the stool under him.

Helmut gasped at the wound aside Hank's head.

"All right, Ivy!" he shouted, as the *artiste* fled the room. "Fuckin' A, nice shot!"

They stood over the tax man, the splintered stool, the spattered-ink wreckage. Helmut's biceps throbbed, and Ivan was jacked completely up.

"Let's do this prick," Helmut said. "Do him up good." He turned to where the ink man was – "Ink man? Where is that dude?"

"He booked, Helmut."

Helmut had an idea. Everyone would know who the tax man was. He was just out cold, not dead or anything, but when he woke up... Ivan giggled at the thought.

Helmut picked up the needle gun, flicked the ON toggle, and that hum filled the room again. And he tattooed...

SKIN TAX

... on the fainted man's forehead.

"That'll teach 'im," Helmut said, the work done. It was sloppy. It barely resembled the words. There was nothing symmetric or balanced about it. Not as fancy as the Ink Man, Helmut had to admit. But it was there, for good, nevertheless.

Ivan had gone white. He looked like he was going to vomit any second. Brouhahas of this sort were just a bit more than he had backbone for.

"We better get outta here before somebody shows up," he said. Helmut thought his best friend might be right. He stood and dropped the needle gun on Hank's chest.

"So long, Hank," he said. "Don't forget to pay your taxes."

In front of Salt Lick's Town Hall, Helmut woke up to a bastard of a headache, blood clotting his T-shirt. He lifted his head up over the level of his truck's window. A full-antlered buck jumped back from the

114

truck and eyeballed him. Helmut froze by habit. The deer sniffed the air. Then it turned and presented its black-rimmed tail and tawny rump. It took a few steps toward the laundromat, stopped, and stared back at Helmut.

Helmut whistled and arced his fingers like a Hollywood monster. The deer crossed Mud Lake Road in three bounds and disappeared into the woods between Lowell's and Juniper Jamison's house.

"Holy shit," Helmut said. Why he'd driven this far and not the rest of the way home... well, who knows why folks do what they do when they're hammered? He looked down at the blood. That dip shit down at Skin Prints must have forgotten to put a bandage on, and then he remembered, and grinned.

He walked to Town Hall's front door. It was open, so he thought Mike Eagle Eye must be around. But it was early – 6:30 by his watch, although the clock on the façade read 6:34. He went down the hall to the bathroom to pee, pulled the sleeve of his T-shirt up around his shoulder, stared at the anchor, at the scroll.

He read *NOT AXES!*, and no matter how he turned in the bathroom's fluorescent light, no matter how much he pinched and pushed the sore skin, that T was not going to migrate across the scroll to its proper place. It was stuck there, for good.

Candace was going to have his ass for sure.

CHAPTER 10
in which Jimmy Bayles, Afro-American, counts coup...

A few days before the Christmas before his ticker blew, Lothar slid off the road in a snowstorm about five miles out of Salt Lick. He was returning from a job site for an end-of-the-day Peacock at Lowell's. Overconfident in his foul-weather driving prowess, he hit a patch of ice coming into a curve on Highway 410 and ran his F250 off into the drainage ditch, smacking his forehead on the steering wheel.

After he said *godammit* and *shit* a couple of times and checked his forehead in the rear-view mirror, he rocked the rig back and forth in four-wheel drive, going from reverse to drive. But this only spun the tires further down into muck. The truck rested on its front axles, the bed sticking up into falling snow like a weirdly canted monolith. He sat in the grounded truck contemplating his next move. Then he saw headlights, quit contemplating, and popped open his door.

A cement-mixer pulled up alongside. Jimmy Bayles, Hoyt Stone's apprentice, emerged.

"You need some help?" Jimmy shouted, with a huge, crazy grin, over the wind.

"Yeah, I needa get pulled outta here's what I need," Lothar yelled, half in and half out of the truck's cab. "Run on back into Naches for me now. Get a wrecker."

"No need," Jimmy said, all lips and teeth in twilight. "Gotta winch'll winch you right outta here in about five seconds." Jimmy hoped his assistance would augur well for future interactions with Salt Lick's primary citizen.

"Fine then, let's get at it." Lothar climbed out of the cab. He looked around through the fat, swirling flakes at the truck's bed in the air and the front tires in the muck. He and Jimmy pulled the cable free from the front of the mixer, threaded the hook around Lothar's rear axle and wrapped it back onto the stout cable. Jimmy got into the mixer, shifted into reverse. The cable drew taut. The hook slipped and caught.

116

There was a sucking sound from under Lothar's front tires. The F250 came free.

"Obliged," Lothar said. "You're O.K. for a coluh'd fella."

Jimmy collected and rewound the winch cable.

And for weeks, believing himself magnanimous, Lothar told everyone he saw about Jimmy Bayles. How Jimmy Bayles was O.K. for a coluh'd fella. He told this to Wellman Kinchlow and Juniper Jamison, to Jacqua Druce and Nick Oxendine, to Gib MacNaughton and Hector Aguirre, to his wife, to his sons.

Gunter – who knows what the boy was thinking? – endeavored to admonish his father.

"You know, Dad, this is the 1990s. You could call him Black or African-American."

Lothar made as if to be mystified: "Well, he is coluh'd, isn't he?"

His son paused, in alien, unsure territory.

"Isn't he?" Lothar's voice rose in pitch. "He ain't a white man, is he, right, he ain't white, so he's not white, he's coluh'd." Lothar's voice quickened and rose again. "That's what he is, coluh'd. And that ain't saying nothing except he's coluh'd, which is a true fact. Isn't that right?"

The sheer determination of his father's will to win, the circling and weaving of his father's attack, was as if Gunter were in the prize ring with Muhammed Ali. Lothar's diatribe was like the Great One's fancy footwork.

"Yes, sir," Gunter said, throwing in his own towel.

"That's right. You're on the right track. He is coluh'd. And that's why I said coluh'd, because I say exactly what I mean. And nothing's wrong with that – it's just a state of being, coluh'd is. A state of being *Ne*-gro. Saying different is sort of communistic, don't you think?"

To avoid Lothar's further wrath, Gunter had to admit that yes, perhaps, stating otherwise might be communistic.

Lothar said, pointedly, "Thank you." He left the room with the bearing of a winner by knock-out.

Sometime after midnight Mike Eagle Eye staggered across Mud Lake Road onto the Pie Apple's porch smashing into things – the vending machine, the *Herald-Republic* box, a bench. Then he bounced off tree trunks between the Pie Apple and Town Hall. Finally he fell amid rotten cedar stumps, all while clutching a fifth of cheap whiskey and not spilling a drop.

What a mess. Boiled as an owl, he regained his feet. He executed a polka across the road's centerline. A spastic commencement tugged at the base of his throat. The summer night spun – the stars, the sky, the trees against it. He looked up. Tree branches flew off into the warm darkness. Reeling, gulping weakly, he purged his supper: Lowell's tavern eggs and kielbasa.

Then Mike was again on all fours, forehead resting in the dewy bunchgrass at the road's shoulder.

He didn't see the cat until it skittered across Mud Lake Road in front of him.

"Hey kitty-cat," he whispered. "Here kitty, kitty. Here pretty little kitty."

The cat stopped on the asphalt. Mike saw the glow of Lowell's windows in its eyes. He wondered whether it would come closer and let him pet its fur.

"Here kitty kitty," he called again.

The cat appeared to consider Mike's summons, then stepped his way. Mike rose – too quickly for his own good – stumbled toward the cat, caught himself before he fell.

But it was too late. The cat executed a sort of feline pirouette, lifted itself onto tippy-toes. Its tail rose with slinky grace. Mike saw too late white stripes down the kitty's back. And then he paid the olfactory price of his massive misinterpretation. A cloud of stultifying odor washed over him.

"Oh, fuck," he grunted. He sat down like a man who has been clopped in the skull with a large, red brick. Load-lightened, already re-manufacturing its own fugginess, the skunk pranced away.

An indeterminate while passed. The scent performed an illusory fade. Mike sniffed the air, then his clothes. Maybe the skunk hadn't scored a direct hit. Mike staggered to a stand, moved in the direction of Lowell's, crossing Mud Lake Road again. His throat burned; a Bourbon and Seven could provide some relief.

He thought he might even sing a little karaoke.

Later, he wondered why, wherever he stepped in the tavern, the way opened before him. He sang in a bubble of space, the circumference of which comprised Lowell's cronies – a drunken jury of raised eyebrows and held nostrils.

After Mike had a go at The Beatles "Get Back," he reeled out from under the blank TV over karaoke corner and pulled up a barstool.

"What is that, Mike?" Nick Oxendine asked. "What'd you get into?"

"Whaddaya mean?"

"You reek, man. Like skunk spray."

"Oh, thas a lil' kitty I run onto."

Kinchlow poured Mike Eagle Eye a drink. Mike lit a smoke, took a sip and exhaled into his glass so the smoke curled and rose, slowly, from the booze and ice. He looked up at the cronies watching him. He thought he heard Jimmy Bayles mutter "damned Injuns."

What Jimmy actually had said was "I think I'll have another Peacock." This sounded nothing whatsoever like "damned Injuns." But Mike thought he heard what he thought he heard. He was in no mood for bigotry, not this night. He dropped off the barstool and bobbled his way over to Jimmy, finger pointed like a pistol. He poked at Jimmy's chest. "Helluva thing callin' me a damn Injun when you the only colored fella around. A *nigger's* what Lothar woulda said."

"Nigger?" For once that I-know-where-the-treasure's-buried grin abandoned Jimmy's mouth. "Colored? What the hell are you talkin' about, Mike."

"You call me a damn Injun, I call you a colored nigger!"

Wellman Kinchlow stepped between them. "Fellas," he whistled. "Here's the deal. You are going to settle down, right now. Ain't nobody here calling names no more. You know you don't mean it – it's the booze talking. I'll cut you off if you can't manage better. Either that or take it outside."

The two men were like a couple of candles, wicks wavering with flame, but otherwise still. Jimmy, by a great measure, was the more sober of the two. So he backed off first. "You don't have to get all up and hard on me, Mike. Lemme buy you a drink." He was eager for reconciliation, but still vexed he had been first, obviously misunderstood, and second, called a nigger. He knew Mike was blasted, but that wasn't much of an excuse. Best thing, though, was to remain affable. "I'm sorry," he added. His hallmark smile blinked like a lighthouse lens.

If what he did through the haze of bourbon could be described as *considering*, Mike Eagle Eye considered this. And agreed. He and Jimmy moved away from the table to the bar, and Kinchlow poured Mike another. The cronies – Hector Aguirre, Gib, Jacqua, Nick Oxendine, Gunter Sturmhund – breathed a collective sigh of relief.

"Crazy," Gunter said after the entruced pair had stepped away. "Both of them, crazy as hell."

Hector, always civic minded, observed that it pleased him that Salt Lick, alone perhaps among all communities, seemed to have avoided all the ugliness, over the years, regarding issues of race. "Number one social issue in America," he said. "Country ought to take a lesson from Salt Lick. I mean look at us." He gestured around at the group. "I'm the mayor – *Mejicano*. We got Jimmy working the cement, African. Gib, here – Scotch. Mike, the best damned town fixit-man in the county, Indian. Kinchlow – white as they get. Jacqua, Irish *and* a lady. Like I say, all four corners of the globe represented right here. Or at least three of them. Only thing we don't got is Orientals."

Jacqua broke out in song. "We are the world, we are the children."

Mike and Jimmy rejoined the group with fresh glasses.

"And, if I remember correctly, Lothar had a fairly matter-of-fact approach to this issue," Hector said.

"You've got to be kidding me," Gunter said. "Dad was as bigoted as they come."

"Well, I just mean he called a black man a black man, an Indian man an Indian man, and so forth."

"He called a black man *coluh'd* as I recall," Gunter said. Jimmy nodded.

"Yep," Jimmy said. "A few months back I pulled Lothar out the ditch up 410 a ways. I heard he run around saying what a nice thing it was, this colored boy pullin' him out like that."

There was an awkward silence. They sipped their drinks, looked up and around themselves at the bar. Mike Eagle Eye lit another cigarette.

It was he who broke the thoughtful silence. "You know, we're all the same, but different. We're like the deer and the elk and the moose."

The group eyed him like an outbreak of forest fungus.

"White man is elk," he said. "Black man is moose. Indian man is deer. Asia man is reindeer."

"Oh good God," said Jacqua.

"Whataya call the Arabs?" Gunter asked.

Mike paused for an instant, seemed to turn the problem around in his inebriated cortex. Then he brightened. "Antelope, I guess."

"If white man's the elk, that would have made Lothar the royal bull," Kinchlow mused through the gaps in his bridgework. "Bugling about, mounting cows left and right – the ruler of the herd!"

120

"I resent having the young females of this fine town and hereabouts referred to as cows," Jacqua said.

"You ain't gotta worry about it unless you're one of those been mounted!" Mike said. Laughter broke out.

But Jimmy felt the horn of aggression rising again. Black man is the moose, Mike had said. So what's a moose? Bloated, ungainly, horselike – always wandering around halfway sunk in muck. Not a pretty picture. Some moments after the conversation had moved on to something else, he said, "I don't like it."

"Don't like what?" asked Jacqua.

"Being a moose. Black man ain't no goddamned moose."

"Oh, for crying out loud, Jimmy, it's just bullshit," Gunter said. "We're just bullshitting here."

"I'm not bullshitting," Jimmy said. He squinted at Mike Eagle Eye with fresh rancor. "Not no more."

"O.K. fellas, that's it," said Kinchlow. "You need to settle this once and for all."

The race was Jacqua's idea. She had recently been to the funny-car trials at Yakima Speedway. It seemed a perfect solution. They could block Highway 410 for four miles from Eagle Rock westward and detour cars along the Nile River Road.

"I know where we have some detour signs stashed," Mike said.

"I'll set 'em up," Kinchlow said.

"What'll we race *in*?" asked Jimmy.

"You drive Hoyt's mixer," Gunter said. He turned to Mike. "And you drive the pumper."

"That piece a shit!" Mike said.

"Hey, Mike, that's a well-maintained machine. You oughtta know, unless you been skimping on the mechanical. I think it rocks."

Mike Eagle Eye could not let Gunter's slap at his mechanical abilities go unchallenged. His besotted pride forced him into acquiescence.

Agreed, then, Kinchlow lifted the phone to contact the crippled man with the cowboy hat, proprietor of The Woodshed at Eagle Rock. He'd need to know there would be some hullabaloo out there tomorrow and could expect some disruption to business. Not much, though, since the eastward detour would spill out right at Eagle Rock, and the westward detour would begin there. And the racers and onlookers would make it up to him, Kinchlow promised. They would dine at The Woodshed afterward and drink probably two hundred bucks worth of beer. It was the few-and-far-between residents between Eagle Rock and the west entrance to Nile River Road who might find themselves more affected. Kinchlow would need to stop by each farm on the way out and warn folks to stay off the road for an hour or so.

"What time we doing this?" he hollered, covering the phone's mouthpiece with one hand.

"10 o'clock tomorrow morning," Jimmy said. Everyone in the room involuntarily glanced at his or her wristwatch.

"Oh boy," Mike said, anticipating his hangover.

The morning sky was clear as an alpine lake. Mike Eagle Eye, unbathed and smelling powerfully, still, of skunk squirt, fed Quoof and Pyewacket, then arrived at Town Hall puffing a cigarette a little after 7 a.m. At least, that's what the clock on the building read, although his wristwatch indicated seven straight up. With hangover camshafts rotating in his head, he keyed the door and walked down the unlit hall to the garage. He opened it to a tableau of small-town municipal junk crowding the bright red pumper.

Mike struggled through some calculations. Racing Hoyt Stone's 1972 International Harvester cement mixer with this 1940 American LaFrance 500-Series pumper garaged for nearly a decade in the Town Hall was a no-shit bleak prospect. Thirty-two years and only God knew how much horsepower separated the two machines. Mike was pretty sure both characteristics favored the mixer.

He recalled applying stencils to the pumper's new red paint more than five years ago, painting Salt Lick No. 1 in gold paint on the door sides. It had seemed at the time to be sort of a joke, but Lothar had sure been dead serious about it. Now, the chrome grille and bumper, the siren, the handrails – everything that ought to be brilliant silver on the machine was, instead, pitted with rust. This included the chrome label, on which could barely still be discerned: *INVADER*, and underneath, *Elmira NY*. But the bodywork was clean and red. For a few minutes, Mike's doubt shifted to a strange admiration whose source – if it wasn't the care he'd invested in the old pumper – he couldn't identify.

Funny, he thought as he lit another smoke, for it to end up here, in Salt Lick, Washington, fifty-plus years old. All the way from New York, a place he could only imagine from pictures in newspapers and stories in books. He couldn't remember how the town had come by the machine, and supposed its acquisition – by Lothar, no doubt – predated him.

The pumper had not been out of the garage ten times, he figured, since he'd painted it. Though he had started the motor, religiously, once every week to keep the oil viscous and the battery charged. He only kept five gallons of gas in the tanks. The leaded variety was getting harder and harder to find. Once every six months he drove the old beast into Naches. There he would siphon off the long-sitting gas and replace it with fresh. But the water in the pumper's tanks – now that was a different story. The pumper's aquifers had last been filled within the past decade. But it couldn't have been much more recently than nine years ago. He checked the chambers' levels for evaporation every so often, but he thought if they ever really had a fire, ever really had to use the damned thing, the old pumper would probably spew algae and scum as much as H_2O.

Mike walked around the pumper, as close as the junk heaped around it allowed. He cleared a few things out of the way as he went. A stack of traffic cones, a PED XING sign he'd never gotten around to posting between Lowell's and the Pie Apple, four three-quarters-empty five-gallon buckets of paint. Pike poles and a couple of axes. He saw that the detour signs, which had been stacked over by the Town Hall's water heater, were gone. Kinchlow had picked them up either earlier this morning or last night after closing the tavern. After a few minutes, Mike had cleared enough around the driver's door and the front to drive out. He unlocked the garage door, hoisted it upward. It rolled onto the ceiling with the shrieks of untended metal on metal.

He tossed his spent cigarette into Town Hall's gravel driveway and rounded the vehicle's bow – in ways, the old pumper was very much akin to a bright red tugboat. He unlatched the driver's door, hauled himself upward and in, temples pounding. He turned the key. Twelve cylinders under the hood coughed once then roared to life. From the captain's chair, surveying all in front of him across the vast, bulbous hood, he thought *yes*, for a moment, *this actually might be very fast.* Funny what a new angle would do for perspective. "This rocks," he said.

Meanwhile, Jimmy rose from his camp-trailer slumber, fed and watered Bastard, and began the process of hijacking Hoyt Stone's cement mixer. Hoyt heard the throaty burble of its idling diesel motor, and emerged from the headquarters of Stoneway Pouring – which also happened to be his house. Hoyt ambled up to the side of the rig.

"Where you off too?" he asked. "Ain't got no jobs this morning."

"Into Naches for an oil check." Jimmy knew Hoyt would find out about the race – there was no question of that. But he figured forgiveness would be easier to get than permission, as the old saw goes. "Back around noon."

The explanation satisfied Hoyt. He stepped back onto his porch and lit a smoke. Jimmy rolled out of the driveway and up the road. Hoyt was pleased with Jimmy, a hard worker, a good businessman. The young man had a bright future in concrete. The mixer's motor echoed around the hills for a while, almost until Hoyt had smoked his cigarette down to the filter, then faded.

The sun had risen high enough over Bethel Ridge that it wouldn't blind the drivers as they barreled eastward on State Highway 410. The Lowell's crowd assembled with Jimmy and the Stoneway Pouring cement mixer. Kinchlow pulled up in his old Chevy Malibu. He announced the placement of detour signs and notification to area residents was complete. Behind them, toward Cliffdell and the mountains, Kinchlow's handiwork – a large kluged-together barrier – crossed the road. Every two or three minutes a car or truck would approach. The anonymous driver would apparently think nothing much more of the barrier than the minor inconvenience a short detour would represent, and turn right onto Nile River Road. The tires of these intermittent vehicles popped on gravel as they geared slowly around the first turn, and then they'd be away and forgotten.

Ten o'clock approached. There was no sign of Mike Eagle Eye and the pumper. Eyes scanned to the east, to the first broad, sweeping turn that followed the arc of the Naches River. Hands shielded the eyes from the sun's glare, eager for the first sign of the fire truck. At ten straight up, there still was no sign of the delinquent Mike.

"He chickened out," Jacqua said. "I just bet you."

"No way," Kinchlow said. "Not Mike."

"I agree," said Gunter. "There's no way in hell Mike would walk away from this."

And Gunter was the first to spot it, what appeared as a fat, red beetle sputtering in the distance. The group cheered, even Jimmy, and the pumper's siren sounded faintly, a lonesome keening like the call of a single coyote. It wafted the length of the valley to them, barely outpacing its origins and warping in tone and timbre as it bounced from foothill to river to ranchhouse to cliffside. The wail notched up a tick in volume and key, and the pumper looked now like a fabulous red rocket blundering toward the group barely under control.

Mike Eagle Eye pulled up to the crowd, the antique fire engine snorting and cranking. When he came to a full stop, it backfired like a blunderbuss.

"Where you been, Mikey?"

"Whaddaya mean? I'm right on time." Mike held his wrist out the window, proffering evidence.

"It's almost a quarter after," Kinchlow said.

"Not by my watch." Mike pointed at his wrist. "It's ten straight on, right now."

"I think maybe you fell on something last night and broke it," Gunter said.

"Well, no use bitching about it now. I'm here, so let's get it on."

"I think you're pointed the wrong way," said Jimmy, from the mixer's cab.

"Funny guy," Mike said, and engaged the pumper. He rolled forward out of a cloud of roiling, farting exhaust and executed a two-point turn in five points. Thus, he configured the pumper's launchpath parallel to the mixer's.

Mike unfolded himself from the pumper's cab, stepped onto the shoulder, fired up another smoke.

"I thought you was ready," Kinchlow whistled.

"Not quite. Gotta do something first." He rounded the pumper to its watervalves, inserted the handle of a side-mounted pickax, and cranked open the valve. A gout of putrescent water sprayed from the unwinding threads and, when they realized what would come next, the assemblage backed away with the same haste and demeanor as they would have shown had he beheaded himself. When the valve finally popped off, water shot in an aquacannon sweep across the twin yellow line. The arc crossed over the asphalt and splashed Stoneway Pouring's single cement mixer. It was exactly as if a big red firedog were having a long piss at a giant blue fireplug. Marking its territory.

"Free car wash!" Mike howled as the fetid water sprayed.

"Oh, you jackass!" Jimmy hollered from the cab. "Get in the damned thing, and let's race." Jimmy had hoped Mike would forget about the water – all that weight would have made the pumper lumber down Highway 410 no faster than a shy, hard turd. The mixer's tumbler can was empty, so despite having a heavier gross empty weight, Jimmy thought he'd have the advantage if Mike forgot the thousands of pounds of water. No such luck, and so the fire engine was lighter, probably by about a third. He'd have to hope the mixer's big Mack powerplant generated more horsepower than the old pumper's motor.

It took ten minutes for the pumper's tanks to drain, the Lowell's crew shouting at Mike to hurry up and get on with it the whole time. The wells finally went dry. Mike gave them a thumbs up. Pronouncing her now a lean, mean fire-fighting machine, he hopped back into the cab.

Jacqua stepped in front of the two vehicles, Mike in the Invader pumper on her right and Jimmy in Hoyt Stone's mixer to the south to her left.

"Gentlemen," she said, "and I use the term with no respect for its meaning, wait five minutes for us to get to the finish line. You may now start your engines."

There was the click and whine of starters, then a rhapsody of bearings, rings, pistons, coils and solenoids. The percussive dual blattings of exhaust filled the valley. The group piled into their various cars and trucks to cover the four miles to the finish line.

As they disappeared toward the east, Mike reached over and cranked down his passenger-side window. He leaned in the seat, craned his neck upward to Jimmy's cab.

"Who's gonna start us?"

"I don't know," Jimmy yelled down over the melody of the engines. "I guess we sorta have to."

"How we gonna do that?"

"I dunno – you decide. Wait five minutes by your watch, and when you start to roll I'll start to roll."

"Sounds O.K. I'm gonna kick your ass."

Jimmy gave him the finger and laughed.

Like two great gas giants spinning through a solar system, a red 1940 American LaFrance Invader Series 500 Pumper and a blue 1972 International Boost-A-Load mixer with eight speeds and an Eaton differential consumed highway approaching a hundred miles per hour. Trees passed in speedlines. Insects pancaked windshield glass. Dead leaves flew up in wakes like rooster tails. But mostly what trailed them was a gale of dust.

Through the windows, both drivers saw a Horizon Air turboprop headed west over the Cascades. In no time the roof rims of their cabs eclipsed its flightpath. It can only be imagined, the spectacle of the startling transit below, that must have been visible from its flight deck.

At first, Jimmy held the clear advantage. The huge Mack motor threw out RPMs like a staccato series of suckerpunches below the pumper's exposed beltline. Mike fell behind by three lengths, Jimmy whooping gaily in his cab, bouncing up and down on the seat, trying to

126

slurp just one more quanta of energy from the motor. The mixer's can revolved emptily down the highway. Jimmy felt the speed deep in his guts, this massive impetus forward, this crude, inexorable purposefulness.

Across the road, Mike fought to hold the pumper together. He was surprised at the rush of wind and counterwind in the cab. Airbursts buffeted him from both the still-open passenger window and dozens of holes and separations in the panels as well. His hair blew around his face, ponytail coiling his neck like a viper. He noticed a hole rusted in the passenger-side floorboards, jetting air as if a pressurized hose fed it. The road flashed by underneath. The engine seemed about to throw a rod, which would be damned near catastrophic at this speed. He imagined the block twisting on itself – all that energy and torque and momentum – turning inside out and throwing shrapnel and gas and sparks everywhere. Like Jimmy, the velocity and risk opened a wide, awesome wound on Mike. It had a certain delicious, wild-ass appeal.

They approached a tight curve a mile west of Eagle Rock. Jimmy knew that with its higher center of gravity, he'd have to gear down the mixer to negotiate the turn. Mike, closer to the road, would probably catch him, or at least make up some serious ground. Jimmy thought that if he got through slowing just enough, and shifted up again at exactly the right moment, he might be able to remain ahead.

All of this flashed through Mike's mind as well. He knew he had the added advantage of hugging the inside of the curve. He'd just track the mixer like a Formula One driver, ride its draft up to the curve, and push the accelerator through the floor coming out of it.

And that's the way it happened. Mike emerged from the curve half a length ahead of Jimmy, who had that Boost-A-Load nearly up on the two outboard wheels. Mike screamed toward the still-open passenger window, offering a one-fingered salute. The pumper's motor shrieked – he felt the chassis shaking violently, as if any minute the whole setup might disintegrate in a huge boom, the Naches River Valley's own Big Bang for Creationists and Darwinians to debate for all time.

Jimmy's mixer seemed to suck more air than fuel, quickly losing ground after the curve. But he didn't give it a moment's rest, raking it up into eighth gear, clutching out, flooring the pedal. The motor surged as if with afterburners. He gained a little on Mike, and saw, finally, The Woodshed in the distance.

Problem is, no one had informed the sheep.

True, Wellman Kinchlow had gone house to house – there weren't many, after all – to warn residents. In fact, several farm families had gathered at their mailboxes to watch the hulking masses roar by.

But who knows what goes on in the mind of a sheep? Who can control them, who can fence them in? Why did the sheep cross the road? To alter the course of history. Or at least of the small matter of race relations in tiny Salt Lick, Washington.

Three-hundred yards from The Woodshed a single, wool-matted male sheep owned by the crippled man with the cowboy hat blundered from the drainage ditch onto the highway. Unshorn, his dirty wool dragged the tarmac like a filthy mophead.

Mike spun the wheel and, like a massive schooner, the back came directly about, so that he lost controlled contact with the road, skidded sideways, ironed it out, and headed for The Woodshed. Jimmy swerved in the next lane just in time, maintained a semblance of control, then tucked the mixer in the minuscule space that separates disaster from victory.

Narrowly missing the crippled man with the cowboy hat's trailer, grazing the most southerly tanks of The Woodshed's propane farm, blasting through an opening in a copse of quickly denuding birches, humping up over the shoulder across the bridge spanning the Naches, crunching through the guardrail, Mike Eagle Eye sailed a fantastic red parabola.

He crashed in a mighty splash mid-stream. A geyser shot skyward from the pumper's bow; a brief rain cascaded on the bank in front of it. The pumper rocked then settled up to its lugnuts in current.

Jimmy coasted to a stop at the finish line, killed the engine, staggered with the intoxication of triumph down from the cab. But all those who had waited, the entire winner's circle, had already spun on a dead run for the river. Mid-stream, a relieved rescue party hoisted Mike Eagle Eye – banged up, nose bloodied, two ribs busted, they'd find out later, but quite conscious – from the pumper's cab. Jimmy Bayles, flushed with victory and bawling at their backs, climbed onto the mixer's hood. He pumped his fist in a Power Salute. Having vanquished the Red Man, having proved the superiority of the Pan-African race, having brought honor and homage to the Kingdom of the Moose, he shouted toward the river:

"You know it! The Black Man is victorious! Hail Mother Africa!"

He lorded it over his foes, as Mike Eagle Eye would have counted coup had their circumstances been reversed. You wouldn't have thought it possible, but Jimmy Bayles' grin of joy grew unprecedentedly large.

But no one paid him any attention, and soon the only sound was the insistent movement of water, as only gravity ever truly wins.

Jimmy pumped his fist in the air, once more, half-heartedly.

CHAPTER 11
in which Mike Eagle Eye shakes and burns...

From the bench seat of his red Ford pickup in the parking lot of the Lucky Six market in Gleed, Lothar Sturmhund felt and heard simultaneously a car door open into his side panel.

In the same way a nuclear detonation produces a slowly broadening mushroom cloud hotter than the sun's core, Lothar went unstable. He flung wide his cab door, vaulting onto the asphalt with the roar of a bull seeing red. He rounded the truck to encounter the tiniest elderly woman in Yakima County – maybe in the wide world. She was a mere frailty of sticks and skin, gray hair wound atop her head in a desiccated bun. She looked as if she weighed two-point-one ounces.

"What is this?" Lothar pointed at a new, minor ding in his paint. The old woman shrunk back into the well of her open car-door, eyes signaling confusion. She paused, unsure whether to speak or sit and lock her door.

"You're on the wrong track, you old bat, if you think you can just pull up here and smash into my truck." Lothar placed his hands on his hips in a way that clearly expected an accounting.

"I'm sorry," she stammered. "I didn't mean to."

Lothar whooped like Crazy Horse.

"What are you, some kind of communist or something? No regard for the property of others. Racing in here slamming into others' vehicles, you old biddy."

The woman cringed under. Slowly she slipped her shoe up over the lip of her door jamb, folding inward.

"Where you goin'?" Lothar said. "Don't you turn your back on me."

She sat behind her wheel, leaned her minuscule body out the still-open doorway.

"You're crazy, mister," she said.

"What? What'd you say to me, you old bag?"

"I said you're crazy – crazy as a bedbug."

And with all her might she hoicked her door shut, slapping the lock in place like one might slap lawn-pocking moles upburrowing from tiny dirt mountains. Lothar gasped for half a second. His intake was like an air-breathing rocket's. Then he bellowed, raised his arms, and delivered a two-fisted blow to the roof of her car. She struggled with keys in the ignition.

Lothar looked up and around the lot, mumbling.

"You nasty old commie." He spied a shopping cart someone had abandoned. He lumbered over to it while her engine cranked and died. He heard her starter whine again as he reached the cart. He spun with the cart before him, wielding it like a battering ram. Her motor coughed, caught, blew a gout of exhaust ass-wards, and pinged to four-cylinder life.

As the old woman shifted into reverse, Lothar launched the cart into her driver's side panel. It caromed off the pressed steel, gouging paint and denting the surface with its impact. He saw her eyes as large as cantaloupes in the rearview. When she turned to look at him, her mouth was the eggshape of a squeezed O.

Lothar grabbed the rebounding cart and made another run, this time from the side as she reversed from the parking stall. The cart bounced off her door, leaving a long streak. As she backed out and turned, her front bumper caught the edge of the cart and sent it rebounding into the F-250. It ripped a long dent along the bed wall. Lothar made a sound like an artillery shell going off.

She punched it then, her four cylinders poinging like playing cards clothes-pinned to bike spokes. Lothar leapt out of the way, grabbed the cart and chased her through the lot. Like a moth that slams itself again and again against lit bulb-glass, she drove in disoriented circles, honking her horn. Lothar rammed and battered her from every compass angle. Finally, she dithered to the curb, lurched over it onto Raines Avenue, and drove off in a cloud of exhaust.

Lothar stood next to the stoved-in shopping cart. He wiped Teutonic sweat from his brow.

Stupid old bag.

As if he didn't have enough of them, Mike Eagle Eye's *real* troubles began in September, when he forswore nicotine.

They began in large form, wide-screen, Surroundsound, Dolby, when he gave up smoking for the fourth or fifth time. It always takes several attempts to quit, he'd heard some self-important, advise-begatter say. *You just keep trying. Yes.* And this time he was making the run cold turkey. No patches, gums, acupuncture, hypnotism: none of that shit.

While Salt Lick's children returned to school and summer waned, Mike resolved to make his lungs as clear and white as paper. While cottonwoods launched their little ships of seed on warm breezes, he resolved to lose his smokers' cough, once and for good.

Then came the day he had marked on his calendar: QUIT. For a few hours that morning, he sat in a hotbox of illusion: "This is easier than I remember," he thought. But by noon, it was as if the pyramid energy had completely crumbled. Bright packs of cigarettes colonized his head like chimeras, effulgent with familiar emblems and totems, typefonts, logos, tax stickers. He mentally unzipped their cellophane wrappers. In the pleasure/torture cells of his imagination he tore the foil tops in straight squares and tapped out the lovely smokes. *My pretties.* By 2 p.m. he felt... *bulgey* – as if he must leap out of his own skin. He realized that he had not eaten lunch, and struggled to escape the gnawing edge of both nicotine and caloric withdrawal. Surely, he soon would blast from his prison of a body. Just swell, then explode. Before the clock on Town Hall's façade recorded another tick, he would surrender to this great coming distension that could only culminate in an explosion of guts and glory. But then, calming himself at the vending machine outside the Pie Apple, he slotted quarters. He bent forward after the *thunk* of the candy, retrieved the candy bar. He consumed it in two bites, maybe twelve chews in all, swallowed the greasy thing almost whole. So quick and Cro-Magnon was his bolting of the bar that he just missed sucking down its wrapper. If a bird would have flown by at that moment, Mike might have ingested it in much the same way as sometimes happens at the intakes of jet aircraft engines.

This ravenousness surprised him. Mike was mindful of all the warnings connecting weight gain and the cessation of smoking. But just one candy bar couldn't hurt. Still, with a bitter cocoa aftertaste, he felt the boundary of urge move closer. As he forced another pair of quarters into the machine, he knew that in only seconds his heart, lungs – the contents of his entire chest cavity – would blast forth through his sternum. He would, with his guts, wash the glass door of the Pie Apple's vending machine. He would occlude all the glammy packaging, the bright, seductive candies, so as to put them, too, out of mind. What a sight that would be for the kids, just returning from their first days of the new school term and coughed out of the bus on the Pie Apple's stoop. The guts of a genuine Indian on the porch-boards!

Still, Mike Eagle Eye made it through Day One by scratching and clawing and gnawing through ropes. He made it in the way rats trapped by fire would, screeching, spinning in circles to catch their naked tails. He made it by sheer motherfucking willpower. But even as he laid his head on his pillow, he wondered whether he might yet suddenly re-dress, jump in the car and drive 95 mph up and down Highway 410, finally spilling out at a mini-store in Cliffdell, Eagle Rock, Naches – anywhere open this late! – to dig with trembling fingers at his back pocket for his wallet. He wondered whether he would yet, before the clocks of Salt Lick struck their various midnights, buy a gorgeous pack of smokes and light two, maybe three at a time. He could still draw into himself, into his body and soul, the clear, clean, crystalline, creosote mercury, throat-cut-with-a-razor love smoke – the very vapor of sweet angels – the tar, the mellifluous nicotine. He could still do it. His skull smiled for it. His dick rose for it. His armpits sweated for it. But he wouldn't. By the hair flowing from the ancestors' beards, he swore that he wouldn't.

And Day Two was twice as bad.

Twenty-four hours later, Mike fell asleep instantly and began to dream. He dreamed he was in a super-megastore – a sprawling edifice so large it probably couldn't even be found in the great metropolis of Yakima, but could only be discovered by trekking further, to Spokane, say, or in the other direction, Seattle – a vast market. It was after hours, tills cleared, weak light from only the EXIT signs. He went from aisle to aisle in the dark pleasing himself with the things he found.

Here was teriyaki beef jerky, and he gnawed on the salt-honeyed meat until his jaws ached. Then he cleansed his palate with fine wines, bottles and bottles of the stuff. He ate bags of pink and white animal cookies, the kinds with the little candy sprinkles. He sucked the chocolate coating from vanilla ice cream bars, licked the sweetness until his tongue lapped at the wood sticks. In Produce, he opened melons and let juice and seeds drip. He moved into Men's Clothing, exchanged his stained, sopping shirt for a clean cotton garment. This seemed insufficient, and he traversed the aisle to Women's, swapped the shirt for a silk blouse, rubbed the feminine fabric against his bare, hairless chest, his masculine nipples, then let the man's shirt drop to the floor in a heap. When he was finished there, he went back to Grocery, opened cans of beer and sacks of snack chips and gourmet cookies. He ran up and down the aisles with his head full of the rhythm of talking drums, potlatch music. He pulled plastic from around steaks, barbecued them over in Homewares, ate the oozing beef slabs without utensils. He did not trim the rich, succulent fat. Then he staggered to Home Electronics and watched videos, switched on several CD players at once. He sat in a

133

circle of sweet and salty junk food, listened simultaneously to Sepulchre and Megadeth and Tool and Nine Inch Nails and Metallica and *Carmina Burana*, at full volume, washing the food down with imported beers and local microbrews. He laid back nude except for underwear in this luxe and rubbed onto his skin fragrant body oils he had brought from Personal Products. He writhed on the slick floor to the wild, large beat of the music. As the interest would possess him, Mike glanced at the red lights dancing on the amplifiers, little bouncing readouts measuring energy as he writhed in oil and cream and underwear and alcohol. He would smile, and smell the smells of jasmine and merlot, honeysuckle peach, cinnamon and chardonnay, and forget about the evil jones for cigarettes amidst all of this. When he arose in the dream his ponytail was a single hank of ointmented odor, a pleasure rope. *This rocks this rocks this rocks*, he kept saying, over and over, until he woke.

Day Three dawned. He wondered whether his – *orgy?* – really had been a dream at all. But of course it had – he was right here in tiny Salt Lick, trying to kick nicotine. Fantasy or not, though, he sensed a key learning: to cope, he would have to constantly seek distraction. He would have to keep smokes out of his head. He would have to fashion a world of shiny objects with which to surround himself and fill that mental real estate. He must place himself safely inside walls that would delight him. It was the only way to throw down cigarettes from their great height.

Working in Town Hall's pumper-less garage that day, he looked out through the open roll-up door at the last light of summer playing across the asphalt of Mud Lake Road. He heard the calls of Canada geese overhead, birds migrating south and east. All of this was good, and he felt determined and strong, and also yet a tiny bit still strung out. And then he thought he felt Lothar's approving presence, just for an instant, so that his flesh leapt into hills and the hole of his ass clenched and gulped like the lips of a landed carp, a rim *koi*. He realized he was terrified of life – the broad span of it he assumed waited ahead – without cigarettes.

That night, he had second helpings at supper. The next day he had an extra portion at lunch. This pattern – bearing the autograph of gluttony – repeated itself. He began to eat breakfast again after a several-year hiatus. And not a politically correct, colorless, mostly bran-featuring breakfast that would make his excrement soft and relentless all day, and would work wonders for his cardio-vascular network. No, this was down-and-dirty *Breakfast*. Sausages. Honey-cured bacon. Eggs fried in butter and bacon-grease, and buttermilk biscuits drowned in lard gravy. Great piles of cholesterol and saturated fat, and coffee no longer black but with real sugar and cream, so much cream the color of the hot drink was that of slightly off, thick, whole milk.

After a week he stepped on the scale and had gained seven pounds. One pound per day. He flung insults at his own expanding image in the bathroom mirror. "I am the Michelin Tire Man! The Pillsbury Dough Boy!" He celebrated by eating an entire package of ice-cream sandwiches, washing them down with a quart of Cherry Coke. He accomplished this gastric feat sitting in a La-Z-Boy rocker in front of the TV, *Pulp Fiction* in the VCR. He had taken, the past few nights, to renting Quentin Tarentino cassettes down at the Pie Apple. He liked the curse-ridden scripts, the heroin addicts, the surprise gunshots and ensuing bloodspray and, yes, of course, the incessant swirling of cigarette smoke. He played a game while watching – to see whether he could spot a single scene wherein a cigarette was actually absent. Last night it had been *Jackie Brown* – Mike just loved it when DeNiro does that spoiled, snotty little hippy chick in the parking lot. Just *POP!* and Bob's-Your-Uncle, she's totaled, she's *through*. She's on pavement, and no matter how many times Mike watched it, he was as blown away as she. It nearly made his ponytail stand erect! Tomorrow night, *From Dusk Till Dawn*, a little *Vampiro Mejicano* action. Then maybe a night off, then *Reservoir Dogs*. Yes! There was never a single microsecond of *that* movie wherein one of two things was not suspended in mid-air: cigarette smoke or a mist of flying, hot blood.

After the first couple of weeks the physical part of nicotine withdrawal had slipped away like a receding nightflux. After a baptism of jagged nerves for three or four days, then a gradual easing, what remained was an astonishingly acerbic ache, a raw loss like the demise of a favored loved one. It was the *grieving* they talk about. He was sacked with depression.

Through this bleakness, Mike began to sense something around him, something in the air growing large and loud, and closer, like approaching attack helicopters of urge. They forayed into his airspace with all the promise and threat of Yul Brynner's *Etcetera*, bare-chested, confident and ointmented, hands on hips. His slavery to nicotine had been like a levee holding back a frothy ocean of appetite. That dike breached, the sea smashed the shore and flooded coastal lowlands. He starting sleeping nude. Little pieces of his superstore dream began to come true.

For instance, he discovered it was no distance at all from the alluring covers of *Cosmopolitan, Shape, Marie Claire,* or *Vogue* at the Super Six checkouts in Gleed, to the downloading of jpeg after jpeg from the prurient palaces of his new Internet connection. He spent hours eating this electronic meat. He'd fight sleep to log on, fight a low baud-rate and shitty telephone lines to stay online, loving her on the screen behind the protection of a modem prophylactic. Her, she, it, that, *there*, open before him with begging eyes – her, who was his own soft, moist, slippery digital girlfriend. Mike woke exhausted with half-circles under his eyes. Lifting his groggy head from the pillow, his reflection seemed to balance twin charcoal briquettes on the high shelves of his cheeks in the mirror across his bedroom. Then he would laze in the warm sheets, reach down to adjust or hold his penis and thus delay rising to urinate. He found his member semi-tumescent and tender. *What had happened?* But new desire would well in him, and his confusion and soreness would pass.

Too, he began to explore the richness of new odors, or to reacquaint himself with old familiar ones. He would make a special point to breathe in through his nose at the precise moment when an encounter with a woman in Yakima would wash him in her smell. In this way, he grew attuned to dozens of perfumes, as well as underlying, other, more fundamental scents. He took, for the first time in his life, to wearing cologne himself.

He sought, mastered, then abused, a Beelzebub's cornucopia of distractions over the course of several weeks: He ate huge amounts of red meat. He bought stacks of crossword puzzle magazines (but never completed a single puzzle). He rented numerous video games, spending hours gazing dumbly at the TV. He purchased numerous skin mags, starting softcore but devolving into freakish, fetish-based effluvia, humans with hardware, animal, mineral, vegetable, *Etcetera*. He gradually increased the recklessness of his driving and sought straightaways in which he could exceed 100 mph or even, on some remote roads, *bury the needle*, as they say (he hadn't learned a hell of a lot from his busted mouth and cracked ribs rocketing Salt Lick's fire pumper into the Naches River). He drank unprecedented quantities of alcohol, including all manners of gins, vodkas, whiskeys, beers, wines, ales, liqueurs, tequilas, mescals (yes, he ate the *worm* in order to resist lighting up) and sangrias. He road-tripped – almost 150 miles! – over Chinook Pass for the sole purpose of visiting strip bars out by Seattle-Tacoma International airport, and coughed up wads of cash to enjoy a very special sort of eye-candy, the Texas Couch Dance. Sure, there were titty bars in Yakima. Damned fine ones. But Mike Eagle Eye couldn't think of one where the women of Thailand and Hong Kong and Macau danced and... well... *did* things with their bodies, with their body *parts*, like over in Seattle.

As he thus coped with the absence of the great and savory god Nicotine, Mike Eagle Eye held his chin and high cheekbones aloft, his countenance erect. He managed, through an admirable enforcement of his own will, to avoid cigarettes. "I barely miss them," he confided with anyone who would listen. "Never felt better." He had gained thirty-seven pounds, and was fond of heralding Angus MacNaughton or Jericho Jenkins, who rode their bicycles up and down Benton Drive or Mud Lake Road. To the pedal-pumping boys he would bellow, "Hey Hey Hey, It's Fat Albert!"

After Mike Eagle Eye had maintained his war on tobacco for a month and a few days, and had comported himself reasonably well, autumn fell on Salt Lick like the lid of a coffin. Windstorms blew power out. Low clouds burgeoned and huffed. Puddles froze for the first time. At the Super Six in Gleed bag-boys were certain to stuff a gray, fat tumor of depression into each grocery sack they packed.

Mike entered the Pie Apple one afternoon to purchase a six-pack of beer. Oh, the tall sixteen-ounce silver cans – how he admired the glinty beauty of the aluminum, the sweat that gathered and dropped as soon as they were lifted from behind the cooler doors. They looked so inviting – Mike gave the can the old Eagle Eye for a moment then, as if resistance was proved, forever, to be futile, suddenly licked the beads of condensate from the containers.

"Something wicked this way comes," he warned Jacqua, as he waddled up the aisle, tonguing the cans.

Jacqua, astounded, annoyed to be distracted from her latest copy of the *Enquirer*, pulled her revolver from under the counter.

"You come in hear thinking you're wicked, putting your tongue all over my merchandise. I don't know what the hell's rung your bell. Maybe you ain't fixed from all the head shaking must have gone on when you plowed into the river. But I *do* know one thing – if you don't put your tongue back in your mouth and off of my product, you can come lick this," Jacqua said, and waved the pistol's muzzle.

"I truly am sorry." Mike left off the tongue action for a moment. "It's the cigarettes. I see the cigarettes there behind the counter."

"What about them?" she asked, from behind the revolver.

"I been quit for a few weeks and it's... it's hard, Jacqua."

"Well maybe you better pick up a smoke before your ass falls off."

"Yes," said Mike. "Yes, I think you may be right." He pointed at a pack while she placed the piece back under the counter. "Yes, that one."

"Matches?"

137

"Oh yeah. Oh yeah, please."

She muttered something like *crazyass-mother* as Mike Eagle Eye left the store, but he didn't hear her. He was already fumbling pretties in his hands.

CHAPTER 12
in which Gib's lawn suffers for his love of cannabis...

Kleine Lothar was twelve years old when grizzle-faced soldiers liberated Erfurt-am-Gera. Russen or Amerikans – little lad Lothar didn't know. And to his small pack of *die fasche Jungen* – bad boys – it didn't much matter. The torn-trousers gang roamed the broken alleys and fractured structures of Erfurt with knives in their belts, daddies all dead and gone, blown apart somewhere. Or rushed under rubble. Or disintegrated in explosions of aviation fuel and aluminum, crumpled fuselages. Drowned in U-boats. Machine-gunned and cannoned.

The morphology of Erfurt, which lies in the state of Thüringen north of the Thüringerwald on the Gera River: all this lack of parental control transformed the blasted city into a sort of *Feiertaglager* – a holiday camp – for the bad boys. Especially those dirty-faced orphans able to rise above the cracked mortar and cloven bricks to discern the needs of conquering armies – tobacco, knives, *das Morpheum, die Jungfrau*. Among church spires fallen like felled timber, the *Jungen*, already rotten to the core, ran the truly damned place.

Lothar spewed from his mother's belly in the year the Fatherland made nasty Adolph its chancellor. As Herr Doktor swabbed birth fluid from the tiny Aryan while Frau Sturmhund bled to death on white sheets through her impossibly ripped core, *Der Führer* fulminated among the fasces and swastikas – O! How the crowds swooned. Baby Lothar clawed his way into this world as *Lebensraum* lashed it. When he was ten, British cannons blew his father, Gerhard Sturmhund, the burg's peacetime Karpenter, to smithereens in the guts of a Panzer at El Alamein. The Danziger nanny fled for her home port in the wake of little Lothar's *Putsch*: one night with the drone of Luftwaffe bombers overhead, the blond-headed monster materialized in her chambers, fumbled with her damp nightclothes. She woke from a dream of moving stars and strange, shifting constellations with Lothar nuzzling. Gertrude was her name – Lothar could barely

139

remember her as a grown man, just as a muddy image of giant, globular cream and moisture.

Her screams trailed her across the old landscape of Prussia.

Soon the boy Lothar was leader of his gang and knew the tricks of provision. It might be argued that this is where he learned the ins and outs of general contracting, which is, after all, simply a matter of making connections. There is need; there is the mobilization to satisfy need. The performance of that effort was Lothar's special little skill. When he began to see fewer German aircraft in the sky and more Allied, particularly when bombs began to drop from their bellies like hornets from long, slim metallic hives to blow the whole fucking place apart, Lothar sensed a sea-change. At eleven and a half, he was dealing wartime tobacco.

Then the soldiers came. He sold them cigarettes. He could find morphine with the medics of one outfit, and trade them for smokes to the shell-crazy junkies of another. He also dealt in playing cards – odd for these ubiquitous gaming decks to be in shortage. It seemed everyone wanted to gamble!

An *Offizier* erected his camp in a crushed hovel across Weissewolfestrasse from the ruins of Lothar's father's apartments and carpenter shop. He brought with him some sort of vassal, a pistol-wielding *Leftenant* with whom Lothar soon made contact, and a beast that might have been a dog or might have been a dragon. It hissed and showed its teeth like a *Berserker* whenever Lothar walked down the street, letting loose great hideous yelps and draining discolored spittle. The boy's terror of this repto-mammal was out of character—there wasn't much those days that gave Lothar Sturmhund pause for worry. Lothar came to have an impression of the officer as Russian rather than American for no other reason than the man's appetite for distilled liquor, a commodity more difficult than most to find. The *russische Offizier* also was partial, after some time had passed, to the morphine.

On a night of particular celebration so near the end of the war that the bombing had all but ceased and the occupying force seemed to be more a drunken sea of men than an army, the vassal proffered to Lothar the problem of his master's sexual satisfaction. The master required the services of a prostitute. Lothar winked at the inquirer. He meant in the wink to imply that he discerned this: the vassal was more tired of receiving his master up the ass than his master, the *Offizier*, actually sought the moans of a *hübsche Mädchen*. Nevertheless, Lothar spawned an idea. There was a young lovely who had already made Lothar a man for the price of a pack of cigarettes, a little girl five or six years older than he who had lived nearby before

Erfurt's general implosion. He could bring her to the officer. Lothar and the girl could split the money.

"Sie ist eine Jungfrau," Lothar lied, but the vassal's eyes glinted with glee: How pleased his master would be to perform an act of deflowerment! Maybe his master would permit the vassal to enjoy a well-reamed seconds! Lothar debarked for the *Mädchen's* street, and collected her with the promise of coins. At first she was hesitant – when she finally agreed, Lothar affirmed her: *"Sie gehen die rechte Richtung!"* "You are going in the right direction." "You are on the right track." Throughout his life, he remembered her heartbreaking name: Uwe.

He brought the *Jungfrau* Uwe to the Russian and turned her over amid the snarlings of the Russian's beast. The vassal dropped a few coins in Lothar's palm, instructed him to go get the *Offizier* more morphine. The master wished to fuck this bitch with the drug coursing in his veins, and he feared the supply on hand was inadequate. The vassal held forth a few more coins. Would Lothar please hasten? *"Ja,"* Lothar said.

When Lothar returned with a pocketful of ampoules, the dog or reptile was going primally mad. It yelped and frothed at the end of its lead to announce Lothar's arrival. Inside, there was the stench of sweat and narcotics. There was Uwe, slammed syringe slapped into her elbow's hinge, blue-faced, on the *Offizier's* lap, cooing, her blond locks in dead hanks. Her hands were fused with the *Offizier's* anatomy. "Wake up, wake up you whore!" the vassal kept shouting as she sailed an ocean of morphine lust – the sea that is flat, the one where ships do, sometimes, fall off the edge into the abyss. The *Offizier* sat in a chair fixing, leather belt tight on his veiny, thin biceps, curl of ecsta-pleasure at the edges of his lips. He swatted at his vassal as if the servant was a blowfly. He thumbed his own syringe as Lothar entered the canvas-walled room.

With this scene splayed before him, young Lothar forgot that his precious Uwe's predicament was one of his own making. Why was this filthy communist's free hand under her garments? Who was he, that she should caress his swarthy flesh so?

"Kommunist scheisse!" He pulled his knife and waved it around the cell. The vassal's kidneys were in close range, but he twisted away, emitting an uproarious giggle. The *Offizier* joined his serf in laughter and clapped his hands at this *Privatspektakal*, hearing in his Soviet brain some sort of warping, pleasant calliope reel. Lothar stepped to his front, still waving his toyish knife. A few months short of his teen years, five years from escape to the West, twelve years

141

from emigration to Amerika, Lothar Sturmhund intended to draw the crimson knife across the bobbing vocal cord of this fucking Russian, this drug-sotted molester of his sweet Uwe, this *Kommunist*. He imagined lifeblood spewing from the slit, and the *Offizier* laughing and laughing while it gurgled down his tunic. *And who is this silly-ass* Deutschlandischer *boy waving his knife around? Why is the lieutenant not slaying him this minute? Why are the whore's clothes still on? Who has some potato vodka?* Forgetting Uwe teetering on his thighs, the *Offizier* tried to rise and investigate all of these things. But he slumped back, morphine coursing through his body. Good night, Oh Conqueror. Then Uwe joined in the laughter, mocking *kleine* Lothar. "What's wrong, little boy?" she said.

Lothar fled.

The dog-thing, in the boy's wake, snapped its enormous mandible and bayed a profound madness into the German night.

As a grown man, Lothar would hunt the valleys and hills of the eastern Cascade slopes until night fell and the moon in its various phases arose in the east. On nights when the moon was a slim-blade crescent, or altogether new, stars would blink into the black space – those of the brightest magnitude first, like minuscule needle-pricks in the cosmos. Then, by the hundreds and thousands, those stars would multiply and bang in the bowl of night a skein of holes, so that the sky reminded him of the overturned cleft of a morphine addict's arm. And he would see, from time to time, if it was very quiet and dark, a small, dim light move slowly from one horizon to the other.

Satellites, he knew. Tunneling through the black like narcolepsy through veins and arteries. *The Russians*, he thought, *always watching. Kommunists.*

Uwe! Uwe!

Oh.

Gib MacNaughton loosed a fulsome belch. Pot smoke curled up from his lips like a pungent, billowing sail. The brain tissue behind his eyes felt as if a concubine's fingertips performed sensuous massage there. His head, wrapped in a wool blanket of narcosis, nodded forward. His chin came to rest on his chest. The stereophones clamped around his ears would have made him, to an intruder, look like a spaceman in the dark, or a dozing chopper pilot. He tapped his toes in time to The Zombies, and floated into stellar space.

The narcosis was fractured when his kneecap was touched. His eyes popped open.

Angus stood, looking as bored as any ten-year-old boy – even with thousands of acres of forest around him to explore, a small lake across the road, and a pet peacock. With all of this potential distraction, his son had been, instead, working a jigsaw puzzle on the dining room table. The boy had been at it for hours, it seemed. Gib had started to help, but grew weary of the pastime when they had finished the main picture and all that was left were hundreds of pieces of blue for the sky. These indistinguishable scraps of cardboard, the same as chips of bark sloughed at the bases of pine stumps, seemed to multiply. Stacks of the intricately cut pieces rose in pyramids inside the completed border, above the partly finished picture. Only the sky remained incomplete, void.

Through the dining room window tree shadows moved across the back yard. Hummingbirds flitted in and out of the branches and leaves of rhododendron bushes Gib had planted beneath the windowsill. Although the blooms had come and gone with spring, the tiny birds still hummed hopefully there.

Gib had watched the birds for a while, then excused himself. He wandered into the semi-dark living room and rolled up a fat joint. He slid the stereophones over his ears, fired the joint, sucked in a first hit and held it in his lungs as long as he could. The volume of his chest seemed to go on expanding even after he stopped inhaling. By the time he exhaled, he felt the first lovely grains of tetrahydrocannabinol enter his bloodstream – along with four-hundred other delicious chemicals – and that was *all right*. Everything was fine, and for all Gib cared, Angus could emplace bits of sky within the straight-edged frame of his puzzle from now until the end of time.

But now, after rousing his father with the knee-tap, Angus seemed to be motioning at the front door. Maybe someone had knocked. Gib couldn't imagine whom. A tiny bit annoyed, he pulled one speaker-cup from around his ear and asked, "What?"

"The grass," Angus said.

"What about the grass?"

"You asked me to remind you to cut it." Angus folded his arms on his chest as if he were a father demanding a chore's execution from a recalcitrant teenage brat.

"Oh, yeah. Thanks – I'll get right to it in a minute." He set the stereophones back around his ear.

Angus shrugged, then skipped off down the hall. From the corner of his eye, Gib saw him return with Petey's ball. It was one of those cored-out, hard-rubber balls with a little silver bell inside. It made a sound like an abrupt cricket-chirp whenever Petey beaked it. It was funny to watch that damned peacock play with that ball, especially when Gib was high. Hilarious – a circus in his own back yard. *Hey everybody, three rings out back of the MacNaughton's double-wide! Step right up!* Gib broke into stoned giggles as the song finished. He set the stereophones down on the couch, rose, and clicked off the stereo.

When he stepped outside the sunlight blasted him. He squinted from the stoop, gathering the bright light slowly, feeling the marijuana kick further in. The high sun made everything hot, and seemed to render all he saw in black and white. His pupils stayed wide. He walked to the truck to get his sunglasses.

Like most people's, Gib's ambition waned when he smoked pot. It seemed to him like another day might be better for mowing the front lawn. Another day might be better for any task.

About the only farmyard chore he liked when he was loaded was working in the garden. Gib loved to tend his plants. In the corner of the backyard, behind Petey's pen under the bluff that provided a reflective warmth for the dungy soil, he'd set up about a two-hundred and fifty square feet of pumpkins, Brussels sprouts, tomatoes, zucchini, carrots, onions, beets, summer squash, bell peppers and his own homegrown stash of pot plants. Behind all of it stood a row of sunflowers, five, then six, seven, eight feet tall with fat brown faces and seeds dropping everywhere. He liked how ravens flew up to them and plucked out the seeds.

But now, unfortunately, the task was grass-cutting. There weren't many tasks Gib despised more than following a noisy gas-guzzling machine in diminishing circuits around a lawn. Gib thought that pretty soon he ought to teach Angus how to mow. He'd be done with it then. The yard wasn't that big, after all, and flat. Anybody who could push the mower's weight could do it, if they were properly schooled in the safety precautions – warned not to wear open-toed shoes or sandals and to keep one's fingers and toes out of the blade's path, that sort of thing. And if they could be made to understand that the wheels simply track the ruts of the last go-round, and grass is dumped from the catcher every three or four times around, out on the compost heap behind the pen. All of that could be understood by bright, young Angus.

For today, though, Gib resigned himself to completing the task on his own. Instructing his son in this labor seemed like more trouble than it was worth. And the day was getting on.

It hadn't used to be this way, Gib thought as he rounded the trailer for the toolshed. He used to have a ball playing with Angus and Petey. It wasn't so long ago, either. He also hadn't used to get high so often – it seemed like now he was perpetually stoned. The long commute to Zillah was getting to him after all, but the real onset seemed to be when Lothar Sturmhund's heart blew. He remembered how weird Angus had acted after that mean old prick had keeled over and obliterated, in his blond-headed fall, their glass coffee table. The Sturmhunds hadn't even offered to replace it.

Gib pulled the shed door open and dragged the mower out. He filled its gas tank. Then he pushed the old mower – squeaking and trundling over the rough sideyard – to the front. Stepping to the machine's side, he placed his shoe on the mower's deck, pushed the choke lever to cold, and yanked the pull-cord. The motor churned and pepped as the cord rewound itself, but didn't fire. He tried again with the same result. He pulled eleven or twelve more times, flooded the motor and waited a few minutes in the heat. This was always the way it went, so he spent a moment staring straight at the sun, defying it to blind him. He looked down at his wristwatch to check the time, but couldn't see its face from the retina-burn.

As he waited, bird calls spiced the August air around him. A raven lit on a cedar branch to the west of the double-wide. Its throaty call went across the road to Mud Lake and was answered. The return call sounded rich and deep, like a very low note tongued across the reeds of an oboe. The near raven called again, and the pair exchanged a baritone chorus.

Then Gib stooped to collect the pull-cord again, and with a full-body tug the motor blasted great gouts of blue exhaust in a series of clouds, then rumbled to life. The overhead raven took wing toward Mud Lake. Gib saw the departing bird as a fleeting, inky arc in the corner of his vision. He stepped behind the mower and pushed it down the edge of the grass bordering the sidewalk. Then he made a ninety degree turn and headed up the shady edge of the yard. Another turn, and he was parallel to the trailer again, but on the opposite side of the yard. Then he completed his circuit, wheeling up the edge of the driveway to where he had started.

Gib thought about this and that. His deliberations spun like a flock of birds. He thought about Angus's puzzle, and hummed a line from The Zombies in tune with his mower. He thought of screwing a woman – no woman in particular, maybe Angus's mom again, someday, maybe somebody else. Then he thought of work again, circling his mind around fully in that irresolute way menial tasks produce. There was no clear ideation, simply a meandering cycling of cognitions and images that dipped and swerved and orbited themselves. The sort of thinking that is much akin to wandering in the woods, growing more lost with the passing of moments.

Gib and his musings circuited the yard in ever-concentric boxes. He paused to empty the catcher every few passes. He broke a sweat. By the time he had maybe two more tight circuits to complete – a small square of unmown grass at the center of the lawn – the mower seized and died. Out of gas, probably, Gib thought, and checked the tank. Sure enough, the cavity was as dry as a popcorn fart.

It seemed like a good time for a break anyway, although there were barely two passes left to complete the yard. He went inside for a can of soda. Then it seemed like a good time to get high again. He rolled another joint and smoked it down to the roach. The pot kicked in again as he sat watching through the window at Petey pushing his ridiculous dingle-ball at Angus. Gib giggled.

Then he went to put his stereophones on and listened to an album by The Guess Who for a while. Angus stepped back into the double-wide and could hear his dad's awful singing voice. It sounded like the croaking of a creek toad.

The next morning – Monday – when it was time to roll out and head for work, Gib realized he'd left the mower dead-center in the yard with the unmown patch. He'd take care of it after work, because he was running late.

Gib's truck guzzled gas as he passed the Y for Highway 12, into Naches and further on past the orchards and grain silos and cow lots, then the feedline that overran the highway. It was a morning as clear as crystal. The rising sun was straight ahead, so that he had to lower his visor and set the sunglasses on his nose the instant he emerged from the shadows of the Naches valley. *Damn*, was he ever tired. It seemed like every morning he grew more weary, so that lately it felt as if he were dragging a shroud of bones from his mattress, stumbling down the hall to perk acrid coffee, stumbling back to wake Angus. He'd stagger into the shower, then dress and drop into the car seat after kissing his son goodbye on the cheek. He wondered whether leaving Angus at home all day in the double-wide was such a great idea. But it was summertime, light all day, and there wasn't much mischief the boy could get himself into. And paying a sitter was out of the question.

Then there was the drive. At first the route to Zillah had seemed interminable. Then, right around the time of old Sturmhund's death –

just before it, he guessed – there was an odd period in which he grew accustomed to the daily trek, where it settled on him like a routine and he imagined it wasn't, after all, so bad. When he took the double-wide off the market and resolved himself to an immediate future of these long commutes, part of the mental exercise was to convince himself that it was manageable. He could do it. He and Angus could manage the fact that he would leave earlier and arrive home later.

But in the wake of Lothar Sturmhund's bizarre death the drive seemed to stretch and warp. It seemed to never end. When he finally reached Zillah it always surprised him. He would then realize that for miles and miles he had simply been numb, driving like an automaton.

Today would be different. He slotted a Led Zeppelin cassette into his truck's stereo, pulled a joint out of his shirt pocket, and lit it. He was loaded by the time he pulled up to his office building. He went straight from the parking lot to the men's room to wash, to the extent possible, the odor of pot smoke from himself.

Gib arrived at his desk, flicked the switch on his terminal, and began to enter numbers and symbols. They paraded across the computer monitor in front of his nose, left to right, appearing from nowhere and signifying nothing as his fingers plonked on keys. Off key, he hummed one of the cuts from the Zeppelin tape.

When the effects of the marijuana faded around 10 o'clock, he thought the day would never end.

On Saturday morning Angus came in from running around the backyard with Petey to make a sandwich of peanut butter, green apple slices, and Wonder Bread.

"Do you want one, Dad?" he asked.

Gib was sitting over the dining room table trying one blue puzzle piece after another for a snug fit. He would move each piece from the pile of "untried" pieces on his left to the pile of "tried" pieces on his right. Over the course of the past half hour, the pyramid of pieces on the left had diminished in height and volume, and the pyramid on his right had grown. When a piece finally fit, he would move the entire right-hand pile back onto the left and begin the whole process again. It was a methodology of iron determination, and whence this determination came, Gib could not have said for a million bucks. But he would be damned if he'd let this puzzle and its endless stack of sky blue bits get the best of him. His rote concentration was so intent that he barely registered Angus' voice.

"Dad!" Angus shouted.

147

Gib's head snapped up. "What?"

"Do you want a sandwich? I been calling you for five minutes."

"Oh." Gib wallowed in a strange mud of confusion. "I'm sorry – I guess so."

Angus brought sandwiches to the table on plates heaped also with potato chips and a raw carrot each, from the garden. The boy sat down in the chair opposite his father, scooted a plate across the table in Gib's direction.

"You don't look so good," Angus said. "You sick?"

"Nope, just tired." In fact, Gib's neck hurt from brooding over the puzzle. And his wrists were stiff from rotating and test-fitting uncooperative puzzle pieces.

"You want to show me how to mow today?" Angus was anxious to learn the mechanics of this adult-looking chore. The mower, with its old oily engine and grass-matted wheels, held for him a certain fascination. Once, in the shed, he had peeked under the mower's carriage. The blade suspended there captivated him. He imagined it spinning like a propeller, whacking grass – or anything else, for that matter – which got in its way. He had reached under and ran his thumb along the leading edge, a rock-scarred pitted surface, bare steel in places, but still honed. He had jerked his thumb away as if the blade were white hot.

"I don't know," Gib said. "Maybe."

Later, after abandoning the puzzle, Gib pulled the mower from the center of the lawn to the driveway. He sent Angus for the gas can while he unscrewed the tank stopper. Angus returned, and Gib upended the contents into the tank. Gasoline gurgled through the spigot and sloshed around inside, raising fumes that, to Angus, were not unpleasant. He sniffed at the air, which only moments ago held the clear, hot pine-scent of mid-August. The tank filled and, too late, Gib pulled the spigot from the tank. Gas splashed over the lip, sloshed his bare calves above his socks and tennis shoes.

He mumbled a curse. "This is the choke." He pulled a button outward from the motor block. Angus nodded. Gib showed him the cord. "You've got to pull it jerky-like, and real hard." He pulled the cord a few times. "Smell that?" An overcarbureted odor wafted between the two. "It's flooded. That usually happens with an old machine like this. You just let it sit a minute now. You might as well get used to it. You understand?"

Angus accepted all of this, again nodding.

"I can't hear you shake your head, son."

"Yes, Dad. I understand."

Satisfied, Gib rose to pull the cord again. The mower caught, spluttered, emitted its blue cloud, and began whirring. Gib showed Angus how to push the choke back in, stand behind the mower, and begin. He got out of the way and offered the pusher's position to his son. "Get goin'," he said, with a proud grin. He followed Angus a couple of feet behind, studying the placement of the wheels and giving Angus' shoulders a nudge for momentum when his son got to a rough spot in the lawn. When Angus had made a complete circuit, his father showed him how to properly align the mower for the next pass.

After Angus had gone around five or six times, Gib started to feel overly hot in the sun. He stepped into the double-wide to bring out a couple of sodas, thought instantly as he passed through the front door of smoking some weed, fetched the Cokes and grabbed a joint from his stash in the kitchen. He returned to the front porch and sat there, smoking pot while his son mowed with increasing competence. By the time Angus came around again to the porch, he motioned for his son to cut the motor and join him for a cold drink.

Angus, of course, didn't know yet how to stop the motor, so Gib rose and flicked the ignition switch on the handle. Stupid of himself not to have shown Angus before he started, Gib thought. Maybe a little dangerous, too.

Angus joined him in sunshine as hard and full as can possibly fall at midday. The sun was at its zenith overhead. Angus' hair was damp, and sweat rolled in tiny droplets down his boyish nape. His cheeks were the color of roses. His father, peering at him in the bright sunlight, developed a sudden paranoia that the boy had overexerted himself and would suffer a spell of heatstroke. So that in spite of Angus's protestations to the contrary, his father insisted Angus quit for the day and join Gib inside where it was cool. Gib even said Angus could have Petey inside for a few hours.

They went inside with their sodas, Gib as high as a balloon whose string had been carelessly let loose, and Angus hot and sticky, but thrilled with the ghost after-vibrations of the mower that made his hands tingle still. The mower sat in the middle of the grass, and the job wasn't quite as complete as, even, the time Gib had mowed before. There was the center patch, four or five inches high, the patch Gib had left unfinished and neglected. And there was a swath around it, two mower-widths wide maybe, neglected this time around. All about it was freshly mown grass patterned by the insistent passage of the machine's wheels. An odd tiered sort of appearance, which would have made its impression on any random passer by, should anyone ever wander up this way, which was rare indeed. A broad, squat pyramid of fescue, an isle of bluegrass.

     Gib MacNaughton's boss asked him to come into the superior's office.

     The older man looked over the top rims of his bifocals. "Gib, what's going on? I've noticed your work has had a few more mistakes than usual."

     "I didn't realize." Gib lifted his hands and stared at the fingers as if they committed data-entry mistakes of their own volition and he must partner with his boss to demand of them an accounting. "If that's the case, I'm not sure what has happened. Maybe I'm just more tired from the drive, you know, I didn't expect the long drive to get to me so much. For a while, it was hard, then it got better. Sort of routine, you know? But then it suddenly seemed to get longer – much longer. It's worse, it seems, now than ever before. I'm just tired all the time, is all."

     The supervisor was mildly surprised to receive such an elaborate response. He'd expected a sullen, monosyllabic answer filled with resentment, with drug use at the root of it all. What puzzled him was that Gib, with whose work he had been very pleased early on, had worked out so quickly an answer that appeared to possess some credibility. And that it had rushed out of him as if carbonated. So maybe it wasn't drugs. This is what the man hoped, because he liked Gib MacNaughton. He wanted him to be successful, to stay on for a good long while. But not if he was taking dope. That was the one thing that drove the supervisor crazy – perfectly normal people with great potential, wrecking their lives and the lives of those around them with drugs.

     "Look," the supervisor said. "I like you. I like you working here. I know it's a helluva long drive, but I didn't pick the job, you did. You came to us and said, 'I want to work.' We said, 'Show us what you've got.' We never talked about the commute and stuff in your personal life. We said, 'We'll pay you if you do the work and do it well.' So far you've done that, but you have slipped a little lately. I want to know why, and if it's lack of sleep then get some more damned sleep. If it's something else, get some help before it catches up with you."

     He hated sounding like such a hard-ass because he was a cream-puff at heart. It bothered him that Gib winced with his words, and that he wouldn't maintain eye contact.

     "Now get back in there and see if you can do something about these entry errors."

Gib rose and left. Before he crossed through his boss's office door, he added, "Thank you – I'll try my best."

"That's all any of us expects."

The next time Gib decided to cut grass was the following Sunday. August was almost through, and there had been an uncharacteristic heavy rain the day before. Now the sun was out again and vapor rose out of the grass and ground with a cloying mugginess that would drain energy from even the most stalwart. Yakima County was rarely muggy – heat there was an arid, desiccating thing, especially at the height of summer. But a rain amidst the hot days would drive the following day's humidity up.

Angus had gone across the road to throw a line in the lake. Gib had just finished a joint when it occurred to him he was overdue to mow, especially the patch at the center of the lawn. He peered at it through the front window. It had sprouted weird leaves, buds almost, as if the long grass were going to seed. He thought about it a moment – whether he had ever seen lawn grass grown this wild. He decided that no, he probably hadn't. It interested him. He exited the front door and waded through the lawn to the center, pulled some blades of grass from the moist earth, held them up in the sunshine for an examination. Sure enough, little seed pods had developed there, and looked as if they awaited a stiff breeze to carry them away. As he was looking, a shadow flashed in the yard. He looked up to see one of those commuter aircraft just past the disk of the sun, and realized he had been hearing its engines drone for several seconds without the sound even registering. The plane continued west. Gib dropped the grass.

Then he bent to pluck a blade of grass-leaf. It was as broad as a sword and tacky to the touch. Its edge was blade sharp – he thought it might be possible for it to cause a fine cut, like the edge of a sheet of paper drawn across a fingertip in surprise. Then he placed the blade between his two thumbs. He blew vigorously through the slot. The grass-blade vibrated, resulting in a raw caw that filled the front yard and startled birds in the surrounding treeline.

Gib started the mower and made several passes before it ran out of gas. Then he abandoned the machine where it stood, engine cooling, having left again untended the lawn's center. He went inside to roll up another joint and listen to music. It was cool in the trailer, at least more so than outside. Cool and dry. He pulled the shades and put on some Pink Floyd.

Summer ran long into September, and three things happened during the first two weeks of that month.

First, Angus was back to school, departing every morning after Gib left the trailer, walking down Mud Lake Road to the Pie Apple to meet the school bus.

Second, Gib ignored Angus' pleas to cut the grass again and, instead, reserved this chore for himself. "You got homework now," he said. But Gib never seemed to complete the mowing, so that the center patch grew taller yet. Sometimes the grass bent in the wind. Seeds burst from it and were carried away on breezes. At other times, when the wind was still, it just stood straight and tall, like at the center of a neglected field. If rain fell, the stalks tumbled and threaded each other in wet green mayhem. Each time Gib mowed he seemed to complete less and less of the job, so that filling the gas tank came fewer and fewer times between. When the stalks were standing dry and tall, the front lawn began to resemble, in its lines, the architecture of one of those temples the Incas or Aztecs or Mayans used to erect. It rose from the flanks to the center.

Third, Gib's boss busted him smoking a joint in the parking lot during lunch. Not very smart of Gib, but the workdays were getting longer and he was frustrated at his seeming inability to properly enter the data. Rather than improving his accuracy after that first conversation with his boss, he had allowed his work to further deteriorate.

His boss pulled in just as Gib flared the business end of a fat bomber. Gib drew the smoke in – a cavern full, it seemed – and held it until his boss's car rolled to the other end of the lot. But it was too late. His boss had seen him sitting there. His boss had correctly deduced his illicit lunchtime activity. The patient man stepped to Gib's window and told him to take the rest of the week off.

"Come back on Monday," he said. "We'll talk about where you want to go, what you want to do and who you want to be in life."

Gib, potent smoke curling from the open windows of his truck cab, agreed, and drove home.

The next Monday – after a Sunday lawn attempt that comprised just one run down the grass abutting the sidewalk and a turn along the woodsline – his boss put him on probation and told him to seek professional help.

Gib agreed that he would.

The first Saturday in October, Gib ran out of cigarette paper with which to roll his joints.

"Angus," he hollered down the hall. Where is that damned kid, he thought. "Angus!"

"Yeah, Dad?" Angus came bounding in the back door with Petey on the heels of his sneakers.

"Angus, do me a favor, huh? Run down to the Pie Apple and get some Zig Zags from Jacqua, you know, cigarette papers. She'll have them behind the counter."

An errand was fine with Angus – it was a boring Saturday anyway. It had just started getting chilly in the evenings lately, and the summer had finally petered out with the birch and maple leaves just starting to turn autumn shades. It meant spending time outside was curtailed somewhat, and on top of that, he usually had his homework. He took Petey out to the pen and returned to the double-wide to get some cash from his father.

Then he hiked Mud Lake Road the three-quarters of a mile to downtown Salt Lick, not a car or truck passing him the whole distance.

When he got within site of Salt Lick's main collection of buildings, he crossed over to the side of Juniper's hat shop and the peacock farmer's tavern. For some reason, Angus preferred not to step alongside the road in front of the Town Hall. It seemed creepy to him, with its large glass windows. They were mostly empty, he thought. The place raised the hair on his neck like scratching the rusty botton of a wheelbarrow with his fingernails would – everytime he walked by – so he made a practice of crossing back over Mud Lake Road only when he reached Lowell's and was directly opposite the Pie Apple.

When Angus reached the Pie Apple he stepped inside to the merry ring of Jacqua Druce's goat bell, which was affixed to the inside doorknob. Jacqua looked up.

"Angus," she said. "How're you today?"

"Ok, I guess."

"A little bored, it looks like. Don't you have no homework to do, or some fooling around to get done with?"

"Yeah, I got all of that, but Dad sent me on an errand. I gotta get him some Zig Zags, he says." Angus dug in his jeans pockets and produced a wad comprising three ones, displayed the crinkled bills in his palm. Flora Navarro slid behind the counter next to Jacqua and whispered something to her.

"Your daddy sent you down here to get his rolling papers?" Flora asked.

"Yes ma'am."

"Well, I'm gonna have a word with your daddy," Jacqua said. "Sending his boy down here to get his Zig Zags. Can you imagine?"

She grabbed a package of Zig Zags from a rack behind the counter and pocketed them. Then she sent Angus down the aisle to the display freezer for an ice-cream bar.

"Flora, you watch the store." She donned a down vest and pulled Angus from the store by the forearm. Her grasp pinched the skin there. No doubt about it, Angus thought, she's mad! At what, who knows? But *pissing* mad! He crammed the ice-cream bar into his mouth, almost finishing it by the time she had situated him on the bench-seat of her pickup. Her tires spat gravel as she lurched up Mud Lake Road, muttering curses, indecipherable to Angus, under her breath.

In less than two minutes Jacqua Druce pulled into Gib MacNaughton's driveway on the leading edge of a cloud of dust. She gaped at the sea of grass there, shaped like a perfect Meso-American pyramid, nicely tended at the sides but wild, tall and jungley at the center. "Sweet Jesus!" she said, and slid out from under the steering wheel through her opening door. "Come on." Angus followed.

She roared onto the porch like a harrier and burst through the front door as if she owned the place. Angus trotted up behind her.

The living room was filled with sugar-sweet smoke. It wafted from the open door in psychedelic shapes, strata of particulates lifting and separating like blankets on a soft breeze. Gib MacNaughton sat on the couch with his stereophones on, oblivious to the arrival of Jacqua and his son. The music was so loud that Jacqua heard it through the earphones as plainly as if it emanated from normal speakers at a tolerable, conversation-permitting volume.

She grabbed hold of the coiling stereophone cord that stretched the room from Gib's head to the stereo stack. And she yanked those phones as if she were hauling in a randy steer for a silver prize buckle. Gib's eyes flew open like shutters eager for springtime. He seemed, for a moment, all eyeballs. Then he blinked and wiped his eyes to verify what he had thought he saw – the Pie Apple's proprietress standing in his living room, looking as righteous and perturbed as the subject of that famous painting of John Brown at Harper's Ferry.

"That was Bob Marley!" Gib MacNaughton said, as if this were all the explanation that would ever, in all the course of human history, be required. But then he added, "Exodus."

She leveled an Abolishonist's finger at him.

"Don't you never," she said, "ever, ever send this boy to get your dope papers. Not from my store. Not never." She reached into her coat pocket, withdrew the packet of Zig-Zags, and flung them at Gib like a fork-ball. Then she dug in her other pocket and tossed his money at him with the same vehemence. She turned and exited the door. Gib didn't utter a word.

Bob Marley and his band jammed in the speakerphones. The highest frequencies of the reggae beat circled Gib MacNaughton's living room like the painted wood horses of a bemirrored calliope.

He looked at Angus. The boy shrugged his small shoulders as if to suggest either a deep personal mystification at the proprietress' actions, or a deep personal indifference to the tongue-lashing his father had just received. What the boy was thinking had, in fact, very little to do with either. He'd liked the ice-cream bar. He wondered how he might be able to get another soon.

Outside, they heard the squealing of tires, and the engine roar, then fade, as Jacqua Druce bounced back down Mud Lake Road.

CHAPTER 13
in which the secession movement meets a sad end...

Juniper Jamison pulled into his driveway. As he rounded Mud Lake Road, he'd seen that Lothar was waiting for him high in the cab of his red Ford. This made Juniper nervous. The hat blocker was late, and no one ever liked to keep Lothar Sturmhund waiting. Not even – *especially* not even – the few who were (or sought to be) close to him. Juniper counted himself in that small, dwindling group, chocked it up to his support of Lothar's idea to break away from Yakima County. He checked his watch, found that yes, he was three minutes late. He'd tarried a few minutes – apparently three too many – at the sportsman's shop in Naches. This might have to be handled delicately.

Juniper put on his best smile and bounded from the cab of his pickup. Juniper Jamison was the hugest man in Salt Lick and had a rosaceous face. "Sorry I'm late," he said. He stuck out his massive hand as Lothar climbed down from his mount. His beefy fist swallowed Lothar's in a clutch that seemed more like sumo match than handclasp. Juniper Jamison had been made fat in his mother's womb, and he, all his life, cultivated it by bolting all the food in sight. At the annual Jerky Fair, for example, it might be reasonable for him to contribute a full one-quarter of the total take for the Reverend's charities. The dish he would bring was creamed corn, in a five-gallon plastic bucket.

And nowhere was Juniper's rotundity more expressed than in the digits of his hammish hands.

Truly, no larger fingers could be imagined than Juniper Jamison's. They were each like the kielbasa sausages Kinchlow sold next door at Lowell's. Peninsulas of sweetmeat that sprouted from his wrists, and the opposing thumbs seemed to have the same circumference as the wide end of a ball bat. It is almost incomprehensible to imagine that these hands could properly articulate, that they could, in fact, be productive. That they could fashion *anything!* But Juniper Jamison was the finest, most skilled cowboy-hat care specialist in the region. That's all he did – nothing else – no leatherwork, no tooling, no bootwork, no saddlework,

156

no crafting of reins or whips. He focused on cowboy hats, and his focus made him unparalleled at the execution of all aspects of cowboy hat work, from the banal to the esoteric. If there had been an *Encyclopaedia Cowboyhattica*, Juniper Jamison would certainly have consulted on the project, if not outright served as its author. All of this was enough so that he could make a living doing only this, and occasionally ordering hats for folks from the Resistol or Stetson catalogs.

"Joop, old pal, it's O.K. I'm in good spirits today. What time you got?"

On the entire planet, only Lothar Sturmhund assumed he could transmogrify that already bizarre given name *Juniper* into the patently absurd *Joop*, then actually let it come out of his mouth and dance on the air. Juniper Jamison would have crushed anyone else who fucked with his name. From Lothar, though, the fat hat guru chose to accept this moniker-monkeying as almost the conferring of an honorific – proof of the Hirsute One's affection. Juniper checked his watch nervously. "Four after."

"You're on the right track. That's what I love about you." Lothar's lips, nested between the red hair of his beard and mustache, formed a gigantic smile. "Let's go in and see what you got for me."

"O.K., but I gotta show you something first." Juniper tugged Lothar around his pickup toward the back. "Now don't bust your milk when you see this." He pointed as they rounded the truck's bed. Lothar followed an imaginary plumb-line from Juniper's pudgy digit, centered on the rusted bumper. There his license plate was newly framed. And the message on the framed license plate, the message that Juniper Jamison apparently wanted to send to the world – or at least the Yakima County area – was LIVE FAST PLAY HARD DIE YOUNG LEAVE A GOOD LOOKIN' CORPSE. "What do you think?" Juniper asked.

Lothar stared at the frame for a good minute without commenting. He disliked this sort of thing – license plate frames, bumper stickers, that nasty boy sticker that said NO FEAR on the pickups and four-wheelers of the area's youth. He especially hated the one where the boy is pissing on the logo of one of the truck manufacturers whose truck the driver's wasn't. He thought those young drivers were on the wrong track, that they perhaps suffered from inadequate parenting. He wondered whether something like this was in Joop's past – an inadequate, communistic father.

Juniper's license-plate frame put Lothar in mind of that on the front and back of a '68 Mustang owned by a certain young woman named Lisa. This young vixen-goddess worked at an old folk's home in Yakima, where he'd contracted with Pete Kecht to do some wallboard repair. Her frame – the one on her car – read, MY OTHER RIDE IS YOUR BOYFRIEND. Now there was a nasty little spitfire. Confident. And competent!

Juniper's auto-witticism also reminded Lothar of a local bumper sticker. It read, "EXPENSIVE, BUT WORTH IT," and was affixed to the back window of Vicki Aguirre's Nipponese-made Toyota car. Lothar had first read it as "EXPLOSIVE, BUT WORTH IT," and thought *Yes, I bet you are,* trailing her into town one day. And all of this reminded him that Vicki was one of the few young women in the area whom he had not yet attempted to bed. He'd have to get right to that. To see just how explosive that lovely little princess could be (and having chosen this goal, achieved it within the week).

If Lothar had acted in character, he would have told Juniper Jamison he thought the license plate frame was asinine. Instead, preferring to get on with things – to get his new hat and confer on Juniper a very important bestowment, he chose to simply grunt, "Hmm," and mumble, "That's something, all right."

But Juniper accepted this as an approval. A grin cracked on his fat face, and he nodded his head up and down so that his wattles swung like those of some overfed, aggressive fowl. "I knew you'd like it," he said. "I just knew it." It was as though Lothar had just baptized Juniper's first son and guaranteed the wee offspring's eternal salvation. "Let's go get your hat," Juniper said.

He led Lothar through the side door to his garage shop and stepped behind his counter. He pulled a box from amid reblocking tools – jigs, steamers, pliers – arrayed on his workbench. He set the box in front of Lothar. "Open it."

Lothar excised from the box a white Stetson El Aguila. He turned the hat in his fingers, feeling the silk. Its traditional cattleman's shape was pleasing to his eye, as pleasing as it had been the first day he'd stepped into Juniper's shop after Juniper had hung up the promotional poster behind the counter. The poster featured the El Aguila, 100-percent fine beaver fur with its gold buckle, atop the head of a very rugged-looking cowpoke. "True Luxury for Your Head," the poster promised. Holding it here in his hands, its five-inch crown and four-inch brim calling his Germanic name, Lothar thought that he would have to agree. He donned the hat, turned to his side, and beheld his reflection in a mirror Juniper had mounted at the end of the counter for just this sort of moment.

"So that's what an eight-hundred fifty dollar hat looks like!" Lothar said. "Damned good, don't it?"

In agreement, Juniper's whole body shook like a barrel of bread pudding.

"You know," Lothar turned back to Juniper, "this is like having a crown, like a king with his crown."

"Tall Tree County!"

"Tall Tree County!" said Lothar. "Next referendum, for sure!"

It was, perhaps, the happiest day of Juniper Jamison's life.

"Grab some birds, get your shotgun," Lothar said. "I feel like shooting me some skeet."

Juniper complied, retrieving a heavy case of clay pigeons. He hefted the case as if it were filled with helium and followed his mentor and his mentor's hat out the door.

Juniper Jamison, Magda Sturmhund, Nick Oxendine, and other members of the Tall Tree County movement, sat together in the Widow Sturmhund's living room and watched election returns come in on the fuzzy black and white set.

"I think we need a Web site," Nick, who was serving as the movement's P.R. man, said from lips nesting in three days of mustache and chin stubble. His shirt was open four buttons. Underneath, he had a T-shirt that had used to be white, but was now food-dappled.

"Yeah," Juniper said from under the El Aguila. "Double-you, double-you, double-you we lost again by a wider margin dot com. Sounds ridiculous, don't you think?" He reached up to push the hat down around his skull again, a gesture he had to perform repeatedly, since the damned thing was too small and always creeping up.

"Don't be cross, Juniper," Magda said. "It's not Nick's fault."

"Well then, whose fault is it?"

As Lothar's successor in leading the county secession movement, Juniper was watching, for the second election in a row, numbers indicating that the referendum to create Tall Tree County would not make it to ballot. It was, in fact, *gaining anti-momentum*, a term Nick invoked to represent lack of success. Anti-momentum measured public disapproval or apathy – Juniper wasn't sure which – an entropy of interest in an independent county that stood for the farmer, the rural support structure and secession from the monolithic, bureaucratic, gone-soft Yakima County.

Then there he was on the screen, in a taped interview. He recalled driving home from Yakima, the county seat he regarded as the home turf of the enemy (the Yakimama's Boys, he called them all). He

159

remembered with dissatisfaction the interview itself. He hated media people. He appreciated their power, of course, but didn't understand it. These were people who distorted, cheated, cultivated questionable sources then ran around as if they were morally, spiritually, ethically and intellectually superior. These were the people who printed, on the front page above the fold, TALL COUNTY WANNABE BRANDISHES 'MUSKET' in DEWEY DEFEATS TRUMAN-sized type! *How could people read this crap*, he marveled. How could they *believe* it? The local papers were becoming more and more like the *National Enquirer*, and every night of the week there was a new entertainment program masquerading as a news magazine. If anything had become apparent since Jacqua Druce set up her 99-channel satellite dish, it was this.

He was working himself up again. And wondering what Lothar would do in his shoes.

In the interview, Juniper had made a trivial reference to the Founding Fathers of the country, how they finally were driven to protest taxation without representation with the business end of a musket. It was a minor comment in the context of explaining the evolution of dissatisfaction among the county's rural residents.

"For chrissakes, man," Juniper had said to the TV reporter, "a man can't plant his shovel on his own land anymore without being *permitted* to death. Try developing your property. You can't do nothing with the parts that have been declared wetlands" – he spoke this word like a curse – "but you sure's hell have to pay property taxes!"

The reporter had poker-faced him, revealing no signal that he understood. He had a great sound bite: *"When the fathers of our country had enough, they got out their muskets."* That's all he cared about, and that's what showed up on TV. Then every media outlet in the state did a second-day story, scavenging from the enterprise work of the TV reporter like crows pecking roadkill.

"When the fathers of our country had enough, they got out their muskets," Juniper's talking head said from the snowy television. The committee groaned, and the referendum scorecard in the screen's corner rolled again and the percentage next to *Yes* – meaning to defeat the referendum – increased, and that next to *No* decreased.

"Shit," Nick said.

"Exactly." Juniper agreed, for once, with his flak. "You are precisely right."

Magda's phone rang. She answered and handed it to Nick. "Oxendine," he said. "Uh-huh. Uh-huh. Sure, lemme see." He turned to Juniper: "Tristan Devon at the *Herald-Republic* wants your reaction to the voting. Just a sec..." he turned his attention back to the caller.

"Uh-huh, hold on..." Again to Juniper: "He's claiming exit polls are showing we're toast. Wants to know whether you'll concede and try again next election. Hold on..."

"Gimme that thing." Juniper snatched the phone. "This is Juniper Jamison."

"Oh... Mr. Jamison, thank you for your time, sir."

"Yeah, yeah. You're quite welcome...Tristan, is it? Tristan? What kinda name's that?"

"Well, uh, Mr. Jamison, sir, it's..."

"I'm gonna call you Moke."

"Uh, well, whatever sir, but that's not my name..."

"Oh, nevermind. You had a question, Moke?"

"Sir, the exit polling shows that the referendum for Tall Tree County will fail, sir."

"Yeah, well don't bust your milk... What time is it?"

"Beg pardon, sir?"

"What *time* is it, I said. You got trouble hearing, son?"

There was silence from the reporter, then, like the weak mewling of a kitten: "7:35."

"Hmm, I got 7:40, but whatever. Either way, the night ain't over yet, now, is it, son?"

"No, no, you're right, the night isn't over. But I wonder if you have been watching..."

"Of course I been watching..."

"Then you see the numbers, sir, right? You see the numbers?"

What to say? "Mr. Devon, the night is not over, and I have no further comment at this time except to add that we are gaining anti-momentum."

"Anti-momentum, sir?"

"*Gaining* anti-momentum. That's what I said."

"Can I quote you on that, sir?"

"Why do you even ask?" Juniper queried the matte-black object in his hand, an article of technology that allowed the living room of his predecessor, and his predecessor's widow, to be invaded by these asses from the press. He slapped the loathsome phone into its cradle.

Two weeks after the defeat of the Tall Tree County referendum, the Tall Tree County committee met again in the Sturmhund living room to start planning for a third run, six months hence.

"We need a plan," Juniper said. Instead of speaking further, he held forth a copy of the *Herald-Republic*: TALL TREE REFRENDUM 'GAINS ANTI-MOMENTUM,' DIES.

"We need a communication plan," Nick said, examining for the dozenth time the raggy newspaper. "We need a plan that sets forth how we will communicate, what our goal is, what our mission and vision are, what our strategies will be, what key messages we will say."

The group was listening to him, rapt.

"What tactics we will use to deploy our key messages. What measurements we will use to judge the success of our efforts."

"That's easy," Magda said, as if solving an enigma. "We'll win!"

"We'll win," agreed Nick.

"What kinds of things will we do?" Jacqua asked. She eyed Nick as if all this talk of missions and measurements were the words of an exotic tongue.

"That's to be decided later," Nick said. "We have to start with the vision, the mission. And from that we derive our goals and strategies, and only then do we entertain the notion of the actual *things* we will do."

"Seems the long way through it," Juniper said. His face was red as a beet. It glared under the white cowboy hat. "We could simplify it right here, right now. The mission and the vision and the goal are the same: an independent Tall Tree County. The strategy is to get everybody in Tall Tree country to think this is the right thing."

"Well, yes, but..." Nick began.

"Let me finish. The message is this: Do you want to be part of Tall Tree County or not, because if you don't, then you've got to be part of Yakima County and pay Yakima County taxes and you can't plant your shovel in Yakima County wetlands even if they're on your property cause Yakima County says so like the rest of the Yakimama's Boys." He paused, face purpling with lack of oxygen, to suck in breath. "Then we get some bumper stickers and signs and get us some T-shirts made and start getting on the phone again. Try harder this time."

"Well," Nick said, and the rest of the council began to discern the makings of an intellectual cow-pie-throwing match, "those are all good ideas, but I think we'd better talk through them all. Really understand what we're about. Yeah, I mean, what are we about? And when we've decided what we're about, then we're ready to tell others, and then we're ready to do the heavy-lifting work."

"Like what I said," said Juniper.

"Like, for instance, I like the idea of having that web site thing," Magda said. "I like it a lot. What exactly is it?"

"I like the bumper sticker idea," Jacqua said. "I could hand them out at the store."

Nick rolled his eyes. It was going to be a long meeting.

"How about a flag?" asked Tina Druce, Jacqua's daughter. "A flag for Tall Tree County. We could have a contest."

The room fell silent for a moment as each member the council turned over this idea in his or her head.

After a moment, Magda broke the reverie: "On the web thing…"

"We could put it on the stickers," added the elder Druce.

"It's a good idea," Juniper said, blessing the notion of a prototype, a component of this unfurling creation – the Tall Tree County flag. He rose to indicate a coffee break.

Three weeks after the pivotal night in which the Tall Tree County committee forsook the machinations of a properly constructed communication plan and jumped right ahead into tactics, specifically, the tactic of holding a flag-design contest, the web site was activated. The URL was www.talltreecounty.org, and clicking on it would bring a home page with a DESIGN OUR FLAG button. The only requirement was that the designer reside in the environs of the proposed Tall Tree County, and that the design have no "underlying questionable content of prurient, lascivious, militantly seditious, or otherwise objectionable content," bazillion-dollar script written by Nick. Within days, the committee had its first designs.

"Look here, an act of vexillological plagiary!" Nick shouted, after printing out one submission.

"A what?" asked the teen Druce.

"I'll wash your mouth out with soap!" Magda said.

"No, see," said Nick. "*Vexillological*. Latin, for the study of flags. I learned it doing research. But this here's a flag that's already been used. I've seen it in a book."

"But her note says it's the Liberty Tree flag, used by the rebel navy in the Revolution," Tina read from the e-mail accompanying the design. "'It's perfectly good for Tall Tree County,' the designer says, 'a green tree on a white field – a Tall Tree,' she says in her note."

Nick reached for the paper, examined the design. A green tree centered on a rectangle of pure white. The words AN APPEAL TO HEAVEN above the tree, in black. Pure and simple.

Juniper came in, fresh from a walk through his barn and a horse-feeding, then up Mud Lake Road and Benton Drive to the Sturmhund place.

"Lookie here, Juniper," Nick said, "look at this flag submission."

Juniper accepted the papers, evaluated the design, perused the letter, handed it back.

"I don't like it."

The group was stunned. It was the first decent thing they'd seen.

"How come?" Nick rubbed his chin, the roots of his flowing beard.

"Too religious."

"Too religious?"

"Yeah. Too damned religious."

"But it fits so well with us, I mean, look at the tree. This is heaven, this is God's country, Tall Tree County is *God's Country*," Nick said.

"It's too religious. People could mistake us for a bunch of whackos."

Nick, glad Reverend Jenkins hadn't been on hand to hear *that*, fished in his back pocket for his wallet. He drew it from around his waist, opened it, pulled a one-dollar bill forth, splayed it in his palm for Juniper.

"Lookie here," he said. "Here's the legal tender of this great country. The father of our country, George Washington, on the front. Like you, like Lothar, the father of a *move*ment. On the back," – he flipped the bill one-handed – "the motto: IN GOD WE TRUST. Good enough for this great country, good enough for us."

Juniper Jamison – so much like his mentor – was unused to being challenged, particularly as Lothar's successor. Especially in this way, witnessed by the entire committee. What would Lothar do? Lothar would likely have subjected Nick to a verbal pummeling, if not physical. But Juniper Jamison didn't feel that sort of power coursing from him yet, and the deficiency burned him. He didn't yet enjoy the committee's support that strongly. They'd probably all bust milk in a dozen directions. So instead, he drew in breath and expanded to his full girth.

"Let me show you something." He snatched the note from Nick's hand. "You take the father of our country and you fold him like so." He made a fold horizontally the length of the bill about a third of the way up the portrait's neck. "Then you fold him like this." He folded the bill again, back toward the original fold at just above the bridge of the first president's nose. "And what you got is you turned the father of our country into a mushroom."

Juniper looked around the room, expecting laughter, but encountering only stillness.

Nick looked down at the twice-folded note in Juniper's hand, Juniper offering it back to him. He looked up at Juniper's eyes again.

"I give up," he said.

"You're fired," said Juniper.

Another week passed, and Juniper was in his shop reloading 30.06 bullets at a counterpress. He was thinking of what a strange thing it was that the people had named Hector Aguirre Salt Lick's mayor and not him. He was thinking – with growing resentment – that he hadn't really seen a hell of a lot of Hector around Town Hall. Juniper Jamison's Hat Reblocking had a window view onto Town Hall's gravel lot. He couldn't think of the last time he'd seen the warden's rig parked there. It just wasn't right. He – Juniper Jamison – belonged behind Lothar Sturmhund's old desk. That's the way Lothar would have wanted it. He had Lothar's hat. The phone rang.

"Juniper Jamison Hat Reblocking," he answered.

"Oh... hello, uh... Mr. Jamison?"

"That's what I said, yeah."

"I'm sorry, I didn't expect to ring directly through to you."

"Well... I'm standin' here by the phone..."

"Yes, well, us, this is Tristan Devon at the *Herald-Republic*."

"Moke! Good for you!"

"I, um, had a coupla questions for you, sir, regarding the Tall Tree County movement."

Juniper shrugged, as if the reporter could see him. He poured a measure of gunpowder into brass while balancing the phone between his shoulder, neck and chin. "I guess you're talking to the right guy, then, huh?"

"Yes, well, sir, I hear you canned Nick Oxendine."

"Yep."

"Can you comment on that for me sir, you are confirming that the Tall Tree County movement fired Nicholas Oxendine?"

"Yep."

"Yes, then, well, any further comment as to why?"

"The Tall Tree County movement is headed in a new direction," Juniper said. "A direction that is the opposite of gaining anti-momentum. We are moving forward."

"Yes, moving forward... in a new direction."

"That's right."

"Any more on that, sir?"

"Think of it like an airplane. You know, one of those damned airplanes always buzzing overhead. They fly forward. Try flying one backward. What you get is a heap of flames. That's anti-momentum for you. Going forward's what we're doing now. You watch and see."

"O.K. ... one additional question, sir, Mr. Jamison, I understand that the Tall Tree County movement is designing a flag, a sort of rallying symbol. Can you confirm that, sir?"

"Yes."

"Yes, sir, that's true?"

"Yes, that's true."

"Well, can you tell me anything about it?"

"Not much right now, no. We had a contest. A design won. We're having it made."

"What's it look like... I mean, do you mind saying?"

Juniper levered lead into another brass shell. "I'd rather not."

"Any details at all, sir?"

"Well... O.K., maybe just one. There's a motto on the flag."

"A motto, sir?"

"A motto."

"What's it say?"

"'Don't tread on me.' Perfect, huh?"

"I guess so, I mean, it's been done you know?"

"Yep. But it's perfect because it's in alignment with our new direction, our moving forward."

"Like an airplane."

"*Exactly* like an airplane."

"I see. O.K. So you really fired Nick, huh?"

"Totally."

"You got an opening for a P.R. man, then?"

"Yeah, why, you interested?"

"I don't know, maybe. Seem to think more and more these days of getting into private practice. Crossing over to the dark side, as we say in the business. Workin' for the paper don't pay shit."

"Why don't you come around to the shop and see me then, sometime, maybe this week."

"Maybe."

"Yeah, I'll show you all about our new direction."

"O.K., sure."

"I'm here all the time."

"O.K., thanks."

"Gimme a call when you're on your way."

"Will do."

Juniper pressed another shell. And another. A cache of ordnance grew, first in his shop, then outgrew his shop, and the munitions mounted, and the new direction moving forward moved forward and negated the *gaining* of *anti-momentum*. Tall Tree County's flag would have a rattlesnake on it, by God, and that was that.

Juniper loaded his rifle and waited for the reporter.

CHAPTER 14
in which Joop Jamison loads and cocks the Fourth Estate...

Gunter Sturmhund was hunting elk, which means that he was waiting. Cold bit into his flesh, through multiple layers of wool and nylon. The hard redwood stump he had chosen as a seat an hour before had become needle-numbing. He felt frozen in place, as if movement – any movement – would be immediately followed by a fundamental cracking. His breath, in steam, flowed out and floated away.

Lothar's youngest son had hiked slowly in for thirty minutes from a logging road in the foggy dark. He paused to listen every few steps for the crack of limbs, the signature of startled game. Equipped with rifle, field glasses, compass, buck knife, wool coat and cowboy hat, Gunter was annoyed with the fog. It made discernment difficult, masking gender and making yearlings and cows indistinguishable from mature bulls. It reduced by a factor of ten the precious seconds one would have to verify that an animal could be taken, then fire a well-placed kill shot.

Gunter had separated from his father and brother halfway back up the hill. Helmut would hunt two ridges to the east, Lothar one ridge to the west and further down. The movement of the two boundary hunters was supposed to spook elk into Gunter's line of fire. This was the theory.

Dawn came up. Shapes that seemed only questions in the pre-light took on definition. Odd mists evaporated in snatches of sunlight – the fog seemed to have broken. The knot of these woods, irresolvable in the darkness, had begun to clarify with the rising of light. Now, in full morning, it looked simple.

Elk-hunting comprises long stretches – hours at a time – of sitting silently motionless on a stump or log providing a secreted, but systemic, view of a ravine or hillside animals might graze upon. Hunters look for fresh sign – moist scat and hoof prints with motes of dry earth in them – that will indicate the recent presence of animals. Then they survey the area for a reasonably comfortable spot to wait, one where two or three hours can be passed before time and failing anticipation overwhelm them and they must move on. This was happening to Gunter now. But he willed myself to wait.

Time stretched out. He stared at the second hand of his wristwatch and counted its long sweep. It seemed an eternity. He glanced up *knowing* an elk was about to wander into the clearing. But five more minutes passed. Then he rose with the creaking and stretching of tendons and bones. He took a step. Still there was silence in the woods around.

He climbed down into the ravine he'd been surveying for ninety-five minutes. Fog was gathering again, deeper than before. Soon he was on a game trail. Its clear cut on the forest floor divided salal and other undergrowth with a ribbon of pine needles, deer and elk tracks, droppings. There were so many trails, like a matrix over the forest. To follow a single one, from start to finish, would be impossible. Gunter wondered, in the presence of such an extensive trail network why game wasn't spotted constantly, deer and elk criss-crossing in front of him every ten seconds. But he also knew that even a small population was capable of making the large number of trails. Their number and proliferation was a false indicator of population.

Moving slowly across the ravine, fog now denser and enveloping, Gunter crossed over some fallen limbs. He rounded a stand of mountain juniper, picked up another trail, and began to climb out of the canyon. He climbed around a nurse-log hosting seedlings, termites, and brilliant fungi. The woods around him gathered and closed. The trail moved into the trees: so did he. Dry lower limbs scraped across his coat and face. Some cracked as he pressed through a tight spot. The trail continued. As the route wound past a blown-down hemlock he spotted a black object ahead, directly in the center of the trail.

A crow, dead, lying on its side with wings stowed and feet tucked in.

It was clearly not a raven. Its size – about ten inches from beak to tail feather – confirmed this. A raven is larger, sometimes more than two feet long.

He paused for a moment and wondered that its body lay here – any animal's corpse in the forest is almost instantly consumed by other animals. It occurred to him that the crow must have just died, maybe only moments ago. He looked up at the overstory. He found stillness only, and no revelation.

His father's voice broke the cold mirror of silence.

"Fine looking fellow, wasn't he?"

Gunter gasped, startled. As he recovered, fog dissipated around him. He looked up at his father and knew that Lothar took delight in the dead crow. That laying there, in the trail, the bird was the same size and color of his father's heart. Saying not a word, with no acknowledgement at all – a dangerous course with his father – Gunter stepped from under the canopy into a clearing.

He heard the drone of an airplane overhead. A hole opened in the fog, and widened. He spotted the aircraft, a commuter turbojet headed west. It preceded the sound of its engines, moved slowly, gracefully. Gunter pulled his rifle from its shoulder-sling, grasped its stock in his glove, hefted it skyward. He brought the scope to his eye. He put the crosshairs on the airplane and tracked it.

Gunter Sturmhund imagined all the possibilities.

"Nice to think about, ain't it son?" his father said. "All that flame."

Tristan Devon stood from his car seat. His breath blew clouds in front of him. He clasped a reporter's spiral notebook in his bare hand. *Goddamned cold*, he thought. He reached back into his car for his split-leather gloves. He started to pull one on.

Then three things happened. Or, rather, Tristan Devon sensed three things happening so quickly in succession as to possess the same time-space. First, a hyperdrilling pressure wave trailing a sonic whine split the air next to his head as rifling lead tore a tunnel in space. Second, the boom of a large-bore rifle discharged in, more or less, his direction. A frisson slid down his spine and bunched at the sphincter, which clenched impossibly tight then opened as wide as a throughway. Third, he heard plate glass explode behind him.

He thought, *Now what am I gonna do?* and *Get Down!* and then waded into a rushing locomotive. He spun to his left from behind the door, knocked four or five yards from the car, felt a staccato hammerblow amid his shoulderblades. He dropped onto frozen mud and stone. His notebook clattered a few feet away, pages rilling in backblow. He saw blood on the asphalt.

Before awareness abandoned him he had time to think that he should hide. But he was low enough now – grounded – to need no further cover.

Flora Navarro looked up from cleaning the chrome pitcher housing on the espresso machine. "That was close." Jacqua was looking up too, at Flora.

"Was that glass?" Jacqua asked.

The two gawped at each other for a few seconds. They listened for whatever would come next. There had been gunfire right in town. But its importance had not yet registered. November was a month filled with rifle blasts, in the hills, anyway. If it weren't for the stream of deer and elk hunters in October and November, none of the businesses in the area – not even the Pie Apple or Lowell's – would make it the rest of the year. A hunter had simply, mistakenly, discharged his rifle too close to town. Stupid, unsafe, but certainly not unheard of.

A second blast snapped them from uncertainty.

"Get down!" Jacqua said. The pair hit the bare wood floor. "Some drunk fool's shooting up the town."

Jacqua reached up into the space under the counter where she kept her pistol. She pulled it down into her lap. She checked the chamber and flicked off the safety. To Flora, it looked as though Jacqua almost willed the shooter to step one boot into the Pie Apple. She'd blow his guts all over the video rack – which might be cool and exciting and a tale that would be told for a long time. Except that Flora would most likely be the one to mop the mess up.

"Jacqua, put that away," she said. It was direction offered, oddly, at her superior. "Nobody's coming in here. We have to call the sheriff."

Jacqua looked uncertain, then silly. Of course no one would come into the Pie Apple, his rifle leveled, here to rob her minuscule till. And Flora was right, the authorities did need calling. Jacqua peered over the counter out the side window. Half-light met her, the only color a flaring neon sign in Lowell's window across the street. Next door, at Juniper's, she saw a strange car. Its door was ajar. There was a person lying nearby.

"Jesus, Mary, and Joseph," she said. "There's a man shot out there!" She scrambled to her feet and vaulted the counter. Flora followed. The women pushed through the door, goat-bell jangling – didn't even pause to brace for the cold as they stepped outside. Jacqua snatched the pay phone from its cradle. She poked 9-1-1. A dispatcher came on.

"There's a shooting in Salt Lick," she said. "Salt Lick, yes." There was a pause. "There are no goddamned addresses in Salt Lick! We're just up the highway from Naches. To the west, yes." After another pause: "My name is Jacqua Druce. I own the Pie Apple grocery. There's a man shot across the street. You need to send the sheriff and an ambulance."

She set the phone back on its cradle. Wellman Kinchlow shouted from across the street. "What happened?" Behind him, patrons emerged from the tavern, hunters mostly in their fluorescent vests and hats, but there was Mike Eagle Eye too, still limping behind strangers, and Gib MacNaughton. It was getting on four o'clock, light falling fast into dusk. Then, even from across Mud Lake Road in the twilight, Jacqua saw Kinchlow's eyes grow wide. She followed the line of his gaze to the Town Hall window or, rather, where the window had hung. There remained only the frame and some jagged shards crimped in seals.

"I called 9-1-1," she hollered. "I think that guy's been shot." She pointed at the lump next to the car, which moved a little. "He ain't dead though." She began to move toward the fallen man.

"Jacqua, be careful!" Flora broke into stride behind her boss. Kinchlow broke toward the wounded man also. The three reached him about the same time.

"Who is he?" Lowell's proprietor asked.

"Don't have a clue." Jacqua knelt. The man moaned. The air around him smelled of shit and blood. "He's losing blood fast." She tore his overcoat flap wide and revealed the bullet's wreckage. He wore a necktie – she fumbled to slip its knot from his throat. His shirt was soaked and torn. She saw sinew and bone behind flaps of skin, and a neat, black-crimson hole at the center of the mess. She wondered what sort of horror the exit wound would be, if the bullet even made it out – she knew bullets did funny things, at least in animals. They could go clean through and just drill a hole neat as you please, or they could hit a bone spur and ricochet around in there for a while at fantastic speeds, liquefying all the tissue they tumbled through and turning guts into a sort of pudding. But this guy's shoulder was a total fucking mess. She looked up at Flora. "This guy is gonna die if we don't stop the blood."

"The deal is, there's no pressure point for a blown-off shoulder," said Kinchlow.

Jacqua leveled a gaze at him that would have melted frozen wax. "You got to push right on the wound, you big dumb-ass." And so Wellman Kinchlow did, took his scrubbed-clean barkeeper's hands and folded them around each other in a massive double fist, and plunged it right into the coursing space. The blood flowed slower, seeping around his hands, but stopped jetting in squirts. "Go back in the bar," he said, over his shoulder, to no one in particular. "Get me about a thousand clean bar towels. They're under the counter." Someone fled to do so.

And then something happened as if Lothar were still alive, as if he still walked among them: the group had a synchrony experience. Simultaneously, at that moment the realization that someone had been shot, and lay at their feet bleeding – perhaps to death – and that he clearly had not shot himself, seemed to strike everyone. This meant, of course, that there was a shooter. Therefore, they all, standing there – the fluorescing hunters, in particular – for the most part represented potential follow-on targets. If someone had gone ape-shit enough to gun down a stranger in the middle of town, what would keep him or her from upping the toll? The hunters broke up like bowling pins, scrambling first to put objects between them and – well, where? – and then sprinting back toward the tavern. They left Jacqua, Flora, Mike Eagle Eye and Kinchlow in a huddle about the man.

"We'd better stay low," Mike whispered.

"I need those towels," said Kinchlow.

Another half minute passed, and the hunter who had gone for the towels called from Lowell's doorway. Flora ran to him hunched over as near the ground as possible and took the stack from him. She crabbed back to the huddle. Kinchlow grabbed a fistful of towels and reblocked the wound. The towels turned bright red and then black in the falling light. Mike Eagle Eye, of all people, started to pray.

The four huddlers shivered into nightfall. And after some time, they heard the first siren.

Detective Pandoulis of the Yakima Sheriff Department slid through the turn onto Salt Lick's main road and floored the accelerator to spin through the curve. It was an unnecessary waste of taxpayer's money – the gasoline that ignited and fed that surge, because he was less than fifty yards from the crime scene. Already patrons had spilled from the tavern at the roadside and were vectoring him toward the problem as if he were some docking vessel. He yanked the wheel toward a huddle of people he saw hunkered down. The aid car, which had tailed him since shortly after Gleed, roared in behind him.

The whole world pulsed with red, blue, and white lights.

Pandoulis pulled his service revolver from his holster as he slid from under the patrol car's roof. "Where's the problem?" he asked of no one and everyone, loudly, as if he demanded an answer from any quarter, the hills and canyons even. It was similar to the way Lothar Sturmhund would have talked to them, believing their existence and presence there was to provide him with facts, and *fast*.

"Get down!" Kinchlow barked. "There's a sniper somewhere." Like a panther, Pandoulis crouched at the patrol car's wheelwell. His pistol and braced forearms stretched before him like the prow of a boat, aiming at anything. Everywhere. Anyone – no, the house.

Juniper Jamison's Hat Reblocking, the hand-painted sign read over the garage. "Who lives there?" the detective demanded. The group turned slowly, as a unit, to view Juniper's front porch. Then they all looked back at the detective.

"Our hat-blocker," Flora said. The ambulance guys shunted up the gravel clutching their kits, swimming in mirrored light.

"You men get down," Pandoulis said. "We got a sniper in there, might still be hot." He pointed over his shoulder at Juniper's house. The ambulance men dropped, then crawled over to the wounded man.

"Whoa," said one of them. "This dude's fucked up." He said this with a stolid admiration, as if a new, fresh challenge presented itself and this was the reason why he existed. To fix a fucked-up dude. "Look at this," he said to his partner, who had just come into the group's view. He pointed at the wrecked shoulder. His partner moved in close with a penlight. In its sideglare, Flora Navarro saw that the second emergency technician was the Breadman, that E. CUBBENS was engraved on his name badge, and that in glancing up away from the wound for a moment he caught her stunned stare and his gaze lingered on her. Her breath caught in her throat. Her heart clenched. So did her perineal muscles, involuntarily.

The EMTs started work in earnest, pulling compresses and ampoules from their kits, fingers flying over blood as knitters of flesh. While Pandoulis cased Juniper's house, Cubbens, the Breadman, fumbled in the wounded man's overcoat pocket and fished forth a wallet. He snapped it open. "Working Press," he read. "Tristan Devon. Yakima *Herald-Republic*."

Pandoulis pursed his lips and moved away from the shadow of his car. Low to the ground, he worked to the base of a tall tamarack pine in Juniper's front yard. He rested there, behind the trunk, to inventory the situation. He heard general busyness behind him with the shot reporter, but a disconcerting silence from the house. If the town mayor had plugged a reporter, there was going to be a shitstorm. He'd better handle this, every jot and tittle of it, by the book. And where the hell was his backup, anyway?

Back at the huddle, Tristan Devon was dying. The EMTs could do nothing about it. The man had simply lost too much blood. The ground was slick with it – everyone in the huddle was soaked through their knees and shins. Still, Cubbens worked madly to stem the flow, shoving compresses deep into the wound. But no matter how hard he pressed, blood seemed, still, to flow. His partner knew he would be a great EMT some day. So what if he'd had some trouble with the drivers' union. Just meant he couldn't pilot the aid car for a couple of years. A shame to have to pull him off this husk. The senior EMT checked the reporter's carotid artery for pulse, found nothing. "Cubbens," he said, "he's deceased." He said this matter of factly, but softer than he normally would have. Cubbens would see his quota of busted-up bodies, exploding pericardial sacs, drunken head-ons on 410, bull-maulings, and kids with limbs caught in farm machinery in the weeks and seasons to come. Might as well have this first death be a gentle one.

Then he pulled the reporter's overcoat slightly to the side, and viewed a fresh horror.

How could they have missed it? The exit would was the size of a fist, exactly in the middle of his torso. Centered just a half inch below the sternum. Merrick looked up, around, rested his gaze on the Town Hall. He looked up the slight rise of Mud Lake Road to the laundromat, then back downhill at the Pie Apple. A second shooter? Or had this poor prick just spun with the shoulder impact and taken a second shot between the shoulderblades? No wonder he croaked – they'd been working the wrong hole! Not that working the right hole, as it were, would have helped. This guy's goose was cooked the second bullet came home.

When Flora heard the ambulance man pronounce the reporter dead she let escape a small sob and collapsed on the seat of her jeans in the man's blood. Jacqua, too, sat back. Kinchlow and Mike Eagle Eye remained on their knees, Mike on all fours so that Devon's life flowed away, downhill, as all that is wet eventually does, through his fingers and palms. Ed Cubbens – the Breadman – and Flora shared another look. He closed his eyes first.

Detective Pandoulis was at the screen door. He decided not to go in until his backup arrived. Soon another car rolled up with lights on but siren off. Detective Jeff Quimby was on the porch with him in less than a minute, the two cops strategizing an assault.

First, there was the problem of location. The shooter could be anywhere in the house, or could have fled out the back. Recreating the shooting scenario, Pandoulis suggested the reporter had exited his vehicle and been immediately fired upon. That would have made the angle better from the shop – the garage, under the sign. Second, there was the problem of anticipating where the shooter might have fled, or if he hadn't fled, where he had hunkered down. As Pandoulis considered this he registered the faint onset of a cloud-borne drone. It grew somewhere above him, enflanneled in the black-gray, an aircraft. What if their shooter took a plonk at a low-flying aircraft? Pandoulis decided they would split at the front door, Quimby to head quietly around the left side of the house to check the back, Pandoulis to proceed low, hugging the foundation, in full view on approach to the garage.

Pandoulis gathered his guts as if he must clench them in his fist. He had never been shot, and had been fired on only once. He had never had a partner shot. He had never shot his revolver at a suspect. He was surprised that he felt less fearful – in the sense that any of these things may, at any moment, happen – than hog-tied. He imagined that even the smallish bureaucracy of Yakima County government would examine closely every step he took, every word he said. They might parse through his actions, especially in a case as high profile as this would surely be, and find something he hadn't done correctly. He reached a door abutting the side of the garage and its roll-up front.

The hell with it. He stood and kicked a large-sized lawman's boot through Juniper Jamison's rotting garage side door. It collapsed as if it had been a screen. He reached through the opening and toggled the light switch.

Juniper Jamison sat slumped behind his reloading bench. His head lolled forward, chin on chest, crammed still into a white cowboy hat. (Weird, all that force of an exploding heart – exactly as the heart of his mentor – and the goddamned hat stayed on his head.) The smell of spent gunpowder was thick in the room. Juniper lit his workshop with fluorescent tubes, so the light was white and pure and stark. On the wall, Pandoulis noted Juniper's posted fee schedule:

Brushing	$5.25
Waterproof	$6.50
Cleaning	$7.50
Reblock	$22.50
The Works	$28.00.

A poster hung from push-pins, some cowboy and his hat. STETSON EL AGUILA, it read across the top. "True Luxury for Your Head" at the bottom, in script. Pandoulis rounded the counter. A rifle lay at the mayor's boots.

He fished a silver whistle from his shirt pocket and gave it two short blasts. Quimby huffed through the door after a few shakes. "Holy Christ," was all the backup said.

"This town does go through people," observed Pandoulis.

Quimby and Pandoulis had stretched yellow plastic tape around Juniper Jamison's house and shop, around Tristan Devon's car and body. The Yakima County Coroner showed up and had to bull his way through all the Lowell's patrons. Camera flashes struck like lightning every few seconds for a while, then ceased – whether the photographs were the work of the detectives or the press, or both, couldn't be said.

Quimby started interviewing folks who may have heard or seen anything suspicious. But he couldn't even establish a time for the first shot. The cute teenage kid from the grocery thought it might have been about 3:45. Her boss thought 4 on the dot. The barkeeper guessed it was about ten to 4. Quimby glanced across the street at the clock face on the town hall's façade, read seven minutes to seven. He checked his own wristwatch: twenty 'til. No wonder nobody in this shit town knew what time it was.

The Peacocks were flowing in Kinchlow's tavern that evening, with all the county rigs, TV vans from Yakima, a helicopter overhead for a while. Reporters stuffed microphones or mini-cassette recorders in the face of anything that drew breath. After they had interviewed everyone, they embarked on the absurd and desperate practice of interviewing one another. One of their own had fallen. How did that make them, as journalists, feel? It was the oddest group therapy imaginable. Top Story, no doubt.

Jacqua had to go back and mind the Pie Apple. All these folks from town needed pops and bags of chips and sticks of smoked meat. For a minute there, she thought one of them might even rent a video. In fact, she was absolutely jumping in the store, damned near breathless. Where the hell was Flora? It had been a rough evening for her, true, but she hadn't said anything about going home.

But Flora was at the crime scene, comforting the Breadman. And oh, the smell of his hair. And her caress on him – his cheeks and hands were so hot, as if he were saturated with fever, but not the fever of illness but of, again, failure. Ed Cubbens must have been older than her by twenty years, but he was like a child in her hands. A certain variety of joy swamped her center.

If there was anything she was interested in fixing, it was this poor boy's broken heart.

The day after Juniper Jamison shot Tristan Devon, the *Herald-Republic* showed up in a strung stack on the Pie Apple's board porch. The headline spanned the top of Page 1 in a typical spasm of journalistic hyperbole: MASSACRE AT SALT LICK. The subhead read, BEAT

REPORTER TRISTAN DEVON FATALLY SHOT BY SEPARATIST. There was an enormous color photo of Wellman Kinchlow and Jacqua Druce being interviewed by Detective Pandoulis – visibility and recognition that probably had the detective shitting razor blades all day. In the photograph, the trio was in front of Tristan Devon's still-open car door. Their features were awash in emergency light, and the vacancies in Kinchlow's bridgework appeared especially pronounced. The story tucked below commented on the life and professional achievements of Tristan Devon, but for the most part dwelt on the devolution and undoing of a man, the bizarre personage whose Christian name was the same as a word for shrub, who made his living pressing leather hats, who had threatened to "break out his rifles," or somesuch, a few weeks back. Though Yakamians were, in general, familiar with the Tall Tree County movement and its failures, as far as anyone in Salt Lick itself knew, it was the first time their town's name had ever been set in type. And elsewhere, wherever readers read the slim paper they would, almost uniformly, ask, "Where the hell is Salt Lick?"

A question that would bounce off the icy November air and echo back unanswered.

CHAPTER 15
in which Tina Druce paints an ugly reality...

The emanation from Gunter Sturmhund's closed bedroom door struck his father like the sound excited deaf mutes make when they attempt speech.

"*Mein Gott*," Lothar thought, "what in hell is the little communist doing now?" Without a knock, Lothar stormed in to his son's room. There, he discovered fifteen-year-old Gunter reclining on his bed with stereophones on. His eyes were closed. His hands slapped an aggressive drumbeat on his thighs. As Lothar took in the initial seconds of this tableau, it occurred to him there was an unwelcome indoctrination under way in his home. It was his fatherly duty to grabble with and destroy it. His suspicion could not have better been confirmed when Gunter, eyes still squeezed shut, palms still drumming, pulled his lips back into a sneer and moaned, "I'm so bored with the U – S – A..."

Lothar reached down and jerked the stereophones from his son's head. Gunter leapt backward with momentary panic, then appeared confused for an instant as if all before him must resolve and construct itself before he could focus. The music came louder from the unobstructed stereophones. Lothar commanded: "Turn that crap off."

Gunter blushed as deeply as if he had been discovered jerking off. He skittered around his bed, keeping a good distance from his father, slid over to the stereo and clicked the power toggle. The CD player shut down; sound from the stereophones ceased.

"What are you listening to?"

Gunter pointed at a compact disc case. His father retrieved it. "The Clash," he said. Three punks on the cover. He turned the case over in his hands, inventoried the song titles. "Clash City Rockers," he read. "I'm So Bored with the U.S.A." "Remote Control." "Com-*plete* Control" – he raised a brow and glanced at his son as he sneered this last – "White Riot." He read on, inflecting this syllable or that when he read words he thought particularly heinous: "I *Fought* the Law." "*Hate* and War" "*Jail* Guitar Doors."

Gunter stood. The old man stared him down. "Give me the disc," Lothar said. Gunter stooped to comply, caught his father's clout about the ear. It produced an instant one-sided tinnitus. "Hand it forth," his father commanded behind a cresting wave of rage. "I'm getting it" – Gunter whined like a tiny puppy – "just gimme a second." Lothar swept air for his son's other ear, missed. Gunter held forth the shiny silver disc.

His father collapsed the disc in his palm. Shards of plastic cut into the old man's hand and blood seeped out. "Not in my house," he growled. "Never."

Gunter made one small attempt to reason: "Dad, it's just music."

Lothar's eyes grew as wide as an expanse. "It's *Hundescheisse*." He defied his son to counter. "Dog shit."

But the boy, although now nearly the size of his father, simply stood and acknowledged his father's will.

"You're so bored with the U.S.A.? You little communist – this music, as you call it, is sapping the strength and lifeblood of young men your age all over this great nation. You're all on the wrong track. What're you gonna do if this mighty country ever goes to war? Who's gonna fight then, you buncha lily-livered liberal wienies? Who's gonna protect the women and children? You pussy." He flung the bloody shards of the Clash's debut album – chords and rhythm a decade and a half old and five major musical movements in the past – at the face of his youngest son. He stormed from the room to his machine shop.

Gunter stooped to gather the pieces.

Of all the colors composing God's palette, of all the hues and shades and timbres with which He chose to drape the eastern Cascade foothills and wash across the juvenile receptors of her eyes, Tina Druce liked best those she thought of as "local."

She had once, as a small girl – aged maybe six or seven – disappeared from her mother's house at the fork of Mud Lake Road and Benton Drive. After she had been absent for some number of hours, Jacqua Druce collected those who had gathered at Lowell's for an afternoon beverage with the promise of free drinks – Peacocks or otherwise – for all later that night. She formed them into a search posse and deployed them in teams to reconnoiter the deep woods about town. Salt Lick's thirsty residents found Tina in no time, at the head of Sanford Canyon, a good mile from her home and up past Lothar and Magda's, up past Ivan's, even further up the road than Stoneway

Pouring. The little girl – whose eyes were the color of the undersides of broadsword fern fronds – sat in the chair of a fractured cedar stump, a giant that had gone over in a windstorm some years back and left, in its rooted base, a throne for nature to carve. In her small hands were an open notebook and a pencil whose nib she had worn down to a blunt stub.

When they asked where she had been, what she had been doing all that time, Tina Druce spoke not at all, but simply produced her notebook. She held the pages open for them. As they unfurled in the light breeze, members of the search party gathered around to read her encolumned notations, entered there very bookmanlike for a girl so young and petite. They were amazed that the lettering was so precise. Where they would have assumed penmanship would not yet have gotten hold of her, they had to admit that the design of her writing – the curls and loops and straight lines – was a lovely thing. A penmanship of grace, one of them might have observed, had the words come.

But nevermind the medium, nor the mechanics of its execution. The content: now *there* was a marvel.

Tina Druce had filled her first column with invented names for all of the hues and shades for what a boring person would have simply called "green." The list included such fanciful notations as fernish, pineneedle, sapcurl, mapleafy and mosshair. On another page she had scribed a list of what those with more limited imaginations would have simply tried to erect – brick by brick – as the edifice that went collectively by "brown." This list included such whimsical descriptors as barkscore, rockbrown, woodsdirt, mushroomskin, conecase and fawn's hide (that last: two words, which seemed to run counter to most of her appellations – single words formed from two poetic components – so that her notebook of the forests colors read like a volume of poetry set in a typeface of refinement.) There was a page for grays: ironflint, granitedust, bleachboard, fogblanket, cloudsky... there were more than four pages of columns for this tedious color. The notebook was filled with hundreds – maybe thousands – of names for the earth-, plant- and skytones that were, indeed, indigenous. Enough so that the town knew from that day forward Tina possessed an eye for color, a heart for the artistic, and could in fact, some day, become an artist of some importance.

Forrest and Jacqua Druce had settled in their home back in the mid-1970s, shortly before the arrival of the Sturmhunds. Forrest had been the sort of fellow who jumped out of perfectly good helicopters. There was a word for the particular color of the terrain his military-booted soles impacted when he landed. The name of that color:

Vietnam. Leaping from a Huey into a paddy in that far-off conflict, Forrest had straddled a color fancifully called *anti-personnel mine*, a color whose characteristics not only included a bright, fulminating burst of orange-yellow energy but also had this crazy property: it blew body parts off of whoever trod thereupon. (He was lucky it hadn't taken more of his leg, or both legs, or both legs and his nuts and cock – or unlucky, from some perspectives, because it hadn't taken his life and left him maimed. If anything, unpredictable, not to mention temperamental, was this color *anti-personnel mine*.) Forrest Druce drank heavily from the moment he returned to the United States with an honorable discharge. He bought cheap land on the eastern slopes of the Cascades in an unincorporated part of Yakima County the few locals called Salt Lick. He settled there with his young wife. She had a baby ten months later. They named her Tina. She turned out to be a neat kid. So it turned out to be a pretty all-right thing that the mine only blew off his foot rather than ankles, knees, thighs, reproductive equipment, and so on.

No one remembered much of Forrest Druce. Jacqua did, of course, as if it were yesterday. But Tina could have been only three or four when he up and walked. Or, rather, limped away, on his one good leg and his bloodless prosthesis. Tina remembered her father only in unformed incidents and shadows at the core of her mind. For instance, she knew her father was fond of uttering a colloquialism involving a certain Dick's Hatband. Tina remembered he would say, "That's uglier than Dick's Hatband," or, "This is sweatier than Dick's Hatband." He would invoke comparisons between objects or situations or people with Dick's Hatband continually – and randomly, it would seem to those within earshot – substituting "dirtier" or "as hideous as" or "greasier" according to no apparent algorithm except as Forrest Druce's moods struck him. Jacqua hated this. Especially when he started to use it to refer to her decisions, ideas, cooking, and so forth. In these instances he would say this or that – her creamed corn or the way she kept house – was as "fucked up as Dick's Hatband."

Tina also remembered that her father used a cane and walked with a limp. She remembered being enfolded in his arms, cuddling in his lap a couple of times. Every once in a while, she would collect a scent from something nearby that would remind her of him, or of an incident in which he was present and involved. She saw washed out, poorly focused photos of him any time she liked in one of her mother's old scrapbooks. He was handsome. But her mother never volunteered any information and offered only monosyllables to Tina's questions about her dad. Eventually Tina got the idea and stopped asking. Because what Jacqua could not reveal in answers other than monosyllabically were the details of the last night she and Forrest cohabited Salt Lick. The night he raised that cane and swung at her as if she were a pitched hardball. How that cane felt clattering across her brow. How she ran him from the house with a leveled shotgun that God only knew by what miracle she had refrained from triggering.

All this hidden from her, Tina wondered about the man and once commemorated him in this way: at the elementary school in Gleed, on the occasion when one of her spelling words was *forest*, she insisted on spelling it *forrest*. When the paper came back the word was red-checked as an error. Tina brought it to the teacher and explained that this was her way of spelling the word. It would continue to be her way, and whenever the teacher saw it written this way – double-R'd – in future, she could anticipate this and not hold it against Tina. It was all very matter of fact. Oddly enough, Tina found her teacher in fascinated acquiescence with this arrangement. Must have been the penmanship. And in follow-on years, Tina would simply arrange a private meeting early in the semester to explain this uniqueness she possessed, this compulsion to honor her dead-beat, dead-limbed dad, to commemorate him in the word for vast tracts of fir, salal, mosquitoes, pine, cougar, ravens, cedar, lichen, elk, spruce, mushrooms, bobcats, aspen, stone, moss, hemlock, deer, vetch, bear and the forbs of the understory. God's most beauteous, cycling creation.

It became apparent that Tina was exceptionally bright. She understood concepts immediately, memorized the dates and places of her history and social studies lessons as if she had been there. Geography offered no challenges – she could find on any globe Benin, Bhutan, Baghdad, Belorus, Beijing, Bern, Bangor, Bogota, Bradislava, Bimini, Boston and Botswana. She excelled in mathematics, conquering geometry and algebra two grades before her contemporaries. Music was an easy thing for her, the reading of staves and the grasping of challenging chords. She played on the elementary school's poorly tuned piano six pieces: Mozart's Allegro in B Flat Major, four Brazilian folk songs arranged by Mary Verne, and Türk's Rondo. Her penmanship only improved.

If it can be said that one subject appealed to Tina Druce above all others, it was the subject of art. Jacqua encouraged this, enrolling her in special courses at the suggestion of her art teachers. "We can only do so much for her here," they said, "teaching this curriculum. Our resources are limited. She really needs a stimulating challenge. A private art tutor could do this." Jacqua, who barely made ends meet at the Pie Apple, had had a notion to begin stocking videotapes for rental. This, she thought, might provide added income so that the artist that dwelled not-so-deep in her daughter could be brought forth and encouraged to fully bloom. Jacqua received tutor referrals, developed her video-rental idea, began to stock the tapes, and found that the videocassettes found a receptive, Hollywood-thirsty, bored audience in little Salt Lick (with its poor reception from Yakima's limited TV fare).

Tina's tutor, Mrs. Gideon, cost her mother twenty-five dollars a week. Mrs. Gideon operated a small gallery in east Yakima and held the awe-inspiring credential of having displayed and sold paintings in Seattle. It was Mrs. Gideon who encouraged Tina to experiment with various media – painting in tempera, watercolor, oils, drawing in charcoal and pen, assembling collages of found materials. Mrs. Gideon taught Tina to appreciate the curves of the human form properly drawn, and to consider perspective issues such as vanishing points and the proper casting of shadows. She taught her how to hold the brush lightly but with purpose. Most of all, Mrs. Gideon taught Tina passion for the articulation of her ideas, to bring forth those things at the core of herself and expose them to the viewer. To offer what was inside her mind to the entire world. Tina, before long, in a single brushstroke before her mentor, could produce a handclap of rushing praise. She discovered that her favorite medium was oil paint upon canvas. And at this point her mother invested in an easel, a palette, scores of paint tubes and various-sized horsehair brushes, solvents for brush cleaning, and blank canvases, procured at an art-supply shop in west Yakima.

Tina's paintings possessed the same fidelity as photographs. Her favorite subjects were the ubiquitous things around her – hillocks, trees, wildlife, fences, logging roads, cattle, the people and places of Salt Lick. Her landscapes were exact replicas of what the eye saw. Every detail was there in precise replication. Tina was no fan of schools of art such as Impressionism or modern, pop art – although it can be said that she truly appreciated the skill behind such creation, she simply preferred to replicate unwaveringly what she saw. She would record on canvas faithfully from her surroundings – a pine stump with the jigsaw bark sloughed at its base, sprouting a clump of orange amanita at its first cleft, with a Parkinson's squirrel shouting forth like a little preacher at its hewn rim. All of this she would execute with stunning detail and perfect alignment, leaving nothing out, the perspective exactly on and shadows falling perfectly where they belonged. She would execute paintings quickly, often in less than an afternoon, without any predrawing or templating, with simply the rapid execution of brushstroke on brushstroke, the mixing and application of mapleafy and ironflint and barkscore, or fernish and fogblanket and mosshair, or every color that split from white light through the prism of her creativity and

184

leached from her brush onto the bare cloth surface. She would lose track of time. It would race past. Her attention to other demands, chores around the house for example, would fade in her earnestness to complete the current canvas. In this her mother was supportive. Jacqua never uttered an admonishment of any sort. That is, not until Lothar Sturmhund died. Not until the residents of Salt Lick went into a tailspin, slowly at first then rapidly, as if one of the Horizon Air commuter flights that perpetually overflew them had experienced a mechanical difficulty and gone corkscrewing into a mountainside.

When this happened, Lothar's death, Tina Druce painted her first ugly thing.

It started out as a beautiful landscape in her mind, an articulation of the folding hills and clefts, forest-swept, up near where the American River wends back and forth under Highway 410. She imagined herself situated on some peak nearby with her easel and painting the opposite ridge. And what appeared at first was, indeed, a faithful and gorgeous replication. Except that midway through its execution, she had a mind to rape the landscape with a gaping clearcut wound. A timber company, she reasoned, would have ripped across the virgin hill an opening of stumps and fallen branches. A glaring scab across the land. She painted the defilement at the center of her canvas with exactness and precision. When she was finished she wept. It was, to her mind, the most faithful art that had ever flowed from her. It was a testament, this ripped hymen of the land.

She believed that all that had flowed from her brush before was a lie.

Her mother found her in the little studio at the back of the house. They had added the room there so Tina could look out the window and see a tree-topped bluff below Cleman Mountain beyond her mother's satellite dish. Jacqua found her there, weeping.

"My God, child, what's the matter?"

Tina looked up from her finished work. Tears coursed around spatters of oil paint that dotted her face like odd colored freckles or teenage acne. "Oh Mom," she whispered. "It's so ugly. Look at it." She gestured at the still-drying canvas.

Jacqua beheld the wound on the face of the land. She misunderstood immediately her daughter's grief as that of a naïve teenager bent on changing the world in an environmental sort of way, as a sort of green concern over the raping of land by timber magnates.

"Honey," she said. "Honey, it's all right. It's just the way things are."

"I know!" Tina leapt from her painting stool. It shot from under her and clattered on its side. "I know! And think of all the lies I have painted." And with this statement she flung her palette at the canvas with such force as to rip out its center, at the location of the faithfully rendered clearcut, a gaping tear – a wound upon a wound – so that the painting was ruined. She stormed from the room. Her mother stooped to gather the mess.

Then it was like she was taken over by a fever. Over the short course of weeks Tina whipped through three dozen canvases and countless tubes of paint. Straining her mother's purse, she sent the Pie Apple's proprietress on several jaunts to Yakima for new supplies – which worked out O.K. since Flora could mind the store. Tina's paintings became simpler, the objects in them more representative. She overthrew old forms, investing her time with brush and canvas in pursuit of the new. She started to embrace elements first of Impressionism, combining styles. For instance, she would render a perfectly faithful forest glade and place at its centered a hare executed Impressionistically. Or on another canvas, a photographically rendered salmon leaping from a stream of vague flowings and bluish-green hues dappled in small, dabbed strokes, so that it was like a large, vague pixilation surrounding the perfectly comprehendible fish. Her work devolved from Impressionism to Symbolism. She did no research, studied no art books, looked up no techniques, read no bios of the great modern artists, yet her work seemed to migrate along the shifts and changes of her century. She rediscovered Art Nouveau and the Nabis, Fauvism, Cubism and the Dadaists, Futurism and Expressionism. Metaphysical painting and Surrealism. She dripped wristwatches over windblown limbs in a desert of clearcuts. She painted the Town Hall's façade, and where the white, lit clockface would have synchronized the town in Lothar's day, she painted a Cubistic rendition of Lothar's face, a countenance recognizable as only his, but strangely unformed yet unmistakably stern. As if a god of new angles now ruled Salt Lick in the wily Teuton's absence.

Tina showed a respite from this madness during the last campaign for Tall Tree County. She inked the first prospective logo for Juniper Jamison, suggested a web site contest for the prospective county's flag. But when that fell apart, and when Juniper Jamison was carried out of his Salt Lick hat reblocking shop on a slab and ferried back to Yakima's county mortuary, she returned to her abstract pictures. She ignored everything else, including the comings and goings of the school bus that collected Salt Lick's children in front of her mother's store and distributed them according to age at Gleed's schools. She simply stayed in her studio all day, and painted. She slopped her oils on the canvas, neglected brush cleanings in between, swirled the hues together until she had no name for them. She replicated the color of Old Man Weesle's putrefying skin – that corruption of plum-purple – recalled from when she had found him a year and a half back, dead and baking and gaseous in the double-wide now inhabited by the MacNaughtons. She named this color bloatstench. She began to splat gruesome colors such as this on without brushes, flinging them watered down with her bare fingertips, or splunted them from the orifices of their tubes like toothpaste onto a toothbrush directly onto the bare canvas, or atop the unnamable colors she had sloshed there moments before. She went through four and five canvases a day in this manner.

Until one day in late November she returned to, at least, a semblance of order. It was a bitter cold afternoon at the height of hunting season, three weeks before Thanksgiving. She saw low clouds threatening another snowfall outside her studio window. Already dirty snow had gathered and fallen in melting and refreezing clumps in the satellite dish, and at its base. She heard, every so often, intermittent rifle blasts from the hills, crossing even the threshold of her closed studio window. She thought of deer and elk falling, red blood pouring out onto virginal white. She thought of how the hunters were artists too, painting the canvas of snow with animal guts as they carved into the fallen beasts with giant silver knives. She thought of steaming entrails slopping forth from those giant, hewn cavities, of stomach sacks and organs spilled in a rush of metallic odor. She had a picture in the eye of her mind of a hunter severing the penis of a royal bull elk and holding it high in the frigid air like a loving cup.

And this led her directly to ruminate of Lothar Sturmhund. Of something in the tilt of his blond head, the Germanic cast of his features. Something that put her in mind of debasement. Tina Druce was, at seventeen, a virgin. She realized in that moment that Lothar Sturmhund could have been the agent of her deflowerment, that she had wasted her time with all this fucking *art*, this goddamned fucking *painting*, these ridiculous shit-ass *lies*, while she could have filled those moments by filling herself with Lothar, with his thrusts, his breath, his cock in her, his slaps and beatings, his absolute rule.

She painted the dead in her mind. In this, not a small part of her wanted to paint a composition of decomposition, to add the purpling Old Man Weesle to her *oeuvre*. Instead, she painted what she always knew she must one day, eventually, paint. She took the image of Lothar Sturmhund from her mind, and translated this to a clear pure canvas.

187

She painted him as she saw it, a perfect articulation of his hirsute, Thüringian goddishness.

Jacqua arrived home after hiking the ice-slippery quarter mile from the Pie Apple to their house with two paper sacks of comfort food. She opened her unlocked front door. "Tina? Tina, honey, I'm home, sweetheart."

She paused in the quiet. A light snow had begun to fall halfway up the hill. She stamped her boots on the throw rug in front of the door, hung her parka on a peg on the back of the door as she shut out the cold behind her.

"Tina?" Silence.

She stepped across her living room, down the hall to her daughter's studio. Tina sat like a statue, a canvas erected between her and Jacqua in the studio's doorway.

"Sweetie?" Jacqua said, "Are you O.K.?"

"Oh yes." Tina sounded as if her voice were under layers of water or some other milky obscuration.

"Have you been painting all day again?"

"Yes – come see." As her mother approached, Tina slid from the stool and grasped the canvas and easel in both hands to turn it to meet her mother. Jacqua gasped.

The canvas was large: four feet by three feet, longer longitudinally, the three-foot side to side. At the core was a perfect filled circle. It was fifteen inches in diameter, and green – not mosshair or fernish or pineneedle, but exactly green. Around it, from each of the four sides and each of the four corners of the canvas, was a field explicitly and only brown. Brown, that is, as only brown can be described, not any of Tina's notebook shades, but brown. It terminated precisely at the border of the green circle. It looked oddly like a flag hung from its lanyard straight to the ground. Jacqua asked if that's what it was, a flag of some sort.

"No mom." Tina smiled, and her smile was like something proffered across a universe of regret, wan and grim, not a smile of joy. "It's a picture of everything that could have been, but never was." She was silent then, an encouragement for her mother to speculate.

"Everything that could have been, but never was."

"Yes."

"For instance?"

"Oh yes," Tina said, as if from the piano chords of a discordant dream. "Such as Lothar Sturmhund and me."

188

"Lothar," her mother echoed, cowlike.

"I'm sorry, Mommy. I'm so sorry."

Jacqua collected her daughter to her bosom. "My sweet baby," she said. "My sweet baby."

Jacqua destroyed her daughter's painting, threw the canvas on the burnpit out back, poured some gasoline she kept on hand for the generator on the disgusting object and flung onto it a lit match. It roared to a brief conflagration, settled and began to slowly consume itself. She had an odd thought she was immolating a grandchild.

She turned to enter the house and saw Tina at the back door, bracing herself in the half open doorway, leaning on the knob with one hand for support. As Jacqua approached, she saw that Tina was crying. "Tina," she said, "it's for the best. Trust me on this one."

Jacqua turned with her arm around her daughter. They watched the canvas curl as flames ate the edges, watched the glowing ashes separate and lift, float up in oily smoke and land on the snow-covered yard. Pieces of ash fell in Jacqua's bootprints. The oily smoke blotted, for a few moments, the ironflint sky. "I wish you would paint me a *nice* picture again," Jacqua said. "Something I could recognize right away. Something I wouldn't have to ask you what it was. Could you do that?" She asked turned, lifted her daughter's wet chin with her fingertips so that eye contact was inevitable, inescapable. "Could you do that for me, baby?"

Tina nodded.

Tina returned to her studio. She sat in front of a fresh canvas measuring 38 inches by 52 inches. She executed a perfect rendition of the way the gauze part of a bandage looks when it has been removed from a supperating cut, dried nasty maroon and deep blood red, with browns and ochres and siennas. The tinctures of a scab ripped open too soon.

"DICK'S HATBAND," she painted in bright yellow block letters at the base, and signed her name in pink. *Tina Druce.*

The dot of the "i" in her first name was a pink heart.

Jacqua Druce knew, now, that it was time to assemble the townspeople at Lowell's and broker a discussion. Hector Aguirre's animal-part, road-kill jerky was one thing. There was sniper fire from

Juniper Jamison rained down upon that poor writer from the *Herald-Republic*. O.K., that was another. Then, there was Gunter Sturmhund's robotic amalgam graven image to his father's memory, and his brother's tattoo: NOT AXES! There was Reverend and Mrs. Jenkins' poor mutt Eli entombed in the driveway. There was Ivan Manley's fascination with female undergarments, and his remarkable inattention to Vicki Aguirre's advances on Jacqua's own living room couch. This latter Jacqua had seen with her own eyes – a man staring blankly ahead with no response while a very desirable woman shoved her bare breasts in his face! There was Mike Eagle Eye incessantly attempting to quit smoking, sliding his snaky tongue all over a six-pack down at the store, smashing the town pumper into the Naches River. There was Jimmy Bayles standing atop Hoyt Stone's cement mixer hollering about the African Mother into thin air. Gib MacNaughton sending his son to the Pie Apple to get his dope papers. Imagine! And Nick Oxendine – that was simply beyond bizarre. Here was the world's most fastidious man fallen to near indigence.

Taken separately, these could have been explained away as the oddities of tiny-town life. Of separation, of excommunication, of the constant necessity of traveling to Yakima for the slightest need. Of the need for all the canvases and paints and art supplies a picked-over, thrice-watched-by-every-citizen-in-Salt-Lick video collection could sustain.

But when it all came home to roost, in Tina, that was too far.

She collected them at Lowell's – Nick the town clerk, Wellman Kinchlow, Jimmy, Mike Eagle Eye, her best friend Magda, Lothar's boys and his daughter-in-law Candace, Gib MacNaughton, Vicki Aguirre and her dad Mayor Hector the Fish and Wildlife warden, Flora, Ivan, Hoyt Stone and his wife, Grace, all of them. She even demanded that Reverend Harland Jenkins cross the tavern's threshold to join them.

"This has got to stop," she said. "What has been happening in Salt Lick must end." She surveyed the group, and each of them stared back at her with dawning comprehension. And they all nodded as if they knew exactly what in the hell she was talking about.

And in no time at all, they did.

CHAPTER 16
in which Jacqua sets in motion a climactic exorcism..

It is generally assumed that never once in his sixty-four years did Lothar Sturmhund consider the likelihood of his own death. His ego would not have permitted such a thing, although he may, once or twice, have come close: when he laid the mantle of Tall Tree County leadership on Juniper Jamison with the promise of an eight-hundred and fifty dollar hat, or when he invented Tough Love – he may have intended those acts, however temporal, components of some sort of legacy.

But on the whole, Lothar would not have believed his own demise to be inevitable. He would, rather, likely have believed this: Should Death dare come, he would simply bully it away – he might, for instance, chase it through a parking lot with a wire shopping cart or point at a desk and say, "See there, that's where we'll see if you're right for the job" – and that Death would have fled tail-tucked from Lothar's Tetragrammatonic countenance.

Of course even Lothar could not, at the hour of his end, refuse compliance. All he could do was be sure that he had left legacies, that he had made meaningful impressions on those around him, that he would be remembered. That his life made – indeed – a difference. The legacies he did, in fact, leave for all those around him were many.

Of course, the moment of cardial cavitation is no time for worrying about all of that.

"The Town Hall?"

Madga Sturmhund assessed her friend Jacqua. Jacqua sat in Lowell's after having gathered a dozen or so of them. "Get over to Lowell's," she'd said. "We have some things we need to discuss."

So now they were all there, even the Reverend. Jacqua Druce was usually the calmest, most level-headed of all of them, and widely recognized as so. But now, not one of them was sure that she hadn't slipped over to the side of madness. Their eyes simply stared as if the ends of this unlikely notion would not connect.

"You've all felt it," Jacqua said. "Don't tell me you haven't. Something has gone very wrong here, and I think it's coming from there." She pointed back around her shoulder, through Lowell's front plate-glass, across the buzzing neon beer tubes, in the direction of the town's clock.

"From Town Hall," Hoyt Stone said.

"Yes... look..." She tried to make an explanation with her hands, as if she were sculpting a solution, but found that her palms came to rest on the table upward. Configured so, she appeared to be frozen in a state of supplication. Her mind spun and clutched for an explanation. Why was she so uneasy every time she passed it? Why, all day down at the store, would she sense a certain presence from behind the wall at her back, the wall that abutted Town Hall? And what, or who, was the presence? She thought she knew, as unlikely, as foreign to her experience as it was, this presence... could it have been *he*? The ghost of that bastard, that old German, that prick? Lothar's spirit, having never fled Salt Lick and lingering, even now, in the boards and insulation and wiring of Town Hall, casting his angry afterpresence about the town, manifesting his inability to access heaven in the haunting and possession of the town's good people?

"You've all felt it," she insisted. "If you think about it. Every time you drive or walk by. Ask them." She pointed at long-bearded Nick Oxendine and Mike Eagle Eye, who had just lit his second cigarette of the gathering. "Come on guys, you work there. Tell everybody what it's like to walk down the hall and feel him suddenly next to you, or to be arranging all that crap in the garage and feel like you're being watched. Tell them what you told me, Nick."

Neat Nick from Salt Lick sat behind a foot-long beard in three days of the same T-shirt and considered the act of broader disclosure. Then he spoke, and his voice was small and thin, as if he uttered his words with great, awed labor and wished to bite them off before they had a chance to form, emerge and slip into the minds of his townmates.

"I was in the john." He stared at the hands he had clasped on the table in front of him. He watched them as if they belonged to someone else, and continued. "I went in to take a leak, you know. I got unzipped and out and all that, and I'm just waiting, waiting for the piss to come. I mean, I had to piss like a race horse when I went in there. And I'm all set to go, standing there over the urinal mint, and it's like I'm stoppered up. You know, plugged." Nick's voice rose, growing disturbed. "I can

192

feel it, way back up in there, in my bladder and so forth. I mean I have definitely got to *piss*." Nick paused and looked up, not at anyone, but through them, as if he were seeking confirmation of new faith across the tableau of a vast plain. "Then it occurred to me – it's exactly how it used to be with Lothar. If I'd be in there to piss and he'd come up to the next urinal, I'd just freeze up. Waiting for him to ask me the goddamned time or something. Or just – I don't know, it's embarrassing to admit – intimidated, I guess."

"An alpha male thing, you said," Jacqua said.

"Alpha male – what's that?" Hector Aguirre asked.

"Yeah, I did, I said that," Nick said. "Alpha male – that means Lothar Sturmhund was the number one, the Kahuna. Leader of the pack. It's from the animal kingdom – everywhere there's animals and herds, there's an alpha male. Think of it as the biggest, baddest bull elk in the hills – the one all the little spike bulls secretly want to challenge but, at the same time, are terrified of. He is the one who gets to mate the most. He's the king." The opportunity to offer this explanation had calmed Nick somewhat, as if exposition had, for him, sedative and restorative powers.

"So anyway," Jacqua said, waving her hand dismissively, "then tell them what happened."

"Well, yeah." The edge of panic returned to his voice. "I guess... well, the point is, he was there. I got cold all over and just wanted to get out of there. I didn't care at that moment whether I wet my trousers or what, I just wanted out. I zipped up and run down the hall..."

"Almost knocked me on my ass!" said Mike Eagle Eye.

"Yeah, that's right, I came around the corner and there was Mike."

"He looked like he'd seen a mountain lion, like a great big panther'd taken a bite outta his butt! You shoulda seen..."

Mike Eagle Eye realized that every eye in Lowell's was on him, and that there was absolute silence, and that it was not a respectful, "yes, go on" sort of silence, but a "why don't you shut up and let him finish!" sort of silence. He turned to Nick. "Anyway, finish your story."

"I guess I have. I mean, I ran out the building and urinated out back, down the canyon. But he was there. I definitely think so. I don't know the how, why, or what of it, but he was there."

The group sat still, a dozen cups of coffee having gone tepid in the course of Nick Oxendine's narrative. Each was wrestling, in his or her mind, with the speculative nature of all of this – weighing odd occurrences and obsessions whose onset could be tracked to the sudden explosion in Lothar's chest. From the moment the Great Thüringian slipped from this world through the glassy gate of Gib MacNaughton's coffee table to his own personal Valhalla, life in Salt Lick had flipped completely out. Could Nick's simple anecdote represent the travails of all of them these past few months? Could his urinal encounter with the specter of Lothar Sturmhund elucidate their own confusion this past half year? Mike Eagle Eye had to admit, for one, that working at Town Hall had been mighty unsettling, with cells or pockets of weird odor and unexpected temperature shifts all summer and fall. He might have described these phenomena as *displacements* – had the word been in his vocabulary – experiences he thought of vaguely as the shifting of piles or wads of space. Things would move – air, would move. As if something inhabited it for a moment or passed through it.

Kinchlow stood suddenly. "Anybody want a Peacock? Because I sure do."

Reverend Jenkins held his wrist in the air: "It's only 10:45."

Kinchlow made as if to be speaking with a child through the missing, whistling spaces of his teeth. "Reverend, thank you. We are all aware that it is before noon, and that no one should ever consume alcohol before noon – probably no one should ever drink alcohol after noon as well!" His sarcasm, propelled melodically through the gaps in his oral fence, produced a peppering of barely enthused laughter. "But, here's the deal. We are going to call this morning an *exception*. I know there are not many *exceptions* in the *Bible*, but today we..."

The Reverend held his hand up. "Wellman," he said, "there is no need to cross that line, son." He smiled and his eye twirled like a pinwheel. His grin split his face like an egg. "You may bring me the first glass." Those in the room gaped in silence for a few seconds, then erupted in a cheer, and Gib MacNaughton slapped the preacher's back heartily. "That's a mountain man!" shouted Jimmy Bayles. "That's a mountain man!" Mike Eagle Eye stubbed his smoke and lit another right away. Ivan Manley giggled through his perpetually shocked rictus and pointed at the Reverend, and even the timid Gunter made devil horns on top of his hands with his index fingers, wiggling them so they twitched and throbbed like little teenaged penises.

"All right, all right," Jacqua spoke into the gale of all these bouncing *bons mot*. "Back to the matter at hand." She called to Kinchlow, "Just bring me a coffee," by which she meant *Put a good, healthy splash of bourbon in a mug of joe, and keep your damned Peacocks.*"

"So Jacqua," Flora Navarro said. "Just tell us what to do. I mean, what are we talking about here?"

"Yeah, tell us," said Hector Aguirre.

"Why don't you decide, Daddy," Vicki said. "You're the mayor."

"Because Jacqua has thought this through, I think," he said, while Nick Oxendine rolled his eyes at Vicki's vapidity and simultaneously recalled penetrating her from a delicious, doggish angle. "Woof!" he whispered, barely, so she could hear. She turned toward her ex-lover – this *particular* ex-lover, Nick, as there were others in the room (and maybe the ghost of one across the street) – and her smile rose, too, in recall. She howled softly, just for his hearing, and rolled her hips on her chair in a sexy, moisture-provoking mini-grind. It's possible that Neat Nick, still a nasty mess, forgot at that moment the scary anecdote he had related to his fellow townsfolk. Most likely he now wished he *was* the vinyl seat under Vicki's salubrious, life-giving crotch-roll. There would not have been room in the dense cheese of his imagination for both, not after the months he'd been through.

Kinchlow arrived with a tray of Peacocks and one mug of fortified coffee, and dealt out the drinks. The Reverend's was half gone in one holy pull. Jacqua sipped her steaming mug, burnt her tongue and fumbled in her purse for something. She withdrew a videotape, set it on the table.

"You've all seen this," she said. "Three or four times, probably."

"More like eight or nine," Candace Sturmhund said. Everyone stared at the cassette box, as if it would at any moment levitate or turn circles. Which would have been perfectly in character for this particular object, since it was the cardboard jacket and movie cassette enhousing The Exorcist, that devil movie with Linda Blair and the pea soup going everywhere.

"You understand what I'm saying?"

A look of comprehension bled into the room and slipped, first, onto the face of Reverend Mallford Jenkins, then to the others. The Reverend's twirling eye fell still and both eyes focused – a rare thing, indeed! – like high beams, on the videocassette. "Jesus Christ, Son of God, have mercy on me, a poor sinner," he said. He belted the second half of his Peacock and demanded of Kinchlow a second glass, voicelessly but with a single look loaded with command.

"Good God," Magda, the spouse of the ghost, whispered. She was struck by the feeling readers of novels get when they have finished a page but cannot remember its contents, or have read the same paragraph fifteen times. A feeling of displacement and irresolution, and desperation.

"Mom, it's O.K. It's O.K." Helmut rose, limped to a position behind his mother, laid his arms around her shoulders. His mother lifted her hands to caress and then lay still against them.

"Yes." Jacqua stared around her at the dumbshow. "Lothar Sturmhund has possessed us. And it's up to us to get out." She looked around the room at his victims as if they were a new product of speciation, those who used to be uncomplicated representatives of *Homo sapiens*, foothills dwellers, but whom Lothar had transformed on the mitochondric, chloroplastic levels into something new, something that had taken a step backward, or if not backward, at least in an unwholesome, damaged direction. It was if, by agency of Lothar's death and the cessation of his iron guidance, they had become slowly unmoored and drifted asea. She surveyed the eyes of each person in the room, looked into their skulls to see lights, slowly at first, then in a rush, toggle on.

"So what are we going to do?" Hoyt asked. The scar where his thumb had been throbbed like the blazes.

"We have to exorcise him," Flora said. For her it was more like a discovery she made aloud than an answer to Hoyt's question. She said it in the same way she would have voiced surprise on stumbling into a forest glen mounded with gemstones.

"Yeah," Jimmy said. His grin turned malicious, bedeviled. "Let's *do* this bad boy!"

"This all sounds so very *Catholic*," the Reverend groused. But with his second Peacock almost gone, he couldn't hold the grudge long.

If anyone had passed outside Lowell's Tavern that freezing December morning, if anyone had trudged the slippery hill from Highway 410 and passed the Pie Apple on the right, wondering why there was a sign affixed to the door with masking tape that read *Gone for a while, will return at noon*, if anyone had then crossed Mud Lake Road to the tavern and arrived at the exact moment Salt Lick's resident's strategized the methods of their freedom from the spirit of their dead, hirsute Thüringian, if anyone had paused as fat snowflakes began to fall that morning and heard a pure roar of happy cheer rise and expand and roil from within the inn, if anyone would have peered through the tavern's window and seen glasses of beer that were not called glasses of beer but Peacocks raised and clinked at the rims in celebration – even in the hands of a minister of the Baptist race – she or he would have witnessed the first gasping breaths of independence.

She or he would have seen, and known at her or his core that they had seen a birth of freedom.

"Yakima Tower, this is Horizon 887, after climbout."

196

"Yes, Horizon 887, level off at nine-zero-zero-zero, heading two-eight-four, over."

"Roger, Yakima Tower. We'll see you."

Horizon Air Captain Malcolm Terwilliger's airplane knifed through sparse clouds at nine thousand feet. His co-pilot, Cole Schantz, trimmed the stabilizer and brought the deHavilland Dash 8 level – or nearly enough level to still allow the generation of lift – around its center of gravity. The horizon in front of their windshield was a tapestry of blood-red and orange, sunset prolonged here, high over the countryside. This is what Terwilliger loved, what kept him flying after all these years: earthbound, the sun set too damned early. Up here, it almost never seemed to slip under the scrim of the earth. It could be pursued, chased, as in a game. He knew this was an illusion – in order to beat the sunset he'd have to push an aircraft well beyond a thousand miles per hour. Back in his Air Force days maybe, if he would have ever got the chance to fly one of those air-breathing half-jet, half-missiles. No – the Dash 8 was a real turd in the sky. But nevertheless, a turd he loved. A faithful, lumbering soldier of the winds. Besides, turd-speed and low altitude gave him a chance to see what he overflew, and he had to admit he liked that.

Schantz's voice came through his earphones. "It's beautiful, isn't it?"

"I never get tired of it, Schantzie." The Dash 8's twin radial engines hunted on the other side of the fuselage, synchronous one moment and producing a clear tone, and asynchronous the next, for a different drone. It was similar to an ever-shifting and returning Doppler effect. The radial symphony slowly cycled as they maintained level flight over the Naches River Valley.

"Folks, this is Captain Terwilliger. Just wanted to let you know we are maintaining level flight for now just below our cruising altitude of 12,000 feet on our way to Seattle-Tacoma. We'll climb a little more in few minutes as soon as we get a closer to the mountains, so please keep your lap belts fastened and tight for now. Time to Seattle is about fifty minutes and the wind is, unusually, at our tail, so we should be on the ground on time or before, about 5:35. For now, sit back, relax and enjoy the flight. You should be able to get a glimpse of Ellensburg through the clouds off the right hand side of the airplane, or Ellensburg's streetlights anyway. I'll come on again and update you in a while. And thanks for flying Horizon Air."

Terwilliger clicked off the intercom. "Well said," his copilot noted. The teeth of the Cascade Mountains divided the panorama ahead from darkness to sunset. At eleven o'clock, to the captain's side of the cockpit, Mt. Rainier broke the regularity of the chain, lifting its volcanic mass high into the atmosphere and trailing ruby altocumulus like a string of gemstones from its summit.

"This is the life," Schantz said.

They fell silent in the flight deck for a few moments, checking gages. Yakima came on to advise them to proceed to their cruise height and hand them off to Ellensburg Tower. Schantz pulled the yoke back slightly – no autopilot tonight, with such a short hop. The airplane tilted nose up and lifted itself further into the twilight sky over central Washington. What cloud cover there had been in Yakima was spotty and low, but the blanket had bunched up as it flowed from west to east over the range ahead of them. It got thicker as the mountains approached – it would be dense as wool on the other side. Here, though, was the transition: the relative clear of Yakima slowly being overcome in a sort of dappled texture below, clouds and holes between them, so that the pilots saw the ground and its features – where there was man-made light, anyway – intermittently.

The Dash 8 leveled off again over the fork of Highways 12 and 410, and Schantz, looking down to the starboard side, spied a particularly intense light through a cloudbreak. It almost blazed – like an amber caution signal, only a million kilowatts' worth. It glinted in the black vacuum of unlit earth like the eye of a panther or an angry sparking topaz.

"You oughtta see this, Mal," Schantz said.

"What's that?"

"It's this huge light, about two-o'clock, almost straight down."

"Bank us. Let me see."

Schantz slowly banked the airplane to the right. The light source dropped out of direct sight behind a cloud, which leapt into orange pulse as the water crystals comprising it refracted the brilliant, orange matter of light. Then they passed again into line of sight.

"Look at that." Terwilliger said. "That's a fire."

"A fire... yes. Yes, it is, you're right."

"That is one big-ass fire."

"In December? Little after forest-fire season, don't you think?"

Schantz leveled the Dash 8 again, peeking over the window rim from instant to instant. "Take over," he said. Terwilliger took active control of the flight. "I don't think that's a forest fire," Schantz said. "It's too compact, it's all in the same place. It's... concentrated."

"What do you think it is?"

Schantz paused for a moment. "An aircraft down?"

"Let's see. Get Ellensburg on."

"Ellensburg Tower, this is Horizon Air 887 heading two-eight-four, we are thirty miles westbound out of Yakima en route to Sea-Tac, over."

There was a second or two of blank air, and Ellensburg answered.

"Ellensburg, Horizon 887 here, we have a visual on what appears to be a massive, concentrated fire on the ground. Do you have any aircraft off your radar in this sector?"

"Negative, 887, but we'll check with the Army over at Vagabond, and Yakima, Moses Lake too."

"Thank you, sir, we are flying out of visual range, over."

"Roger that, 887, thank you. We'll take it from here. And let's hope not."

"Roger, Ellensburg. You got that right."

"And 887? Godspeed."

Schantz placed the radio on scan, craned to look, once again, at the fire. "Goddamn Malcolm, I hope that isn't an aircraft."

"You and me both, bro," the captain said. "You and me both."

The Dash 8 droned on toward Seattle through thickening, rising nimbostratus. Snow clouds.

When the world needed a fire, there was perhaps no one on its face who could oblige quite like Mike Eagle Eye. Whether this was something indigenous about him – smoke lodges, ceremonial powwow dances, that sort of thing – really can't be said. What can be said is that the citizenry of Salt Lick, Washington, decided it needed a fire. And it was happily serendipitous that Mike Eagle Eye was there to oblige. Because more than anything, it was fire Mike Eagle Eye loved to design, construct, tinder and execute. Whether it was that simple action of flaring matchtip to a fresh smoke, or a vast conflagration of slag-burn up in the clearcuts while moonlighting for the Forest Service – the Yakama man loved flame, smoke, char and ash. Fire, in his estimation, *rocked*.

Yet at first he offered more than a dozen reasons why the particular fire Salt Lick's ghost-plagued citizenry desired was not such a good idea.

Chief among them was this: he and Wellman Kinchlow had just three days ago spent almost six hours – nearly an entire shift! – hanging light bulbs of variegated hues about the eaves and soffits and rain gutters of Town Hall. Christmas was coming, all right, and no better way to celebrate than to exhaust almost half of Salt Lick's total annual kilowattage spinning merry yuletide colors off across Mud Lake Road and into the empty woods. Still, folks took their cheer where they could get it. Knowing this, Mike and Kinchlow had taken special pains each year to design more elaborate and *artistic* (if such a word could be used in conjunction with these two fellows, one wonders what descriptor, then, is left, for an artist like Tina Druce?) variations on themes. Patterns of alternating-colored bulbs that cycled on timers would knock out a Here-Comes-Baby-Jesus rhythm (or a Baby *Hey*-zoos rhythm, for Hector, Vicki and Flora) into the frosty night. If Magi were to visit this Bethlehem bearing gifts, they would stumble about giggling – not having a name for the apperceivance of being high on acid, but grooving on the choate lights just the same. Because if it was anything, Mike's and Kinchlow's light display was a psychedelic extravaganza. An *Experience*. If Jimi Hendrix would have lived to see it, he would have cut a Christmas album.

That's how excellent were Mike's and Kinchlow's light hangings on Town Hall. They even circled the clock's face with an orbiting, pulsing wreath of mini-lights that chased, speckled, veri-cycled, waxed and waned in pulses, flashed like quasars and generally caused eyes that peered too long upon them to simply bug out from overstimulation. Even Reverend Jenkins' eyes stood up and saluted the spectacle.

And then there was the matter of the polystyrene nativity display canted akimbo upon the mossy shingles of the roof. A pair of floodlamps lit the fading plastic icons in a way that to an outsider would have seemed grotesque, but to the people of Salt Lick served as reminder that the season of the birth of love was upon them. Twin, three-foot-high candy canes – also plastic, and bulb-lit from within – framed the door like perpetually screwing barber columns.

So all that labor – the work of assembling all of this, replacing failed bulbs and fuses, running extension cords hither and yon, making sure there were no untied ends that could be tripped upon, no frayed wires that might short out or electrocute the innocent – the fact that all this work had been accomplished and might go for naught gave Mike Eagle Eye pause. It must have been a horrible dilemma for him. On the one hand, the glorious light display. On the other, a bonfire without, in his experience, precedent. Although the two options were as different, both held certain… attractions.

Then Hoyt Stone brought up the matter of insurance. Wouldn't they invite trouble, torching a perfectly functional Town Hall? "It's like this, see. There are laws against such things – laws against arson." And this seemed particularly problematic for Hector Aguirre, who felt, in an increasingly visceral manner, that the civic well-being of the citizens was his serious duty, one that could not be shirked or abrogated. After filling their guts with unconventional jerky, he was still – months later –

slightly unsure of his mayoral footing. And it seemed to Mike that if Hector was concerned, then Mike would most certainly be concerned, Hector being his boss and all.

But it was Nick Oxendine who settled their collective nerve on this one: "Are you kidding? That place isn't insured! Never has been. Nothing in it, as far as I know, has ever been insured, not even the fire truck..." – at this, he glanced menacingly at Mike – "so I wouldn't worry about that."

"Are you positive?" Jacqua asked.

Nick tried, as best he could, to affect upon his own muzzle the facial characteristics of a soon-to-trumpet royal bull. It wasn't a leap of any distance at all, given the coarse beard that sprouted from his face, exactly like the deep brown shag dangling from the neck, withers and brisket of a male elk. All he needed was a nice rack of antlers. "Lookee here," he said. "I think that I, as your town clerk, would be expected to know definitely these kinds of things. And this I definitely know. The Salt Lick Town Hall is not, and never has been, *insured*." At this he stopped swelling, but still looked around as if expecting a challenge. Receiving none, and comfortable there wasn't a vote of no confidence in the offing, he then looked calmly at Mike Eagle Eye as if to demonstrate that he had dealt *that* excuse a deathblow in the way that only a competent and faithful public servant can. In fact, as a result, Nick began in that moment to feel *neater* again. In the simple act of cleanly dispatching fact he threw down his figurative shovel, stopped digging his metaphorical hole, and started an archetypal climbing-out process.

Next, Flora brought up the proximity of the Pie Apple and the laundromat. Wouldn't the flames and heat jeopardize those structures? And what about the forest around them? Could the fire escape their control, fly out of hand and off into the night? Might the forest, indeed, their whole world, go up in a blaze as well? Although Mike Eagle Eye believed he would have considerably more control over a blaze of his own authorship than this (he in fact discovered the tiniest mote of resentment indwelled him after Flora aired this rather ridiculous concern – that he might lose control of his own fire and loose calamity on them all – good God!), he didn't want to leave any objection to the notion of razing Town Hall without the benefit of a full dialogue.

But it was Gib MacNaughton who stepped up to the plate to face this curveball. "Flora, lass, we live in the most sodden, moist, wet, murky, bloody-hell saturated state in the United States of America. And it's the most sodden, moist, wet, etcetera month of the bloody-hell saturated year. I believe we'd be lucky if we can get the Town Hall itself to catch."

But Mike Eagle Eye chafed at this as well. Of course he could ignite Town Hall! He could set a bucket of water ablaze! Honestly, these hacks at his pyrotechnic abilities – although surely unintended – were beginning to grate. And so, finally, after much dithering and wallowing about in irresolution, after the full accounting of pros and cons and precautions had been exhaustively discussed, after all the real and imagined barriers had been thrown up and then felled like trees before Paul Bunyan, it all broiled down to this: Mike Eagle Eye's own ego rendered it impossible for him to be anything but foursquare on the issue of burning Town Hall. He would burn it to the ground. It would be the coolest damned campfire ever!

When Mike Eagle Eye parked the American-LaFrance Series 500 Invader in the Naches River, Salt Lick couldn't afford to have the aged pumper towed off the rocks. And Kinchlow, despite his broad connections, had not yet been able to locate any ranchers up around Eagle Rock who might altruistically winch the old red carcass, *gratis*, from the current. The state agency responsible to ensure dangerous chemicals didn't make their sinister ways into the environment made them siphon the gas and oil and tranny fluid out of the antique vehicle, as well as swab grease from axles, pedal springs, bearings and certain hinges and other mechanisms. So while Washington state allowed them to let the pumper rest there and continue its slow process of reduction, presumably for eternity, what it would not countenance – in a baffling application of *reductio ad absurdum* – was the release of any salmon-killing, wetlands toxifying, ozone-depleting, waterfowl-sinew-poisoning muco-detritosa to leech into the area's biosphere.

In this, a macabre transaction resulted. The citizenry of Salt Lick were deprived of 1 (one) antique fire-fighting apparatus, but gained 5 (five) five-gallon tanks of leaded gasoline and approximately 12 (twelve) quarts of a carbon-based cocktail comprising various refined and additive-laced excoriatingly flammable liquids, or near-liquids, as it were. This admixture was like a variation on napalm – an explosive gelid that made its viscous way into the happy inventory of town fix-it man Mike Eagle Eye.

Therefore: 1 Salt Lick − 1 Antique Pumper + 5 Gal. Gas + 12 Qts. Blow-up Jello = 1 Big-Ass Fireball of Freedom. Now *that* rocks!

And this happy, rocking equation summed the exorcism of Lothar's *geist* from their lives.

On the Ides of December the people of Salt Lick gathered at their Town Hall and checked their watches for the last time against the chronometer on the façade of Lothar's Keep. They discovered that their synchrony varied, across all of them, as much as forty-two minutes. They looked to His Honor Hector Aguirre for adjudication. The Mayor took a very mayoral gander at his wrist. "It's 5:52," he proclaimed, and they all cheered and condensation from their collective exhalation rose into the freezing evening. They ceremoniously reset their wayward timepieces.

The night sky was patchy. Stars could be seen through cedar and pine branches, except when folks looked directly at Town Hall, which was most merrily lit. The lights shimmered and danced in a frigid breeze. Their electric ropes swayed a little as wind lifted and dropped them with no apparent predominant direction. Folks stood about in their down coats, wool trousers and snow boots. They drank spiked coffee and Peacocks in the street. There were seven inches of snow on the ground, but it was neatly compacted in the road, slushy in spots.

At Mike Eagle Eye's direction, Jacqua and Tina Druce, and Flora Navarro, with the help of Ed Cubbens – who had come to town at Flora's suggestion to help and, probably, snuggle later – fixed precautionary hoses from the Pie Apple's spigots. Kinchlow screwed a couple more hoselines coming out of Lowell's, and one from Juniper Jamison's lightless house. Mike Eagle Eye humped some traffic cones down to the turnoff from Highway 410, blocking off the town.

Nick retrieved the town's computer and one vertical file of records from his office inside, transported them to temporary stowage in Lowell's, then went home and cut off his beard. He brought the clippings back in a large plastic seal-top baggie, which made a sort of hirsuteness pillow. He stowed the monstrosity in his top desk drawer. It lay there exactly like a deceased, cellophane-encoffined muskrat.

Liar-nosed Ivan Manley borrowed ex-Juniper Jamison's pickup and returned in half an hour with a load of cardboard cartons. While he would not say precisely what they contained, he accepted the assistance of half a dozen of them toting the boxes into the American-LaFrance's now-nearly empty hangar. While he wasn't looking, Vicki Aguirre lifted a flap and found a sheer under-thong with the faintest leopard-print woven into the fabric. Underneath it, further into the nest of the box, was more fabric, more pairs of lovely underthings. A pang of jealousy infested her briefly, then she shrugged and pocketed the diaphanous thong. When others left the garage and she remained with Ivan, who forlornly eyed the boxes, she fished them from her pocket, held them in her palms and approached. "Let me wear these for you," she said, and he agreed. The panties lay across her hands like spun sugar. The two exited, fingers laced.

Meantime, Lothar Sturmhund's boys and Tina Druce left on a mission of gathering-in as well. They arrived first at Magda Sturmhund's and soon were busy grunting and hefting the newly minted idol of Lothar that Gunter had built in his daddy's shop. Soon the automaton was prone in the back of his daddy's Ford pick-up. They drove to Jacqua's and filled the rest of the bed with Tina's repulsive paintings and the giant satellite dish. All of this they brought and carried into the Town Hall, placing the robot in Nick Oxendine's desk chair.

Hector Aguirre needed two trucks and six men to bring the remainder of his frozen beast jerky. Gib MacNaughton climbed furtively back up Mud Lake Road and retrieved a garbage bag full of his recently harvested and dried home-grown marijuana and, turning down inquiries as to its contents, placed the bag squarely in the Town Hall's men's room's urinal, and pissed on it, so no one would be tempted to have a look. Angus MacNaughton tossed in some fireworks he had saved from Fourth of July for New Year's Eve. Jacqua Druce scattered all the Pie Apple's remaining copies of the *National Enquirer* amongst the building's interior. "Just to make sure," she said, "the place will go up." They liberated Juniper Jamison's reblocking shop of its tools, posters and price schedule, and his garage of its handpainted sign, and chucked all of that in the Town Hall. And Wellman Kinchlow tossed in his karaoke machine to boot.

Each of them sacrificed something to kindle the coming conflagration. And when they were finished, and stood in the cold eyeing Mike Eagle Eye expectantly, he made a solemn declaration: "I promise from this day forward I will never, ever try to stop smoking ever again!"

Their cheer could not have been greater if the Seahawks, Cougars, Mariners and Sonics all won championships in the same year. And this positive affirmation had the further result of prompting Wellman Kinchlow to hop, also, on the resolution train: He declared that a Yakima dentist visit was in the offing.

Mike Eagle Eye sloshed the leaded gasoline and spledged pumper-jelly on the Christmas-glistening structure, and the fumes of all this filled the air. He directed all of them across the road to the lots in front of Kinchlow's and Juniper's. He poured the final quarts of the last gas can as he retreated with them, so that a ribbon of gasoline laid itself down yellowly on snow. He produced a book of matches.

"Wait!" the Reverend shouted.

"What, Daddy?" asked Jericho Jenkins. The whole crowd turned to the preacher.

"A prayer. Surely an exorcism cannot be completed without a prayer."

They fell silent and stared at the snow. Some closed their eyes.

"Great Lord," the Reverend began, and his voice rose to the sparse clouds, and rose above them into the ionosphere and into the reaches of space and sped toward Arcturus and the boundary of the universe. There it found St. Peter's portal, and the Reverend's prayer gained admittance. It ricocheted across avenues of gold, into the Inconceivable Palace with its platinum columns and Judgment Bowls, and resonated in the Ear of God. And when, back on Earth, Reverend Mallford Jenkins had prayed thusly for almost five minutes and folks began to grow cold through inactivity and stamp their feet in the packed snow, Mike Eagle Eye began to worry for the evaporation of the gasoline. He stepped respectfully to Jenkins' side and whispered this concern in the minister's ear, who stammered, "Of course," and wound up his intercessory with "Oh, save us from, and rid us of, *him*. In the name of our Lord Jesus Christ, everyone said..." – and he paused, and on this cue, the citizenry of Salt Lick articulated the Hebrew word for *Make It So*: "Amen."

"Hallelujah!" added Reverend Jenkins.

Mike bent to strike a match. The Reverend grabbed his forearm. "One last thing," he said, and his lazy eye whirled like a pinwheel, mouth cracking egg-like into a massive rictus of glee. He pulled from his parka a notebook, crossed Mud Lake Road into a stultifying wall of gas-funk, and flung the notebook at Town Hall's front portal. "Notes from his eulogy," he explained, as he re-crossed to join his flock.

Mike Eagle Eye struck the match.

In nature, fire can result from volcanic activity from the bowels of the earth or electrical activity descending from the heavens above it. It is supposed that humankind's first use of fire was to locate and husband some flame-source whose genesis was in one of these occurrences – lava or lightning. The fire would be cared for and transported with the troupe of barely-beyond-apes with an awe and respect reserved for the deities. Fire became sacred, holy. Purifying.

The hominids began to tame it, to mold it to their uses and employ it in the achieving of their goals. It warmed them, gave them light, protection from those huge-toothed cats and savage bear-things and other terrifying predators. It allowed them to smelt ore, bake clay, climb the ladder of proto-technology. To hammer out blades and spears and warheads. It can be argued that this taming of fire – which was successful, mostly – was the catalytic agent for the gathering of nomads into cells, and from this arose the notion of political and social collections of hominids, permanent homes, hamlets, towns, cities. The megalopolis flared from one spark.

Humankind – in the same way it learned to replicate natural deposits of salt that animals might like to lick, and form this salt into bricks called salt licks – learned to assembly sulfurous chemicals in a hard nut on the end of miniscule piece of lumber and give it the name match. Scraped along a rough surface, the resulting friction produced the same natural miracle as the engine driving supernovae at the edge of the cosmos: the rapid expansion of gas and heat resulting in combustion. This, in turn, resulted in the generation of light in the form of flame.

Fire.

Flame leapt from Mike Eagle Eye's match tip and rolled across Mud Lake Road on the gasoline runlet. It licked at the foot of Lothar's Keep and detonated. The concussion and wall of flash-heat knocked most of them on their asses. It blew out two of Lowell's plate-glass windows and one pane from Juniper Jamison's shop door. It left their ears keening with tinnitus. A fireball as wide across as half a hillock boiled a hundred feet skyward, turning on itself like a lofted ball of roiling, orange plasma. A second wave of heat filled the onlookers' universe. The echoes of the initial blast caromed off the hills and thickening clouds and returned, and set out again.

Flame licked like the tongues of coyotes at the fresh carcass of Town Hall. The pops and snaps of exploding pitch came as siding was consumed and decades-old pine studs became fuel. Insulation ignited and tiny glowing eyes of breeze-driven coals chased each other through its melting filaments. Angus' fireworks went off, throwing sparks in to the night and sending fountainous columns skyward again to join great chucks of ash that pitch and whirled like ghost ravens.

Town Hall sighed and wheezed, its dry lumber going up like leaves of newsprint. Enormous sheets of flame climbed higher on the walls, and the Christmas bulbs popped in delightful explosions, each a tiny kinetic model of the initial blast. The nativity melted and flowed into the gutters, then through the opening holes in the roof's failing matrix. The candy canes oozed down the door jambs. Gouts of flame could be seen dancing around the interior while beams failed and dropped onto terrain. Gunter could see his superheated metal father glowing at Nick's flaming desk, and had to bury his head in Helmut's shoulder while Candace slowly rubbed the nape of his neck and Magda clung, without strength, to all three of them.

Cinders flew around them like camp robbers and settled black on snow. Everywhere was the smell of charred fuel, wood, paper, toxins, cardboard, old paint, gunpowder from the fireworks, the sweet syrupy odor of Gib's burning dope contaminated by the deep, inky scent of melting plastic and oil paint, burning canvas, women's undergarments, Nick's lunch sacks and whisker coils, cleaning unguents and agents, copper pipes re-smelting, insulation around wiring bubbling down to small pools. A circle of melted snow opened around the conflagration, and the odor of steam joined the miasma. The beacons of a commuter plane blinked, alternately blue and red, overhead, but the engines could not be heard. The fire roared like Jehovah.

Salt Lick's Town Hall collapsed into itself, harming not one shingle of the Pie Apple or the laundromat. It imploded in a heap of sparks thrown like a bursted mega-hive of golden hornets, collapsed on the fading weight of itself and slid, ass-end first, off its rear pilings, into Sanford Canyon. The horned specter of Lothar Sturmhund, some say, hovered above it for a moment, rose, bayed at this outrage and at the lack of moon, and dissipated.

A light snow began to fall from a sky that had grown overcast. It mingled with tumbling creosote, the residue gathering in the folds of their clothing and upturned faces.

Jacqua held her daughter. Ivan's arms enfolded his *Latina* goddess, Vicki Aguirre. Her father stood with his hands on his hips, grimly, in a group with the Reverend and his wife and son, and Kinchlow. Gib and Angus MacNaughton, Jimmy Bayles, Hoyt and Claire Stone, and Mike Eagle Eye and his two Doberman's Quoof and Pyewacket, stared from under the cedar in Juniper's front lawn. Flora Navarro and the Breadman shared a passionate kiss. Nick Oxendine stepped up to Mike's side. "Nice work, partner," he said.

The Sturmhunds clung as a unit at the center of Mud Lake Road. Magda Sturmhund flinched and moaned as Town Hall settled in the ravine. "Goodbye, my love," she whispered.

Then snowfall quickened. Its flakes grew enormous and covered the aching world with white silence.

Detective Pandoulis of the Yakima County Sheriff's Department stroked stubble and stared into the steaming crater. Nick Oxendine and

Hector Aguirre were with him, Hector supremely irritated because he'd had to chain up in order to drive over and meet the sheriff. A foot and a half of snow on the ground, and the Detective was demanding *he* come give an accounting of what had gone on in *his* town last night. Who the hell did this *detective* think he was?

Nick was busy explaining that there was no insurance, so the Detective's concern about insurance fraud had no foundation, when Hector slid up the road, slipping, sliding, fishtailing. He failed to stop in time and there was a crunch of chrome and steel as his bumper met with the Detective's patrol car. Pandoulis rolled his eyes – these people in Salt Lick were something else!

"Then what about a fire permit?" Pandoulis turned to the emerging mayor. "Did you guys even have a fire permit?"

"You'll have to ask him," Hector snapped, and slipped ass-over-teakettle in the icy road. Nick staggered gingerly over to help him up, had his boss on his feet in no time. Both of them now fumed. "Lookee here," Nick said, "I write the damned fire permits around here, Detective." He wagged his finger at the lawman. "And you can sure as hell bet I wrote one for this." He gestured at the steaming hole.

"And where might it be at this time?"

"I left it on my desk." Salt Lick's town clerk stood with his gloves on the sides of his belt. In this posture was, perhaps, the first defiance Nicholas Oxendine, Neat Nick from Salt Lick, ever exhibited in his generally fastidious life.

Pandoulis gave up. "O.K., O.K., that's enough for me." He spread his hands and walked around the two, giving them considerable birth, as if whatever was odd and funky and slightly out of whack about them, about this bizarre place, about Salt Lick, might jump from them to him like some strange, poisonous tick. "I'm going to get in this car, and I'm going to go back down the hill, and I'm going to get on the highway, and I'm going to go back to Yakima, and I'm actually going to get, I think, a coffee and a donut in Naches on the way, and enjoy it. I'm going to pretend I never was out here today, and I'm going to hope I never have to come out here again." As the Detective made this embarrassing speech, he employed the same tone he might adopt for instructing second-graders. He slid into his car and glared at them through the windshield.

Salt Lick Mayor Hector Aguirre turned to Salt Lick Town Clerk Nicholas Oxendine and asked, "Fine with you?"

"Fine with me!"

Lowell's front door squeaked open and Wellman Kinchlow emerged with a snow shovel. "What was that all about?" he hollered across Mud Lake Road.

"Nothing important," Aguirre shouted back.

"Tell you what, though," Nick added, "why don't you pull a couple of Peacocks and we'll be in a minute. Tell you all about it."

Lowell's proprietor waved his acquiescence, smiled that grin which so astoundingly resembled piano keys, and stowed the shovel, blade down, next to the door. He didn't much feel like shoveling snow right now, anyway.

AFTERWORD

Oh, the dreams Lothar dreamt.

Like mammals that existed before God imposed order on the world, dreams bounded through Lothar's sleeping skull. Inchoate, brutish, his nighttime visions fueled his goings forth into the world, and his wanderings east to west and north to south. Each night manifested a brilliant confirmation of his greatness. Each period of darkness informed Lothar's Teutonic cerebellum with the manifesto and imperative of his suzerainty over all.

One night he dreamed like an ancient Hebrew abandoned, basketed, floating. He rose from the wilderness and leads his people with a staff. He overcame the Pharaoh and split a sea. Lothar climbed a mountain, chiseled rock from its summit in a mannish act of diminution, and descended into Salt Lick with stone diptychs to lay down the law. Homunculi – his citizenry – eagerly tongued up his mandates, the smell of wet pines filling the air.

Another night he engaged in a sort of mesmerism, and females from every town, every foursquare, every habitation and ethos and corner of the planet would succumb to his magnet. Their needles pointed urgently in his direction in a sort of bone game, as if he were a monad of persuasion. When he finished with them and cast them aside, Lothar scorned their small agonies. They dropped, one after one, from his bed through interstices into an indefatigable, bottomless oblivion.

Lothar dreamed that he commanded an army. He dreamed he had an alchemist's touch. He dreamed the wisest sought him out for counsel. He dreamed he was dressed in a coat of woven silver, filaments of precious metal pulled thin, the weaving shot through with strands of platinum. In his dreams he saw that the warp and woof of his household and kingdom were built upon immovable rock. He dreamed he was a tsunami and annihilated a shoreline. He reached out, in his dreams, and sucked yellow light from the sun. He ripped the face off a black bear and claimed it as his own. He pulled a loaded coal-car with his teeth, squeezed sand into glass in his mighty grip. He breathed the rarified air

210

of faultlessness. He dreamed he possessed the morning star in all of its splendor. He dreamed that he stood upon Everest's cap and challenged God.

He dreamed that he wrestled with an angel, but woke up before the angel was overcome.

Redeemable? Irredeemable? All of us. Lothar. LTHR. It is impossible for any of us to say. In all of us he dwells.

The time has come. All our timepieces say so. A commuter flight drones overhead – even those people know. Town Hall has burned.

Lothar time.

Put an end to this man. Put an end to this time circling upon itself.

We will tell you something, we who survived him. Of the going-on six billion people who roamed the planet, thirty-eight lived in Salt Lick, Washington, when Lothar walked among us. We know, now, that humankind evolved not out of Africa's great valley, but from the shale and feldspar and granite of Yakima County. From beneath the forest floor, from under the boles of lodgepole pines, in the pallid gaze of owls. Within earshot of the long, low language of elk. It is there that evil entered the world.

Do not let it draw breath.

Do not let it be born again.

Take this match.

Light it.

Burn.

ABOUT THE AUTHOR

Brian Ames is the author of three collections of short fiction; *Smoke Follows Beauty*, *Head Full of Traffic*, and *Eighty-Sixed*. He lives and writes in a suburb of St. Louis, Missouri.